GATEWAY TO ARISHA

UNCERTAIN BEGINNINGS

VIRGINIA ROSE

Book Cover by Virginia Rose

First edition, 2024

ISBN 979-8-9906107-0-5 (paperback)

www.virginiaroseauthor.com

To Him who gave me this story and the words to write

Contents

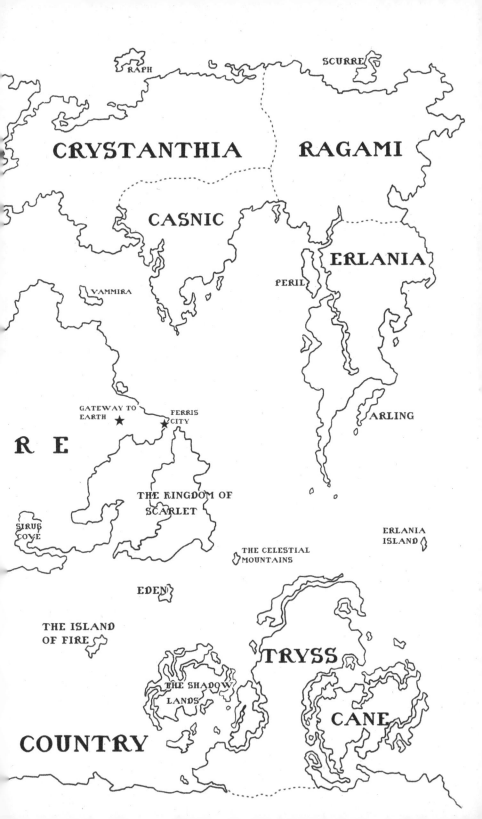

A Note from Me to You

I HONESTLY DIDN'T FULLY believe the tales my parents, brother, and their friends told me growing up. They were just silly little adventure stories made up to entertain me and Dylas while we were little. Dylas and I are actually the same age despite technically our relationship being that of an uncle and nephew to one another. You already may be thinking our family is a bit odd, but you'll understand in time. We grew up with one another and, as children, we were riveted by these adventures in which our parents took on the roles of heroes, fighting for another world despite the uncertain situation into which they had been thrust. But once we started going off to school every day, that's all they ever were—just silly little adventure stories our parents had come up with for our entertainment. I tell you the truth, the excitement in them never ceased to burn out for me, despite how many times Dylas and I were mocked for believing such foolery. Although, maybe I was a fool for telling some of the stories to our classmates in the first place, I couldn't stop myself because of how much the stories meant to me as a child.

The existence of another world? Of abilities unnatural to humans? Even I knew the ideas were absurd. But I also didn't want to believe them to be lies either. Something within me said otherwise. Maybe it was a longing that they were real, or maybe it was my gut telling me that they must have been. But I felt that too many things pointed toward them being the truth. How was I to let some children at school convince me my parents were lying to me when they said it really did happen? I have seen many people cave under peer pressure. Even Dylas gave into it. Although he has continued to support me no matter what, and part of me wonders if it's all just an act to please others, all while he still believes in them. Not me. I won't let people change me, no matter what insults they throw at me. All my doubts aside, they must be real, and I'm going to determine that.

Recently, as I near the end of high school, I have begun to wonder: *why on earth would so many people back up a tale my parents made up for their children?* Sure, if it were only Dylas's parents and my parents, then the whole thing was probably made up. But all of their friends seemed completely in on it, too. To me, such a thing seemed all too elaborate. So I came to a decision to write the whole thing down and make sense of it all. I wanted to see if all of their accounts of what happened lined up. For if they made it up, surely there would be some major variation in the tale from person to person that went past just a person's memory being slightly different on matters than another. The underlying tale would remain the same. So I set out on my own. I spent time with each of those claiming it really did happen, and created a master story with all of their accounts. Even if you don't believe it, as my classmates did not, I still hope you will enjoy what I have written. I tried to carefully shape out this story so dear to me, in the same way it excited and amazed me, but I will let you be the judge of how I did. Now let me begin with Genesis and River...

Chapter 1
That Night

THE MOON SHONE THROUGH the sliding glass doors, as the small family settled down in their apartment for the night. That night, the moon bathed the wood floor in its light, revealing the many children's toys strewn about. Genesis heard her parents' muffled voices as they turned the living room lights off to go to bed themselves. But sleep was yet to find the small girl, despite the hours that had passed since her parents tucked her in bed. Perhaps she couldn't sleep because she couldn't stop staring at that bright moon. Or perhaps she sensed something amiss as well. For the moon had shone brightly through those glass doors on many nights before and she had had no problem sleeping then. Tonight was different, and every night after, a bright moon would always keep Genesis up.

She heard a crunching beneath the covers beside her and glared back over her shoulder at the disturbance in the night's calm. Then, in a swift motion, she threw the sheets off the bed to unveil her little brother River nestled in between his stuffed animals as he munched upon the snacks he had snuck into bed. Yet again! Lately, it had become a nightly occurrence, and already it irritated his older sister a great deal. There was no question at all as to why he was such a chubby little child. I tell you the truth, he could never stop eating! His parents had tried all they could to regulate it to a healthier degree, but River could be quite cunning and knew it didn't take much to entice their dear old grandmother to buy them for him. Their parents believed eating well was a very good thing, but to such an excess could be quite detrimental to his health.

"What did I tell you about snacks in bed?!" his sister scolded. As a response he merely looked at her, the moonlight reflecting off his eyes so that they glistened in the darkness. He mumbled some baby gibberish, all while hugging the bag of chips tight against his chest. He very well could be a hidden genius. His schemes at obtaining snacks became more and more elaborate by the day. Sometimes he managed to get away with it without their parents ever realizing it until they wondered why the pantry's food supply so swiftly dwindled. But he was five years old and one still couldn't understand a word he said most of the time.

Genesis snatched the chips away, crumpling the bag up. Their eyes locked in the darkness. River's filled with betrayal, Genesis's with apathy, not tearing her eyes off him for a second as she tucked the bag in the nightstand drawer beside her. River's lips began to tremble, his eyes fixated on his precious chips as she drew the drawer slowly shut, his late night snack now officially confiscated.

A whimper escaped his lips beside her, evolving rather quickly into a ghostly sort of low wail. You see, he knew quite well how afraid of ghosts and the dark his sister was, and hoped that in doing so she would just deliver the snacks back to him in order to get him to stop such a horrid sound. But in such an idea he was sorely mistaken. She knew his schemes quite well and so instead threw the sheets back over both of them and lay down with her back to him. His plan of winning back his bag of chips had failed.

"Brat," she scoffed.

River stopped his morbid wailing. He found it not a pleasant task to perform, plus he was getting nowhere with it. Oh well, how might he attack next?

Genesis's eyes wandered up to the paper cranes that dangled from the vent above her nightstand. She wondered why she had to have a little brother and not a little sister, for he did nothing but annoy her. She thought of when they folded those paper cranes with their mother, another example of his petulant behavior. He had whined and clung to Genesis's arm the whole time, as she tried desperately to match the movements of their mother's long, delicate fingers folding the square pieces of colored paper. All of her cranes were perfect and neat, while Genesis's looked like crumpled up paper, and it was all River's fault! Their mother had not minded in the least. In fact, she loved their imperfectness a great deal. They had remained arranged on her desk ever since that day, so that whenever she looked up from her work, a smile would come over her lips. They were made for her by her precious daughter, and so it didn't matter that they were imperfect in the least. However, Genesis could only feel anger toward her brother when she looked at them. If he had just stopped clinging to her and whining for a moment, maybe she could have made some pretty ones like their mother's.

River now sobbed beside Genesis, trails of salt forming lines down the edges of his pudgy cheeks. Genesis was up in a swift motion, pillow in hand. "Oh, shut up!" She chucked the pillow at his head, his cries muffling beneath it. He'd be fine. She hadn't smothered him. He may have acted like a child, but he did have the intelligence to remove a pillow from his face before suffocating. That conclusion reached, she flopped back down to continue her moon watching.

River's weeping died down and, after a period of peaceful silence, he got up—as he so often did—and started to wander about the room. His sister, on the other hand, returned to her thoughts. She wished most that she wouldn't have to share a room with her brother anymore. For she knew it was going to get weird pretty fast. Alas, their current apartment proved too small for them to have separate rooms. Their parents did intend on moving in the near future, as Genesis was now the age of seven, and they both agreed that soon enough it would no longer be appropriate. In addition, there had been talk of a new baby possibly in the future, in which case the apartment would be far too small for a family of five. She hoped God would bless her with a baby sister next time. While on that thought, she clasped her hands together to make her desperate plea.

River now ventured over to stand just in front of his older sister by the nightstand drawer. She kept her eyes shut and pretended she had gone to sleep in hopes he would follow suit. But he made no move to do so. A moment passed. Then came the crinkling of the bag from the nightstand drawer. Genesis sprang into action. He let out a startled gasp as she seized his hand and the bag fell to the floor with a crunch as several of the chips within broke.

"Gen-gen... You broke my chips..." he whimpered. Gen-gen—he always called her this since "Genesis" was too much for him to say.

"Get back in bed," she ridiculed.

"B-but... but... hungrrrry," he whined.

"I don't care! Get back in bed before you wake Mom and Dad!"

River stalked across the floor and sat down defiantly on his little stepping stool, to glare at his sister in the darkness. She fell back against her pillow with a harsh sigh, returning his glare right back at him. He only remained seated a moment longer before he got back to wandering the room again. She clapped her hands over her eyes with an even more exasperated sigh, for she could not take such nonsense from him any longer. The room reeked of potato chips, and while others might like the smell, Genesis found it quite repugnant when she was trying to fall asleep.

"Gen-gen," River murmured. She glanced over at him, lifting her hands from her eyes to see where he stood by the window now, his fingers in his mouth as they so often were. He was still such a baby.

"What is it now?" she scoffed.

"People." He pointed out the glass doors with his wet little finger.

"There aren't any people up this late. You're the only one. Now get back in bed already!"

He looked at his sister, his wide eyes glistening in the moonlight again. Genesis sighed and tossed the sheets off in irritation. She caught hold of his stout little body, about to toss him back into the bed as best she could, but then she stopped, her eyes wide in surprise. Just as her brother had pointed out, there were a bunch of men in the back garden. Not only that, but their faces appeared to be covered by dark masks, and rifles were slung over their shoulders. A man motioned and they started through the overgrown grass around the building. Genesis knew little about guns and men lurking in the night at such a young age, but fear pricked up within her in an instant, and she had a deep sinking feeling within her stomach.

"Gen-gen." River poked at his sister's cheek to get her attention.

"Shush, River," she hissed.

Both children jumped as a loud banging sounded at the front door. It was so loud it seemed to rattled the whole apartment. Fear gripped Genesis and her hold on her little brother tightened with it.

"Lee, what is that? Is there someone at the door?" their mother said from the other room.

"I don't know... At this hour?" their father doubted. Their voices drew nearer as they went into the main area of the apartment from the bedroom to investigate the situation.

"I don't think you should open the door, Lee..."

"Who's there?" their father shouted.

Silence.

"Let's call the police... I don't feel right about this situation..." their mother said.

"Yeah, you're right... I don't want to act rashly, but something isn't right."

Genesis stared at the door to their bedroom. It stood ajar and through it Genesis could see her father's dark hair as he stood by the kitchen phone. Another loud bang came and then the soft dialing sound of the phone. Their father lifted his head to look in the direction of the now silent door, phone still in hand.

"I'll go check on the children..." their mother began.

"Gen-gen?" River grabbed his sister's arm, shaking her as she stood in a fearful daze.

Suddenly, a loud crash filled the room and their mother screamed. Genesis saw fragments of glass shoot past their father, and the kitchen phone fell to the floor with a crack. Then, a dark figure descended upon him from the direction of the now shattered window, and the sound of many boots squeaked on the wood flooring of the other room as it flooded with faceless men.

Genesis grabbed River again and dove under the bed. Only a few seconds of the new situation under the cramped bed had passed before River began whimpering. The difference from earlier was that she felt no apathy—how could she when she felt just as scared and wanted nothing more than to start whimpering as well? But, as the older sister, she had to keep her composure, so she clapped a firm hand over his mouth to muffle him.

"What do you want? Let go of my wife!" their father demanded in the other room.

"Sorry, sir, but your wife is a security threat. She is a danger to *Arisha*, so we will be taking her, along with you...wait...are there children in this house, too?" a man said in a calm, snake-like voice.

"No, we don't have any children..." their mother answered.

"Then what is with these children's toys?" A clattering followed and Genesis could only guess the man had knocked some of River's toys off the coffee table. "Don't lie. This house says there are children here all over it."

"We were preparing to have children. We have wanted to have children for a long time, but haven't been able to have any," their mother grasped at whatever she could in a desperate attempt to protect her two children. In truth, she knew her words would probably do no good in their current situation. But still, as a mother, she had to try at all costs to protect them from whatever evil had just invaded their home.

"I do not believe a word you are saying. I will have the house searched."

Genesis started to crawl toward the nightstand to get the phone located there, but her brother grabbed hold of her and would not let go. She couldn't see him in the dark, but she could sense the utter fear pouring forth from him all the more. She stopped and realized he was no longer whimpering. He understood the situation now. *Be quiet. Don't let them know we are here at all costs.* That meant don't even risk trying to get the phone.

She continued to lie under the bed motionless, the smell of dust filling their nostrils, to a point that made it so hard not to sneeze. Their bodies both trembled. If they could just have their mother. If she would come in and pull them out from under the bed, hold them both tightly to her, and tell them everything was going to be all right. Then Genesis knew the fear would leave her. She'd wake up crying in her mother's arms and her mother would tell her it was just a nightmare. But could one be so lucky? Maybe sometimes one could wake from such situations and find that it truly had been all a nightmare. But not now. No, now a harsh reality had arrived.

The door to their bedroom flung open, and time seemed to stop. Genesis felt as if she couldn't breathe. Not from the dust filling her lungs, nor from her brother's tight hold on her. No, all that filled her now was fear.

Boots thumped across the floor, the sound amplified to their ears pressed against the floorboards, as a man walked about the room. Genesis reached to her throat to clutch the cross necklace her father had given her for her last birthday. She gripped her brother tighter as well. River held his breath, whether due to her grip or his own terror, she was unsure.

The man continued to walk around the room. The children could hear his rifle shift on his shoulder with his movements. At last, he crouched down and they could hear his breaths as he drew closer and closer to the underside of the bed. Genesis turned her head sharply to see the shadow of his hand through the bed skirt, back lit by that crisp moonlight she had lain admiring only ten minutes earlier. She gripped her necklace even tighter, her face pressed against the floor again.

"You're under here, right?" the man whispered in a gentle voice. The spell broke and they both gasped for air after holding their breath for so long. The kindness in his voice was like none other they had ever heard. Still, Genesis could not bring herself to lift up her head again. Maybe it was a trap...

"Don't be afraid. I'm not going to let them take you. Your parents managed to call the police so they will be here in a moment. I'm so sorry this is happening. I wish there was more I could do to help you." His voice was faint. If he got caught, it would be over for all of them, including him.

Police sirens sounded in the distance, gradually drawing nearer and nearer. What he had said was true. He really did want to help them. That kindness had been no deception on his part.

The man stood up in a swift motion, so that the bed skirt bellowed where he had been. "Agent Ashford, we must leave this instant. Did you find any children?" A gruff voice drew toward the room, but the man exited before the other man could enter.

"No, sir, I think they told the truth. There are no children here," he answered.

"All right. Let's not delay any further then."

The children stayed frozen where they were as the footsteps died away down the front steps. Then a stillness fell over everything. River started to whimper again and so Genesis continued to hold onto him, still under the bed, both too terrified to venture forth for a time. The sirens grew louder and louder until they were right outside.

"Come on, River," Genesis whispered as she moved to crawl out from under the bed. He refused to follow, his body still trembling. She couldn't blame him though. No, her brother could do no wrong now. She felt just as terrified. She stared down at her own shaking hands as she reached back under the bed and dragged him out. She paused as he began to sneeze from the dust he had inhaled, then took his hand in hers. Her thoughts reverted back to the wish that she'd had as they lay under the bed...the wish for their mother to come and comfort them.

"It's going to be okay, River... We'll stay together no matter what. So don't you ever let go of my hand. Stay by my side." She looked directly into her brother's terrified eyes, until he slowly nodded. Then she rose to her feet and they walked through the empty apartment, out through the open front door. Flashing lights shone outside, and car doors shutting behind the police as they got out of their vehicles sounded in the calm night. She stopped at the top of the steps and her grip on River's hand tightened as the policeman came up the stairs toward them.

Chapter 2

Entrance Exams

THE SILENCE AND TENSION in the hallway made Genesis feel as if she might suffocate. She stood near a window that looked into a small gym room where River was currently taking a physical test. She watched as he stumbled to a stop on the other side of the room having just run as fast as he could across it. His face was beet red, and she could see how hard his chest heaved. He managed to keep his posture straight in hopes of disguising how physically out of shape he was, but he wasn't fooling anyone, that was for sure. She had told him over and over that he needed to train for the physical aspect of the exam, but he hadn't listened. She knew he had assumed that his mixed martial art skills would be all he needed, but that had been hopeful thinking on his part. He was now 12 and excelled in academics, but he didn't care for sports in the least.

"River! At this rate I'm not sure if you'll pass!" Genesis muttered to herself. She watched as the examiner motioned River over to the center of the room again and seemed to be asking him some questions. Genesis's only hope was that he had scored high enough on the academic examination that they had finished a little while ago to outweigh his deficiencies in the physical portion. He always had his nose in some kind of book, both fiction and nonfiction. He loved school and learning in general and, as a result, he had consistently ranked at the top of his class since he was seven years old. She felt quite proud of him in that regard, to say the least.

"Miss Deadlock," a voice broke the silence of the empty hallway, and Genesis turned to see a woman standing in the doorway of one of the nearby rooms. The woman smiled. "Let's finish up your exam. Right this way." The woman disappeared around the doorframe again, and so, with one final glance through the window at her brother, Genesis turned and quickly hurried to follow her.

Genesis had already finished both her academic and physical examinations, so she had figured she was done. Apparently she had been mistaken and there was one more aspect of the exam left. The room she now entered had an examination table in the center, like you would see in a doctor's office. Since the building wasn't a doctor's office, however, and didn't belong to the examiners, for that matter, the table was collapsible so that it could be easily transported from location to location as they traveled to different cities to hold their exams. The room was not all that interesting; it was mostly empty with a few gray chairs, and a table where the woman, who Genesis assumed to be a nurse or a doctor, had all her equipment laid out. The room reeked of sterilizing chemicals.

"I'll just be doing a quick health check and gather some samples the school will need while processing your application," the woman explained.

"Samples?" Genesis questioned, patting the table a moment to ensure it was stable before she took a seat upon it.

"Yes, I'm sure you understand the nature of the school. We do classified tech work for the Mirrorick government. As such we take a number of security precautions, one of which will be taking DNA and blood samples. We will use those to confirm you are who you say you are. Understand?"

"Yes, ma'am," Genesis answered.

"I'll proceed with the blood sample first, just to get that over with."

"Thank you," Genesis said. The woman got to work preparing to draw some blood. Genesis really did hate the idea of being stabbed by a needle. I am sure none of us really like the prospect, but it is, on occasion, necessary.

"What made you interested in our program?" the woman asked to distract Genesis from the needle.

"Arisha University..." Genesis murmured, her brain swimming with the anticipation of the coming prick. "I guess I was partly intrigued by the mystery surrounding your school. It's not easy to be accepted into and launches you into the high end of the tech world. After the college portion, I'll be able to get a good job at a Mirrickian tech corporation. I think the results speak for themselves—all the students that graduate get really good jobs and are able to work with brand new technologies that could help a lot of people. My little brother River wants to take the same path and we're hoping we'll be able to go together." she answered half in truth. Most of what she said was repeating what the school made itself out to be. She really didn't have that much interest in tech. She just wanted to go because of the name, *Arisha*. She was going because she wanted to find her parents and it was the only lead she had.

"There! All done," the woman said, holding up a small vial of Genesis's blood. "Now that wasn't so bad, was it? I'll need to swab your cheek now. Hold on."

Genesis opened her mouth and the woman proceeded to wipe a Q-tip on the inside of her cheek. "What do your parents think about this? I know that's what makes a lot of students decide not to enter in the end. Unless their parents are the ones pushing them to go, that is." She laughed. "The entire program is eight years—four years for the high school portion, and four years for college—and we don't typically let students leave, unless it's an emergency. Again, due to our security precautions."

"My parents are no longer here. My brother and I were raised by our uncle, and he has been very supportive of us. He's an MMA teacher and so a lot of my physical skills I learned from him. I'm very grateful to him."

"That's wonderful. I'm going to check your lungs now so try to give me some deep breaths." Genesis nodded. The woman did a few more tests after that, all tests you'd normally receive in a physical exam with your doctor, so I don't suppose they are all that interesting to mention!

"All right! That is all I need from you. You can head back down the hall to wait for your brother in the lobby. We'll get back to you with your results in a couple of weeks. Do you have any questions?"

"None that I can think of right now. Thank you, ma'am," Genesis answered.

Genesis made her way down the hall and out into the lobby as she had been instructed. River shouldn't be too far behind her. She guessed that he would have the health check shortly after her. She hadn't waited long between her physical test and the medical exam.

After collecting their bags, Genesis immediately pulled out her phone to text Uncle Ferris to let him know she was done and that River would be done soon. Then she dropped her phone onto her lap, and gazed sleepily at the red and black tiles that were arranged to make patterns on the floor. The venue seemed very fancy, which demonstrated the wealth of the school that they could afford such a location to hold their annual entrance examinations.

"Why does that sign say Arisha University on it?" A couple students sat on the far side of the room. A gloomy girl had asked the question to the guy seated beside her.

"B-because th-the s-school has t-two names," the guy beside her stammered. "A-arisha University and the m-more c-common name

D-driscoll University."

"Are you doing all right?"

"Y-yes... just n-nervous... I n-need to make it in."

Genesis's phone vibrated with Uncle Ferris's response, confirming that he was on his way to pick them up. Genesis took a deep breath and sank lower in her chair. The tension was pretty high even though the room was not all that crowded. Most of the applicants had just arrived and still had their examinations ahead of them. She at least had the relief of having done her part, and so it was all out of her hands moving forward. She really wanted to make it, too. She had been working so hard toward that test ever since the day that she and Uncle Ferris had discovered the existence of Arisha University, or perhaps I should say Driscoll University. I will be referring to it more often by Driscoll for reasons that will be clear later!

Several minutes passed and other students were called back to start their exams. For Driscoll to test each student individually, there must be only a few brave students applying at each test location, which further demonstrated the seriousness of the school to Genesis.

Genesis straightened up as River sauntered down the hallway toward her, his image reflected in the glistening tiles of the floor. He heaved an exasperated sigh before sinking heavily into the chair next to her. Genesis didn't dare ask him about it. She didn't really need to though—his attitude said it all.

"I don't think I'm going to pass..." River said sadly.

"You don't know that..."

"But I do! I did terribly on that physical test. I could totally see my failing scores in the examiner's eyes! Plus, he even reminded me that I was a bit young for the program, and they rarely accept students who aren't entering high school next year! He was basically telling me nicely that I didn't pass! The only part of that test I did halfway decently was the martial arts. I had my frustration driving me to easily overtake that examiner...if only that were enough. You're so strong and smart I'm sure you won't have any problem making it in. After all, you gave up having friends in middle school just so you could focus all your attention on preparing for this exam. I guess I should be prepared to say goodbye to you next fall." River was not usually so negative, thus Genesis knew his harsh words were only out of frustration over how he felt he had done.

"I won't go without you, River. Even if I have to go a year late, or even two years late, I'll wait for you. *Yes*, I want to find our parents more than anything and *Arisha* is our only clue right now, but above that I promised myself that we'd do everything together and that I'd never leave you behind. We can't even know for sure that this school will even have the answer, so you come first."

He flushed a bit, quite embarrassed over his sister's words. They must have cheered him up, however, for he seemed in better sorts after that as they waited for their uncle to arrive. After a bit, it was almost as if he had forgotten all about his misfortune and began undoing his sister's black hair from the bun in which it had been secured. Genesis was too nervous about whether or not he had passed the tests to really mind him playing with her hair that much. She really wanted to go to Driscoll sooner rather than later, but she couldn't break the promises she had made to her brother. She wouldn't go if he couldn't, and right now the odds were looking pretty grim. She wouldn't give up until their family was back together again. Of that, she was certain.

Chapter 3
Results

GENESIS HELD ONTO HER trembling little brother *that* terrible morning at the police station. Though at the time his speech was not very good, he kept repeating *Arisha* over and over again, until it sounded strange from his mouth. Each syllable became clear and understandable. The only constant sound most of that morning was that one word from his lips as the sun climbed higher and higher into the sky. For hours Genesis either looked outside to see the day's progress or fixated her eyes on the clock hung up on the stark white wall across from where they sat. Occasionally the sound of a phone ringing somewhere, or a conversation between two officers would pass by them, but River's small voice was the only important thing to his older sister. Then suddenly, River paused, his round eyes lifted from the navy seat cushions to look up at his older sister just as her lips began to quiver.

"Those men..." she whispered, "They said mama was a danger to *Arisha*. I don't know what that is... When they asked if she had children she said *no*. Why would Mama and Daddy leave us like that? Why would they pretend like we didn't exist?" she asked as tears started to roll down her face.

"They took Mommy away. She loves us," he mumbled, his fingers in his mouth. Genesis brushed aside her tears with her wrists and took a deep sniffling breath as it dawned on her what he meant. She realized she was being irrational. She knew then that she had to find them. She had to stop crying and being scared. She had to protect her little brother at all costs. She was the older one, which meant she had to be strong.

The police investigation had turned up nothing. The children had even brought up "Arisha" to them, but that seemed to do little good. That is why when she heard of Arisha University for the first time, she knew that would be their first clue to find their parents. Genesis would probably get further on the inside as a student, but she couldn't know if she was on the right track for sure unless she made it in.

Waiting. Something I think we can all agree is never an easy task, especially when that thing you are waiting for is uncertain. Like a verdict or an acceptance letter. This is where Genesis found herself now, after the completion of her entrance examinations. The process of waiting. A process of building anticipation with each coming day that they did not receive that important call.

The day came at last a full two weeks after they had taken the entrance exam for Driscoll University. Genesis and River had just gotten home from school to find Uncle Ferris talking on the house phone in the other room. Of course, he was a teacher so it wasn't like he didn't get calls regularly from his adult students, but they mostly called him on his cellphone so him being on the home line did spark their curiosity.

On a side note, at this point I feel I must explain that Uncle Ferris did not like children all that much. Despite that, he had still agreed to move into the mansion after their grandmother passed and their grandfather grew too sick to take care of River and Genesis himself. That was when Genesis was eight and River six, just a little over a year after their parents had been taken. After their grandfather passed as well, a little over a year ago, Uncle Ferris then inherited the mansion and so they had all remained there. Genesis wondered if the reason he encouraged them to go to Driscoll University was so that he could get them off his hands and have someone else finish raising them. He never talked about such things, though, so how were they to know?

Genesis and River stood anxiously behind him as he answered whoever was on the other end with brief "yeses" and "thank yous". River, of course, was panting after even just the short sprint from the front door to the kitchen at the very back of the house. Their uncle's mansion was quite large, after all, so the distance was probably a great deal longer than what you and I have from our front doors to kitchens.

"Thank you so much. Yes, I'm sure we will be requesting the materials.... Yes, I'd like to confirm everything with the children first and get back to you on your offer to Genesis....again, thank you..."

At last he hung up the phone and turned around to face them. Genesis clutched the dark stone countertop, her eyes examining his expression as she tried to come to some sort of conclusion over the news. Uncle Ferris was in no way easy to read, however, for he always smiled brightly at the two of them in a rather pleasant manner. I guess one could say he could be quite secretive, and that smile was a method of making himself as unforthcoming as possible.

"Genesis made it in, didn't she?" River asked with enthusiasm. He had not missed the part where Uncle Ferris had mentioned something about an offer to Genesis, but neither had Genesis. Her mind was already swimming and she couldn't tell if the suggestion of an offer could be good or not. Perhaps she hadn't made it but they were offering something else instead?

"If River didn't make it, maybe you shouldn't tell me either. I'm not going without him," Genesis said, although she didn't in the least bit enjoy the thought of not being told what the news was.

"There is no need. I'm pleased to tell you that you both made it in," Uncle Ferris said in such a casual manner that neither one of them could really react for a moment.

"Wait... we... What? Even *I* made it in?" River finally blurted out in disbelief.

"Yes, we didn't hear you wrong, did we?" Genesis added, to which River shot her a look. It was meant to be teasing, but did she really have to make it seem so obvious that she had doubted his abilities to do so?

"You did indeed, my lad. They said you almost failed the physical test, but your perfect academic scores made up for it. They are sure that in their program the physical aspect will come with time."

"Oh, bother. They'll force me to run, won't they?"

"Running is good for you," Uncle Ferris said.

"Yeah, I'm sure it will be good for you. I hope they make you run every day," his sister teased, to which she received a jab in the ribcage from him in response.

"Enough of that. You both made it! So I expect to see at least some more smiling around here..."

"We did!" River declared. Taking up each other's hands, the two of them then began to jump up and down with a series of excited ramblings that Uncle Ferris could certainly not even half understand.

"Alright, alright, alright, let's take the passion down a few notches," Uncle Ferris told them. Genesis turned her head, unable to control the smile that turned up the corners of her lips now that the news was starting to fully set in. "The school seemed particularly interested in you, Genesis."

"I knew they would! Genesis worked so very hard, after all," River said, clapping his hands together in quick succession.

"They have actually invited you to come early during spring break, and take the last month and a half of middle school classes with the students at the House of Arisha," Uncle Ferris finished. The smile faded from Genesis's lips and she grew more serious over the new information. "On top of that, they are giving you a full scholarship including room and board. I'm quite pleased about that, given that we were going to have to use up a great sum of your parents' money to pay half the tuition cost, since I was planning on paying the other half."

"That's so amazing!!! Didn't I tell you you would pass no problem?! That's a huge scholarship!"

"Yeah... How is that even possible? In all my time researching the school, I've never heard of them ever giving out scholarships..." Genesis stammered. She was truly happy, but honestly she was starting to feel just a bit overwhelmed by the news.

"What is the House of Arisha?" River asked.

"Right, you wouldn't know since it didn't seem relevant to bring up before now..." Uncle Ferris said, clearing his throat. "Like the school, little is known for sure about it. But what we do know is that the House is an orphanage run by the school, probably on the campus or near it. Of course, that doesn't make much of a difference, as the exact location of both is unknown. Hence the reason that a chauffeur will be coming to pick you both up and take you when it's time. They are going to email all that information to me after I confirm your acceptance, though." Uncle Ferris waved it off. "Anyway, nothing about the kids at the House is known well by those of us on the outside. They do receive a great number of donations every year, due to how noble people think it is that the founders of the school—the Watts family—have taken in orphans and educated them so well. Honestly, I've been wondering this whole time if the mystery of the place called the House of Arisha was just some made up rumor spread for the school to receive the donations. I guess being that Genesis was invited to go there, that must not be the case, however."

"I assume the students who came into the University from the House will probably be treated better and be above the other students since they have been with the Watts family for a lot longer," Genesis added.

"I see! I never realized there was such a place!" River said in surprise.

"Yeah…" Uncle Ferris started again. "What we do know about that place are mere speculations since most people don't know exactly what goes on in that mysterious school with the whole classified thing. At least people get enjoyment out of conspiracy theories. Where there is more uncertainty, the wilder the conspiracy can get. There are no tours of the campus and the government only goes once a year to make their inspections. I'd honestly feel more uncomfortable if not for that. The Mirrorick government has sanctioned their operations and so I'm certain it's not a bad place. In the end, the decision is up to you, Genesis. I will write up the email confirming your acceptance tonight unless you need some more time to think it over…"

Genesis shook her head. "Nope, I don't think I need to think it over. I'm not going to go yet… Spring break is not that far away so that would give me little time to prepare… More than that, I promised River we'd do this together…"

"No, you don't have to… It's really fine if you want to go sooner…" River stopped as his sister grasped his shoulder and shook her head.

"My mind is made up. As long as it won't affect my scholarship I'd like to enter in the fall with River. We'll go into this together. I wasn't going to go unless River made it so I'm not going to leave him behind now either. That's what I've decided."

Uncle Ferris nodded in understanding. "Very well, but I better not hear any complaining about how long summer is this year," he teased.

"We won't!" they both said in unison.

"All right. Well, run along now. I expect you to keep up with your studies...and I also expect more running from you, young man."

"Never!" River declared, at the same time fleeing from Genesis as she made an attempt to tickle his ribs.

Uncle Ferris smiled gently to himself, glancing over at a picture he had set up on one of the floating shelves where he kept all of his wine glasses above the bar sink. The picture was of his brother and sister-in-law on their wedding day. Where on Earth were the two of them now?

Chapter 4

A Silent Journey

COME THE END OF that summer, Genesis and River packed all of their belongings into boxes and shipped them off to Driscoll University. Once the boxes arrived, they would be put into their new dorm rooms in preparation for their arrival at the school the following week. All they had left with them was anything that could fit into their suitcases.

Time dragged that last week, as Genesis and River made their final preparations. The two of them handled the anticipation quite differently though. While River bubbled with all the excitement in the world—as he so often did about a great deal of things—Genesis harbored some doubt over whether she really had made a wise choice in going to the school.

Why was the school so secretive to the public? What had those DNA and blood samples really been for? Why was the acceptance rate so incredibly low...yet both she and River had made it in? What was she getting her little brother into?

All she could do was grasp at her vague hope—the hope that she could uncover the truth about her parents' disappearance. She couldn't know for sure if going to the school would really, truly unlock that mystery, but she had to try. The government approved the school, so she held onto that knowledge and kept telling herself that there was no way they would let the school hurt them. As a side note—I, for one, believe strongly that feelings of doubt and dread, such as those that Genesis experienced back then, can often act as a warning and should never be taken lightly.

At long last, the week came to an end and the morning they were to go to Driscoll arrived. The car was scheduled to be there in the late afternoon, so, after an early dinner Genesis and River went out onto the porch and started waiting.

About half an hour had passed when a rumbling welled up from the long gravel driveway, and the two of them bolted to their feet. Genesis stood completely still as she listened, while River rushed over to the stone steps that lead down from the porch. He watched as the car rounded one of the hedges and continued up the driveway toward them. That was it—the car sent there to take them away from the house they had grown up in since the loss of their parents.

They turned as the front door opened and Uncle Ferris joined them on the porch. The time had arrived to say goodbye to his niece and nephew. Uncle Ferris clapped his hand down on River's head and ruffled his dark locks of hair. In turn, River tried to wrestle from his grasp, but even with all River's strength, he was no match for Uncle Ferris. As soon as their uncle had his arms locked around River's chest he could not escape until their uncle had released his hold.

"When I get back, I'll be able to beat you! That's a promise!" River declared as he spun back around to face his uncle. Uncle Ferris responded with a slim smile and moved to embrace his niece as well, but not quite as roughly as he had done for River.

The driver waited patiently by the vehicle as they finished their goodbyes. Uncle Ferris shed no tears over their departure—at least not until the car was a safe distance down the driveway. Genesis had expected that from him, though. She thought he must be relieved to have them off his hands, as guilty as that relief probably made him feel. After all, he had never been too fond of children in the first place. He mourned the thought of how poorly he had treated their father when he was a child, but that didn't change his regard toward young humans. At least, that is what Genesis believed.

Genesis waved over her shoulder at Uncle Ferris one last time as she stood in front of the car door. He just continued to smile as he returned the gesture. His golden hair shone bright in the afternoon sunshine. *Would she see him again? How long would that be? Would he be all right living in that mansion all alone?* She tried to engrave the image of him in her mind, so that no matter how long it was until she saw him again, she would always remember how he looked standing on the porch as they left.

At last she tore her eyes away from him and slipped into the back seat of the car beside her brother. The smell of the new car filled the air within, much to River's pleasure as he was quite fond of such smells. The driver slammed Genesis's car door shut as he passed from packing their luggage in the trunk to the open driver's door. After he had taken his position back at the wheel, the car started forward, marking the start of their journey. After all that time spent trying to get into the school, they were finally on their way.

"I can't believe we're actually going!" River said as he struggled to fit the seat belt across his lap. His sister helped him find the buckle on which he sat. "Thank you, Gen-gen!"

"My pleasure," she beamed.

"I wonder what kinds of people will be there! I'm sure everyone will be super talented!" His head whipped around to flash an enthusiastic grin at her. "Didn't you hear? My favorite actor decided to go to Arisha... Driscoll... whatever! Anyway he's starting around now, too! We might even see him on the campus!"

"Who would that be again?" his sister asked, uncertain. She hadn't really kept up with things like that. I fear she had been far too focused on her training the past few years, which left little time for TV and other leisurely activities. In other words, she didn't know much about famous actors and other celebrities of the sort.

"Hiero Caddel, of course!" he exclaimed. She gave him a blank stare in response. She wanted so desperately to please her brother by knowing exactly who that was, but she had no idea. The name certainly had a familiar ring to it as there was not one person at the time who hadn't heard his name—especially if you were a girl in middle school, no matter how antisocial you might be—but she still couldn't match a face to the name and so felt far from being able to say she knew the guy.

River sighed and shook his head. "You're so uncultured! How do you not know about him? He's a famous kid actor! The talk of the times! He started acting when he was very little and gained popularity over the years! He's one of the best in his field, plus he's even got his own band and everything at only 15! He's the same age as you, for goodness sake! But anyway, he announced last year he was shooting for Arisha University for high school, since it was really hard to get into. The thing is, he actually made it and decided to go! I can't believe you don't know anything about him, though! You're a girl and his age! You should be drooling all over him, like every other teenage girl on the planet! He's super good-looking and all!"

"Sorry, River...but I don't really care about whether or not some famous guy will be attending school with us." She scratched her temple in a nervous manner as she spoke. His expression fell the next instant, so she swiftly took hold of his hand on the leather seat between them and gave it a tight squeeze. "But I'm happy you admire him so much. I'm glad you were able to have as normal a childhood as possible."

He nodded and his expression brightened again. "I really hope I can get his autograph!"

"I'm sure you will. We're going to the same school as him, and, from what it sounds like, there won't be that many students in each grade since it's so hard to get in."

"Yeah... I read somewhere that only like 100 kids made it this year, not counting the kids coming from the school's orphanage, of course."

"That's not very many at all..."

"Yeah, we got very lucky, I guess. Especially me, since they obviously wanted you pretty badly with that full scholarship. I'm just glad that our parent's money was able to cover the cost for me to go as well..."

Genesis glanced up at the front seat of the car where the driver sat in silence, the corners of his mustache twisted up on either side of his face. She thought it very strange that he hadn't uttered a single word to either one of them the entire trip. He hadn't even said anything to them as they entered the car.

"How long will we be driving, sir?" she asked. No response followed. Like a robot, his eyes stared straight ahead at the road, a blank expression on his face, from what she could see in the rear view mirror. A sigh escaped her lips and she sank back against the seat, her gaze directed out the car window.

The day grew late and the sun began to sink lower in the sky. Still the car drove on to carry them through the city of Mirrorick and out into the countryside beyond. River fell asleep since he had barely slept the night before in his excitement, but Genesis, on the other hand, continued to stare out the window lost in her own thoughts. Eventually, the car drove onto a dirt road surrounded by willow trees on either side. Their long draped branches bent against the wind as the vehicle drove straight through them for a good 10 minutes more before a tunnel appeared and the vehicle plunged onward.

Genesis blinked as her eyes tried to adjust to the dim lighting provided by lanterns every few yards in the tunnel. She marveled that they lit only when the car drew close to them, like they had motion sensors. The lights had a soothing effect on Genesis as the vehicle was never fully cloaked in darkness, almost like someone was welcoming them in.

The car slowed as it entered a cavernous chamber filled with dim lights that hung on the many pillars that supported the ceiling above them. The room was mostly empty with the exception of a few vehicles, like the one they were in, as well as some buses, parked along the back wall. Four tunnels led out of the chamber. The walls were of worn bricks and the ground was cracked concrete. Other than that, there was nothing more to the room.

Genesis nudged her brother in the ribs as the car approached one of the tunnels that sloped up out of the chamber. River stirred from his sleep, blinked in the dim light, and muttered something incoherent under his breath. Gravity then forced them back against their seats as the car heaved its way up the steep ramp toward the dimming light that now filtered down from the exit above them.

"Are we there?" River asked, clutching his armrest as the car reached level ground again. Just in front of the vehicle, their path was blocked by a closed gate that led out of the tunnel. The gate was iron—an electrical one that could slide open and closed on its own. Genesis could not see any signs that they had arrived at the school, but that made sense for a school that wanted to keep its location a secret.

"I'm guessing so... I can't say for sure..." Genesis answered hesitantly.

The driver rolled down his window for a man approaching the car and handed him an ID card. The man scanned it with a scanner device before he leaned over to gaze into the back seat. "Genesis and River Deadlock," the driver spoke for the first time. The man made a motion with his hand and the driver rolled down both of the back windows so that the man could look in.

"Can you hold out your hand, missy?" the man asked in a kind voice. Genesis nodded slowly and held her hand out the window. The man clamped some kind of machine around her pointer finger and she flinched as her finger was pricked without warning. Next, he removed the machine and gazed at the screen. Although she wasn't really bleeding too much, the man handed her a cotton ball to hold over her finger. He then performed the same test on River.

"All right. You are free to go," the man told the driver. The gate screeched open and he took a few steps back, while still staring down at the screen.

"That was a surprise!" River said. His eyes were fixed on the small bead of blood that welled from his pricked finger.

Genesis didn't say anything for a moment as she weighed what had just happened. She could only come to the conclusion that it had been done to ensure they were indeed the same individuals that had been accepted into the university. The school continued to be mysterious!

The car drove through the gates and entered onto a gravel road. They bumped along always on a slight incline. Thankfully, the incline was not anywhere near as steep as the ramp they had taken to exit from the tunnel. All that Genesis could see out her window was a large cliff face that loomed high up over the road. Outside River's window were trees.

They passed by a driveway down to a large mansion situated in the midst of the forest. "What's that?!" River exclaimed.

"The House. You shan't be going there, so pay it no heed. In fact, it is preferred if you don't dwell on what lies outside the windows at this time. You may grow confused," the man answered in an abrupt manner of speech.

Ignoring the driver, Genesis responded, "It's so amazing to see in person!" She kept her gaze on the top of the building and once they were a bit higher, she could see the tops of several other buildings around the house, as well as the cliff that rose up behind the property. Soon trees blocked her view, and she lost sight of the buildings all together.

A little while later River grew weary of the trees and bumping motion of the car and started to sigh repeatedly, which his sister tried to ignore. On Genesis's side, they passed some docks along the river bank and then the road turned and they were surrounded by trees on both sides. At last they reached another gate, at which the driver handed over his ID again. The difference here, however, was that the woman stationed there did not have to do anything else to confirm the identity of the Deadlock children, much to their relief. After handing the driver back his ID, she let them through the imposing gate. They had finally entered the campus of Driscoll University.

Genesis grew excited to observe more interesting scenery, but the journey had indeed come to an end. The car stopped in front of the first building, a whitewashed brick building with a sign that read "Medical Department" over the main doors. A garden surrounded it, including some crepe myrtles that still had a few flowers left on their branches.

The driver got out and removed their suitcases from the trunk. Neither Genesis nor River spoke as they waited for permission to exit. River could not stop fidgeting in his seat, though. They had driven all that way already and so even just those brief few minutes felt like an eternity. At last, the driver opened Genesis's door and directed them to get out.

They stretched their legs in the evening sun that now filtered in between the trees to bathe the sidewalk in its golden light. The sky looked so lovely, like a watercolor painting of bright oranges and purples. They had made it! The driving was done and therefore the most difficult part must be completed! Now they just needed to adjust to life, meet the other students, and attend classes until they got some clue to the whereabouts of their parents. If only that were truly the case...

The driver rolled their suitcases over to them without a word. "Thank you so much, sir," Genesis said as she grasped the handle of her suitcase while bowing to the driver—a gesture of gratitude that had been adopted into Mirrorickian culture.

Perhaps I should pause here for a brief geographical explanation. Mirrorick, for those who may not know of its existence, is an area between the United States and Canada that broke away to govern themselves in the early 2000s. Most people just thought of it as being a city back then, but it actually included a large area of wilderness as well. The school was located somewhere within the Mirrorickian borders, and so it was the Mirrorick government that had sanctioned it.

River, remembering the polite thing to do, followed his sister's example, but he was too caught up in the fact that they had finally reached the school, to utter a word of thanks. In the end, it didn't matter that much since the driver said nothing in response. He merely motioned for them to follow him up to the front doors of the Medical Department without any explanation as to why they were going inside.

Past the automatic doors, they found themselves in the lobby of a medical center. A nurse stood at the front desk and so the driver handed both of them off to her before he took leave of them. In general, Genesis thought he must either be unfriendly, hate his job, or didn't like children, much like their uncle, although she knew it wasn't right for her to jump to such conclusions. He could have any number of reasons why he had barely said a word to them for the couple hours they had been together in a closed space.

"You two can sit down if you want. You'll be called back in just a few moments," the nurse told them, with a gesture over to a few seats not far from a floor to ceiling length window that looked out to a side yard.

"Thank you, ma'am," Genesis answered, and the two of them moved to do as directed.

Chapter 5

Dr. Cherith

THE LOBBY WAS SO quiet that only the soft voices of the nurse and the receptionist behind the front desk could be heard while River and Genesis sat waiting. River sighed again and rested his chin on his hands, leaning forward on the handle of his suitcase in front of him.

"Tired?" Genesis asked.

"Yeah, I want to get to our dorm rooms soon so I can make my bed and sleep for a while. Do you think we'll start classes the day after tomorrow? It's Saturday, so I figured that would be most logical," River answered.

"Yeah... That was my thought, too... We didn't receive the official start date for classes. Just the day that the car would come to pick us up, so I'm not sure. If we don't start the day after tomorrow, then I guess it won't be for another week. We could have some sort of orientation at some point this week, don't you think?"

"That would suck! I want to start classes as soon as possible! The summer has been so long and I miss school!"

Only River... She was looking forward to starting school at Driscoll University as well. The school was mysterious, so of course she was! Despite her own excitement, she couldn't think of too many students who were as excited to get into academics with the same enthusiasm as River. Genesis sat, lost in thought, as she leaned on her hand to gaze at some birds through the window beside her. They hopped about the grass where some crepe myrtle petals had gathered, jabbing their beaks down among them to catch bugs. How strange to see crepe myrtle trees growing in Mirrorick. She had only ever seen crepe myrtles that one time Uncle Ferris had taken them down to North Carolina for vacation one summer. Now that she thought about it, the purple petals were quite unique as well.

She heard a door shut down the hall, followed by some quick footsteps over the white tiled floors. Both of their heads lifted as a male doctor with long, straight, black hair entered the room and approached the nurse at the front desk. After a moment of conversing with her in a low voice, he turned his attention to River and Genesis.

"Miss Deadlock, would you please come with me?" he requested, his voice breaking the silence that had hung so heavily in the room.

Genesis glanced over at River before she stood, grasping the handle of her suitcase. The doctor turned to start back down the hall as he had come, but her steps grew uncertain as she tried to follow. She kept stopping to glance back over at River again, her mind swimming with anxiety.

"W-wait..." she spoke up. "What about my brother?" Her voice trembled. The situation seemed strange to her. Why were they in a medical building instead of an administrative building, or their dormitory, for that matter? And why was she being taken away from the only person she felt completely comforted by? She didn't like it at all. It was not that she sensed danger—every single individual that they had interacted with, other than their driver, had been very kind to them, and the doctor seemed just as kind—but that didn't change the fact that they were in unfamiliar territory. Genesis wasn't quite sure what to expect going forward.

The doctor turned around again. "Don't worry," he assured her.

"You will only be separated for a little while, and then we will be sure to reunite the two of you. We were sure to put you both in the same student group, so you will only have to be separated for a short while here at the beginning of your studies. Otherwise, while you are here, the two of you will be attending classes and living in close proximity to each other." Genesis looked back again, but River gave her a confident nod to show he was all right on his own. She took a deep hissing breath to calm her nerves, before she continued down the hall after the doctor.

Her legs shook beneath her as he led her to an examination room. He held the door open to her and she stepped inside. "I left a gown for you on the table to change into. I'll be back in a moment with another doctor. You can leave your suitcase by that chair in the corner—one of the female nurses will take care of them, so don't worry," the doctor said.

"Okay. Thank you, sir," Genesis answered. He gave her another smile and shut the door, then she was alone for the first time since that morning.

Her eyes wandered the room as she pushed her suitcase over to the chair in the corner. The room she was in now smelled of sterilizing alcohol, which wasn't in the least bit pleasant to her. In fact, she found it quite suffocating. She picked up the hospital gown folded neatly on the examination table and hastily put it on in fear that he would come back before she had finished changing. Her speed was unnecessary, however, for she spent a great length of time seated in silence on the table as she waited for his return. She wondered what kind of examination she was going to receive. She didn't really enjoy going to the doctor much at all, but I wonder if anyone really enjoys going to the doctor. Sorry, my dear reader, if you yourself are a doctor.

At last the knock came at the door, and the doctor reentered accompanied by a younger doctor with a brisk stride. "Dr. Das, at your service," the young doctor quipped with his hand extended out to Genesis.

"Please don't say anything to scare or alarm our student," the main doctor told him, almost before Dr. Das had gotten his words out completely. You see, the young doctor was a resident who had recently graduated from the university himself and often spoke out of turn.

"Don't worry! I won't do what I did last time. I was just introducing myself!" Dr. Das said, hurrying over to take a seat beside the monitor that was situated on a desk behind the examination table.

The main doctor flipped through Genesis's file as he made his way over to the counter along the right wall. The longer he delayed, the more anxious Genesis felt. Both men seemed quite friendly, though, and that did put her mind somewhat at ease.

"All right, Miss Deadlock, I say we get straight to it," the doctor said as he set his file down on the counter and took a seat on a stool. Genesis swallowed and shifted on the examination table so that she faced the doctor.

"I suppose I should take an example from Dr. Das and introduce myself. I'm Dr. William Cherith, the lead medical personnel here at Driscoll University. Today, we will start the awakening process with you!"

"Ooh, exciting!" Dr. Das said.

"I cannot go into the details of what the awakening process entails at this time. You will understand far better once it is over, but I wanted to start the process by assuring you that you are safe. We are here, and we are not going to let anything happen to you."

"Maybe," Das added, clicking his computer mouse as he looked over Genesis's medical records on the monitor.

"Don't listen to him. You will be all right, we won't let you die."

"Maybe."

"Dang it, Das. I'm going to make you leave."

"I won't say another word, promise!"

"Anyway..."

"Um..." Genesis started. Her stomach had twisted itself up and she felt like she might be sick. Dr. Cherith left space for her to speak and, as a result, a heavy silence hung over the room.

As the silence progressed, Dr. Das could only beat himself up more and more. Why could he not just keep his mouth shut? They were about to have a repeat of what had happened during one of last week's awakenings! Because he hadn't kept his mouth shut that kid had started crying and begged to be allowed to go home. In the end, Dr. Cherith had to tell the kid everything and it ended up messing up the entire order of things! He had tried to refrain from speaking this time, but sometimes he just couldn't help it! The words just popped right out before he could really think about them!

"What exactly *is* the awakening process...?" Genesis asked.

"Like I said, it will be much easier to explain afterwards. I will say that it is a process all of our students go through. We wouldn't have let you into the school if we did not think your body could handle it. I can't say it's going to be entirely pleasant, but I think you'll find it worth it in the end."

"Why, though? What's it for?"

"It's like a rite of passage!" Das spoke up. Surely he could say that much and redeem the situation he had started to create! "It will all make sense soon, so trust Dr. Cherith. He's been doing this for quite some time! Sorry if I scared you! I need to get better about that, but Dr. Cherith and I have both done the procedure, so we trust the process completely."

"Thank you, Das," Dr. Cherith said warningly.

"I'm still not sure... I don't like not knowing what is going to happen to me..." Genesis said in a low voice.

"I understand, and I wish I could explain things better. Honestly, you are probably not going to believe me if I do. That's why I want you to trust me. I know all of this might seem a little weird to you. You aren't at a normal school—I'm sure you realize that by now. We have reasons behind everything we do, and so I want you to understand that and trust that we really don't intend to hurt you in any way. We are your allies here and we are going to try to help you get the most out of your experience here at Arisha. Now, is it all right if we proceed forward? I want your permission first."

Genesis hesitated for a long time. Her head felt like it was swimming. She had been independent from such a young age and had learned to be wary of a lot of things. She hated the idea of casting caution to the wind and letting them proceed with the so-called "awakening" that she knew nothing about. At the same time, now that she was there, what choice did she have? If the process was necessary for entrance into the school, then there was nothing stopping them from proceeding anyway without her permission. At least if she did give permission, then she would be working with them and not starting her time off at the school at odds with them. In her current situation, she was probably right. I believe that situations like this should never be taken lightly, however. One should never throw caution to the wind as I believe Genesis had already done many times up to that point. That said, I am not suggesting that she was headed down a path to her own destruction, but I am also not suggesting the path she headed down was all sunshine and rainbows either.

"Okay... I'll trust you... I made it this far, after all, and you promise I'll be all right, right?"

"Yes, I promise that we will do everything in our power to make you feel safe and unafraid the whole time."

"Okay. Then I give my permission. We can start this awakening process..." she answered.

"Very well. I'm going to put you under anesthesia for a bit. It will just feel like taking a nap, all right?" Dr. Cherith said. Genesis nodded slowly in understanding. "Very well." He made a motion to Dr. Das to hand him a small syringe that the resident had been preparing behind Genesis. "We administer this kind of anesthesia through injection, so I hope you don't have issues with needles."

"No, sir," Genesis answered.

Dr. Cherith wheeled his stool close to her. She drew in a deep breath as he prepared to administer the drug. What kind of place had she gotten herself into? Was she really on the right track? Was she certain she could trust them? She had always thought herself a decent judge of character based on minimal interaction, and she didn't feel uncomfortable with either of the two doctors. They both had a safe, warm presence about them that put her at ease, even while the things they said stirred her with worry.

Dr. Cherith had already finished administering the drug and she started to feel a bit dizzy and faint. Dr. Das took hold of her shoulders and slowly reclined her back on the table as her vision began to blur. If the path she had taken turned out to be a mistake, what would she do then? She couldn't keep the doubts out of her head, but if this was what it took to find her parents then she was willing to do anything. She just had to find them. Her entire body numbed to the world and the white ceiling clouded before her eyes. The last things she saw were the shapes of Dr. Cherith and Dr. Das standing over her as she fell into unconsciousness.

Chapter 6

Awakening

GENESIS PULLED IN AND out of reality, unaware of how much time had really passed. She must have been out for a while, and, when she finally regained consciousness, she found herself reclined in a chair in a different room. The smell of chemicals filled the air around her. Unlike the examination room, this one was dimly lit by only one light that shone down upon her.

She struggled only to discover her arms were locked down securely to the arms of the chair. Several masked doctors stood round about her, but she could only make out their general shapes and forms as she blinked to try and focus her vision to no avail. Her mind felt fuzzy and her body seemed to be unable to function properly at all. She turned her head to see needles stuck into her arms, and from the needles were tubes with dark fluids running through them. She lifted her head a bit at a time, for everything felt so hazy that even such a small task proved difficult for her to accomplish. Her eyes at last came to rest upon a bag of blood which filtered into her veins through the tubes.

"No," she murmured as she began to struggle, too scared, confused, and weak to do anything else. Then she began to scream and sob without control, her entire body convulsing. "What are you doing to me? Stop it!" She jerked against her restraints until her wrists rubbed raw from the metal. "River! Where is my little brother? Are you hurting him, too? Please stop! Don't hurt my little brother!"

The sounds coming from monitors buzzed in her ears until they rang with their sound. She shouted and her arms yanked at their restraints again, but a man rested his hand on her shoulder. His voice was muffled, but his tone was kind. Yes, she knew it was Dr. Cherith again. He was right there next to her trying to calm her—actually all the voices around her seemed to. They were all there for her, she was going to be all right.

Another doctor hummed and waved his hand in front of her face several times until her body relaxed and her eyes shut. She thought they must have drugged her again to calm her from her outburst, but maybe the man had done something she still did not yet understand.

She fell deep into dark waters of unconsciousness. Claw-like hands reached out to grab at her arms, legs, and face. She opened her eyes in some nightmarish place and began to struggle against the hands as she heard voices all around her. The voices were not just ghostly, but also filled with terror—like screams from the pits of hell. The fear induced from them only made her struggle against the hands all the more and use every ounce of strength left in her body. She broke free.

She found herself in a mystical kind of place, almost knee deep in water that glistened against the darkness. Where the light that allowed her to see in the darkness came from was unbeknownst to her. Everything was like a black void that stretched out around her on all sides without end except for the water and another person who stood with his back to her. To be more specific, a strange man with an unusual shade of dark olive green hair. She took a step forward on unsolid ground, like the bottom of a lake or swamp; the water sloshed about her knees as she did so and the sound echoed through that dark place. The man turned his head to look back over his shoulder at her, a smile breaking over his slim lips. Her arms and legs began to tremble as she stood just a few paces behind him. A single other person in that cold darkness. His smile was so comforting that it seemed like the only kind thing in the dark dismal world around her. She sank down onto her knees in the water and lifted her hands toward him. That place smelled terrible, like the mud at the bottom of a bog, yet even that could not keep her from gasping for the breath that came so reluctantly to her lungs.

"Please... I don't want to die yet... Please get me through this... Help me..." She could barely get those few words out, but her intense desperation for his help drove her on toward him.

"You're finally here... I've been waiting..." the man whispered, his voice airy and faint like a wisp on the wind. He strode toward her, his hand outstretched. The water did not ripple with his movements through it, as if he dwelt outside of even that imaginary world around them. She extended her shaking hand toward his fingers. Her heaving chest felt as if it would cave in, but still she reached. Their fingertips met and then his soft palm came to rest upon hers. His smile and red eyes were so calm and kind, that in a moment tears rushed down her face, and she let out a few despairing sobs. Still he smiled, his eyes cast upon her face. She wasn't sure who he was, but she just wanted him to help her and make the pain stop. Never in her whole life had she felt so weak and pitiful. She always tried hard not to cry and to be brave for her brother's sake, but now she couldn't restrain herself. She just knelt in the water and sobbed like a small child at his feet.

"You can do this, Genesis, because you're strong... I will protect you for as long as I can. Now take on your father's power and strengthen it until you have perfected the valta of shapeshifting..." She had never seen him before in her life, yet he knew her name. She was overcome with deep confusion. What she now saw and felt, it all felt so real, but that place couldn't possibly be. Was she awake? Or was she dreaming?

A strange sharp energy passed from his hand into her hand and up her arm, then through her entire body. The power pushed her backward into the glistening water with its force, but instead of hitting the muddy ground she had stood upon, she began to sink. As she sunk into the darkness her black hair, which floated in the water around her, changed to that same strange olive green of the man's hair. Valta coursed through her entire body, as she continued to sink deeper and deeper into the darkness, but yet she didn't run out of air. That place really must have been a dream...

Chapter 7

Valta

GENESIS WAS STARTLED AWAKE, completely lucid and in reality. Her body sunk into the soft floor of the room she now found herself in. She was in a room like one of those that they put mental patients in, with cushioned walls and floors. But unlike that type of room, there was an observation window in one of the walls. Her awakening must finally be over.

Her breaths came slow and short as the room spun round about her. The lights had been dimmed, so that the stark whiteness of the room would not be so hard on her weary eyes. Her attention drifted to the observation window along the back wall, where some doctors stood on the other side. Their eyes studied her like some sort of scientific specimen. She could not bring herself to move at first, but bit by bit she gathered the will. I believe the desire to figure out what had been done to her grew too strong to hold her back.

She sat up, but her body cramped sharply in various places, and so she jerked back down to the floor with a painful gasp. Her head pulsed from dizziness and exhaustion. The answers to her many questions urged her on, though, and so she tried again. She dragged herself over the uneven floor toward the window. Once she reached it, she paused, in an attempt to catch her heaving breath, then rose up on her feet. Her hand gripped the edge of the cold window through which the men stood, stunned looks on their faces. One mustered a smile. You see, they had done the process with so many students who entered the university before, but never once had they witnessed one able to stand up so soon afterwards. She truly exceeded their expectations after such a short time. Just as she had reached the window, her body gave way and she sank back to the floor, breathless. The room began to spin again and she felt quite grateful for the cushioned floor, as the fall might have hurt otherwise.

The door now opened and one of the doctors stepped into the room. At first she didn't recognize him because of the mask he wore over his mouth, but after she noticed the long, dark, straight hair that reached down to his waist, she knew exactly who he was. Dr. Cherith pulled his mask down upon his approach so that Genesis could see his face. With a kind smile, he knelt down beside her and so she gathered her strength again to sit up in a slow, painful manner.

"W-what's going on?" she stammered.

"It is all right, Miss Deadlock. The awakening went smoothly! Now I am here as your teacher to teach you the basics of your valta and answer any questions you might have these first few months of your studies here at Driscoll University. Now, before we go into your first lesson, what would you like to know?" he asked.

She didn't answer him at first; her eyes remained fixated on his expression. She felt more confused than ever after he had spoken. She wondered if she heard things wrong due to an aftereffect of the drugs he had given her. He acted as if nothing was wrong with the situation they had put her through at all. For goodness sake, she just wanted him to answer her question as to what was going on. Why on earth were they doing something as terrible as whatever it was that they were doing, to someone not yet an adult like herself? Sure she had given permission, but in general, what had been done didn't seem right.

"What is going on?" she repeated with more firmness in her voice.

"We just finished your awakening... Or I suppose we still have one test to run before we're finished. In that case, we are in the process of awakening your valta, which is the valta known as shapeshift."

"What is a valta?"

"All right then. I'll be sure to explain it all now that the process is over. There are currently 14 different forms of valta. These are: water, fire, vegetation, earth, wind, ice, shadow, light, electricity, iron, energy, psychic, blood art, and shapeshift. By far, shapeshift and blood art are the most rare of these. Blood art is exclusive to a place called The Kingdom of Scarlet. Energy is not as rare, but is exclusive to a place called Tryss. As for you and I, we would fall under the category of shapeshift, which can be found about anywhere, but is a rarer valta."

"I don't understand what that all means..." He wasn't very good at explaining things, especially not shapeshifting. You see, he had never been granted his own valta student before, as there were rarely any shapeshifters to train. As a result, he had never really done the part of the process where he had to explain everything. Even so, he was ever so pleased to receive not one but two shapeshifters that year! Genesis knew nothing of that world so she wasn't sure how she should understand any of the elements he had just named. She wanted to know what the valta thing *was*.

"Valta is power. Within each person there are what we call valta cells which lie dormant, usually for the span of a person's entire life. They are undetectable except when awakened due to how incredibly small they are. We took samples of your blood and by mixing it with a certain substance were able to awaken these cells and conclude that you possessed the rare valta of shapeshift. Then, upon your arrival, we injected the awakened blood back into your body, which caused a chain reaction in your valta cells, awakening them all so that you might access their power. As I said, every human possesses dormant valta cells within them, but not all are the same. The types I listed before are all the current valtas out there. While there are more that have either become extinct or banned, these 14 types are what we list as our valtas today. The name of each type implies the power they wield. Yours being shapeshift gives you the ability to change into any creature whose DNA you have ingested. This works like cloning. Your cells change to be coded as the DNA of the creature you want to turn into—this turns you into an exact copy of that creature. I can go into further details on the science behind it in our first session. For now, why not put it to the test?"

She stared up at him in astonishment for a brief moment. "This all sounds kind of insane to me..." she faltered.

"Let me show you first, and then you can attempt it yourself." He set down his clipboard and pen as he moved to stand. Her eyes lifted to watch him throw his lab coat off, underneath which he wore plain black clothes of a very strange-looking material. The material was infused with his DNA and so it became an extension of his body. In the next moment his whole body condensed down into a spiral of blue light. Genesis flung herself back against the wall in shock as a bird landed gently on the cushioned floor and, with a sharp turn of its head, looked over at her. All that remained of the doctor was his pair of spectacles, which now fell onto the cushioned floor beside the small animal. Genesis swallowed; her mind and heart in a tumult as she thought she might have a heart attack.

As you know, things like people turning into birds don't happen in real life, as far as we are concerned. Genesis was just like us at the time and so she could not believe the notion of someone turning into a bird right before her eyes, just as you and I probably couldn't believe it either. She first thought that she might have lost her mind. Then next, that she was in some sort of awful nightmare and must wake from it. As a result of such thoughts, she began to strike her head several times with her hands. But then the bird's body began to warp and the doctor reappeared, with a chuckle at the stunned expression on her face.

He picked up his spectacles and replaced them on the bridge of his nose. "Now, there are some important things to note: regular clothes can not shift with you. You will need special garb infused with your DNA so that you will not be in...in the natural state...every time you shift back into your regular form. Also, you can only retain a few forms at a time. So be sure to return to your regular form frequently so as to not lose yourself. If you lose your original form, we do have your DNA so we can change you back. But if you were to be away from the school and not have DNA as back up, you could end up forever remaining some other creature. Just take this as a warning.

"Also, about the garb. We did send some of your DNA to a tailor who specializes in making such garb. But it will still take a few weeks to complete. You see, shapeshifting garb is not easy to make. The materials used are hard to obtain and the fusion process takes some time. Plus, we had to artificially grow more of your DNA from your samples. But what can be done? In the meantime you will have to be sure to have a blanket or something to cover yourself until then. Would you like to give it a try now?" She shook her head hard at the question. "Why not?" He seemed stunned by her reaction, his head tilted to the side with confusion on his face.

"It sounds super sketchy, if you ask me," she mumbled.

He let out a short laugh. "This all does seem pretty sketchy, doesn't it? But you did sign agreement forms saying you would let us do anything we wanted to you. Plus, you have an objective in coming here, right?" Those words made her cease breathing, for she remembered that she must find her parents at all costs—that was the reason she had ignored all of her fears up until now. With a hard swallow, she nodded. "Then using this valta, the valta of shapeshift, is the key to that goal. Your valta cells have already been awakened. That is why you are shaking so much. So why not give it a try? I will even let you pick your first animal." He motioned to a man who stood not far away in the doorway to the room.

The man now wheeled a cart in behind him, the steel frame shaking on the unsteady, soft ground. On the cart's racks were several cages with animals in them. In the first cage was a black cat. In the second, a Pomeranian dog. The third had a white bunny. The last, a blue bird with a yellow throat.

"You may choose the first animal you wish to change into."

She hesitated in another moment of doubt. The question that echoed through her mind now was whether she should resist a little more? Or should she move forward as they wished her to? She also felt very curious about valta. If he was telling the truth, the nature of the school was far wilder than she could have ever imagined it to be. No wonder they only let in a select few people. With that realization, her mind was made up for sure. She had made it into the school, had she not? She would indeed try shapeshifting and see if it was really true. She still had doubts despite everything she had just witnessed pointing toward its truth, but her actual change would confirm it, unless she was, indeed, just in a fever-induced dream.

All that in mind, she crawled over toward the cages and looked at the animals within: the bunny with its fluffy, soft fur; the dog with those round eyes; the bird as it hopped about the cage. The one that caught her eye, though, was the cat with its twitching whiskers. She had always loved cats, and wondered what it would be like to be one when she was little. With that memory, it only seemed right for her to choose the cat first.

"I see you have your eye on the cat," Dr. Cherith broached.

"Yes, sir," she answered with a nod.

"All right, excellent choice." He got to his feet and took the cat out of the cage with care.

"Wait... I don't have to eat it, right?" she protested.

He burst out into a short fit of laughter. "We would never make you do something like that! While our valta can be a bit disgusting with the need to ingest the DNA of the creatures we want to shift into, we only need a very small amount to do so. Here, pet her if you like." He held out the cat to her. She hesitated yet again, before she reached out with caution and ran her hand over the cat's sleek fur. "Good, now look at your hand." She lifted her hand, as instructed, to see she now had small strands of fur stuck to her palm, in part because her hands were sweaty from all that had happened. "You see that? Those small strands of hair contain the cat's DNA. Ingesting just one strand will be enough for your body to be able to copy it. That is how powerful valta is. Go ahead, try it."

She stared down at her hand for a long time. The longer she delayed, the more anxious she became about this whole scenario. The thought occurred to her that if she did change like he said she would, what if they couldn't change her back? Plus, licking the palm of her hand was already gross enough. But licking it with cat fur all over it was another level of disgusting. She glanced up at him.

"I can change back, right?" she asked.

"Of course you can. We can give you a substance to make you change back. Don't worry you won't be stuck like that forever."

"How do I shift after I swallow the strand? You didn't explain that part to me. I don't know how to go about it like you did."

"So many questions! Don't worry, when you first ingest the DNA of something you will automatically shift into it. That is, until you have further training that will ensure you can control your valta better. After all, we don't realize how many strands of animal fur and bugs we swallow without realizing it! Does that make sense?"

"Not at all! I don't understand how I won't be constantly shifting into things!"

"I see... Well, shapeshifting can be very sensitive at times. Although our bodies do get good at differentiating between consciously and unconsciously ingested DNA. It's kind of an amazing thing that our bodies are able to do! The more you train your valta, the less likely you will be to accidentally shift into something. I'm going to go into this more in our first scheduled valta session. Best to save me something to teach later! Why not try it now? Or do you have any more questions?"

She continued to stare at her hand another moment before she pulled off one strand of the cat fur. Then, with a brief, nervous gulp, she put it into her mouth and swallowed it. She found it very strange to intentionally do such a disgusting thing, but in another moment the room began to warp and then she felt as if she was falling. The room grew bigger and bigger and colors changed—more muted and strange to her new eyes. Only a few colors—the blue and yellow feathers of the bird—stood out with their same boldness.

She wriggled her way out of the hospital gown and looked about at the faces of the two men in the room, hazy and strange in appearance. She could sense every movement they made with the long whiskers that extended out from both sides of her face. The experience was so strange that she almost couldn't express it in words. She was scared, but also fascinated and wanted to know more. She wanted to fully embrace the new power and make it her own. She wanted to use it to find her parents in the strange world she had just walked into.

"You shifted very well for your first time. Would you like to change back now?" he asked. She opened my mouth to say *yes* but all that came out was a *meow*. The sound startled her so that her tail bristled. She really had become a cat. "Since this is your first time and you did so well, we will not put any more strain on your body. Let me give you this."

He put something into her mouth, a substance that tasted disgusting, like medicine. She began to feel extremely drowsy in an instant. Then she felt herself shift back into her normal state and a blanket was quickly thrown over her. She was unconscious again before she could really take in anything else.

Chapter 8

Zuri

WHEN GENESIS REGAINED CONSCIOUSNESS, she found herself in a bed covered with a thin white sheet. She blinked in the natural sunlight that filtered in through an open window just beside her bed. This was the first natural sunlight that had touched her eyes for several days, so it stung them. What she had learned in that cushioned, white room was her reality now and she had to face it. She still didn't know much about the place she now found herself in, and she knew it would take her a while to fully wrap her mind around everything that had happened, but somehow she could change into animals. Such an idea seemed impossible, but apparently she really could.

Suddenly a realization hit her and her heart felt as if it might stop. She sat up in bed, startled. "How had I forgotten that?" she whispered.

"Gen-gen!" a familiar voice greeted. His voice came like music to her ears after so long in the dark—her little brother she had worried so much about during the whole ordeal! I fear I can not quite say he was all right though, for as she lifted her eyes up to see the boy who sat in the bed across from her, she was rendered momentarily speechless. Her dearest little brother, who had been rather chubby his entire life, was as thin as a rail. His cheeks were sunken and his arms, which nearly disappeared into the sleeves of his hospital gown, as thin as twigs. That wasn't the only thing that had changed about the young boy: his hair had changed to a navy color, and his eyes were a deep red.

"River?!" Genesis cried.

"It's weird, right? I think that awakening thing was pretty hard on my body since I lost so much weight. But hey, look on the bright side. Now I can eat as much as I want and not put on any weight at all," he said with a laugh.

Genesis felt like crying, but she remembered her promise to herself to stay strong as the older sibling. She had already cried far too much since their arrival and it had only been a week, although they did not know that—they had been unconscious for so much of it that they both thought it must have been only a couple days.

"I suppose that is an advantage... What is your valta? You're not a shapeshifter, are you?" she asked her brother.

"Nope! I'm an energy user! Which means I can revert my gravity and have super strength if I train my body harder. Apparently, my valta type is the reason why I lost so much weight. In fact, excess weight is necessary for it so I wouldn't have been accepted as an energy user if I had not been a bit chubby! I heard that awakening a thin energy user is guaranteed to kill them. It was kind of scary to be told all that right after being awakened, y'know?"

"Yeah, that is scary... It sounds like what our mother might have had," Genesis suggested.

"Our mother had valta?!" River blurted out in shock.

She nodded, for that was the realization she had come to only a few minutes before. "She used to tell us stories when we were little about how she used to have super powers. I, of course, never believed any of them until now. Any parent could tell a story like that to their kid for fun."

"Wow! That's so amazing! I guess we are on the right track then!" he beamed. She nodded again, but then she caught movement out of the corner of her eye, and she turned her head sharply to see a boy in the bed next to her own. The boy's round, pale-blue eyes met her eyes and he smiled an innocent smile. He had a ghastly pale complexion and white hair, sort of like an albino. After all the talk of people possibly dying during awakenings, his ghostly appearance made Genesis's heart beat a bit faster, and she wondered what she looked like now. She reached up and grasped a strand of her olive green hair. Right, she did look different, like in her dream.

"Hello, miss," the boy said in a voice as soft as a snowflake.

"Right! Gen-gen, this is my new friend Zuri!" River exclaimed.

"I see you're already making friends. It is nice to meet you, Zuri," Genesis responded with a short laugh. Zuri pulled himself up slowly to turn and face her, letting his legs dangle lifelessly over the side of the bed, all of his body's movements were slow and languid, as if he could only move with great effort. Genesis wanted to implore him to lay down, but felt it was not her place.

Even if she had said something, Zuri probably wouldn't have listened. His greatest grievance was that he could not get down on the floor to offer a beautiful lady his most respectful greetings, as he wasn't sure that he would be able to get back up again. A bow of just his head would have to do. Already he felt relief that no members of his family were there to see his disrespectful behavior.

"The pleasure is mine. May I know your name?" he asked in hesitant English.

"I am Genesis Leigh Deadlock," she answered.

"So you are River's sister then?" She nodded. "Wonderful." He placed his palms together with a bright smile. "As your brother already said, I am Zuri... Zuri Whitlock to be precise. I originate from Southern Country. Please excuse my rough English, it is not my native language. I grew up learning it so I could come here, but I fear I have not had much experience using it among too many native speakers."

"It's all right... but where is Southern Country?" Genesis asked in confusion.

"Far to the south as the name would imply. I am Arishian so I know little of your world, but I think it would be equivalent to your Antarctica... At least that is what your brother suggested."

"So...very cold?"

"Yes, my people would specialize in the ice valta. I have always loved the snow very much. I came here to the university to learn the abilities of my people since my culture has been fading out over the years,"

"That doesn't sound good... What does it mean that you are Arishian? Did you grow up in the House of Arisha?"

"No, no, Arisha is a place, much like your world called Earth, or Driscoll as we call it in Arisha. This university is built around the portal to my world—the Gateway. This is where they train new valta users to enter Arisha on missions as valta agents... I am ashamed to admit my world has fallen quite a bit, and is now swarming with monsters... Your world has been kind enough to lend a hand in our world's revival."

Genesis sat with her mouth agape in her shock over what had just been said. "You're telling me there is another world other than the one I know?"

"Yes. I find it funny that the two of you know nothing of it! Arishians are raised with this knowledge. It is a dream of many among my people to make it to the university, so that once we graduate, we might enter your world and live peaceful lives."

"I wouldn't say our world is entirely peaceful, though," River stated.

"It must be better than my world," Zuri objected, his fingers curling tightly around the fabric of his bed sheets. "Everything is bleak there. It's always cloudy, so the sun is rarely seen." Zuri got up as he spoke and stumbled toward the window catching himself on its sill. Ice spread across the length of it and a bit up the glass of the window. He paused a moment in his description to stare down at what he had done, then he broke the stunned silence with a soft laugh. "I suppose valta is not so easy to control. I shall work hard not to do such a thing again..." He sighed and lifted his eyes up to the blue skies outside the window. "This is only a little bit of your world and it is truly beautiful..." His last words caught in the air for a moment in a sort of icy wistfulness as he finished what he had intended to say.

Genesis and River remained silent, as they both gazed at the ice rather than at the sky beyond. As I am sure you have guessed, the two of them were not quite used to the idea of such powers existing, even though they both possessed similar powers themselves.

Abruptly, the door to the room opened, breaking the cold mood of the moment as two men entered. One was the other doctor, Dr. Das, who had been with Dr. Cherith before Genesis's awakening; the other was a tall, lean man with a friendly countenance. Based on his pale complexion and white hair, much like that of Zuri, Genesis wondered if he must also be a user of the ice valta. On top of that, he did not appear to be a doctor. He wore a black suit, unlike all the doctors who wore all white.

"Their vitals are normal, so they are perfectly good to go. That concludes the awakenings for your class, so you can go ahead and take them to the dorm," Dr. Das informed him.

"Wonderful," the man answered. He looked over at the students with a kind smile. Dr. Das nodded before he left the room, leaving the three students with their new teacher.

Chapter 9

Driscoll University

"It's nice to meet you three," their teacher said. "I'm sure you will want some time to wrap your minds around everything you have learned. It is a lot to take in, from what I have heard. I, of course, grew up in the House way back when I was a kid, so I've known about valtas as long as I can remember. I don't know what it's like to find out so suddenly at your ages. Don't worry, it all sinks in eventually. If you have enough energy to walk we can head on over to your new dorm..." He started to turn away but stopped with a laugh. "Oh gosh, I nearly forgot. I should probably introduce myself. I am your class professor, Zenry Glazunov. My wife and I will be like parents while you study here, so don't ever be afraid to ask either of us questions or tell us your concerns. Wait, let me help you..." River had been attempting to get up off of his bed by himself, but as he almost fell over, Professor Glazunov knew he must take action. Energy users were so fragile in the early days of their valta training. He would not want River to hurt himself. River's legs seemed frail beneath him as he stood up on them for the first time with the professor's assistance.

"It is just a little hard to stand... I'm okay..." River said with a weak smile. You see, he was trying very hard to make light of the situation in the only way he could. He had to appear positive and not show how much fear he truly felt due to his weakened state. He knew his sister well and did not want to worry her too much.

"You are probably hungry. Energy users must keep up a high food intake. I have a lot of valtas to keep track of, but I will try and meet your every need. Always remember that I am your ally," he told them as he held River on his feet. Genesis believed what he was saying. She realized she could trust the kind-hearted man now with them. He had been a student just like them once upon a time. "I will carry you to the dorms on my back, if you like."

"I feel embarrassed, but I think I might take you up on that offer, sir," River responded.

"Are the two of you able to walk?" Professor Glazunov asked with a glance over at Genesis seated on her bed and Zuri who still stood by the window.

"I think so," Genesis answered as she pushed the sheets off of her. Gripping the bed frame, she eased herself up onto her feet. Her legs felt weak, but it was nothing she couldn't handle after everything she had already gone through. She was in far better shape than her brother, after all, so she felt she had to walk. I often wonder what Professor Glazunov would have done if Zuri and Genesis had not been able to walk on their own. I am sure he had a plan in mind, but I also think that he might have been confident in the strength of his students, even before he really knew them.

"Good. Let us be on our way then. The dorm isn't too far away." The professor guided the three students out of the room with a motion of his hand.

He directed them into separate changing rooms across the hallway, where they found their clothes set out neatly for them. Their suitcases had apparently been taken to the dorms. Genesis noted that the clothes smelled of a different detergent than what they had used back at Uncle Ferris's house; she guessed that they had been washed for her during her awakening. River had the greatest problems with his, however, for he felt like he was swimming in his t-shirt and his pants would not stay up. Zuri lent him his belt as he felt he could manage much better without it than River could.

A few minutes later, they reached an elevator that took them down to the first floor of the medical department. Here, Professor Glazunov stopped at the front desk to check them out with the lady stationed there. With that done, they were free to depart through the automatic doors that opened onto a sidewalk.

As they exited the building, Genesis paused mid-step, mostly because she was already so tired from just that small amount of walking, but also to take in the campus that would be her new home. She had seen some of it upon their arrival a week prior, but she had been too nervous at the time to really observe everything in detail. It was beautiful—filled with flower gardens and willow trees. The buildings had a warm appearance, made of bricks with dark red roofs. As they began to walk, she looked about at everything to try to take in the sights that would grow so familiar to her. She noticed several students around the campus as they passed the buildings. She also noticed a large number of cats as well, for she saw at least five along the way. Perhaps they were strays, or maybe the principal really liked cats.

As they cut through the center of campus, they passed an observation tower and then a group of young girls who were tending a garden. Genesis paused to watch as some of them put their hands into the dirt of the garden bed and new flowers instantly sprang up, while one of the other girls let a gentle misty rain drizzle from her fingertips. Genesis's mouth hung agape and she began to wonder if she would ever get used to the way things were there—people using strange abilities as if it were just a normal part of life. She could not imagine herself shapeshifting as she went about her day, yet the students she passed by seemed to use their valtas quite naturally.

They reached a building that appeared much like many that dwelt along the same street—a building like a tall house with a large front porch. These buildings were housing for the students, dorms if you will, although they were a great deal smaller and more homey than your typical dormitory. The last one on the street sat beside an open field directly to its left. Up the hill from the building stood a great willow tree, under which was a tea table. At that particular building, the professor turned up the cobblestone path and onto the front porch. Genesis stopped and gazed at a small golden sign beside the door, which had *Freshman Class 1, Group A* engraved on it.

Zuri and the professor, who still carried River, continued into the dorm and, after a short pause, Genesis followed. She felt as if she took a big step at that moment as she crossed the stone threshold. From that moment onward, that building was home to all of them.

"Let me show you to your rooms. You should rest up, I'm sure you're exhausted after all that you've been through. Real classes will begin tomorrow. I know that is very little time for you to recuperate, but you are the last group in my class to be awakened," Professor Glazunov explained as Genesis joined them inside.

"I'm excited to be back to school!" River declared with as much energy as he could muster in his current state.

Genesis glanced around her. They stood in a large open room that made up the foyer, kitchen, and dining room. The kitchen area was to the back right of the room and the long dining table that could seat up to 16 was to the left directly beside it. To their right, she found an open doorway leading to some sort of stairway/elevator room to the upper floors, and to their left were two doors—one labeled "Professor Glazunov's

Office" and the other an open doorway to a communal lounge area. Although they could not see it from where they currently stood, in the lounge was a door that led to the basement where the dorm's gym and laundry room were located. There was a closet and a bathroom in the lounge as well. Last, beyond the kitchen and dining room, you would find the pantry and the back door to the dorm.

Overall the whole building held a warmth to it that made those who entered feel immediately at home. The wood furniture, as well as the floors, were made of dark cherry wood, and floral wallpaper covered the walls in small red flowers. All the furniture was accented in that same red color as well, adding to its warmth. Even though the building was not all that old, to Genesis it felt like a visit to a grandmother's house. Although, since Uncle Ferris's mansion had been their grandparents' home before their death, she did not really have such an experience. I guess she supposed that stepping into that dorm must be the closest thing to that feeling. Zuri held a very different take on it, as he merely thought of how strange the Driscollian manner of decorating was!

A girl hummed while rinsing dishes at the kitchen sink. As the three new arrivals came in with the professor, she looked up and turned off the water, wiping her damp hands on her skirt, before she all but skipped over to them with a gleeful expression on her face.

"Mister Glaz! Did you bring some more friends to our dorm?" She beamed in a childish fashion, although she appeared to be around their age. She had green hair the color of the underside of a leaf and wore a flower hair pin to clip back her bangs on one side. The flowers on the hair pin were all real though, but because they were infused with her valta, as long as her valta willed it, they would never wither nor die. The flowers were pink and so matched her huge, round eyes that were filled with childish delight and innocence. As you might imagine, she smelled like flowers as well, but not in an overwhelming way, like many perfumes. The scent was a gentle, pleasant smell that hung around her in the air.

"Of course, Miss Driscoll. This would be the last group for your class," the Professor informed her, "This is Zuri Whitlock, River Deadlock, and Genesis Deadlock." He motioned to each of the newcomers as he introduced them. River now held onto the professor's arm for support as he stood on his weak legs.

"Wow! So many '-locks'! It's a shame two of them have to be dead though." Mae released a short sporadic laugh over her own joke.

"Now settle down, Miss Driscoll. Since Miss Nenna is out picking up a shipment, would you take Miss Deadlock to her room on the girl's floor?"

She nodded with great enthusiasm. "Aye aye, Mister Glaz! It would be my pleasure!" She spun on her heel again but then stopped abruptly and turned to face them. "Wait– you didn't introduce *me*!" She pointed to herself in a dejected sort of manner.

"You may introduce yourself then, Miss Driscoll."

"Yay! Well then, I'm Mae Arisha Driscoll! It is a pleasure to meet you! I hope we can all be friends!" She held out her hands to the three of them. Arisha Driscoll? What was that about? Not yet! In its own timing, all shall be revealed about her name. That I promise, my dear readers. "Now that that's over with, would you follow me dead-lock?"

An anxious look passed over River's face and he reached out to grab his sister's arm as she stepped away from him toward Mae.

"I don't want you to leave again. We've already been separated," he panicked.

"It's all going to be all right, River. You knew you would have to gain a bit of independence once we got here. I know you're used to being close to me, but things are different now, and so you are going to have to have time away from me. We can't be in the same dorm area after all. Just think of it like back at home. We're still in the same house, we just have to go to our respective rooms at night," Genesis soothed.

"But what if more happens? I don't want them to hurt me. I'm scared, Genesis." He used her real name which alerted her that he wasn't fooling around. She rested her hand on his shoulder, about to speak, when Mae piped in.

"You got past the icky part already! Now it's all parties and study!" She clapped her hands rapidly together. Genesis smiled down at him, for she had to be a big sister even though she too felt terrified after everything that had happened. She had to be strong and smile for her little brother no matter what.

"I know you are scared, but it's all going to be fine. I'll see you soon, River," she said in as calm a voice as she could manage. He nodded, his eyes cast to the floor. She gave his shoulder a tight squeeze before she departed to follow Mae into the elevator room.

Chapter 10

Mae

INSIDE THE ELEVATOR ROOM, Genesis found a staircase on the left wall to the second floor and to their right was the elevator. Mae hurried up the wood stairs in front of her, the sound of her ballet flats tapping on the steps in a soft manner. She held herself so lightly, it was as if everything about the girl lifted up and stretched toward the sky, much as a flower grows up out of the earth.

Above, on the second floor, Genesis glanced down over the railing that overlooked the room below. Professor Glazunov was now helping River and Zuri to the elevator to head up to the fourth floor. Genesis followed Mae around the perimeter passing by the second floor elevator until they reached a door that would lead them into the girl's hall. Mae advanced over to the door and swiped her student ID card through a keypad on the doorknob. Her fingers moved swiftly over the keys to type in a unique code she had memorized, which unlocked the door for them to enter the floor. This system was instituted so that no one of the opposite gender could steal a student ID card and go onto a restricted floor. Genesis glanced briefly over to her right at the staircase that continued up to the third floor, before she followed Mae through the open door.

"So what's your valta?" Genesis asked, not quite enjoying the silence between them. She also felt kind of curious about such things since she had only just learned of the existence of these abilities. They entered into a hallway with doors that lead to various rooms, like any normal dormitory.

"I'm vernal as I like to say! Saying vegetation just sounds all weird, ya know?" she chimed as she held out her hand and a plant instantly sprang forth from her palm. It was already impressive to see a plant grow at such a rapid pace, but also out of someone's hand was a whole other kind of amazing in Genesis's eyes. Yes, she had seen those other vegetation users planting a garden on her way to the dorm, but she hadn't had much time to truly take it in.

"Wow!" Genesis gasped. She also felt surprised at how fast the girl had mastered her ability, assuming she was also new to the school. Genesis knew there was no way she could be shapeshifting with as much skill as Mae had just presented her vernal abilities. She didn't even know how to go about shapeshifting back into the cat at will.

Mae let out a short, nervous laugh, as Genesis stood gaping at her. "What about you?" She closed her hand over the plant so that the leaves withered away.

Genesis grinned, excited to be able to share her rare valta with Mae. Of course, she wouldn't be able to do such a demonstration, but still Dr. Cherith had made it out to be very impressive that she possessed such a valta. "I'm a shapeshifter!" Genesis beamed.

Mae straightened and a shocked look passed over her face. Her expression didn't display the same kind of shock and astonishment Genesis had over Mae's valta, however. In fact, it almost seemed negative—something very strange from the overly positive girl.

"That's rare," she murmured, averting her gaze from Genesis. Unease crept over Genesis as she continued to follow Mae down the short hallway of doors. Mae's stride had grown heavier and the general aura around her had shifted. Had Genesis said or done something wrong?

She knew she wasn't the best at interacting with others her age, but she couldn't think of anything wrong with what she had said. All she had said was that she was a shapeshifter.

Mae glanced through a door that was ajar as they passed. All Genesis could see was a girl seated at a desk with a long waterfall of bluish gray hair cascading down about her shoulders, and droplets of water lingering in the air around her. Mae looked at Genesis with anxiety, but said nothing. Confused, Genesis tilted her head, a questioning look on her face.

The two of them came to a door at the end of the hall that was propped open. "Well, this is your room, so get yourself settled in!" she informed Genesis in a stiff manner. She turned to leave, but paused in her stride to glance back over her shoulder. Genesis didn't move to go in, a bit uncomfortable by Mae's sudden shift in attitude. Mae bit her lip then sprang back toward Genesis at an alarming speed. Mae grasped her arm, cupping her other hand up to whisper into Genesis's ear. "The girl in that room we passed I have known since I was a baby. She told me to ostracize the shapeshifter, but I don't want to be mean to anyone. You'll just pretend like I'm ignoring you, right?" She drew back with a sad look in her round eyes. "I like you, Genesis, but I've known Mist forever. I feel so conflicted. You won't tell, right?" Genesis felt stunned by the new information, but shook her head hard even so.

The bright smile returned to Mae's lips. "Okey dokie. Well, I hope very much we will become close friends eventually. For right now I'll just keep away a bit. It's nothing against you. I just don't want to make Mist angry" Her voice remained low the whole time she spoke.

"I understand. It would be hard to go against what a childhood friend asked of you." Even though Genesis said those words with ease, the thought that someone had been told to ostracize her before even meeting her stung all the same.

"Thank you for understanding. I hope she stops being so mean."
Mae then departed down the hall.

Genesis remained alone in her doorway for a few minutes after Mae
had disappeared, still quite disconcerted by the turn of events. Why had
Mae been told to ostracize her? Had others been told the same thing?
Did it matter that much in the end? Genesis hadn't gone to the school
to make friends after all.

The door across the hall abruptly opened, startling her from her
daze and back to the task at hand: seeing her new room. Her attention
was drawn immediately away again, however, as from within the dark
realm beyond that door across the hall, emerged another girl, one that
could not be any more the opposite of Mae. She trudged away from
Genesis, without even a glance in her direction, passing down the hall
toward a door that was marked *bathroom*. Darkness exuded forth from
her, sending shivers up Genesis's spine. Now even more uncomfortable
than ever, she swallowed and slipped into her new room. What strange
girls seemed to live in this hall!

As for the shadow girl, upon catching sight of Genesis, she paused in
the bathroom doorway to look back over her shoulder at the new arrival
to the dorm. She lifted her hand and brushed the dark hair from her
face to see better, right as the new girl disappeared into her room. "Oh
gosh, I hope she didn't see me like this. She probably thinks I'm all weird
or something. I really hope not. What chance do I ever have of making
any friends if I exude such an aura?" she muttered to herself, her hands
clapped to her face in embarrassment. "I must be more careful from now
on..." She then continued on into the bathroom.

In Genesis's room, all the boxes she had shipped, along with her
suitcase, were in a heap in the center of the room. The room was not
too big, of course, but that didn't matter much. It was a good size, and

would serve its purpose as her own personal space. A long desk stretched across the entire back wall of the room. Over the desk, natural light was let into the room through a window, and to either side of the window, floating bookshelves hung on the wall. Against the wall to the right was an unmade bed, and just above that was a shelf on which one could set an alarm clock, or anything else to decorate the room up a bit. Her dresser was located against the left wall, as well as a standing lamp and some hampers for her laundry. Finally, on either side of the doorway were large closets in which to store her belongings.

She slipped off her shoes and found the gray carpet to be surprisingly soft beneath her feet. The room felt small compared to her room back at her uncle's mansion, but that made it feel more cozy. Yes, this would be a nice room to live in for as long as she studied there.

Genesis still felt super exhausted from everything that had happened that day, but she couldn't stand her room remaining unorganized like it was. She just had to make a little headway on unpacking. Of course, she knew her strength was going to dwindle too fast for her to get all of it done, and on that she was quite right. Sure enough, she had only finished making her bed when she fell upon it in defeat, her body far too weak and excited to handle any more activity. So, she decided to rest. A deep sigh welled up in her as she rolled onto her back to look up at the ceiling fan spinning round and round above her. Her eyes shut and she fell immediately asleep.

Chapter 11
Dusk

THE GIRL FROM ACROSS the hall stood in the open doorway of Genesis's now dark room, as the sun had already gone down for the day. She swallowed hard and stood debating whether or not to knock or just enter the open room. "All I must do is act like the sun. Like Dawn. Then I shall get along just fine with her! If he can, despite his stutter and despite being homeschooled, then I certainly can be like the sun, too," she said in a low whisper. Then, without further ado, she cautiously walked across the room until she stood over the bed where Genesis lay sound asleep.

Genesis was startled awake by the strange presence now so close to her. As her eyes fluttered open, she observed a dark figure stooped over her bed, silhouetted by the hall light. Fear gripped her heart as the shadow stepped even closer to her bedside. Her breath caught in her throat, and she could not bring herself to move, even if she hadn't been too completely exhausted to do so anyway.

"What is your name?" the shadow girl inquired, in the best sunshine voice she could manage. I fear she did not do her best performance, however, for her voice still sounded rather dark and mysterious to Genesis.

"Gen-Genesis," Genesis stuttered in response.

The shadow girl sat down on the bed beside Genesis, the bed springs creaking beneath her. She thought to herself that she was really doing quite well indeed at behaving like the sun. Naturally it was quite difficult due to both the darkness of the room and the darkness that exuded from her. I must say, if she really could be like the sun, what an accomplishment that would be!

"I'm Olivia Elrod, but please call me Dusk. It's a pleasure to make your acquaintance. Sorry I didn't greet you earlier when I saw you in the hall," she said in as cheerful a voice as she could muster—her voice still had a ring that you probably wouldn't want to hear in any sort of unfamiliar dark place, though. No...for that matter you probably wouldn't want to hear it in your room late at night either, even though that is a familiar place.

"Oh...that's all right..." Genesis recalled passing this girl in the hallway. She had thought her rather strange, and now faced with her, still thought so. But, she now felt a bit guilty for thinking this. You see, Genesis was beginning to get the picture that the girl did not seem to realize how chill-inducing she really was.

"I hope that we can be friends. You see, I am just across the hall from you."

Genesis was not quite sure how to respond. She thought later that she ought to have agreed with the girl, but the fog of sleep still hung over her heavily, and so a moment of unbearably awkward silence proceeded. Dusk, sensing all her work about to go to waste, hastened to break it again. "So, where do you come from?"

"Mirrorick," Genesis answered as she moved to sit up with much difficulty. Her body almost hurt more after sleeping for a while.

"Wow. Same for me. I've lived there for as long as I can remember. What is your valta?"

"I'm a..." Genesis paused, for she thought of how Mae had been told to ostracize her. On the other hand, Dusk was going to find out eventually, so there really wasn't any point in trying to hide it. Genesis gathered her wits again to answer. "A shapeshifter..."

"Oh...I heard that one was rare. You sounded hesitant. But don't be afraid to tell me. I'm not from the House. I'm not snobbish and jealous of other people's valtas," Dusk answered.

"Mae's from the House then?"

"Oh, yes. She and one other girl are the only girls from the House in our dorm." Genesis knew, as soon as Dusk said it, that she must mean the girl Mae had referred to as Mist. Mae had mentioned knowing that girl for a very long time. "I've visited everyone like this since I arrived in my room a few days ago. While we haven't really gone over introductions yet, I observed the others from our class during meals down in the dining room, and when I have run into them throughout the day. My research has uncovered that there are five students from the House in our dorm, out of 14 total. From what I've been able to gather, our dorm makes up half of the Freshman Class 1 and the dorm next door houses the other half."

"Oh, so you already know the classes, too?"

"Yes. Our dorm is students in Group A, who will be taking classes in Freshman Class 1. I think it's up on the board in the lobby downstairs. The dorm next door is for students of Group B who are also in Freshman Class 1. All of the classes are divided up into two groups. I don't know how many Freshman classes there are in total." Genesis nodded as the girl spoke. "We are on the girl's floor for our group, while the rest of the floors in our dorm are the boys'. I have figured out who in our group is from the House by asking Mae mostly. I have found her to be the only nice one from the House. The two girls from the House are Mae and Misteria, who's a water user. The three guys, who I don't know as much about, possess the valtas of fire, earth, and blood art. I'm sure you've heard blood art to be one of the rare abilities like your shapeshifting."

"Yeah, that is what the doctor said during my awakening," Genesis answered her.

"Did you meet anyone in the recovery room for our group?"

"Yes, my little brother and a boy with ice valta."

"An ice user you say? Splendid. This will be good information to add to my collection. Can you turn on the light?"

"O-oh, of course." Genesis slowly got up, readjusted to being on her feet again, and then flicked on the light switch. She turned back around to now observe Dusk in the faint light that radiated from the lamp in the corner. She sat bundled up in a dark blanket, her dark wisteria-colored hair draped over half her face. From deep within the depths of her blanket, she withdrew a notebook and pen to begin scribbling. Genesis eased herself back down beside her on the bed.

"Do you know the name of the ice user?"

"Yes, his name was Zuri Whitlock," Genesis answered.

"Okay. Zuri is an ice user," Dusk whispered aloud as she wrote. "And you mentioned your brother?"

"Yes, his name is River, and his ability is energy."

Dusk paused to stare down at her notebook page. "Interesting... Our group has all of them except for iron. We should have one more student coming, though, since that only adds up to 13." Dusk turned the notebook to show Genesis. Genesis, of course, glanced down the list, but the names written there left her mind almost the moment she saw them. "While on campus the last few days, I've gone to a few of the other dorms, and I haven't found a group with all 14 different types. In fact, some are very out of proportion." She stifled a sinister laugh, although she had no sinister intent. "One of the upper class's groups is half water users. It would be very interesting if we got an iron user as the 14th student and were therefore made up of all different users." She clutched her notebook to her chest. "That was fun. I'm really looking forward to being here, especially after learning about valta. I just came here because it was a good place to escape from the outside world. How exciting." Her voice sank and she looked down at the folds of her blanket around her.

Genesis felt tempted to ask her what was the matter, for Dusk looked so sad all of the sudden, and her dark aura only got all the more intense. In the end, Genesis thought it was really none of her business. She could also not distinguish if the girl was actually upset about something, or if that was just her resting energy. No matter which it was, Dusk's life before she met Genesis at the school was her private matter.

"What do you think of the dorm rooms?" Dusk asked.

"They're nice," Genesis answered with a nod.

"Yeah. I was kinda hoping I would have a roommate. I guess it's probably better this way. I hope people don't mind if I hang out in their rooms. I feel lonely all by myself in the dark." Her voice cracked. "I wish I could go hang out with my friend Dawn, but I'm not allowed on the boy's floor." She laughed darkly to herself.

Genesis thought of inviting her to come to her room whenever she wanted, but she quickly brushed the thought away. She wasn't there to make friends. She wanted to find her parents, and she was determined that she would do it all on her own. Back in middle school, she had discovered that as she started to get close to some of the girls in her class, her grades began to drop and she had trouble keeping up with everything she needed to do to get into the university. For that reason she made the decision that it was better for her not to make friends and to just push herself on her own. Even if she wasn't trying to get into the school anymore, she couldn't let that interference happen again. She had to focus on her mission before all else, otherwise she might never obtain her dream of having her family together again.

"It's late, so I think I'll go back to my room now. We start class tomorrow," Dusk said.

"Wait, before you go...I was wondering what *your* valta is?" Genesis asked, although she thought she had a good idea, if she remembered the types of valta correctly.

Dusk paused in her stride toward the door. "I'm shadow... I'm not very good at the ability right now, so I can't really show you..."

"*You actually **might** be good at it...*" Genesis mumbled to herself.

"...I haven't tried using it again since they had me test it out during my awakening. I heard we will have special valta training at the end of each day, so I'm sure we'll get to practice tomorrow."

Genesis thought back to when Zuri grasped the window sill in the hospital room and ice had spread across it. Dusk's valta was doing the exact same thing. Her valta was slipping out even if she didn't realize it.

"Shadow sounds pretty cool though...although I'm not quite sure what that entails..." Genesis answered with a laugh

"I suppose so... I'll go now."

Dusk's heavy footfalls faded away back across the hall, and then Genesis heard the door click shut. For a little while after, she sat lost in thought, but eventually she lay back on her bed again, still feeling the effects of the last week. She felt a bit better informed, but the conversation had ended rather abruptly. While the encounter left Genesis with an unsettled feeling, she brushed it off and shut her eyes to drift back to sleep again.

Chapter 12

New Faces

GENESIS WOKE TO FIND a package upon her desk that she had somehow missed the night before. Due to her nerves over starting class that day, she had awakened quite early before the sun had fully risen in the sky. She found she had far more energy, so she decided to see what she could unpack before breakfast. Upon discovering the package though, she promptly opened it to find a uniform inside, along with the school rule book and her daily schedule.

In general, the schedule seemed rather ordinary, like the schedule at any other school, with academic classes as well as a PE class. After 4:00 things seemed to get more interesting with a class titled "Special Valta Training." This must be the training that Dusk had mentioned. Genesis was listed as being in Lab Room 3 of the Valta Department. The only other interesting thing she noted was a language class on Saturday mornings. It was listed for *"all students from off-campus (Earth-side),"* which presumably meant only students who were not from Arisha or the House. She guessed that they must need to learn a language from Arisha in that class, which sounded sort of fun to her. She had only just learned of the existence of another world, and it only made sense that they would speak another language, not English. As for Sundays, those were free days with the option of a student-led Bible study held at the religious center. Along with her schedule was a map of the campus.

By the time she had finished reading through all the material in the package, it was still only 6:00. Looking around the cluttered room, she decided to organize some of her belongings until she needed to get ready for breakfast. Then, at 7:00 sharp, after taking a deep breath, she set off to the bathroom down the hall to start her first official day as a student of Driscoll University.

After she brushed her teeth and took a shower, Genesis changed into her uniform for the first time. Based on how perfectly it fit her, it must have been custom tailored for her. The school had asked for their measurements on the registration forms so she supposed that must have been for the uniforms, along with her shapeshifting garb. She wished that her garb had been finished before starting. She was sure special valta training would be awkward without it. Based on what Dr. Cherith had said to her, though, it sounded like they were making it as fast as they could.

Genesis drew in a deep breath as she exited the shower stall where she had just finished changing. Standing at one of the bathroom sinks was the fifth and only girl she had not encountered yet. If Genesis hadn't known that valtas seemed to change everyone's hair to unnatural colors, she would have been quite thrown off by the girl's bright pink hair. She had no idea what kind of valta such a color could signify... She knew from what Dusk had said that they had all 14 types except iron in their dorm. She might have guessed vegetation, since maybe the pink color would be like flower petals. That was Mae's valta though. The color reminded her more of butterfly wings, even though she couldn't really remember seeing a butterfly of that color before. The train of thought was pointless and suddenly seemed rather boring to her...she could feel herself getting sleepier the longer she stood there staring at the girl. She knew it couldn't be blood art, fire, earth, water, shadow, ice, energy, vegetation, or shapeshift, as all of those were accounted for already. Her head nodded down, but she snapped it back up again, blinking swiftly in surprise at her own rudeness. She had slept for hours, so why was she suddenly so tired to the point of almost falling asleep on her own feet? For that matter, the pink-haired girl herself looked rather tired. Genesis supposed that was somewhat to be expected, because they had both gotten up pretty early—both had had trouble sleeping with anxiety over the coming first day of classes.

The girl glanced drowsily over her shoulder. Genesis smiled sleepily at her and waved to try and be friendly. To the kind gesture, Genesis received nothing back. The girl didn't even smile, she just turned back to continue washing her hands. A bit nervous at the lack of response, Genesis made a quick exit from the bathroom, her strange sleepiness leaving her almost immediately. What Mae had said the evening before came to mind, and Genesis could only wonder if the girl had been told to ignore her as well.

What Genesis didn't see was that as the bathroom door closed behind her, our poor, currently-nameless pink-haired girl stood with her forehead down on the bathroom counter in an attempt to ease the constant headache she had had since the day of her awakening. Was it because of the language barrier that her brain hurt constantly? Or was it because her new valta would not stop slipping out?

Genesis returned to her room down the hall.

"Good morning, Genesis," Dusk whispered from her darkened doorway. Genesis jumped mid-step as the sound of the girl's voice sent a shiver through her body. She tried hard to conceal any other expression of unease. However, in her attempt to guard her emotions, she made no answer, as she set her shower things back in her room and grabbed her room key before returning to the hall. Only then did she realize her mistake, and how rude she must seem for ignoring Dusk's greeting.

"Good morning, Dusk," she answered in a measured voice. Dusk released a murky laugh at the long hesitation on Genesis's part. Much to Genesis's relief, she did not seem at all upset over the delay.

"Do you wanna head down to breakfast together?" Dusk suggested as she drew out of her room. Despite the unsettling aura still hanging over her, she looked very nice that morning. Her hair was pulled mostly back from her face so it didn't close her off as much. She also had a little hood on her uniform to block out the sunlight, but it was currently thrown back while she was inside.

"That sounds good, thank you. I wouldn't want to go down alone. I'm a bit nervous honestly," Genesis answered.

"Yay. Let's go together then."

"Yes."

"Did you sleep well?" Dusk asked as they went.

"For the most part. I feel much better this morning," Genesis answered, pushing open the door to exit the hall. "But I did wake up pretty early... at least I got to organize my room a bit."

"I'm quite nervous about class starting up today, too. But I am grateful that I got here several days ago and could get settled in first. I feel bad for those of you who have to jump right into classes without fully recovering yet." Dusk hit the button for the elevator just as Genesis was starting for the stairs. The two girls stared at each other in awkward silence for a brief moment, until Dusk tittered. "I know it's silly when we just have one flight of stairs to walk down. But I like meeting people in the elevator. And since pretty much everyone goes downstairs at the same time, it's common to run into a few of the guys." Genesis let out a short nervous laugh and decided to just go along with Dusk, even though she could see the downstairs over the railing, as well as hear voices of other students down in the main room. Taking the elevator seemed ridiculous to her, but she didn't want to go down alone, even though it would have been a lot faster to just take the one flight of stairs. She honestly wondered why they even needed an elevator in the first place.

The elevator dinged as it opened up for them. Three guys stood inside, two of whom were talking to each other, while the third leaned back against the wall with an irritated look on his face. In that brief moment, Genesis's eyes were drawn toward the guy who seemed to be doing most of the talking. He had the most wild, frizzy hair she had ever seen—like static, but he also looked kind of like a dandelion. When he snapped, a small bolt of electricity passed between his fingers. Genesis thought it was amazing! A new valta ability revealing itself before her eyes. He must possess the valta of electricity! She was certain that it had been one of the 14 types. The guy himself, however, didn't seem entirely pleased about his new predicament, as each time that it happened he would give his hand an irritated shake.

The boy who was listening turned away from our static friend's long-winded story to gaze at Dusk in the elevator's entryway. He looked as if he saw a ray of light—despite her dark aura. It was as if the fact of her very presence brought an end to the constant stream of words that had bombarded him since the moment he stepped from his room to find "Sparky" also on his way down to breakfast. Dusk, his dear friend, with whom he had come to the school, shone as a ray of hope and sweet escape.

"Oh, i-if it isn't my o-o-oposite..." he stuttered. Dusk's face lit up in a way that it had not done since the moment Genesis had first seen her. She reached out to give him a high five as she stepped into the elevator beside him, his light seeming to overcome her darkness and envelop her. Then the moment of brightness ended as tension filled the small space. Not at all because of Genesis's entrance behind Dusk, though. No, the tension was all induced by our sparky friend, who had been so rudely interrupted.

Dusk and the young man, who had so readily escaped his conversation with Sparky, were quite comfortable with each other already. As I am sure you have already figured out, dear reader, he was Dusk's friend Dawn who she had mentioned the previous night. The other guy, who had been talking *at* him, looked quite irritated at the interruption. Based the energy emanating from the two other boys, Genesis figured the conversation had carried on for far longer than it ought to have. At the very least, she gave Sparky a sympathetic smile, which seemed to satisfy him briefly, as she was very beautiful in his eyes.

"And-d wh-who...who is this?" Dawn asked in a soft voice.

"This is Genesis," Dusk introduced.

"That's-s a nice n-name." Dawn fidgeted nervously as he spoke and avoided making direct eye contact with either of the two girls. Despite that, the expression on his face was filled with serenity and light. In the midst of his awkward mannerisms he shone. Genesis would have imagined the light user to be more similar to Mae: sunny and energetic. She supposed that the ease she felt reminded her of the sun, too, though.

"This is Dawn," Dusk introduced him to Genesis.

"Nice to meet you," Genesis said as she took the hand he extended toward her.

"M-my real n-name is, A-alexander, b-b-but I like t-to go b-by D-dawn."

"All right, I think that we're good on introductions now. Nice to meet you and all, but this particular story has a very interesting end, and so I would like to finish it," the young man said with another staticky snap of his fingers.

"Here we go again," Dusk murmured under her breath as the guy started up, speaking of some drama that took place backstage during one of his performances. Genesis did not put two and two together yet, for her conversation with River over the famous actor and musical artist Hiero Caddel had long since faded from her mind, like a fever dream. One couldn't blame her after all that had transpired over the past week, and, for that matter, how many fever dreams had she actually had during that time?

Unlike Dawn, who fumbled over his words, Hiero had the steady voice of someone who was well used to talking in front of people and obviously had no problem speaking exactly what was on his mind. Knowing he was an entertainer, though, could you find any surprise in that?

The elevator doors dinged and opened again, which was Dawn and Dusk's cue to exit the elevator as fast as humanly possible to get away from Mr. High-and-Mighty as he continued to prattle on and on even as they fled away from him. Genesis, who still didn't want to walk into the dining room alone on the first day, moved to hurry after them, when suddenly she felt a hand on her shoulder and was yanked back mid-step. She had forgotten about the third guy on the elevator until that moment, for he had been silent and kept to himself the whole ride down.

Her head turned sharply and in the next instant her eyes locked with the most brilliant, piercing eyes she had ever seen in her entire life. Her heart fell into her stomach, and she felt tingles run through her entire body.

"So, you're that shapeshifter," he muttered under his breath.

"Y-yes?" she stammered. He released his tight grip on her shoulder without a word and stalked past her off the elevator. She swore some flames licked up at the corners of his grin as he went, but, after blinking a few times, she concluded she must have imagined such a thing. After all, if a fire user let his valta slip out, that would be real trouble, right? She didn't doubt that was his valta, though, as the heat from his touch still lingered on her shoulder for moments afterwards. She swallowed hard before she, too, left the elevator and entered the dining room alone, as she had not wished to do.

Chapter 13

The Small Gentleman

As GENESIS ENTERED THE dining room, several sharp looks shot in her direction. Truthfully, she hadn't wanted to go in alone partly because of Mae's words from the evening before about ostracizing her. She wanted all the more to just disappear from sight and return to her room where she could wait alone for it to be time for class. Despite these thoughts, she mustered up her courage and continued on into the dining room.

A good number of students had already gathered for breakfast. She saw Mae in the kitchen helping a woman prepare the food. The woman looked to be in her early thirties. She had dark hair and a kind expression fixed upon her soft, unusual face. Genesis wondered if she was Arishian. Her suspicions only grew when she spoke to Mae in words that didn't sound like any language Genesis had heard before.

Misteria stood with a young man who, upon first glance, Genesis mistook for a girl due to the long wavy hair he had pulled back in a ponytail. Upon her second glance, she noted the male uniform he wore as well as the sharpness of his jaw bone. He also appeared to be of a race she had not seen, although different from that of the woman cooking. He had an almost elvish look to him with pointed ears and very pale complexion. Without a shadow of a doubt in her mind, Genesis determined that he must be Arishian.

Nearby, Genesis saw Dawn, along with his companion Hiero Caddel, who was still sharing the same story from the elevator. It must have been tremendously important to him that he wouldn't let it go. Dawn was trying to look interested, but kept glancing around the room to see what Dusk was doing.

Another student she noticed was a tall boy with dark, magenta-colored hair. I have heard he did not care to shave back at the start, for he had a slight mustache—it was not as bad as other boys who attempted to grow a mustache at that age, but still made him look a bit unkempt. Some young lady in that room could change that...but perhaps I am getting a bit ahead of myself for suggesting such a thing!

Genesis continued to gaze around the room until she caught sight of Zuri and River seated next to each other at the long dining table talking animatedly. Seeing that her brother had already grown close to one of the other boys in their class made her feel greatly relieved—she had been so worried that it would be hard for River to make friends. After all, he was a good bit younger than everyone else and could get rather wound up and childish at times, but he seemed to be doing just fine.

River must have sensed her gaze upon him. He looked up quickly and as their eyes met, he bolted to his feet. "Gen-gen!" he exclaimed. A sheen of ice spread out over Zuri's chair in surprise at River's voice lifting so suddenly. Then a hush fell over the room as all eyes turned to watch the siblings.

With no awareness of the stir he had just caused, River hurried from his seat and threw his arms around his older sister. Embarrassed that he had just called her by that nickname in a room filled with so many unknown people, she grew rather red in the face. She knew she shouldn't be embarrassed by something like that, but she didn't like having all that attention focused on her, especially in the current situation. Undoubtedly, River didn't know that some of them had decided to ostracize her, so she couldn't really be upset with him.

"I'm glad to see you're doing well this morning," she whispered with a quick but awkward glance about the room. She felt very unaccustomed to him being so very thin, but was glad that he seemed to have more strength and energy after getting some sleep. Yesterday she had been quite worried about how feeble he had grown from the awakening. He could now stand and walk all right, even if he still seemed a bit unstable on his feet.

"Yeah, Zuri and I had so much fun last night! Look! My uniform fits me just fine! They must have known how much weight I'd lose! Oh! I wish you could have been there!"

"Well...I can't go into the boys' part of the dorm...but, even though I wasn't there when you first tried it on, I think it looks good on you now!" He nodded in response. To her relief the others had gone back to conversing and no longer looked in their direction.

River's energetic smile whipped away rather suddenly. "Did I embarrass you? Your face is red..."

"Maybe a bit. But it's all right. You know how easily I get embarrassed." He gave her an understanding nod. Despite her saying it was all right, however, he still couldn't help but feel a little guilty. There he went acting super childish and embarrassing his sister in front of all their new classmates on the first day. His body still hurt so much, but he could sense that he had an unusual amount of energy in it that he hadn't had before. He felt like his head was swimming in a sea of that energy, and, if he stopped restraining it, he felt as if he might start bouncing off the walls—quite literally since his valta allowed him to defy gravity!

"I'm sorry. I'll try not to call you that when we're around other people! It's just a habit! You know? Habits are sometimes hard to break out of! I'll try to be better! Really! Honest, I will! I wouldn't want to mess up our relationship ever by making you feel uncomfortable! I know

I'm a bit young for this program, so, if I cause any problems, you have permission to give me a sisterly slap!" River was speaking so fast without pausing for breath that Genesis finally grabbed both his shoulders and drew in a deep breath like their mother used to do when they were whining. The sound that she made had always had a very soothing effect on them as children and was never in any way impatient.

"It's all right. So breathe a moment. I wasn't going to ask you to stop calling me..." With a sudden gasp, River grabbed his sister's arm and pointed with his other hand at Hiero Caddel—a.k.a. the guy who was still talking at Dawn.

"What?" she asked, startled by his reaction to someone who seemed so full of himself.

"Th-that's... That's Hiero Caddel..." River clapped his hand over his mouth to muffle his words, as he found it quite difficult to speak quietly.

"That guy?!" Genesis blurted. She finally remembered what River had told her during the car ride there about how Hiero Caddel, one of his favorite actors, would be attending their school in the freshman class.

"Yeah! Don't sound so disappointed, Gen-gen!" he scolded from under his hand, pouting up at her.

"He just seems a bit...full of himself..." she muttered.

"I barely recognized him for a moment! If his expression wasn't so distinct, I wouldn't have, since his hair used to be dark brown and straight! He must have some sort of cool valta!"

"Wasn't electricity one of the valtas? Because his hair certainly looks staticky... plus I'm pretty sure I saw some electricity spark from his fingers... Hmmm, now that I think about it, I guess that's why everyone's hair is such unusual colors here. It must be something to do with their valta..." She fingered a strand of her bangs as she spoke, lifting it off of her forehead so that she could peer up at it. With her hair pulled back into two buns, this was the only way she could see the olive green color.

In the next moment a hush fell over the room as Professor Glazanov entered from his office. "Miss Deadlock and Master Amana are setting the table today. Master Ferrari and Master Immogen are clearing. The dishes and utensils are in the pantry behind the kitchen for those who don't know," the Professor instructed. Genesis nodded as she glanced toward a curtain strung across a doorway behind the kitchen.

"Well...good luck, Sis!" River exclaimed, before shuffling back over to his place next to Zuri. Genesis watched her brother go, then turned her attention toward the pantry and drew in a deep breath. She really hoped Amana wasn't one of the ones who had decided to ostracize her, since she would be in the pantry with him.

She entered the cramped, dimly lit pantry a moment later. Her eyes lifted up to the top of the wood shelves to either side of her and then to the one light that hung down from the ceiling. The air around her felt musty and dry, but not in an entirely bad sort of way. She moved forward slowly toward one of the shelves, then stopped and drew back a pace as she caught sight of the utensils and napkins out of the corner of her eye. To her surprise, she bumped into something now behind her...or, should I say, someone.

"I would appreciate it if you would refrain from stepping on me, Lady Deadlock," an elegant voice said below her. She lowered her gaze to look down into a small boy's face as he strode past her into the room. She had not noticed him in the other room, since, because of his short stature, he had probably been completely hidden behind someone taller.

"Oh! Sorry I did not see you..." she started. She had not sensed his presence at all when he had entered the small space behind her. He tightened his lips, his eyes cut up at her. "Sorry... I didn't know that people were allowed to come to this school so young... My brother is young but you must be..." She paused as he seemed to have gotten all the more agitated by her words. "Please forgive me. I didn't mean to offend you..."

"You are digging yourself quite the grave there, Lady Deadlock!" He chuckled to himself with a shake of his head. "I'm much older than anyone else here, after all. I turned 17 two cycles ago! While 'tis no secret that I have quite the small stature—for I measure exactly four feet three inches in height—calling me a child is quite another matter in and of itself." He lifted his narrow eyes up to meet her gaze again. A sly smirk spread over his lips, and he crossed his arms over his chest. He seemed to be quite a serious little gentleman by his manner of speech and the maturity in his demeanor...yet the fact that he wore a pair of bunny ears on his head really didn't make him all that intimidating. In fact, quite the contrary, he could not be taken seriously at all! He was just so short and harmless looking that it was impossible!

"I'm sorry...but it's just that..."

"No, ifs, ands, nor buts!" he sighed.

"I really didn't know... I'm very sorry. Now that I'm speaking with you and have gotten a better look at you, I do realize you are much older than I. Again, I am really sorry."

"Apology accepted, since you are quite beautiful. Could you hand me some plates?" he asked, his hands lifted up toward her, as he was far too short to reach the shelf.

"Oh," she said, startled at his sudden change in subject and demeanor. She had half expected him to call her a stupid shapeshifter and leave. He didn't though, so that made her hasten to comply with his wishes and reach up to take down a small stack of plates.

"You think me weak? Give me at least a dozen more! I can carry all the plates myself."

"Sorry." She reached up to grab more.

"No need to apologize. 'Twasn't that I was seeking to shame you. I feel quite grieved if I have offended such a fine lady like yourself, Lady Deadlock."

"You are very formal, Mister Amana."

"'Tis the respect I ought to give! Women deserve the utmost from us gentlemen. If I were to treat you harshly I should be the one quite ashamed of myself! I am not sensitive about my height. For who needs to be tall to be strong? But calling me a child is quite another matter. So I do apologize if I got a bit agitated. It shan't happen again, milady."

"You're apologizing to me now, when I was the one that offended you!" she laughed.

He smiled in that same sly manner again. "Listen, to you especially, I give my utmost respect. You are the new shapeshifter, after all, are you not? I know that those few students from the House are already treating you quite poorly. Therefore, I shall try and compensate."

"N-no, it's all right..." she stammered.

"I want you to realize that I may be from the House, but my master and I have no intention of ostracizing you in the least, as others have decided upon. I am at your service if you ever need anything at all."

She paused briefly, before she spoke again. "Why did they decide to ostracize me before they had even met me?" He seemed like the right person to ask the question that had been at the back of her mind since Mae had broached the subject the night before. Mae hadn't been the right person to ask since she seemed so in the middle of it all.

"You see, it has always been quite competitive at the House. There was talk of you transferring into the House last spring, since you possess such a rare valta, and the school wished to start your training early. Such a thing has never happened before to someone coming in from Earth-side.

Truly, you are a rarity. So, they have found you to be a threat in their scramble to be the best to graduate from the school and also to gain a coveted position as a research agent, an honor given only to the top students. As for me, you being a shapeshifter does not bother me in the least. So I do not wish to ostracize you. Here, we are all together in one class. I am not one to take such connections lightly. While my duty is first and foremost to my Master, Haise, I wish to watch over you all. I may be short, but I am the eldest, and so I wish to always be here to help you through your times of misfortune. I hath always tried to help those around me to the very best of my capabilities, so I shall continue to do the same for you. I wish people could be less competitive. Valta is valta. This school is a place to learn and grow—that does not mean you must be the best. But those other three shall not let it go. Even Mae in all her sunshine and sparkles wishes to be the best." He let out another sigh. She placed the rest of the plates down onto his stack with care. "Thank you. You shall take care of the utensils, will you not?" She nodded and he turned to leave the room.

"Thank you. It means a lot to me, because I can't help but notice that a few of them seem to already dislike me."

He glanced back as she spoke and gave her a tender smile. "'Tis also good that you did not end up transferring to the House last spring. I do not think they would have been welcoming in the least. But I shall say this: they are nice people, although...a bit on the mental side at times..." He let out another short chuckle. "But 'tis beside the point. I am sure, once they get to know you better, they shan't be so cruel... I'd like to get to know you better myself, for you seem to be such a fine lady, Lady Deadlock."

"I would like that," she answered. He eyed the napkins on a bottom shelf and she quickly moved to grab them.

"They called you Deadlock, but what name do you prefer to be called by, milady?" he asked.

"Oh, I'm Genesis."

"Lady Genesis, then. You certainly have a lovely name."

"And what should I call you?" she asked.

"I am Kazumae Amana from the Kingdom of Scarlet."

"What is the Kingdom of Scarlet?"

"It's a country that specializes in blood art in Arisha. I am a user of the earth valta myself. Quite strange that they call it earth, don't you think?"

She laughed. "So you're from Arisha, then?"

He nodded. "I came here with my master when he was quite young, and the two of us have grown up in the House ever since."

"You must be really close then."

"I do not know about that. 'Tis more like a duty, so I am quite stuck with him." He shrugged his shoulders.

"Oh..." She looked at him in bewilderment. He flashed her a charming smile and started from the pantry. After gathering up the silverware, she followed him out into the dining room where they began to set the table for breakfast. The others still stood around the table, as they continued to wait for the food to be served. But now there was another in the room: the girl who Genesis had seen in the bathroom upstairs that morning.

Chapter 14
Introductions

As soon as Genesis and Kazumae had finished setting the table, the woman—I shall refer to her as their dorm mother for the time being—and Mae brought breakfast over to the table from the kitchen. As that day marked their first official meal at the school, their dorm mother had gone all out with eggs, pancakes, French toast, sausage, bacon, and pretty much anything else you might find in a typical American breakfast.

"What are those round golden disks?" Zuri whispered to Genesis as he pointed discreetly at the mound of pancakes. Zuri now stood beside her not far from the table. River seemed to be engaged in a conversation with Dawn and Dusk, so Zuri decided what would be better than going to chat with his new friend's very beautiful sister?

"Pancakes?" she questioned.

"Ah, pancakes...sounds rather interesting... We do not have such things back in my country in Arisha," he stated.

"Oh...well, they are really good. They're sweet and best served with syrup and topped with whipped cream."

"Sounds delightful indeed. I do love that whipped cream. Once an agent from the school came to our town and he had some whipped cream that he let all of us kids taste. It was only a small spoonful but it was truly wonderful." He lifted his hand to his chin, beaming as he thought back on those times.

"If you would all take your seats now," Professor Glazanov instruct-ed. Each chair had a student's name hung on the back, so there was a scuffling of feet and scrape of chair legs on the wood floor as the students all moved to find their seats. Genesis found her seat pretty easily beside—who else?—but the hothead from the elevator whom she had decided to avoid at all costs!

When she sat down, he made a hissing sound through his teeth. He didn't look at her, but she could sense that he was just as unhappy about the seating arrangement as she was. Honestly, she wasn't even sure how to feel anymore with such strong personalities around her, some hating her, some treating her with an overabundance of kindness, and others not seeming to notice her at all—the last kind she preferred most.

The dorm mother stepped over to the other end of the table and waited for all of them to settle down in their respective seats. As she didn't know much English, she could only smile sweetly at everyone as she waited for Professor Glazunov to speak. After all the students had taken their seats, she followed suit and sat down.

"Now, since it is the first day with everyone here, and the first day of classes for that matter, we would like to get to know everyone who will be living and taking classes together for the next four years. I'll start and then we'll go around the table," Professor Glazunov explained. "But first, please serve yourselves. My wife prepared quite a feast for us today!"

The clanking of utensils followed as the students began to serve themselves from the large ceramic dishes. Everyone was pretty hungry, for the most part. Genesis, of course, did not put much on her plate. She still felt terribly nervous, with it being the first day, and she hated to not eat everything that she put on her plate.

Once everyone settled down, Professor Glazonov began. "As all of you know, I am Zenry Glazunov, and Miss Nenna is my lovely wife

Nennima Glazonov. I am a professor here at the university and also your homeroom teacher. Miss Nenna and I will be your dorm directors while you study here at the university. I thought I would begin your first day by telling you a little bit about us. I'm an ice user, although my ability to use that power will probably fade as I'm now in my thirties. I'm half Arishian but spent most of my childhood at the House. I have been teaching ice valta at the school for about five years now. Before that I worked as an agent in Arisha." He glanced at the hothead for a second, his lips tightening, but the boy seemed to not understand the glance at all. At least not yet. "As for Miss Nenna, she never got her valta awakened. She is pure Arishian and does not know much English, since she just moved to campus about a month ago. I am a class director and can no longer commute to work through the Gateway every day, but luckily it all worked out. She's been hired as your housekeeper and will see to your every need, if at all possible, while you are here, although you might need to get me or a House student to translate if you need to talk to her about something. She wants to create a warm living environment for you while you study."

He paused for a moment to let the students take in that introduction. "Now, starting with Mae, we will go around the table and you will introduce yourselves by name, age, valta type, where you are from, and then share something interesting about yourself," he instructed.

Mae, who sat to his left, smiled as she set down her fork, ready for her introduction. "I'm Mae Arisha Driscoll. I'm 14 years old. Vernal... or, I mean, vegetation is my valta, and I'm from the House. I'm sure you might be curious about my name, though, since I bear both names of the school! I'm actually a daughter of the school, born and raised so that I can eventually do specific tasks for them, such as eventually assist at the House and Agencies! I'm not sure who my parents are, but that's okay because in a way the principal and Miss Bates—the House Director—are like my parents! But if you were curious I have been told that I am completely of Arishian blood, and am a daughter of a special bloodline known as valta servants. I don't know much about the bloodline, so you can't really ask me about it. But I do know that being in that bloodline means I was born with my valta already awakened! That's all for me!" she said, flashing them all another smile as she picked up her fork again to resume eating.

Misteria, next to her, swallowed a bite of food. Her long eyelashes fluttered as she lifted her gaze from her plate. By far, she had the most beautiful face out of all of the girls in their group, and she didn't even wear a bit of makeup. She was simply a natural beauty, so perfect in every way that she almost seemed like a doll. With a melodic intake of breath she began her introduction. "I am Misteria Remington, 15, and a water user. I am also from the House and have been there my whole life, but I am not an orphan." Her voice was calm and serious, almost filled with a coldness like deep ocean waters, and her words flowed from her lips like a rumbling brook. Her manner of speaking actually made you feel quite intimidated, to say the least. She gripped her fork tighter as she continued to speak. "I'm half Arishian, since I heard my mother was born somewhere in the East in Driscoll. I mean Earth, as those of you from this world call it. My mother is a research agent working in Arisha right now, which I think is pretty amazing. When I graduate from here in four years, I hope to join her in her research, which means I have to do my best to become a research agent."

The hothead beside Genesis clenched his teeth and gripped his fork tighter, so that his hands began to shake. If he was really the fire user, then both he and Misteria were from the House, which meant that they had grown up together. She supposed that growing up together did not necessarily mean that they liked each other.

The boy next to Misteria was the pretty boy with the long, wavy, dark hair and elvish appearance. "I'm Haise Imogen, and I'm a blood artist. I came from Arisha along with Mister Kazumae." He looked up to meet the eyes of Kazumae, who sat across the table from him, and immediately averted his gaze again in a nervous manner. He kept his chin low to avoid eye contact with anyone at the table. His face held the elegance of a prince, despite his bashful behavior. He also had the deepest scarlet eyes, like that of blood, and when he spoke you could see his sharp teeth, much like those of a vampire.

"We've been at the House since I was seven and I'm 15 now, so I've been here a while, and am pretty good with my English. I would rather not be asked about my past. Forgive me," he finished. He had an elegant softness in his voice, and his speech was smooth, but he was not nearly as formal as Kazumae.

Zuri sat beside Haise. "I'm Zuri Whitlock and I'm about to turn 14. I was born in Southern Country in Arisha, but grew up in a country known as Shield Alliance. I know little about this world since I have just come here to Driscoll to enter the university. I am an ice user, like everyone else in my bloodline, and probably not surprising at all, my favorite things are to play in the snow and to ice skate," he said. He had such a kind, innocent voice that made everyone at the table smile while listening to him talk. Finishing his introduction, he turned to look at River.

"I am River Deadlock!" River proclaimed, bursting forth with all the energy that he had struggled to keep control over as he sat still in his seat, "I'm 13, and I come from Mirrorick!"

"Hold up a minute... Two thirteen-year-olds in a row? What's going on here?" Hiero Caddel interrupted from where he sat on Genesis's right. River grew visibly tense at Hiero's disruption. He idolized him, after all. Everyone stared at Hiero as he set down his utensil with a clatter and leaned back in his chair. "I mean, don't you think that's a bit young to be coming to this place? You're still a child and you've left your parents? There is so much more you can do out there before deciding to escape from the world for so many years."

River continued to smile. "No way! I'm happy to be here! I came here because I wanted to stay with my sister! I feel quite honored you think that I could have done more before coming here...but I'm sure I couldn't have made quite as many accomplishments as you! I know I'm young, but I'm really happy I came!"

A thick silence descended over the room as Hiero stared across the table. His eyes pierced into River's with a serious expression that was not at all kind.

Chapter 15
Dispute

RIVER LAUGHED NERVOUSLY AS the tension in the room grew uncomfortable. Hiero continued to glower at him from across the table.

"That's quite enough, boys. Let's continue," Professor Glazunov suggested.

"I'm not done! I just want to know why people so young are let into a high school program? I thought this place was hard to get into, but from the looks of things we have three children sitting at this table," Hiero continued

"Three?" Mae asked and pointed to herself in confusion.

"Fine. Four, if we're counting 'naturegirl,' too. There's the ice kid, and we got that little pipsqueak over there, as well. That's who I was actually referring to as the third," Hiero gestured over at Kazumae with a spark of electricity zapping out from his thumb. "And now this kid. With the nature of this school, I wouldn't think that they would accept people so young."

Kazumae stopped mid-sip of tea and very gently and deliberately set down his tea cup on its saucer, trying to keep his cool after this insult. He then spoke in a deadly calm, yet elegant voice, addressing his master Haise, "Sire, permission to kill this young a–"

"Permission denied, Mister Kazumae," Haise interrupted him. "And what have I said about that kind of language?"

"Enough! We won't have any arguments on the first day!" Professor

Glazunov shouted. When everyone was quiet he continued in a level voice. "Don't be so fixated on age. You are all children as you are still high school students who have a good deal of growing up to do. Everyone has their reasons for being here, so please do not question one another when it is information they might not want to share freely. We wouldn't let younger children into this school if we didn't think they could keep up with the rest of the class. Now, if you could finish your introduction Master Deadlock..."

"Of course, sir! Like I said, I'm 13 and from Mirrorick... My valta type is energy, which I think is quite exciting! I really like food a lot and now I can eat as much as I want without it affecting me at all! Also, I came here with my sister, Genesis. Even though I'm the youngest in the class, I'm going to do my very best to keep up with everyone. I'm super excited to start school today and I hope we can all become close really quickly!" A silence followed, which Hiero filled with an exasperated sigh as he muttered something under his breath.

"Miss Blanchet, it's your turn," Professor Glazunov prompted.

The girl Genesis had seen in the bathroom nodded at the sound of her name and stood from her chair with a slight bow to all of them. "My name is Ellie Blanchet, I'm 14, and I'm from Marseille, France," she said in a thick French accent. "My valta is psychic, hypnosis. I am very glad to be here." On that note she took her seat again. A yawn escaped Hiero's mouth and they all turned tired gazes in his direction.

The chair at the corner of the table next to Ellie was empty. Miss Nenna, at the end of the table, having already been introduced, looked toward Dusk, who sat on her other side. In response, Dusk lowered her fork, as she prepared to begin her introduction. *Like the sun, be like Dawn,* she thought to herself as she lifted her darkened gaze to glower around the table—without the least bit intention of doing so.

"I'm Olivia Elrod, but you can call me Dusk. I am 14, and my valta is Shadow. I come from Mirrorick," she uttered in a rasping voice. "This will sound strange, but my favorite thing in the world is the sun." She glanced over at Dawn, who sat beside her, and a smile spread over her lips. The expression on her face softened as she stared at him for a few moments, and in only a matter of seconds, the dark cloud that seemed to have descended over the table lifted. "That's all." She lifted her fork again to her lips and continued to eat.

"I-I am D-dawn, I'm 15 an-and my v-valta i-is l-light. I also c-come f-from M-mirrorick. I p-play v-video games..." Dawn stuttered. Everyone stared at him for a moment as he turned bright red in the face. "S-sorry, a-about m-my s-stutter. It sh-should improve once I-I g-get to kn-know you all b-better."

"It is alright, you sound just fine!" Mae chimed. He smiled in gratitude to her, which in turn made many of the others around the table smile as well.

The boy beside Dawn was the young man with the scruffy face. He now took the silence as his cue to begin his introduction. "I am Grisham Ferrari. I come from an art school in Italy and I am 16 years of age, I possess the wind valta, and I most enjoy painting and writing in my spare time. Now that I have gained this ability of wind, I shall create beauty with it as well. Let me apologize in advance if I accidentally sneeze. If you could see the state of my room right now, I am sure you would understand. I hope to learn to control my valta so such things do not happen again."

A few at the table laughed over the statement as many felt the same way about their lack of control over their own valtas. Grisham seemed nervous, but their laughter set him at ease. On another note, his English was exceptional. He had only the smallest trace of an accent in his words, so he must have been either bilingual or had become very proficient at speaking English before coming to the school. Grisham was by far the tallest student in the class. He was shy but not all that awkward. He just simply liked to keep to himself and create art alone. You could say his presence was as fleeting as something caught in the wind... Excuse me, I fear I make a few too many puns in my descriptions.

Next was Hiero Caddel, who sat beside Grisham. Hiero let out another sigh, as he cut his eyes over at Genesis. He was not at all ugly—his reputation for being handsome held up—but he was far from the handsomest in the group. No, Haise, Grisham, the hothead, and even Kazumae had better looks than him. Even so, Genesis had to admit he was good-looking; however, after the way he had reacted to her brother and how he seemed to monopolize Dawn, she wasn't quite sure how she felt about him. Of course, being that I am not as kind-hearted as Genesis, I fear the answer to how I would have felt about him is quite clear. He had a slim smile and eyes that seemed relaxed in an arrogant sort of way.

"I'm Hiero Caddel," he started. "I'm sure you all have already heard about me, though. After all, I'm pretty famous as an actor and musical artist back in California. I have my own band and everything, and I'm sure I have some stories that I can tell as none of you have performed as much as I have in front of millions of people. That all said, I've come to Arisha University because it's super hard to get into. But don't worry, just because I've had such different life experiences doesn't mean we can't be friends, am I right? I'd love to tell you all about my career and if you want tips for when we all go back to society, I'm sure I could get you connected to people. Anyway, I'm 15, which is pretty impressive with all I've already accomplished in my life," he chuckled to himself. Genesis saw Mae make a face at him across the table. In response, he winked at her in an extremely flirtatious manner. "Anyway, I now possess the amazing powers of electricity, so..."

At that point, the hothead had had about enough and began to grumble all sorts of atrocities under his breath in a language neither Genesis nor any of the other students from Earth-side understood, bringing Hiero to a stop mid-sentence. He was taken aback! How could someone start talking when he was still in the middle of doing so himself?! First Dawn getting distracted from his story earlier and now this?! Sure, the hothead's voice was barely audible, but still! How rude!

The hothead stared down at his food, his grip tightening on the utensil he held in his hand again so hard that they all thought it would snap in half. While it did bend a bit due to the extreme heat of his grasp and the flimsiness of the metal, it remained in one piece. Switching to English, he spoke, not evening glancing in Hiero's direction, "I'm going to be the best valta user in all of Arisha, no question about it. Maybe you've had everything handed to you on a silver platter your whole life, but that's not the way things work here. What makes you assume you can just come in and be the best?" Everyone looked about the table uncomfortably.

Hiero made a clicking sound with his tongue in irritation and a spark passed between his fingers as he snapped them a few times in close succession. "Now, now, I'm not trying to take your crown or anything, Your Highness. But I will be trying my very best to improve myself like I always have. Since I pretty much excel at everything I put my mind to, I very well might surpass you. Even so, what does that matter? I guess you'll just have to try harder as well," Hiero responded.

Genesis sat in stunned silence for a moment, her heart racing as she wished for a way to disappear. The hothead's body temperature had risen so high that she could feel waves of heat hit her as he moved to stand. His one hand slammed down on the table as flames licked up from his other.

"Master Ashford, that's quite enough. Using valta to threaten another student is strictly prohibited," Professor Glazunov said in as calm a voice as he seemed able to muster. Understandable, as the situated at the table was quickly getting out of control. The flames surrounding the young man's hand flickered out and he slumped back down in his seat. " Now, Miss Deadlock, you may introduce yourself," Professor Glazunov suggested.

Genesis hesitated a moment, the stunned silence at the table lengthening as the time passed and she still did not speak. She knew her voice would come out shaking because she hated when people got angry. Why did so many at the table seem so angry? Especially the two she sat between?

"O-kay..." she uttered at last and drew in a deep breath. "I'm Genesis Leigh Deadlock. I just turned 15, and I'm a..." She swallowed hard, afraid to admit the next part out loud. Her eyes lifted up to meet River's across the table for strength. "I'm a shapeshifter... I think that's all I need to say... I just hope that everyone gets along, perhaps. I mean we're all in this class, right? We'll all be studying together for the next four years, so why argue about who will be the best? In the end, we'll all come out as agents for this school, right? I mean, I've only been here a day... so I'm still unsure about the details. But in the end, does it really matter who's the 'best' when we're all aiming toward the same goal?" She couldn't believe what she had said for a second. Her chest tightened and she thought she would be sick. She didn't look but she was sure that she had only made Ashford even angrier and now Misteria was eyeing her sharply. However, the smile Mae flashed her across the table reassured her that she had said the right thing. Even if she made two—perhaps more—of her new classmates angry.

Ashford muttered something beside her in that other language, and his chair slid back as he violently stood again. "I can't agree with anything she just said. I will be the best here whether you guys like it or not! I'm not here to make friends!"

"Breathe," Kazumae muttered between sips of tea.

"My name is Alric Ashford, and I'm from the House of Arisha! I'm a fire user, been one since I was seven years old." Kazumae let out a short laugh. Alric grabbed his glass tightly, the water within violently boiled off, and a puff of steam shot up into the air forming a cloud around him.

"Do you dare burn me?" Kazumae said in a lighthearted voice, the confident grin never wavering from his determined face. Alric continued to glare down at his plate of food until at last he set down his glass, yanked his chair back into position, and took his seat again.

"I wouldn't," he muttered.

"We'll need to have a word in my office after breakfast, Master Ashford," Glazuov said.

Genesis lifted her hand to her chin thoughtfully. The name *Ashford* sounded strangely familiar to her, but she couldn't quite put her finger on it at that moment.

Kazumae cleared his throat and climbed up so he stood on his chair, so that all could see him with ease. "I am Kazumae Amana, that is pronounced KAH-zoo-may, so please do not mispronounce it. I am a user of the earth valta. This shall be of a great surprise but I am by far all of your senior, being 17 years of age. So I wish to be respected," he glanced over at Hiero as he spoke. "I am not small, just not super tall. I enjoy my tea, so if you ever wish to speak, we shall have it over tea. As I am elder, I hope to be a shoulder on which you could lean. If you have any troubles, any at all, please come to me and I shall provide a listening ear. 'Tis all, fair people." With that he got down to finish his breakfast.

A silence filled the room as everyone did the same. The awkwardness resulting from the introductions and arguments rendered everyone speechless. It was not even nine o'clock on the first day and already the tension between everyone in Freshman Class 1 Group A was high. Genesis's anxiety levels had skyrocketed again so that she could barely bring herself to eat another bite. She tried to brush off the hate-filled glances that were sent her way. After all, she wasn't there to make friends either.

Chapter 16
Off to Class

AFTER BREAKFAST, HAISE AND Grisham stayed behind to clean up while the rest of the group returned to their rooms to get ready for their first class. Back in the solitude of her room, Genesis packed her bag for school, although she really wasn't sure what she would need. They didn't have any of their textbooks yet, so she assumed they would receive those during class. She planned to wait until River came down to go over to class with him. That way she wouldn't have to figure out where to go by herself. Still, she examined her map as she waited in the foyer of the dorm, seated on a bench by some cubbies and coat racks. The academic building where they had their first class wasn't too far away from their dorm.

She slipped her map back into the front pocket of her bag as two students came from the stairway. To her great relief, it was not students from the House who came down first, but River and Zuri, just as she had hoped. They both greeted her with cheery smiles when they saw her waiting for them.

"Did you wait for us, Sis?" River asked in surprise.

"Of course," Genesis answered.

"Yay! I'm glad the three of us get to walk over together!"

"Best to figure things out as a group on our first day, am I right?" she said.

"Quite so," Zuri agreed.

The three of them departed the dorm together. As they stepped onto the stone path from the dorm's porch, they all paused. They had seen the campus already on their walk to the dorm the day before, of course, but now that they had had more time for everything to sink in, they could thoroughly enjoy its beauty—Driscoll's campus was more beautiful than Genesis could have ever imagined. The trees and buildings were filled with goodness and warmth that put them all at ease. No matter what they faced on their first day, they were going to be all right.

"We're really here, Gen-gen!" River declared as he grasped his sister's arm. "We're going to find our parents! I just know it!" Genesis nodded in agreement.

Zuri, on the other hand, stood beside them with a wonder-filled look in his pale-blue eyes. He was staring up so that all he could see was the bright blue skies above them. "It's so beautiful and blue," he said in a frosty gasp.

"But the sky is always like that!" River claimed as if it was no big deal.

"Not in Arisha..."

"Most days it is blue here! Only on stormy days or when the sun sets or rises is it not blue."

Zuri took another deep breath. "Your world is truly amazing," he whispered.

"Not really. I think your world sounds *way* more interesting! Oh! I'm very excited to eventually go there! Even though I just learned of it yesterday, I have this feeling in my stomach! Like all tingly with excitement... Kind of like it feels akin to me! Ya know?" River clapped his hands together in quick succession as he hopped up and down in place a few times.

Footsteps sounded on the porch, but the three of them were too engrossed in the sky to notice. Alric paused behind them, as they blocked

his way down off the porch. With gritted teeth he began to grumble under his breath in the same manner as earlier. *"How absolutely annoying."*
He only stood a moment more before he grew fed up with waiting for
them to move and shoved past them as they stood loitering. Genesis took
the cue, and the three began walking so that they wouldn't be in the way
of anyone else coming out of their dorm. I find it quite unfortunate that
Alric, rather than someone kinder, came out while they lingered!

"How is it that my world sounds more interesting to you?" Zuri
asked, falling into step beside River. Genesis perused her map again to
make sure they were headed in the right direction since the other two
seemed to be too distracted to do so. As the oldest, she also felt that it
was her duty.

River's eyes gleamed. "I mean, valta is widely known in your world,
right? Isn't that, like, super cool and all?"

Zuri shrugged. "It's just normal for us. Pretty much everyone has
been awakened, but few have gone to school to know how to use their
valta, and even fewer are very powerful with it. Plus, you've never seen
my world. The truth is, it's pretty terrible. It's always bleak and gray,
plus there is always the fear of monsters attacking the towns...so I don't
know if it's very cool. Everything I've heard about your world has been so
interesting. I mean, for me, the weirdest thing was you knowing nothing
about Arisha during awakening. I assumed everyone here would already
know of the existence of my world." He shrugged again with a smile,
until he saw River's face. "Don't look sad!" The innocence in Zuri's voice
as he talked about depressing things, only made the depressing things
sound all the sadder.

"Now your world sounds like a sad place..." River's voice dropped.

"Well, that would be why I am grateful to your world and this
school, because the Driscollian researchers have come through for quite

some time now, and they have always tried to help resurrect our world."

Kazumae let out a short laugh, which made them all jump in mid-stride, for they had not realized that he and Haise had been walking not far behind them nearly the whole time.

"Mister Kazumae..." Haise cautioned as he looked down at him.

"I know, Sire, and I shan't say a thing on the matter. But it would seem they have very little self-awareness if they do not even know that they are being followed," Kazumae answered.

The three stopped and watched as the two Arishians continued past them. They had now reached the academic building. "It would seem that they are able to conceal their presence well. Curious are those two," Zuri observed.

Hiero, Dawn, and Dusk also stood just out front of the building. Of course, Hiero looked irritated again as Dawn and Dusk were talking to each other with bright expressions on their faces and their backs turned to him. It seemed that they could not decide if they were in the right place or not, which clearly bothered Hiero. Upon seeing the new arrivals, he turned swiftly and strode toward them. He thrust his shoulders back so that his chest was lifted, and he looked down his nose at them even as he drew closer and closer.

"If it isn't Genesis the shapeshifter, whom I get to sit next to at meals," he said. His eyes looked Genesis up then down, in a way that made Genesis feel quite uncomfortable. She drew her bag tighter to her as if it would hide her from his wandering eyes. Thinking about how uncomfortable she would be seated between both him and Alric, she wondered if she could request to change her seat at the table. After all, there was that empty chair next to Ellie...

River, on the other hand, beamed beside his big sister, despite the incident earlier with Hiero at breakfast. River was academically smart, otherwise he wouldn't have made it into the school at such a young age, but he did have trouble picking up on social cues. He had thought Hiero's words were kind earlier, suggesting that he could have done much more before coming to the school. He failed to read between the lines, so to speak, as it had been obvious to everyone else at the table that Hiero did not like the idea of attending classes with a little 13-year-old.

"Are you *really* Hiero Caddel?!" River beamed.

Hiero glanced at him, a heavy exasperated sigh escaping his lips. "Of course! Are you a fan or something?"

"Yes! Totally! You were super cool in your last performance! You really went out with a bang on that one... I was really sad you didn't do one last solo tour this year! I was really hoping you'd do one so I could go see you perform live! I guess you haven't really performed in a while. That makes sense though, this isn't an easy school to get into so you must have been more focused on your studies! Although, you seem to be naturally smart, so I'm sure it wasn't that difficult for you! At the same time, you've always talked about how hard work gets you great places! Oh! But you and Casey Brumming always made the best duo up on stage! I wish I could have seen the two of you performing together! If I had known your performances would have been cut short so suddenly, I would have made more of an effort to try and go see!" River fanboyed. Hiero's expression changed, his lips drawing into a tight line before he turned away without another word and strode back toward Dawn and Dusk. "Hey... but wait... why...?" River stammered.

Genesis caught her brother's arm as he took a few steps after Hiero. "Sorry, River..." Genesis muttered. If she were to guess, Hiero probably didn't want to be told that he performed best with another person. Still, his reaction seemed strange since River wasn't meaning to imply that.

"Come on. This is the building, so stop being cowards and let's get to the classroom already," Hiero said as he grabbed Dawn by the tie and yanked him after himself.

"A-all right..." Dawn stuttered. "C-come on, D-dusk..."

"Guess we'll follow them," Genesis suggested. Pouting beside her, her brother kicked a pebble to send it skipping across the stone path. She sighed. In the end, he was still younger than everyone else, even if he was academically smart. She headed for the door.

"I just don't understand," River whined. Genesis stopped and glanced back at him as he continued to pout. "Every fan I've talked to who's met him in real life, said he was a really nice guy, and always treated his fans respectfully. Even if they ran into him on the streets, he always gave out his autograph and took as many pictures as they wanted with him. So why don't I get to meet the nice Hiero Caddel everyone talked about? I could even be friends with him since we're going to the same school! And although he does seem a bit prideful, that only makes sense since he's famous! I still want to talk to him!"

His sister sighed, retracing her steps back to place her hand very gently on her brother's shoulder. "I know it's rough. But he's famous, and being at school, he only wants to hang out with people his own age... I'm sure you can still get his autograph and listen to his stories. He might love someone to just sit and listen to him...but...hmmm..." Genesis was at a loss for words and wondered what she was even trying to accomplish by that point. She didn't want River getting hurt if Hiero got fed up with him trying to be his friend. She was sure such a thing could be annoying to someone like him, even if he was prideful and liked praise. "I know it's rough," she repeated. "But in the end, it's the harsh reality. Think back to what he said to you earlier at breakfast 'There is so much more you can do out there before deciding to escape from the world for so many years.' In a way, he might be trying to use this place as an escape. If you want to escape the world..."

River nodded slowly. "I know, I know. I shouldn't bring up things from his life outside. Just listen to his stories about things that interest him." He pulled his bag back over his shoulder as the strap had started to slip down.

"Yeah...that's my only guess as to why he reacted like that to what you said... Let's go to class."

"Yeah."

Chapter 17

Earth and Arisha

THE CLASSROOM WAS QUIET even before Professor Glazunov entered. Most of the students had been too nervous to speak with each other, since this was the first time their entire class was together as a group. I am sure it has been mentioned before, but I feel I must remind you that those we met back at the dorm were only half of Freshman Class 1! Genesis and River dorm in Group A, but those in Group B are located in the dorm adjacent to them. Basically, if meeting a bunch of people for the first time at breakfast wasn't difficult enough, now they all waited in a classroom half made up of nameless students. For your own sanity, I shall only divulge the names of the few who are relevant to our story when it becomes necessary.

So the room was rather quiet and tense with a few exceptions. Mae and Misteria were at the back of the classroom with a bunch of the House students from Group B. They had grown up with them, so naturally they all gravitated toward one another as they waited for it to be time for class. Most of the House students were assigned seats at the back of the classroom, which made it easier for them to talk between their desks.

Genesis had found a desk marked with her name without much difficulty. She was seated close to those from the House, as she had been at the table for breakfast. *Great way to make them hate me even more, by grouping me with them all the time,* she thought. To distract herself from her discomfort with the nearby students, Genesis looked about the room. Much like the dorm, the dark wood tones of the walls, floors, and furniture conveyed a feeling of warmth. In a way, Genesis felt it looked more like an old-fashioned school room than the modern ones she was used to back home.

"I think it's time to explain some things to you in more depth," Professor Glazunov began. "Of course, I know those from the House know most of this, but it is time for a little history lesson on the Gateway, Arisha, and our worlds in general. In this class, I will mostly give you information on the school and events, and, in a few days, I hope you all will be more comfortable with each other and me, so that we can make this more of a discussion time to practice speaking Arshin with one another once the Earth-side students have learned a bit of it. You have an official class for that on Saturday mornings, but you'll be given homework to do throughout the week as well.

"Some of you may have seen the schedules, so you know that you'll be having an academic class after this, followed by physical education class, then lunch at the cafeteria, followed by the rest of your academic classes. Then, for your special valta training at the end of the day, you will be in classes consisting of only teachers and students with your valta type, so that you can learn how to use your specific abilities with other users. Then, after that, the rest of the day is yours. Dinner is at 7:00. You can help in the kitchen of your dorm if you want, or train while waiting for dinner. Whoever is setting the table and doing clean up will be assigned each meal, though. Everyone has to do it, so I would rather not hear complaints on the issue. On another note, your dormitory's gym will be unlocked at all times. The gyms are pretty nice, so check them out. They are located in the basements of your dorms, and the staircase to get down is off the first floor lounge. As for the lounge, there are board games if you need something more relaxing to do in the evening. I'm sure you also brought your own things to do as well...

"I already mentioned the class on Saturday mornings... I suppose I should clarify that Arshin is the language most widely spoken in Arisha, and nearly everyone knows it there. The class is mandatory for all students except, of course, the Arishian students who already speak that language, and for students from the House who grew up learning it. That is the main info on that. Does anyone have any questions before I go on?" He looked up at the class as he finished speaking. The room remained silent. "Well, I can see, you're going to be a boring class." Murmurs of protest around the room followed, and so he smiled. "Okay, let us get on with the history then. You are welcome to raise your hand at any time to ask questions." He stood up and started to pace the floor in front of the chalkboard.

"Since the beginning of time, Arisha and Earth were connected by what they called the 'Tunnel of Worlds.' Two worlds that lived together and shared each other's ways for thousands of years. But Arisha discovered valta, which was power hidden within every human being on both Earth and Arisha. As they were unwilling to share their discovery with Earth, tension grew between the people, and eventually a war broke out between the worlds with Earth on the losing side. Then a global flood took place on Earth, and after that, all connections were lost. Our two worlds had been sealed off from each other.

"In Arisha, the use of valtas grew, and so it became a way of life there. They would awaken their children at young ages, so their children would never know life without their valta. Of course, in Arisha, there are more natural ways of awakening a person that are not quite so painful and forced, but they take a great deal of time to produce any valta at all. A few hundred years after the Tunnel of Worlds was sealed, a new type of valta user appeared in Arisha. Many called this valta user the 'valta phantom' or the 'valta priest.' But, when people discovered the abilities the valta priest possessed, it was not long before he was considered dangerous. You have all probably heard by now, a person is born with one type of valta, and one type of valta only. Someone can not gain more types, or one that they have not been born with, in a natural way. But that was not the case with this person. This person had the ability to use all types of natural valta, plus one specialty valta, with no problems and at full force. Some wanted to worship this person as a god. Others realized the danger with having such a person around, as such a person could easily take over the entirety of Arisha, or even open up a new way to Earth—and that was the last thing they wanted. So a war broke out within Arisha between those who thought that this person should live on as a god, and those who thought only of the dangers of doing so. This may not seem like an important story to most of us who are from Earth, but in reality, this is important for you to learn as a student of this school." Professor Glazunov glanced about the class, for there were those (such as Hiero) who looked extremely bored. Hiero sighed and the professor gave him a sharp look before he continued.

"So in the end, the valta priest was put to death, and his wife and children were thrown into prison. Their eldest son grew up and eventually was released when he was able to prove he could only use one valta. Much later, however, it was revealed that the abilities of the valta priest had been passed down to his grandson. The family tried to conceal this, but, according to the written accounts on the matter, the boy was wild and so it grew too hard to contain him. After it became known that a new valta priest had risen, the people realized the ability could be passed down the generations after all, and therefore, they had not snuffed out the power of the valta priest.

"At first, there wasn't another war. People thought they could use the power to their advantage this time, and tried to use the valta priest, seeking to change the world so that *everyone* could use all types of valta. But such an idea was of little use, for after countless tests, it was realized that there could only be one valta priest in every other generation of his bloodline. So, yet another war came, for many determined that there should not be someone who could use all types of valta, as that was too much power for one person to possess. The war carried on for a hundred years, ending when the valta priest disappeared into the Shadow Lands."

Zuri gasped and the professor met his eyes. "The Shadow Lands!" he exclaimed.

"Yes, Master Whitlock. As those from Arisha know, when one has entered the Shadow Lands, they do not usually ever come out again. That is why no one followed to make sure he was dead. The Shadow Lands are considered too dangerous. For those of you who don't know, the Shadow Lands are a grouping of islands in Arisha, where a city known as the City of Lost Souls is located. Legend says that if you go there, your soul will be sucked out of your body by the thousands of ghosts that mindlessly wander its shores.

"Anyway, the war finally ended, but the land was devastated. Things began to slowly crumble apart in Arisha after that, and while Arisha had always been more beautiful than Earth, it was not anymore. Despite this, life in Arisha went on as usual. The people went back to their old ways, and the valta priest became a legend of older times. Maybe a thousand more years passed, and then reports started of sightings of the valta priest...but these never became more than rumors of the people. Governments did take action eventually, however, and there was a search, but to no avail.

"A few hundred more years passed before the valta priest was finally discovered in a major kingdom to the southwest called Tryss—where you will spend your senior year in our destination studies. The citizens of Tryss confirmed that there was indeed a valta priest in their kingdom, and so the search quickly heightened. Arishians worried that war would break out again, and the tensions were high, but the difference now was that everyone in Arisha agreed that the valta priest should be put to death, along with the rest of his family, to ensure the bloodline ended.

"In the confusion, someone dear to the valta priest was killed for her involvement, and that broke him. His power was unleashed and, in the process, he tore a hole in the fabric of our worlds, reopening the Gateway between them. That was how we regained access to Arisha.

"Of course, the Gateway on our end wasn't discovered for quite some time after. Around 200 years ago it was discovered very close to here by Fredrick Watts, and then relations were started between our worlds again. This was a time of peace, though, as the Watts family promised to help resurrect Arisha without making it known to any of our world's governments. That way, the Watts family could ensure that all interactions were done through peace rather than to gain power. Thus far, secrecy has been maintained, and we intend to keep it that way.

"So, that brings us to the history of this school. Driscoll University was established, now 98 years ago, to awaken and train people to go in and help Arisha. Some go to do research on the lands; others to help defend villages from monsters that have run rampant since the great Arishian Wars. Bit by bit, we are helping them rebuild their world..." His voice faltered over those last words before he continued on. "Now, if your chosen life path is not to help Arisha, we ask that you do remain in our school and carry out the missions until your eight years here are complete—that's four years in the school and four years as an agent in the field. After that, you are free to go back to your former lives with the promise that everything you have learned will remain classified, and your valta cells shall be destroyed, which means you can not get them back ever.

"Now, does that all make sense? I know it's a long story, but it's also important to know all that happened to put Arisha in the state it is today and to understand about the Gateway. Any questions now?" he stopped his pacing as Dawn raised his hand.

"Yes, Master Viotto?" he smiled, pleased to have a question.

"I-I w-was w-wondering... W-what h-happened to the v-valta p-priest?" Dawn stuttered.

"Oh, well, releasing all of that power was very taxing, so he died in the process. I heard that when he tore open the Gateway, he used up all his valta, which took his life as well. There has never been another valta priest. So that is the end of that chapter. No one can have more than one valta."

"Oh, th-that's s-sad, th-that h-he died."

"Not really. Sounds like the guy just caused a whole lot of conflict, if you ask me. He deserved to die," someone from the other half of the class remarked. Genesis heard a few sighs about the room.

The professor took his seat at the desk at the front of the room. "Any more questions?" River raised his hand. "Yes, Master Deadlock?"

"So...you said we would have to protect people from monsters...but how exactly did these monsters come to exist in Arisha?" River asked in a nervous voice.

"From what we know, a few of them originated from a chimera creature that could take on characteristics of its food. Such creatures had been carefully monitored so that they could not devour larger, more dangerous creatures, since they themselves were a vicious kind, but with the distraction of the wars, the situation was forgotten, and, as a result, grew out of control. Others speculate that some of the more formless monsters came about from demonic activity that many people practiced during the war in the hope of gaining more power. In those situations, the monsters may have once been human. As for some races, like the Sirus—a vicious race of merfolk—the Fairies, the Blood Artists, the Soul Snatchers, and a race known as the Angels, their origins go back way too far for anyone to know how they came about. It is often wondered, however, if the reason why Earth has legends about such creatures is because at one time Earth was connected to Arisha where such creatures and people actually existed. Just so you know, there are dragons as well, but there are currently only four known to be alive today."

"I have a question as well," a boy asked.

"Go ahead, Master Clive."

"What is Arisha exactly? Is it like another planet and the Gateway is a wormhole? Or is it another dimension?"

"Let me see... Well...that's a good question and one I'm not sure I can answer, if I'm to be at all honest..."

"It's not something we can know," a boy in the front row said in a serious tone. "It could be another planet or another dimension. Unless we found a way to explore the entire galaxy, we might never know if it's another planet or not. We also don't know what the true nature of the Tunnel of Worlds was like. Maybe if we knew that, we'd know the truth about the Gateway."

"Thank you, Master Watts," Professor Glazunov answered. Dusk raised her hand this time. "Yes, Miss Elrod?"

"How does the awakening process work?" she asked.

"Oh, yes. Why don't I have someone familiar with this process answer this one. Master Watts, you often assist during awakenings, could I ask you to explain this one as well?" he suggested.

The boy in the front row stood from his seat, all eyes drawing again toward him. He was very small in stature, although not quite in the same way as Kazumae. While he was much shorter than other guys, his small stature was mostly because he was a very lean boy. He had stormy gray hair and Genesis could not help but notice the lonely look in his gray-blue eyes, as he turned to face the rest of the class. He cleared his throat

"So, in Arisha, the subject is exposed to the element of what is supposed to be his type of valta, along with drinking a liquid found in a certain tree in Arisha. The combination of these two begins the awakening process. Unfortunately, this method ends up taking a long time before even a little bit of valta is produced in the subject. Arisha developed another method—the one that we use now—and that is by processing a sample of the subject's blood in such a way that the dormant valta cells are awakened. The blood is then injected back into the subject where the cells multiply and quickly awaken the whole body. This process takes about a week before the subject can be safely brought back to their senses from such an intense, fast awakening. This can only be done on people who have strong enough bodies for it, because it is very dangerous. We wouldn't have let you into the school if we didn't think you would have survived the process. Death is a strong possibility for those who aren't strong enough. After the valta cells are awakened, all that is left is to activate the power by being exposed to the power's element... Maybe I phrased that in a weird way. When I say element, I mean the requirement to activate your valta. For water users, enough moisture in the air. Fire, enough heat and oxygen. Ice, cold and moisture. Hopefully that is more clear." Watts lowered his head before he took his seat again.

"Thank you, Master Watts. Anything else?" A silence proceeded, for they were all shocked to learn that they had been out for a whole week during their awakening. Except, of course, for the ones from the House, who had long ago endured that process. "Okay then, if there is nothing else you want to know, you may get ready for your next class." Professor Glazunov then stood and took his leave of the room.

Genesis looked back toward Watts as the class began to get up and disperse. She guessed that he must be the principal's son, based on the fact that he had the Principal's last name. But then why did he seem so sad?

Chapter 18
Roland Watts

NEARLY EVERYONE IN THE class took PE seriously. As in their first class that morning, no one really spoke; they all just did as the instructor told them to do without commentary or discussion. Maybe this was because it was the first day and very few of them knew each other all that well. Even so, Genesis already felt like she belonged there, more than she had ever felt at any other school she had attended. The other students seemed so determined to improve themselves, just like she did. She felt like they were all there because they truly wanted to be, not because they had to.

After PE, it was time for lunch at the school cafeteria. Genesis took a shower first in the locker room, and, by the time she had finished changing, everyone else had already gone off to the cafeteria. Luckily, she found it fairly quickly on her own, toward the center of campus. Once inside, she looked from table to table, but didn't recognize anyone from her class, even though she hadn't taken that long to get ready. She guessed that it didn't matter that much if she ate alone. She was the one who had delayed, but she still felt sort of lonely eating by herself on the first day. She had hoped at least her brother would have waited for her.

Genesis picked up a food tray and walked down the cafeteria counter choosing her lunch food. Near the end of the counter was a long table filled with students who wore darker-colored uniforms. She thought they must be upperclassmen, although they all looked a little too young.

A boy stood up from the table and approached her. "Are you from

Freshman Class 1?" the boy asked. Genesis looked at him, startled that he had addressed her. He was pretty handsome, in all honesty, and those charming eyes he fixated on her were filled with kindness. After a few seconds of hesitation, she nodded in answer to his question. "I think your class has already left. You can sit with us if you want. We're all in Freshman Class 3." She looked past him to see the other students at the table eyeing her suspiciously. She swallowed and gave him a bright smile as she considered taking him up on the offer.

Just then she caught sight of Watts from her class sitting down at a table by himself, and her mind was made up. "Thank you. I appreciate the offer, but I think I'll be all right," Genesis answered.

"That's a shame. With our lunch start times staggered by half an hour, I don't think our classes will be able to get to know each other very well."

"We have four years, and it's only the first day," she pointed out.

He clapped his hands together. "You're right! I should have thought about that. But, it isn't right for you to eat alone. If you distance yourself from everyone, you'll end up like Alric Ashford or Roland Watts," he said with a mocking laugh. A few at the table behind him began to laugh with him—those from the House who knew Alric and Roland, of course.

"I will not distance myself...but I am also not here to make friends. Again, it is only the first day."

"Okay. If that's what you want, I won't argue with you. But we're right over here if you wanna sit with us." He paused and then leaned toward her, lifting his hand between his mouth and her ear as he whispered conspiratorially, "I'll tell you this, though. We have the best students from the House in our class. You got all the snobs."

Startled, she took a step back away from him. "I don't see how that's a problem. I couldn't care less about something like that. I'm not here to make friends, anyway, like I said."

"Alright, alright, just saying! We're super cool and won't ostracize you just for being a shapeshifter. So if you're ever done with them being mean, head on over to either of Class 3's dorms. We'll sorta adopt you."

"You bet!" a girl exclaimed from the table behind him.

"I will remember that." Genesis smiled and nodded as she turned away from him to where Watts sat alone. She wasn't all that sure why she felt such a need to sit with him, but she could not ignore the loneliness she felt exuding from him. She wove through the rows and rows of dining tables, filled with boisterous students, until at last she stood at the table where he was seated. He didn't even lift his head or in any way acknowledge her approach.

She took a deep breath and set down her tray across from his, and only then did he lift his head. "I hope you don't mind. It seems the rest of our class already left and I don't like sitting alone very much," she told him.

"It's fine..." he answered briefly, lowering his head again. She took a seat across from him. He sent a glance over his shoulder as some students looked in their direction and began to whisper among themselves.

"So I take it you're Principal Watts's son then? I think they said your name was Roland?" Genesis asked after a moment of awkward silence. Roland only nodded, creating another awkward silence. Genesis continued to eat as she thought of another question to ask, but she felt her nerve leaving her as he seemed to have no interest in talking what-so-ever.

"What kind of valta do you have?" she asked at last.

He paused to finish chewing. "It's complicated..." he answered.

With that, she lost her nerve completely. She was really not sure how to respond to that answer. From everything she had heard, answering what type of valta you had seemed to be pretty uncomplicated...say some kind of element and then be done with it. He had no interest in talking to her—that had become obvious—and so the rest of lunch passed with that heavy, awkward silence between them. Only when Roland at last got up and left without a word, was Genesis able to feel at ease again. She had gotten nowhere with Roland Watts.

Suddenly, there was a commotion on the other side of the cafeteria that drew Genesis away from her thoughts. From the sound of it, a fire user had caught one of the table decors on fire and so about every water user in the room rushed to put it out. I suppose the occurrence was not uncommon in a school where children were still learning to control such strange abilities.

Chapter 19

Shapeshifting

THE REST OF THE afternoon proceeded rather uneventfully—academic classes at Driscoll were like academic classes at any typical high school, after all. At last came the time for Special Valta Training, the class Genesis had been looking forward to all day. Unsure what to expect, she followed the rest of her class to the Valta Department building to find the room listed on her schedule. Anxiety mixed with excitement washed over her as she lingered in the hallway outside the designated lab room. Finally, she took a deep breath, and, without further delay, she opened the door and stepped into the room.

Inside, she found a room that smelled strongly of cleaning chemicals. Every surface was sparse and dusted. There were several desks on which research was done, and three desk chairs were arranged in the center of the room facing one another in a small circle. Air purifiers had been set on about every surface, as well as some attached to the walls and places on the floor. I am sure you can guess that, as this was the lab room for shapeshifting research, it was necessary to keep the air as pure as possible for the shapeshifters who might work or learn in that room. Especially when you took into account that the back wall of the room was lined with cages in which animals were kept. Some were rather familiar to us—animals of Earth—while others bore resemblance to them, but Genesis could tell there was something very different about them than any ordinary creatures she had seen—you guessed it, animals of Arisha.

Furthermore on the subject, be assured that the animals that were kept in that room were treated with the utmost kindness. In fact, they spent very little time in their cages at all. When research was not being done on them, or they were not holding the shapeshifting classes, they were allowed free range of the Vegetation Research Lab in the basement, as it most closely resembled their natural habitat.

Two men stood in front of a bird cage, one lowering a bowl of bird seed down into it, while the other hovered just behind him. She quickly realized she was looking at the same man, the only difference being that one wore a school uniform and did not have glasses. Not only were they the same, but they were both Dr. Cherith, whom she had met during her awakening. Yes, that long, straight, black hair that went down to his waist was unmistakable. She stood in the doorway, lost in her own confusion, as the one who did not wear the school uniform slowly turned around to look at her. His eye must have caught the man standing beside him, though, for his head turned sharply in his direction and a surprised look passed over his face.

"Good heavens! What are you doing?!" he demanded of the other him.

"Whatever do you mean, Reiss? You are the one behaving oddly! Whyever would you take *my* form?" the other man, who wore the uniform, questioned. The corners of his lips twitched as he tried to conceal a mischievous grin.

"Now, now, Reiss, that is quite enough. Would you please shift back now?" Dr. Cherith said in a serious tone, to show he was not playing around.

"Oh, come now, you're no fun!" the other Cherith retorted just before his body was engulfed in blue light. When the light dissipated, Genesis saw a boy that she recognized from Group B. He was very memorable for his shock of white hair with red tips. Honestly, Genesis had guessed him to be a fire user when she had seen him in class, with his gold eyes and red-tinged hair.

"I apologize, Miss Deadlock. Good evening, and welcome to your last class for the day," Dr. Cherith greeted her. "How are you feeling?"

"I am feeling much better, thank you," she answered, still quite in shock at witnessing the art of shapeshifting right before her eyes. In truth, she was doing quite well. Her body still ached a bit, but she had made it through all her classes all right. River had to sit out for most of PE, however. She had thought about asking to sit down a few times herself, but she had pushed through, determined to complete the class.

"So, you'll be my student for this class, along with Reiss Gatlin here. You should really introduce yourselves properly since you two aren't in the same dorm group." He closed the bird cage and turned around to face them again, glancing from Reiss to her.

Reiss let out a quick laugh, and started toward her with his hand extended. "I'm Reiss Gatlin from Freshman Group B. It's a pleasure to meet my new shapeshifting buddy," he said as he took her hand. She smiled, for he leaned forward and kissed it, leaving her to guess he must be from Arisha where they had different forms of greeting new people.

"Reiss..." Dr. Cherith cautioned, seeing an impish smile flicker over the boy's lips. As Reiss withdrew his lips from her hand, his eyes cut up to look at Genesis and, in the blink of an eye, she looked down into her own face. The olive green hair and red eyes still felt a bit startling to her, as she had not seen her own reflection more than a few brief times since her awakening, but it was her face nonetheless. She drew back a step.

"Reiss! Quit that this moment!" Dr. Cherith demanded.

Reiss shifted back again, clapping one hand to his head. "I'm sorry, Mister Cherith! You know I couldn't help myself! She just offered me her hand!"

"No shifting into Miss Deadlock! You may think it's funny, but it makes people feel uncomfortable. Especially a young woman." The doctor took a seat in one of the desk chairs situated in the center of the room and motioned for the other two to do the same. Genesis obeyed, more nervous to have another experience like she had had the day before with the cat, than she was about Reiss shifting into her. She still had trouble wrapping her mind around the fact that she had really turned into a cat!

Reiss sat down beside her and the two of them waited for Dr. Cherith to begin that day's lesson. Even with the vast number of air purifiers in the room, Genesis couldn't help but notice how restless she felt inside. She got a tingly sensation in her fingertips as she inhaled even just the little bits of fur and feather in the air. In truth, while animals were good practice for shapeshifting, placing new shapeshifters in a room filled with them was certainly not ideal. To Dr. Cherith that was all just a part of the training and a test to see how well they could control their valta.

"Let me see...shapeshifting then..." he began. "Once you get the hang of changing back and forth, it should get a lot easier. The thing that will be difficult will be retaining the shapes you've changed into. Basically, for almost every valta there is a side effect and a requirement. As far as shapeshifting goes, there aren't really any major side effects."

"I always feel sleepy if I do a lot of shapeshifting practice all at once," Reiss said.

"Yes. I guess it is important to remember that you are still a human being, and that your body can only take so much strenuous activity. Moving on, there are some restrictions...like, for example: the number of imprints your body can store is limited until trained further. That will actually be our main focus: to increase the number of available shapes you can shift into. I know you are already pretty fast at changing back and forth, Reiss, but you do have trouble retaining more than just your regular and wolf forms, so you will benefit from this training, as well."

"Of course, Mister Cherith! After all, I have never gotten any formal training, even though I have had my valta for a long time now. Plus, I was awakened naturally, so my valta is definitely a lot weaker than the students awakening here." Reiss released a sheepish laugh.

"Yes, yes. I will continue now. We talked about the side effects of shapeshifting, so now let's talk about the requirement. You see, for shapeshifting, the requirement is ingesting the DNA of whatever it is you want to shift into, as I explained during your awakening, Genesis. So, for an example, I gave you the cat. You could simply swallow a bit of fur and then shift into a cat form. Easy, right? But you might not have access to DNA in the exact moment that you need to shift into a certain creature. Fortunately, you don't always have to ingest DNA immediately before shifting. Because the cat was the last thing you turned into, you are still able to shift into that cat. If you are able to make your body change, that is. It's a bit harder to change at will rather than right after ingesting the DNA. Especially as a beginner. So, we'll start there by having you try to bring the cat to the surface. From there, I'll show you how to change back.

"Shapeshifting isn't that difficult, but it is considered a weaker valta if you don't have access to the right forms. That is why I highly recommend you become physically strong on your own, in order to do well in combat training next semester. Eventually, once you both are juniors, we will have some DNA samples from stronger creatures brought in for you to try out, but for the time being, we want to be able to prepare you for not having access to such resources when you're out in the field. It helps to know the strengths of the primary creatures you will be shifting into, but if you get used to different creatures, it should be easier to adapt quickly to new forms you have to spontaneously take on.

"Genesis, try thinking of the cat now," he said. She nodded in understanding. Dr. Cherith interrupted himself, "Oh, and one more thing... You can change into other people, as Reiss demonstrated earlier. So while you are first learning how to control your valta, I recommend you not share food or drinks, lick anyone, kiss anyone, or eat anyone's hair. As I'm sure you noticed today, it's not easy for students to control their valtas when they first obtain them. Shapeshifting is easier than other valtas, but you can be extremely sensitive at first and change at the slightest intake of someone else's DNA. I am quite impressed by your body's apparent ability to suppress the reaction to accidental DNA contact. We swallow so many things without realizing it that I have been expecting some sort of call for you since your discharge yesterday. Even just accidentally swallowing a cat hair in the air can make a beginner shift in an instant. That all said, even if your body already has a good handle on your valta, you should be careful, especially since you don't have your shapeshifting garb yet."

"I'm honestly kind of jealous! I still sometimes struggle not to shift at times! That's why I always wear some light shapeshifting garb under my clothes!" Reiss piped in.

"That seems weird... Why don't I shift so easily?" Genesis questioned.

"You ask that like it's a weakness, but I'd certainly call it a strength! I'm one of the doctors that works most closely on the awakening process. Your valta cell count was a lot higher than the average Earth-side student. You had about the amount Arishians who are born to a mother with active valta have. Such a thing is truly curious in someone from Earth."

A strange feeling crept over Genesis as she was reminded that her mother had once had valta. That had to be the reason why her valta cell count was so high—her mother's valta must have been active when she was born. She wondered if River had the same thing, but her instincts made her hesitate to ask. She didn't intend to bring up her missing parents until she knew the situation at the school better. After all, she didn't know yet who was responsible for their disappearance. Instead, she would try to veer the conversation away from her high valta cell count.

"I'm still a bit worried about shifting into other people," she said.

"Don't you worry! Once you realize how fun shifting into other people is, you'll be doing all those things that Mister Cherith mentioned before, just to change into 'em!" Reiss jested. "Oh, but kissing anyone...well, I haven't done that yet!" Reiss wagged his finger in the air as he spoke. Dr. Cherith let out a long sigh.

"You just kissed Miss Deadlock on the hand a few minutes ago," the doctor reminded him.

Reiss blinked a few times, before color flushed into his face. "On the lips! I meant that I haven't kissed anyone on the lips before!"

"I think *your* main area of training for this class is going to be shapeshifting *manners*, Reiss," Dr. Cherith said.

"Why do I have to learn etiquette?"

"Because it's rude to shapeshift into people just for fun! You're going to get yourself in trouble and seriously upset someone. I just want to try and stop you before that happens..." Reiss sighed, turning his gaze to the ceiling.

"Now, Genesis, back to thinking about the cat."

She nodded, closed her eyes, and took a deep breath, remembering how it felt to transform...that peculiar clench in her chest as her body warped into that form. The feeling was so strange that she thought if she could figure out how to summon that sensation, she could make herself change.

"Good... You partially transformed," the doctor said. She opened her eyes, and reached up to find she now had cat ears. Reiss held his hand to his lips to stifle a laugh, which received a sharp look from Dr. Cherith. "Okay, try focusing some more to transform the rest of the way. Think about the form of the cat, in order to extend it to every part of your body."

Genesis shut her eyes again to concentrate, her hands clenched against her knees. As she focused intently on what it felt like to be a cat, she could feel her body changing as she fell forward toward the floor and landed on all fours. When she opened her eyes this time, it was to the muted colors seen through the eyes of a feline, rather than the bright colors perceived by humans. As on the day before, she was aware of the whiskers on either side of her face, which picked up the slightest movements in the air...such as the flapping of the bird's wings and other movements from the animals in the cages nearby, Dr. Cherith's breaths, and the vibrations of an insect buzzing about the room. She lifted her paws slightly from the floor, as if to be sure she had completely transformed. She became aware of the weight of her uniform on her back, and had to weasel her way out from underneath it.

"Nicely done!" Dr. Cherith congratulated. "I must admit I am a bit jealous as well! It took me several weeks until I could fully transform at will. The transformation back shouldn't be hard, but if you ever get stuck, I have that substance I gave you during your awakening that will revert your DNA back to its original state. Don't worry, you won't ever be stuck forever." He got up and grabbed a blanket from the back of his chair to put over her. "Reiss and I are going to leave the room for this one, got it? Do the same thing you just did, but now think of your own form instead of the cat's. Your shapeshifting garb should be done in about two weeks. For now, Reiss and I will leave the room anytime you need to change back into a human form. Come get us when you have succeeded. If you aren't able to, don't worry, that is all right. If you haven't come to the door within five minutes, I will knock and then enter to assist you." His expression shifted and he shook his head. "Actually...on second thought, a cat can make noise. Instead, how about you yowl for me if you run into any trouble?" He finished with a kind smile and then took his leave of the room, much to her appreciation. Reiss glanced back at her as he followed. His expression seemed a bit shocked. Based on their reactions, she guessed that transforming fully so soon was really quite unusual.

After the door had closed behind them, she shut her eyes to begin concentrating again. A minute or two passed as she sat crouched under the blanket. Finally, she could feel the sensation of her body changing back, and, in a moment, she sat under the blanket fully herself again. She stood up and approached the mirror that hung on the back of a closet door beside one of the desks. There she gave herself a once over to make sure all of her had changed back. Only then could she rejoice over her success. She had really done it! She had thought it would be a lot harder to do, but she did it! Smiling to herself, she began to put on her school uniform.

Dr. Cherith smiled at her as she came out. He was quite impressed. Really, he never truly had doubted that she would be unable to shift back again after how quickly she had shifted into the cat.

"Awesome! That didn't take you long at all!" Dr. Cherith greeted her. "You can practice switching back and forth for the remainder of this class period. Reiss and I will work on his shapeshifting in another room. I'll knock when we come back...and wait for you to open the door. Just because of that little issue that comes with shapeshifting," he laughed. "Once your garb comes in, we'll start doing some more in depth training. For now keep doing that over and over again. That way you can get the hang of switching forms. I bet you'll be transforming like it's second nature by the end of the two weeks! We'll start learning how to transform between different creatures next week, which isn't much different, and get a few more under your belt. Then we can keep practicing and hopefully strengthen your valta enough so that you will be able to retain the DNA of more creatures. I am quite pleased with your progress so far!"

"Thank you, sir." She felt a bit shy about being praised so much.

"Of course! I will talk to you at the end of the period." He then turned to walk briskly down the hall away from her.

Reiss grinned at her. "Good luck!" he beamed. She smiled, giving him a slight nod of her head.

After they had gone, Genesis turned back toward the lab room, excited to get back to work. She was determined that she would master her new ability, no matter how absurd it still seemed. Maybe it was finally starting to sink in for her, and it felt amazing!

Chapter 20

The Challenge

WITH SPECIAL VALTA TRAINING done, the first day at Arisha University came to a close. Dinner back at the dorm passed in awkward silence, since Professor Glazunov and Miss Nenna ate their meal at their house behind the dorm. As a result, no one forced Group A to make conversation with one another. The only break in the silence was Mae's occasional comment on how awkward it was, or her asking someone at random about their day. When Mae did that, she and the individual would go back and forth a few times before the conversation fizzled again. Of course, she chose her targets carefully, saving Hiero for last as she knew asking him would force the table to sit through a long story.

After everyone had finished eating, most of them dispersed for the night, so Genesis decided to finish her homework and then take the opportunity to go down to the gym. Dr. Cherith had told her she would have to train her body physically to be good at combat. She had always worked out at night back home when trying to get into the school, and to stand a chance against River in an MMA match, so it wouldn't be that difficult for her to keep it up. In fact, it might feel weird if she didn't. Furthermore, her body had weakened during her awakening, so she would have to rebuild some of her muscle mass.

After she finished her homework, Genesis changed into her tracksuit and walked down the dorm hallway toward the stairs. As she passed by Ellie's room, she glanced in the open doorway to find the girl seated on the floor with a cage filled with butterflies, watching them intently. She looked rather happy for the first time that day, but then her eyes turned and she looked back at Genesis with a blank look on her face.

"Sorry," Genesis muttered, embarrassed she had been caught staring at her. Ellie looked back at the butterflies and then at Genesis again. "I will go." Genesis began to turn away

"*Excusez-moi*. I am not good at the English... I have studied two years for the school... but I do not speak confidently," Ellie told her. Genesis loved her French accent, although its thickness did make it hard to understand her to a degree.

"Oh...well, you aren't bad at it at all, based on the way you speak. I am sure you will gain more confidence in your abilities soon enough studying at an English school."

Ellie nodded. "*Merci*."

"Well, I'm heading down to the gym, so see you later." Genesis waved before she turned to go.

"See you later," Ellie echoed and waved back with a bright smile.

As Genesis resumed her journey to the gym, she thought about the brief exchange. The encounter had been awkward, but she did feel bad for Ellie. If Ellie was afraid to talk to anyone, she would have trouble making friends at first.

Genesis went through the kitchen and dining area where Mae sat smiling and nodding as Hiero continued to talk. Electricity snapped about his hand. "See! It's annoying and zappy! How am I supposed to get a girlfriend at this school when I zap everything I touch? Plus, I didn't realize how much I snap my fingers while I talk until..."

"I know! Find a girl who likes being electrocuted! Not me, I like to sit in silence sometimes. It can be nice!" Mae chimed in.

"I don't think anyone would enjoy being electrocuted, that sounds pretty fatal, if you ask me. But I guess finding a girl who doesn't mind the occasional zap wouldn't be a bad idea..."

Genesis continued on through the lounge where Dawn sat alone with some kind of video game pulled up on the TV. He was so engrossed in his game that he didn't even look up as she passed by. As she descended the staircase into the basement, she felt determined that she would conquer her weakness and be strong again. Then she would go to Arisha and find her parents. If they really had been captured by Arisha, that was where they must be. The shapeshifting part had sunk in, but thinking about it now, she wasn't so sure about the whole "other world" thing. Everything else they had said seemed to be true, though, so it must be as well...and if it really *was* real, then that must be where her parents were.

Genesis descended down the narrow stairway that led to the dorm's gym. As she turned into the room, she hoped that no one from the House would be down there at that hour. With how serious they all were, however, she had a feeling that might be unlikely. Perhaps she would be able to figure out their schedule, so that she didn't end up down there at the same time in the future.

The dorm's gym was pretty spacious. The school provided some workout equipment, plus there was an area with sparring mats. Unlike the rest of the school, which was made up of warm homey colors, the gym was very bright and white, much like the cushioned Awakening Rooms.

Genesis could hear the sound of someone running on the treadmill across the room. She glanced over and her heart stopped, or at least it felt like it did, since if it actually stopped she'd be dead. He might have been the last person she wanted to see down there—Alric. Out of everyone from the House, he was the one she most wanted to avoid. He seemed to hate her more than any of the others, which he did, even though he had only just met her that day. She knew being in close proximity alone would be awkward, but she wasn't about to bail and not follow through with her workout just for that reason alone. How bad would it look if she came down, saw him, then turned around and went back up the stairs? She knew that she'd feel terrible if someone did that to her, so she took a deep breath and found a spot where she could get started.

Alric had taken notice of her as she came around the corner, causing the rage that constantly simmered inside of him to spike. *"Why her of all people?"* he gasped in Arshin—the language spoken most widely in Arisha, as you know—under his breath, too quietly for Genesis to hear him.

Genesis warmed up with some stretches and a brisk jog around the sparring mats like she'd done in her uncle's mixed martial arts classes back home. Ready for her workout, she decided to use the small weights to work on her biceps. By that point, Alric was no longer on the treadmill but had moved to the leg press machine. She must not have felt his daggered eyes upon her, for she relaxed a bit thinking he simply ignored her. He was probably too caught up in himself to notice her. Little did she know that that was not the case at all. Without thinking, she shut her eyes and started to hum to herself. She was used to playing music as she worked out in her uncle's gym, so it was only natural for her to hum a bit while she worked out here—tomorrow she would have to remember to bring her earbuds.

In only a short time, she became completely lost in her own world. Her thoughts went back to her parents and the night of their disappearance. Then, for some reason, she remembered the agent that night and realized she hadn't thought of that strange occurrence since it had happened. The agent had protected the two of them. She and her little brother would have been discovered if he hadn't told the leader they weren't there. She wondered why he would have done such a thing, and she began to remember that the leader had said his name. She set down the weights, engrossed in her own thoughts now. "What was his name..." she muttered under her breath.

Meanwhile, the whole time, Alric had been having his own thoughts...thoughts about the new shapeshifting girl. The fact that she was considered naturally skilled enough to be invited to transfer into the House the semester before entry into the university, was enough to make his blood boil. Perhaps quite literally with the nature of his valta. He had one advantage, though, and so a crazed grin spread over his lips.

Genesis was startled from her thoughts when she suddenly realized how quiet the room had gotten. Before there had been some noise as Alric worked out—the clicking of the metal equipment and his labored breathing. She opened her eyes to see Alric standing several feet in front of her, staring at her intensely with his vibrant, flaming eyes. Flames started to fizzle up his right arm. She held her breath, reminded of when Professor Glazunov had told them they could not threaten other students with their valta. Alric hadn't said anything yet, but he sure did look like he was threatening her. He grinned again and took an aggressive step closer. He did so to try and intimidate her, and it certainly worked wonders, for she could feel the bloodlust radiate from him. She also knew little about him and worried what his intentions were. Perhaps she had fallen into a very bad situation by remaining in a room alone with a boy she didn't know. Alric, of course, was not that type in the least. In fact, such things never even crossed his mind, nor did he see women as anything more than annoying little emotional creatures that were likely to start crying at any moment.

"Hey, Shapeshifty. Wanna fight me?" he uttered in a menacing tone.

"Not in particular..." she answered with a sheepish laugh.

"Why not? You're obviously the only other student taking it seriously at this school. I've come down here every night since those of us from the House got in this dorm at the beginning of summer and you're the first person who's ever come down! You have an air about you that I know you'll be down here every night now, won't you? I'm going to be the best, and in order to do that, I have to take down the competition. I know you got a full scholarship and I know you were almost transferred into the House to start early without a bit of training! I can't stand that!" He took another sudden step closer. He was so aggressive, that she pulled back away even though he was still several feet from her. He didn't dare go further, however.

"My plan was to come down here every night... yes..." she faltered.

"Well then, let's fight!"

"But, it wouldn't be fun for you at all. I'm so bad at using my valta right now that you would win in like five seconds. Plus I don't have the proper garb yet."

He gritted his teeth hard. "But I want to fight..." He said so in a lower tone, but that did not make it any less intimidating. If anything, she felt more intimidated. She wanted to flee, but he was standing between her and the only door out of the room.

"But...but I don't want to," Genesis answered. He continued to stare hard into her eyes. She had only had her valta for two days. She was just getting started on how to transform back and forth between herself and the cat. Plus there was that unfortunate side effect of her clothes falling off after shifting. She just couldn't fight him using her valta yet. Since she couldn't use her valta, that left her with just raw strength, and she wouldn't stand a chance against him. While he was thinner than some of the other guys, despite working out nightly, he was still a guy and she was still a girl. She would have to figure out a compromise to appease him for now.

"How about this? Give me two weeks. Two weeks to work on my shapeshifting, and for my garb to come in, then we'll fight right here after class," she bargained. He stared at her as he thought hard about her proposed compromise. Finally, he extinguished the flames on his arm. Only then did she feel she could breathe again.

"Fine. I guess I have been using my valta since I was seven, after all." He turned abruptly and sauntered away from her. She had just begun to relax again when he abruptly paused. "But that's a promise, so you better not chicken out in two weeks..."

She mustered a smile back at him. "It's a promise, Alric, and I don't break promises," she answered. Her voice was soft and kind as she said his name. He glanced back at her again, as if the sound of his own name said without scorn came as a shock to him. However, she had already returned to what she had been doing before his interruption, so he continued out of the room.

Why had she agreed to such a thing? She wondered after he had gone. Making such promises to him was only a distraction from her true objective: finding her parents. A few things had come to mind, though, as she had been speaking with him. She knew little about the world of Arisha she now found herself entangled in. Dueling him once might help her to understand valta better and set a goal for her own improvement. She also hated to be seen as a threat when her goal wasn't to be the best to ever graduate from the school, like his goal was. He had far more experience than she did and so it seemed inevitable that he would win. After that, she figured he'd leave her alone. She just really hoped she was right and that it would be only one duel.

Chapter 21
A Ridiculous Plan

AN ENTIRE WEEK PASSED, in which Genesis drowned herself in her studies and the mastering of her new valta. Then, on Monday morning of their second week, Wayland Cherith transferred into their group. Cherith?! Why, isn't that the name of Genesis's valta instructor? Yes, but you must know that Cherith is not that uncommon of a last name in Arisha. That said, I can neither confirm nor deny there being a relation between the two individuals at this time.

When they all came into class that morning, he sat in the back row, his feet thrown up on the desk. He had an edgy look to him: long dark gray hair tied carelessly back from his face, some piercings, but not on his face, just his ears. The only thing on his face was a scar that ran under his left eye, which accentuated his drained appearance. He said nothing to any of them as glances were shot in his direction. Other than the interesting look, he seemed like any of the rest of them. His unexpected presence, however, made everyone look at him with curiosity as Professor Glazunov came in and started to rifle through some papers.

"Not much in the way of announcements today," the professor started. "Just that you will be having an Open Hall, not this Saturday but the following, so make sure your rooms are clean. I'm telling you now, and every morning leading up to the event, since my class didn't seem to want to clean their rooms last year and then blamed me for not offering enough forewarning. Anyway, all doors must be left open during the whole three-hour period of Open Hall. There are security cameras in the public hallway areas and Miss Nenna and I will be watching the feed, so don't even think about doing anything." A pause. "Oh, and also Wayland Cherith will now be joining your class in Group A. He was delayed from coming the first week for personal reasons, but he'll be moving into Dorm A tonight after class. He's an iron user, so the admissions office decided to put him into your group since you were down one person who had decided not to come at the last second. Also, with the addition of Wayland, you will become one of the few groups in the whole history of the school to have all 10 types of natural valtas, plus the four specialty valtas currently at large. So, congratulations on that one." Mae, River, and a girl from Group B began to cheer.

Wayland didn't say anything the whole time Professor Glazunov spoke. He just had to get through class and then he could be alone. He sighed very softly as Professor Glazunov and the other students began a discussion on valta techniques. Finally, the class came to an end and he moved to grab his books in order to put them away. The voices of the other students surrounded him. He wasn't used to so many people talking at once, and so he felt overwhelmed by all the fragments of conversation swirling around him.

"This girl is my girlfriend, we started dating over the weekend and felt ready to make the announcement," Hiero informed Dawn, who was far too distracted by something Dusk had been in the middle of telling him to respond.

"What? Already? But you just met???" Mae cried.

"Live with it," Hiero's obnoxious new girlfriend from Group B answered. We will learn more about her in due time, but for now just know she was quite obnoxious and was as arrogant as Hiero if not more.

"Well, congratulations! A match made in heaven as they say!" Mae chimed.

"Being that I can't stand either one of you, I can only agree," Misteria added.

Wayland covered his ears with his hands, as he stared down at the eraser dust sprinkled upon the smooth surface of his desk. Why was he there? Could he get used to being around so many rambunctious people his age? They were all foolish!

"*Enchanté*, nice to meet you!" Ellie said as she came to his desk. She had been practicing gaining confidence in her introductions, so she thought that with a new student in the class came a perfect opportunity. Wayland lifted his head, startled that he had been approached. Had he acted too weird and drawn attention to himself? What had she asked him?

Ellie noticed the confusion on his face, and so she repeated her statement again.

"Oh... Nice to meet you..." he mumbled in response.

She smiled. "My name is Ellie. I'm 14."

"I'm Wayland," he answered, his eyes averted to the side as he avoided making eye contact. He did so for his own reasons, but it was also best he not directly look at her with how little control she had over her hypnosis.

"Thank you... I'm still studying English right now."

"I see."

She hesitated for a long moment as she thought of what to say next. "I'm from France!"

"I've never been."

She hesitated again, unsure of what he had mumbled. She continued, "Where are you from?"

"Arisha."

"Oh! Arisha! *Magnifique*! Will you help me with the English?"

"Yes... I'm bilingual, so I suppose..." He gripped the strap of his bag tightly. He really had no intention of it. How was he supposed to help her?

"Oh, *merci*!" she giggled, before she turned to go. "*Au revoir*!"

He said nothing as she hurried off through the door. Still seated at his desk, he rested his chin on his hand. She did seem sweet, and he had somehow managed to have a brief conversation. He'd have to see what happened from there. Just one day at a time... His eyes fixed on Roland Watts who still sat at his desk organizing his belongings. Then Wayland's lips drew into a tight line.

Genesis sat alone in the lounge after her trip to the gym that night, reflecting on how much she had improved in a week. Her nightly visits to the gym consisted of working out while trying to ignore Alric's occasional glances at her as if she was a great nuisance to him. She tried not to let that get to her and continued to work out night after night.. The sessions were intense and stressful, however. She felt like she had to work out faster than she wanted to, just to get out of there as quickly as possible. She had even tried going later, but he was always there, no matter what time she arrived. She had started to wonder if that was all he did after dinner before turning in for the night. With the exception of that first night, she always left first, too, so she wasn't exactly sure how long he spent in the gym.

She had gotten a whole lot better at shapeshifting as well. She still didn't think she would beat Alric next week, but she would last longer than she would have that first night. She now had three animals mastered: the cat, the bunny, and the bird. She found the bird to be quite enjoyable because she could fly all over campus, seeing it from a totally different angle. Dr. Cherith had given Reiss and her strict instructions that they were not to fly higher than the top of the observation tower located in the direct center of campus, and, for that matter, not past the fence that ran around the perimeter of all the buildings. She had hoped she could fly down to see the House, but what could be done? She wasn't going to disobey her teacher when he had made himself quite clear. She and Dr. Cherith had established that, as of right now, she could only retain three different creatures in addition to her own form.

A chill ran up her spine and she turned her head sharply to see that Dusk stood above her, cloaked in her dark blanket. Without thinking, Genesis drew in a sharp breath, as she felt a tingling sensation in her toes. Everything was fine, it was just Dusk, nothing more. Then, in the next moment, the lounge suddenly flooded with almost everyone who wasn't from the House. The exceptions were Hiero, who was probably still sitting out on the front porch with his new girlfriend, and Wayland, because he was still moving in.

Aware of their effect on people, Dawn and Dusk took their seats on either side of Genesis on the sofa, balancing out the light and darkness around her to place her in a more comfortable realm. River and Zuri sat down on the edge of the coffee table, which Genesis thought quite rude, while Ellie and Grisham remained standing expectantly. The four of those immediately around her looked at her with desperation in their eyes, for they had all discussed a scheme and Genesis was the vital piece in it.

"What is it?" she asked as she set down the book she had been reading.

Dusk grasped her hands. After a whole week, Dusk felt quite confident that their relationship was off to a great start. Little did she know that with each inch closer to Genesis she got, the more her dark aura consumed Genesis until the very blood in her veins seemed to run cold. Not even Dawn's soft warmth could protect her from it.

"Will you please go undercover for us?" Dusk rasped. Dawn smiled and gently motioned for Dusk to move back a little bit to give Genesis more space. With just this minor adjustment, the dark aura seemed to dissipate a great deal.

"Please, dear sister, we'll do anything! I'll even give you a bit of the last allowance Uncle Ferris gave me! Or! Or! I'll do something even better! I'll let you challenge me to a match even though my little twig arms are still too weak for MMA! All because I know how much you like rolling!" River pleaded. The others nodded in unison with a *hum* of agreement.

"Ehm... no... I told you to take it easy while you recover, and no, I will not be taking any of your money either... What is it that you want me to do?" Genesis hesitated over the last bit as she worried that River was willing to put important things on the line in order to convince her to do whatever it was they all wanted. She knew how precious River's money was to him.

"Dawn and I were talking, and we can't help but notice how divided our group is," Dusk said, tilting her head so that her hair spilled over her shoulder to cover one of her eyes.

"Y-yeah, i-it's d-divided b-between H-house s-students and us-s," Dawn stuttered.

"Exactly! It's as if they think they're better than us!" River chimed in.

"We have a plan," Ellie stated, impatient for them to get to the point. They had drawn out the plan for her in the form of pictures beforehand, to make sure she understood so that they could get her opinion on it, too. In truth, she would have rather they told her in words, so she could practice listening. The drawing had taken so long that her struggling to translate their words probably would have been faster, especially when River and Zuri kept nodding off mid-pencil-stroke.

Dawn nodded over to Zuri. "Oh, my turn?" Zuri asked.

"You're the one who came up with it!" River pointed out.

"Oh, right! So we are hoping to unite the dorm! But first, we want you to do some undercover work. You can shapeshift into people, right?" Zuri asked.

Genesis nodded, with much hesitation, for she didn't really like where the conversation was going. "I've never done it before, however..." she stated.

"Okay, well, awesome! We were thinking we would kidnap one of the House students, then, you could shapeshift as him or her, and then find stuff out that can help us get closer to them!"

"Yeah! I really think we can all be friends!" River pipped in, "I feel like we can through Mae! She's more outgoing and friendly than the rest, and I think her staying distant is only because she's a follower and has known the others from the House for a lot longer than us. Kazumae and Haise aren't entirely unfriendly, but they do seem to keep their distance from everyone in general. I get the impression they have many secrets or something! I think this would be a good idea! We'll work on Hiero and Wayland later, but I feel like a major first step to reaching our goal is to get rid of the wall between the House students and us! Won't you do it for us, Gen-gen?" he grasped her hands swiftly, his eyes sparkling with excitement over the plan they had devised.

Genesis let out a gentle sigh. "Let me get this straight... You want me to kidnap a House student...and then shapeshift into them so that I can spy on the other House students?"

"Yes! Exactly!" River drew back, clapping his hands together rapidly

.

"And that's a good plan...in what universe?"

"Gen-gen! Won't you at least have a little faith in us?"

She sighed again. "I don't even know if I can shapeshift properly into another person..." She really wished to get out of doing such an outlandish thing. With the already existent tension between her and those from the House, doing such a thing would probably only make it worse.

"Why not try on your brother then?" Zuri suggested. Genesis realized that they were pretty determined, and her attempts at excuses weren't working.

"Great idea, bud!" River declared.

"Very well... I'll give it a go then," Genesis grumbled. She did have a bit of interest in seeing what it would be like to turn into another person, after all.

On a side note, she wondered why they had approached her in such a public area rather than waiting to find her alone somewhere else. If their scheme was really so secret and undercover, they wouldn't want to risk someone from the House overhearing, right? Not to fear, dear readers, I do believe that River was sure to confirm the locations of all the House students in advance. Haise and Kazumae were sharing an evening tea along with some House students from other dorms out on the lawn. Alric was down in the gym as usual. He could not even hear their voices above, because the second he saw River's energetic eyes peering through the doorway at him, he had quickly covered his ears with headphones to make himself as unapproachable as possible. As you are aware, River had to pass right through the lounge by his sister to get to the gym staircase, but she was far too engrossed in her thoughts at that moment to notice him. Ellie and Dusk were able to confirm Mae and Misteria's location on the girl's floor, and deemed them too deep in conversation for either of them to be making an appearance downstairs anytime soon. So they felt safe to divulge their plans to Genesis without fear of interruption or eavesdropping.

"Can I have a strand of hair...unless you're okay with me licking you?" Genesis jested with a playful smirk at her little brother.

"Ew, gross, never!" River objected.

"What? You used to try and lick me all the time when you were little. I would literally have to wrestle you down to the floor to prevent you."

"We don't talk about that, Gen-gen!" River laughed in a nervous manner as he combed his fingers through his navy hair, then presented his sister a strand with a flourish of his hand. She stared at it glistening navy blue in the light. She already found herself adjusting to his hair being that color. What actually proved way harder for her was to adjust to her own hair color change, since she only saw herself when she passed a mirror. She put the strand into her mouth hesitantly, for it still felt gross no matter who it belonged to. Then she took a deep breath, aware of strange changes in her body that she could not describe as comfortable. She wondered why she hadn't shifted into a girl like Dusk or Ellie for her initial attempt. First, she noticed how much smaller and bonier her hands had become. River had lost a bit more weight this past week, which she hoped would stop, since it wouldn't be good for him to lose any more. What she did feel surprised about was to find that his skin had no sag to it whatsoever, despite such a drastic loss of weight in such a short period of time. Almost as if he had always been that skinny. Such a thing didn't make sense to her in the least—his skin really should sag in at least a few places...

"Holy crap!" River exclaimed, clapping both hands to his mouth.

"What did Uncle Ferris say about saying that?!" his sister snapped, then stopped, unaccustomed to the deeper tone that came out of her mouth. River's voice wasn't all that deep yet, but it was still deep compared to her own voice.

"Even my voice transferred over? You're like an identical copy of me!" River said in astonishment.

"Yeah, it's pretty crazy. My valta instructor described it like cloning," Genesis explained. Zuri just sat there blinking in awe of her. Even though he came from Arisha, he had never seen a shapeshifter's ability at work. Genesis was truly amazing in his eyes. The others seemed equally awed by the talent.

"It almost f-feels l-like an invasion of p-privacy," Dawn stuttered.

"I think so, too! You may be my sister, but I feel really uncomfortable right now!" River said as he stared at her wide-eyed. She stood up from the sofa in order to walk across the room to a mirror that hung on the wall. The only problem was that as soon as she stood, her track pants started to slip down. She stopped mid stride and grabbed hold of them to keep them from falling. Then she paused, glancing back in hopes that they hadn't seen that, but they all burst out laughing as River turned bright red.

"You almost exposed all my secrets! Change back quickly!" River cried as he clapped his hands over his eyes.

"What secrets are you keeping exactly?" his sister teased.

"You know what! There are two other ladies in this room, so you better hold onto those pants real tight!"

Genesis laughed and continued to walk the rest of the way to the mirror where she could observe her reflection. How strange it must have been to look out through his eyes. She could even see slight color differences in the sofas, as River was slightly colorblind to some colors, such as red. Considering how many red accents were used in the decor of the school, the difference was quite noticeable.

"We're going to have to borrow a boy's uniform if you shift as one of the guys," Dusk pointed out.

"Yeah, definitely. At least I was in my tracksuit now so I didn't shift in a skirt," Genesis said with a wink at River.

"Thank the Lord for that! I don't want anyone to see me like that, even if it's you shifting into me!" River stated. "Anyway, can you please switch back now! I can't take any more of this!"

"Okay, River, I'll respect your wishes." She changed back with ease. She actually found shifting into another human a lot easier than shifting into animals since the bone structure stayed consistent. But, overall, she was getting a lot faster and more efficient with the ability after a week of practice.

"W-well I s-say it's a g-go then," Dawn stuttered.

"Yeah, let's do this! We'll capture the victim tomorrow after class!" River declared as he bolted to his feet. The others nodded in agreement.

"Hold up... Do you have a person in mind?" Genesis asked.

"Nope! Not at all!" River declared.

"Can we maybe pick one? Like maybe a girl?" Genesis suggested.

"Well... You know...kidnapping isn't easy...so..." Zuri started hesitantly.

"We're going to take what we're given!" River declared. "It's far more fun that way, too! Don't you agree?"

No, she couldn't agree at all, but she didn't see herself talking any sense into any of them as they all seemed equally excited about the element of chance in the scheme, and so she said nothing. If her brother was happy and fitting in with the rest of the group, then she would do whatever it took to keep it that way. That was right up there with finding her parents in levels of importance. She just hoped that River and the others thought better of it before they actually went about "kidnapping" a House student for such a shambled together plan...

Chapter 22
Seeing Double

GENESIS SECRETLY GAVE UP and hoped the others would forget all about their little scheme. She hadn't really wanted to do such an outlandish plan from the start anyway, but had agreed because she didn't want to let her brother down. Over the next few days, the chance never arose for her to shapeshift into one of the students from the House, and she certainly wasn't about to go out of her way to do something she didn't really want to do.

On Thursday afternoon, however, Zuri stood in the hall after the last class let out. He had one of his spare uniforms folded up in his hands as he waited for Genesis, but her special valta training was late getting out that afternoon.

At last the door slid open and she stepped into the hall, lost in her own thoughts over shapeshifting. The moment she saw him, she paused, her eyes meeting his, before she glanced down at the uniform he held. *Oh no.*

"Good evening, Genesis," he greeted with a gleeful smile.

She began to take a step back into the lab room, but Reiss came out behind her, preventing her from doing so. He caught her by the shoulder and gave her a playful shove out into the hall before his eyes met Zuri's.

"What's up? Oh! I've seen you before! You're in our class, too, correct?" Reiss asked in an excited voice.

"Yes, I'm Zuri Whitlock," Zuri informed him.

"Sounds pretty Arishian. I'm guessing Southern Country?"

"Yes, yes. You are quite right. Are you Arishian, too?" Zuri asked. Genesis began to scoot herself away, hoping that Zuri wouldn't see so she could make a quick escape from the situation she knew was about to transpire. Alas, Zuri's eyes locked onto her and so also locked her into place beside Reiss.

"Yes, I'm from Scarlet. I transferred into the House when I was seven though."

"Oh! You're a House student then?" Zuri said in surprise.

"Yeah, I suppose so. But I try not to be like them! Being strong with my valta doesn't really matter that much, you know? I think life is far more enjoyable if you aren't so uptight and focused all the time! You've got to play around a bit! We have these cool abilities that Earth doesn't have, right? So why not use them to have fun all the time? We should be friends, Zuri!"

"How right you are..." Zuri murmured, lifting his hand up at the same time to flurry some snowflakes round about it. "I would very much like to be friends!"

"It's a deal then. You are now my new friend!" Genesis made a face over the interaction. Reiss was definitely a strange one. She could only wonder if it was his being Arishian that made him that way around people. All the guys his age she had met would never say something like that to another guy. From every interaction she had seen Reiss make with other students from their class, he seemed to kiss up to everyone and use childish phrases of flattery. She had no intention of passing any sort of judgment on him, of course. As someone from Earth, she just couldn't help noticing the strangeness in his behavior, which many of the other students didn't seem to openly acknowledge as strange whatsoever.

"I'm friends with River, too. Can you be friends with him as well?"

At that point, since his eyes were off of her, Genesis began to turn away again, but Reiss caught her arm to prevent her from going.

"Of course! I can be friends with him as well! I'm happy to have everyone be my best friends!"

What, were they in the first grade? As it was, she wanted to get out of there before Zuri could force her to shapeshift into someone who probably hated her!

"I've got some homework to do, so I really should be off," Genesis muttered as she tried to withdraw her arm from Reiss's.

"But Zuri was waiting for you, right? You won't let the guy down, will you?" Reiss said.

Genesis let out a deep sigh. "I suppose not..."

"Awesome! Well, I'll be on my way now! Nice talking to you, Zuri!" Reiss swung his bag over his shoulder and strode off.

A silence proceeded in which Zuri gave Genesis that same gleeful smile, flicking his wrist to bring his flurry of snowflakes to a quick stop. "Yes?" she hesitated, still worried about why he was standing in the hallway outside the lab room with a uniform in his hands.

"The truth is, Alric fell asleep in the classroom just down the hall, so I was wondering if you'd like to try the plan now? I brought you one of my uniforms... He is a good bit taller than I am, so it might be a bit small, but I think it will work as long as you don't wear my tie since it's not the right color... Our colors match our valtas after all... Hopefully that won't be suspicious, since I've never seen Alric without his tie..."

"Oh, okay." She took the uniform hesitantly from his hands. She really didn't want to follow through, especially not now that she knew who it was. Alric might kill her if he found out she had shifted into him. "Let me change first." She turned to enter the bathroom just down the hall. Alric very well could be the worst possible choice for this scheme.

That thought faded from her mind as she became far more curious as to why on earth Alric had fallen asleep in one of the classrooms? That didn't really seem like something he would do. She knew she really didn't know him or any of the others from the House all that well, but still... She thought over how he never seemed to leave the gym. Maybe it was because he didn't! Maybe he stayed up all night training and so that made him tired during the day. She brushed off her thoughts, as she felt she was getting way too ahead of herself.

When she returned to the hall a few minutes later, Zuri had already left. His uniform felt a bit big on her, but she knew it would be all right once she shifted. She left her belongings under a nearby bench and looked into the classroom where Zuri had directed her. It was the room for the fire users' special valta training so it made sense that he would be in there.

A wave of heat hit her as she opened the door. On top of the heat, it looked a bit different than the other classrooms—the walls, ceiling, and floor were lined with a flame-resistant stone to contain the inevitable fire. The desks were also made of some kind of flame-resistant material, found only in Arisha, that was rough to the touch. All the valta training rooms were different from each other because they were designed to be good and safe environments in which the students could learn and train in their different valta types.

Sure enough, as Zuri had said, Alric lay with his head on his desk, sound asleep. Genesis swallowed hard as she entered the room and sat down sideways in the chair in front of his desk. She held her breath, a bit scared to touch him in fear that he might wake. Very hesitantly, she reached out her hand toward his fiery red hair. Trying to be as gentle as possible, she ran her fingers through his hair in hopes that there would be a loose strand. Because she feared waking him, she did this in quite a timid manner, which was probably why she got nothing. She did make the discovery that Alric, surprisingly, had really soft hair.

Since she was unsuccessful in her attempt at abstracting a hair by that method, she knew she would have to figure something else out. Her heart pounded so fast now. She tried to reassure herself for a moment, then shook her head hard as the thought that she might have to lick him popped into her mind. She already felt too afraid to touch him for fear he would wake up...licking him would definitely do the trick. She could not risk him waking up to that! He probably wouldn't just fume with anger, he would certainly kill her.

As she scanned the area around Alric, desperately searching for an alternative, her eyes alighted on his water bottle sitting on his desk. That was it! She grabbed the bottle very carefully so as to not disturb him, then she unscrewed the lid and looked about the rim to try and find where he had sipped. She used to do the same thing when she was younger, because she wanted to find the place where River *hadn't* sipped, if they were sharing a drink. Now she did the opposite.

She found where she thought was the right place and took a hesitant sip. Much to her surprise, what was within the bottle wasn't water—it was the blackest, most unsweetened tea she had ever tasted in her entire life. She nearly choked from the shock and had to hold her hand over her mouth to stifle her cough. Her body felt hot and then the uniform started to feel a lot smaller on her. She looked down at her hand and ran her fingers through her hair which had that same softness she had just felt a moment before on Alric's head. Her vision then got extremely blurry until she could barely make out her surroundings at all. That was going to be a problem. She couldn't take his glasses, but his eyesight was so bad she grew uncertain that she could walk anywhere in such a state. With how sharply his eyes pierced her, she never would have guessed his vision to be that bad. Although, she really should have expected as much since he did need glasses. Furthermore, her body had started to feel strange, each breath heavy and strained. Yes, it was due to his lung capacity, and that wasn't something she could do anything about either. After changing into him it had become hard to breathe. She suddenly felt so tired, too, and wondered if the exhaustion could be from shapeshifting so much in the past hour... Surely ailments wouldn't transfer over... There was no way that the way she felt now was how Alric felt all the time, right? He seemed all too lively for that, and she doubted it could be an act.

She brushed off these thoughts because another matter came to mind. She realized that she was not sure how to behave like Alric in a believable way. The whole plan was such a bad idea in the first place. No one had accounted for her possible lack of acting skills!

She sighed and glanced down at his glasses for a moment as she considered whether or not she should try to take them anyway. She quickly thought better of that idea, however, as the likelihood of her imminent death at his hands dawned on her yet again.

Seeing him asleep was probably the calmest she had ever seen him look since she had met him. He almost looked normal for once, bundled up in a hoodie that he often wore over his uniform. Now that she thought about it, the room almost felt chilly. She wondered if fire users felt the cold more than most people and that's why she now felt cold in such a heated room. Honestly, she would have thought it to be the opposite, as she figured their active valta cells would keep them very warm. She supposed the opposite made sense, too.

Curious, she lifted her hand up. "Can I use his valta too?" she muttered, as she concentrated on her hand for a moment. Then, thinking better of it, she lowered it back down and considered him again. She hadn't even seen his valta in action to safely attempt such a thing. Her eyes rested on him a while longer, before she turned and quickly left the classroom.

A few moments passed after she left the room. Alric lifted his head and his eyes scanned the empty room. He sighed, brushing his hair where Genesis had touched him, then reached to take a sip of his tea. "Not again... Stupid head putting such stupid dreams in it. My mother would have never touched me like that..." He drew the bottle back violently. "Something smells like shapeshifter! Was she here?" His jaw clenched, as he began to think of what reason she could have to come near him while he was sleeping. Had she been touching his hair while he slept? She was mocking him and trying to mess with him while he was vulnerable. That creepy shapeshifter!

Chapter 23
Kazumae's Tea Table

GENESIS DESCENDED DOWN TO the lobby of the Valta Department and scuttled into the bathroom to prepare herself before stepping outside. How was she going to make it back to the dorms as Alric? She squinted but it did little good to clear up her surroundings. She had made it onto the elevator and down all right. She certainly hadn't wanted to try her luck with the stairs. Was she imagining it, or had her sense of smell improved? She noticed the smell of the air purifier in the lobby more clearly, as well as the heavy scent of chemical cleaner upon entering the lobby bathroom.

She leaned close to the mirror until she could see her reflection in it clearly. Even though Dr. Cherith had compared shapeshifting to cloning, and when she had shifted into River and the cat her vision had changed slightly to match their vision, it was still crazy to her that she was, in all respects, Alric now. She looked a bit off without his glasses, but there was no mistaking those sharp yellow eyes of his. They looked a whole lot calmer on her, though, and so she guessed that the severity must be a projection of his emotions. As she stood there, contemplating her situation, she decided that since she had his form, she could just shift back into herself, and then, once she got to the dorms, shift into Alric again. That way she would be able to see where she was going as she walked across campus.

A giggle escaped Mae's lips. "And what are *you* doing in here?"

Genesis's heart jumped and she spun around. Mae's face was a blur, so that her green hair was really the only way to distinguish her as Mae, other than her childish voice. "I lost my glasses somewhere," Genesis answered quickly. She paused, startled because she had expected her voice to have that growling edge to it like his, but it hadn't. His voice sounded so much calmer when she used it, making her realize he must really have a normal voice but just spoke like that because he wanted to, or because he was so angry all the time. She knew she would have to try and make her voice sound more like his when she spoke, though that would be challenging. She had to remember that they would think she was Alric, so she shouldn't feel self-conscious at all about sounding like him. Still, she wasn't sure what to do and she had to figure it out right now!

"That's not good! Maybe that's why you came into the girls' bathroom instead of the dudes' bathroom? It's okay, pal! I understand! And I won't tell anyone!" She giggled as she pressed her finger to her lips.

Genesis's face turned red as she realized she had gone and done such a thing without thinking. She felt so stupid for going into the girls' bathroom shapeshifted as a guy! She swiftly covered her face with her hand.

"Can't promise I won't tell Mist, though!" Mae added with a nervous laugh.

Genesis wasn't sure what to say for a moment, partly because she hadn't expected to be thrust into a situation right off the bat where she would have to interact with one of the students from the House. She had needed time to mentally prepare and figure out some things before meeting Mae...or really any of them. She knew that Alric would probably have some fiery response to what Mae had just said, but she couldn't think fast enough. Now she realized how little she really knew about Alric. He was aggressive but that was all she could tell. She had only known him for about a week and a half, and, based on everything she was feeling right now, she only felt more and more confused about exactly who he was. She knew how it felt to look out through his eyes, but what went on inside his head? She tried to shake off the thought, feeling greatly disturbed by how creepy such a thing sounded.

"You're not going to scold me or anything? Are you feeling okay, Owl? Are you having an attack? I was trying to hold it together, but please don't die on me!" Mae cried. You ought to know that Mae often liked to give people nicknames after a while, and to Alric she had given the nickname Owl. Her reasons? Because he barely slept at night and had wild eyes like an owl. Plus, she felt it went well with his name.

"I'm not going to die..." Genesis muttered, trying to force some aggression into her voice.

"Really?"

"Yeah..."

"Then it must be mental trauma from special valta training! I heard Professor Alex could be a hard instructor! Come on, let's go get some therapy from Mister Kazumae!"

Mae grabbed Genesis's wrist and because Genesis was at a loss over what exactly to do, she let Mae lead her out of the bathroom. Genesis knew that Mae must be taking her to that table on the lawn where Kazumae always sat after class. She had heard some students referring to it as Kazumae's "tea table." Keeping the plan in mind, that would be the perfect place to go. Kazumae and Mae would be by far the easiest people for her to talk to since she knew more about the two of them than she did the other three House students. Gosh, she hated this plan.

Once they reached the table under the willow, Mae stopped. Kazumae had seen them approaching and made haste to pull out two more tea cups from his basket. He had various ceramic teaware spread across the table. Some plates held cookies, but not of the overly sweet variety. His teapot rested at the very center. Kazumae had always said that tea should be the very center of any gathering that involved the partaking of food into one's body.

When at last the two of them had stopped in front of him, he greeted them with a cheery smile and motioned swiftly for them to sit down. "Good afternoon, Lady Mae and Sir Alric. Would you care to join me for a spot of tea?" he said in his eloquent voice. I think he felt quite pleased to have company, which was a rarity. Isn't tea best enjoyed over some light conversation? Or is that just how someone like Kazumae would feel on the matter? I for one, being the introvert that I am, like to drink tea alone with my writing open before me.

"Of course, Mister Kazumae, magical bunny therapist!" Mae chimed in as she lunged into her seat with so much force that even Genesis, who could barely see a thing, worried she might topple. Mae's secret was a slight trick of her hand, which rooted the chair legs into the grass beneath it so that she could dive into any chair on the lawn with as much force as she deemed necessary. Genesis felt around for her chair and, upon finding it, took a seat as well.

"It seems you have lost your glasses, Sir Alric," Kazumae pointed out, his eyes locked upon Genesis.

She gave a brief nod. "The blasted things broke during class today." She attempted to growl like Alric did, but it sounded rather strange instead.

"Owl seems down in the dumps! He needs therapy!" Mae leaned on the table with her hands outstretched, flowers springing up from various places in her hair and around her arms, although the flowers looked rather droopy due to her concern for Alric.

"He does seem sad indeed, Lady Mae. Sit down and we shall get right to the bottom of this!" Kazumae assured her. He held out a cup of tea toward Genesis. "Here, black, just how you like it." She hesitated a moment with it in her hands, before she took a forceful sip to try not to look suspicious. To her great surprise and relief, the tea was strangely satisfying this time. She smiled slightly as she marveled that she even had Alric's taste buds. Shapeshifting into a person revealed wilder and wilder aspects of her valta than she had ever imagined.

"'Tis quite rough adjusting to things here at the university. At the House we only ever met a couple new students at a time, but now the majority of our class is new to us. Or—I know this shall grate on your temper, so please refrain from shouting—but 'tis rather about your parents, perhaps?"

Genesis wasn't sure how she should answer such a question. Alric's parents were dead, right? He was from the House, after all. That was a realm she knew nothing about. She guessed she should just look pained perhaps? Asking him about his parents was probably painful, but she had also heard Kazuame ask her not to shout... She ought to do so then.

"Don't bring up my blasted parents!" she finally snapped.

A smile pierced Kazumae's lips. "As I have always said, who needs them? If they really thought their work more important than their own child, then why should you be bothered that it led to their ultimate demise? You are here, and we are friends. But I do not know 'tis what this is. You have always been so hard to read, Sir Alric."

He paused and stared at Genesis a moment, considering what else could be bothering Alric. "Ah... then 'tis because of the rest of the class, no? I told you we ought to all just be friends. You are making it quite the unpleasant scenario with your cruel attitude toward them. They do not like any of us—not at all—because of your impertinent behavior. If only we had Lady Genesis on our side, then perhaps we might infiltrate and learn the truth for ourselves... I feel as if you really made quite a bad first impression by trying to shun her. 'Twas really you, Misteria, and Mae's doing. She seems really quite nice and very beautiful indeed. The fairest lady in the class, if I do say so myself." He looked over at Mae, then at Genesis, who smiled shyly at the compliment to her true identity. He turned to Mae. "Oh, but, of course, I am not meaning you are not quite beautiful as well, Lady Mae. I am only speaking of my own personal attraction, I find our Lady Genesis the most lovely of all."

Genesis must have begun to turn scarlet, for Kazumae outright said he was attracted to her without knowing she sat right there at the table with him.

"Yeah, you're right. I'm kind of sad about how we've treated her," Mae started. "She *is* really pretty and I like the things she says, but I was mean to her the first night. Now I just want us all to be friends. I wish she'd come to the House sooner, then we could have found a way to all be friends. I hate how competitive we've always had to be. But I wanted Mist and Levine to like me, too, so that's why I always went along with what they were doing." She gently tapped the bud of a flower she had been in the process of growing up through the lattice work of the metal table. With that simple touch, its petals peeled back so that the flower rested before her eyes in all its glory and beauty.

Just so you know and are not confused by the new name, I will explain. Levine is a girl from the House, who, like Mae, bears the surname Arisha Driscoll, as she also has no knowledge of who her parents are. She went into Group B of Class 1 when they entered the university. For that matter, she is not all that important to our story at this time.

"Yes, indeed. The environment of the House was always rather competitive. But Sir Alric hated the idea of her joining early, is that not so?" Kazumae pointed out.

"Yeah, but now everything is different. Alric's always by himself and seems so sad and lonely."

"Whatever are you talking about, milady? Has he not always been so?" Kazumae laughed and shook his head.

"He used to be really sweet back in the day. That small-for-his-age kid that everyone just wanted to cuddle. It wasn't until Reiss arrived at the House that he became mean all of a sudden..." She sighed. "We could have all the friends in the world if the rest of our group liked us more... I wish I wasn't from the House... I just want to be their friend..."

"Stop talking about me like I'm not sitting right here!" Genesis snapped. She found the role-playing kind of fun now that she felt she was understanding Alric a bit better. She already had her own way of interacting with others established and didn't feel comfortable stepping out of that box. In someone else's body, she felt less inhibited and began to wonder if that was why Reiss enjoyed shifting into other people so often.

Kazumae turned to look directly into Genesis's face. "We would not be speaking of Sir Alric right now like we are if 'twas he sitting here with us, now would we, Lady Genesis? But I would very much like to hear why, of all people, you chose to shapeshift into Sir Alric?" Kazumae inquired, setting down his cup of tea and proceeding to rest his chin on his clasped hands.

Chapter 24
Genesis

"WH-WHAT?" GENESIS STAMMERED, COMPLETELY caught off guard by Kazumae's words.

"With shapeshifters at this school, one shan't ever be too cautious, and, besides, you are a truly terrible actress. You should have chosen to shapeshift as Lady Misteria or maybe even His Highness. But *no,* you chose perhaps the most difficult student in our class to impersonate. You did get close to his voice by the end of this conversation, I shall grant you that. But you said far from enough most of the time, and interjected things at times when Sir Alric would certainly have said nothing at all."

He paused dramatically to organize his thoughts. "Let me elaborate on my thought process. Firstly, you made that comment on not bringing up your parents. The topic is very sensitive and so Sir Alric would probably have said nothing, pretending it had not been said at all. That is why I put in the part 'please do not shout,' because from the moment you took your seat at this table I was already suspicious of you, and so this would undoubtedly trip you up. The rest was only to confirm my suspicions. I then went on about his parents, but to this you chose to remain silent. If it had really been Sir Alric, he would have eventually quit the table in disgust and walked away, not wanting to hear anymore on the matter. Next, I began to opine on the rest of the group and sought to ridicule him for treating them so poorly. Sir Alric would have criticized me back at this affront. My subsequent tactic was to express that I found Lady

Genesis attractive. 'Twas because I was fully confident that indeed you were not Sir Alric, so this statement would confirm my suspicion that I was in truth speaking to Lady Genesis, if you blushed. Which you did. Lastly, I spoke of Sir Alric as if he were not present at all, which made you realize your mistake in staying silent and that you should interject something into the conversation to avert suspicion. All of these reactions led me to realize that you were indeed not Sir Alric Ashford but..."

"What?! Don't tell me I got it all wrong! This isn't Owl?" Mae interrupted, in shock, the flowers withering from the table as she sat up straight in her chair.

Kazumae cleared his throat in a manner of frustration over the interruption. "Yes, my dear, 'tis an impostor. None other than Lady Genesis Leigh Deadlock has infiltrated our ranks. You may change back now, milady. Put all fear from you, we shan't chase you away... Let us have a little chat over tea. For even though I used these tactics to weed you out, most of what I said 'twas true, including the part about you being quite attractive."

Genesis looked down in embarrassment as she changed back. Pleasantly, her vision cleared up so that she could now see Kazumae seated across from her, a smug smirk spread over his lips—he seemed quite pleased with the success of his investigation. He had changed out of his uniform for the day, dressed pretty nicely for his afternoon tea under the willow tree.

"Now, now, what is it that you wanted, Lady Genesis? Why have we engaged in this charade?"

"Oh..." She hesitated as it wasn't really for herself that she had come. She had come because everyone had asked her to, and she hadn't wanted to say *no*. "The rest of our group sent me because they want to get to know you guys better. They thought that I could get information that could help unite us. They don't like how segregated the group is," she finally answered in truth.

"I see." He set his tea cup down on its saucer again and cut his eyes over at Mae who pouted back at him. "We are not completely to blame for this, however. While those two—Lady Misteria and Sir Alric—have been a bit standoffish, the non-House students in the group tense up whenever any of us comes near or tries to speak to them. 'Tis not as one-sided as they may believe. The only person I was truly trying to shun was the one who called me a child. Now after a week has passed, surprisingly enough, 'tis Sir Alric who had obviously dropped the shunning of you first. He must have decided you to be of no threat to him. It shall be a slow process, but eventually I do believe they shall not be so indifferent to you, Lady Genesis. As for the rest of the class, I suppose we can get close to them in time, but they ought to treat us like regular human beings, even if we are more powerful. 'Tis not to be prideful, 'tis clearly only stating a fact, since we have already had years of growing familiar with our valta."

He paused to lift his tea cup and take a sip. "I can say for myself that I would be fine with a few more friends, and for the class to be united. But for the others from the House, that shall be a great ordeal. I shan't go into their personal details, but Sir Alric and Lady Misteria do struggle with abandonment issues and so are very slow to accept new people into their lives. Although, I do believe you have a far better chance with Lady Misteria than Sir Alric at this point. I do think that if Lady Mae and I started spending time with you more often, bit by bit the others shall follow in time. The five of us have known each other for quite a long while now."

"Owl, Mist, and I were in the cradle together. I've never known a time without the two of them," Mae interjected as she proceeded to grow a few more flowers into the latticework of the table.

"You'd do that, Kazumae? Personally, I'm not too focused on making friends here... I have one objective coming to this school, and one only. I intend to complete that objective at all costs. Even if it means I have to train till I break," Genesis stated.

Kazumae laughed. "If that is truly your intention, you might want to work on friendship with all of us at the House then, otherwise, when that happens and you do become powerful, you shall be shunned again due to being competition. Just a friendly word of advice, milady. As I said before, I believe that Lady Misteria would be far easier for you to pull out of her shell. While she may seem cold and unfriendly, she does not usually dislike people. She is just focused. You see, she seeks to become a research agent like her mother, and in order to be deployed into such a field, she must rank at the very top of our class. Perhaps if you can prove you are of no threat to her..."

He took another sip of his tea. "Now, now, let us get to know each other a bit better now that that is all out of the way. What is this objective you spoke of?"

The branches of the willow tree rustled above them as Genesis remained in her own thoughts. She wasn't sure if she wanted to tell too many people about why she was at the university. The situation between her parents and the school was uncertain, so she had been pondering it a bit over the past few days. As students there, they were being trained to become agents for the school. Those men that night seemed like they could be agents of some sort. But whose side were they on? Why had they whisked her parents away in the dark of the night? With that speculation in mind, she had decided not to bring up the matter, in case the school was possibly involved in her parents' disappearance. She just wished she could remember the name of the agent who had concealed their presence that night.

"You can tell us, milady. I shan't feed information to the faculty. If anything, quite the contrary. I may have done much growing up here with my master, but as soon as the time comes, I shall be free of this place and the two of us shall leave as we came. This place does not have the ability to keep us here. Now, what is it you desire? What objective brought you to this school?"

Genesis glanced over at Mae, who sat humming to herself. Truthfully, the conversation had become rather dull to her, and she had not been paying much attention since Kazumae had been talking about Misteria. Still, Genesis did not feel so certain about saying anything in front of her. She was quite chatty, to say the least, and while she felt she could trust Kazumae, could she really trust Mae?

"Do not worry about what Mae shall say. I shall institute some manner of bribery or threat to ensure her silence," Kazumae said.

"You wouldn't!" Mae cried.

"Then you promise not to let a word leave this tea table?"

"But what if I'm sitting at the tea table with other friends?"

"Let it not be! It remains between us three, and us three only."

"Then I do promise! I will carry all secrets to my grave!" Mae cried.

"See, nothing to be concerned about. Now... Lady Genesis..."

"My objective..." Genesis muttered, still uncertain. She looked down at the black tea, which she had no desire to drink anymore, and weighed the benefits of explaining her true objective. Kazumae was well familiar with this world, and had a mature take on things that she could not get from River. At last she cleared her throat. "I want to find my parents. They were taken some years back. The people who invaded our home had said that my mother was...a danger to Arisha, and then they took her and my father... I wonder if they were speaking of this school, because she had had valta when she was younger but lost it, and would tell people about when she did have it, even if they never believed her. I wondered if it was because she was leaking classified information without knowing it... The only reason they didn't take my brother and me was because an agent, whose name I can't remember, pretended we weren't there... I still don't understand why, because he knew we were under the bed, and the room was so obviously occupied by two children. But he left the room and told them that we weren't there."

The two of them listened with interest as she spoke. Yes, Mae was now fully paying attention as she was intrigued by mysteries. The school possibly kidnapping adults? Now that was something!

Kazumae leaned back in his seat, pensive. "That would make sense," he said at last. "First of all, they would not want people to start thinking that valta 'twas possible. Especially being that the Watts family wants Arisha to remain a secret from the government. And yet, taking your mother away seems quite extreme. I would have thought they would just tell her the truth and that she mustn't ever speak of it again under threat of death. But they took them away...which is quite peculiar. The agents were once students just like us, and for the first four years after graduation, they must be agents for the school. That is why you must be away for eight years when you enroll in this school. I know there are a lot of agents, including our professor Sir Glazunov, who do not agree with everything the school does. The agent that night may have been someone like that. Whatever they were taking your parents away for 'twas probably not good, and he was trying to protect you from it."

"Do you think you know where they took them? And is there a way to find that agent? I really want to thank him some day," Genesis questioned.

"I have no idea how to answer either of your questions, Lady Genesis. For finding that agent, I would ask Professor Glazunov, who knows the agents better. I think it shall be very difficult if you can't remember his name or what he looks like. As for your parents, if they are holding them somewhere, it would not be on campus. If they really do have them, they would be on the other side of the Gateway, in Arisha. That or they're dead."

Genesis's chest tightened.

"That was blunt and terrible, Mister Kazumae!" Mae criticized.

"'Twas only being brutally honest with her... but I suppose there is a possibility that they were not taken by the school at all... I know not if I can trust the school, but I'm also not sure they would do something like that. The situation is rather sticky for sure. Could there be any chance that you were mistaken about what they said?"

Genesis looked down without a word. The thought that she might be on the wrong track weighed heavily on her. Why was she even at the school if there wasn't a possibility of finding her parents?

Seeing Genesis's distress, Kazumae took another long sip of tea while gazing over her shoulder down the lawn behind her. He returned his cup to its saucer again and met her eyes. "Say, Lady Genesis, do you take any interest in the prospect of marriage?"

Chapter 25

Misteria

HAISE SUDDENLY SAT DOWN at the table, which made Mae and Genesis both jump and look up at him with startled expressions on their faces. They had not seen him come across the lawn toward where they were seated. Kazumae, of course, was not surprised in the least, as he seemed completely aware of everything going on around him at all times.

"Mister Kazumae. What have I said about trying to propose marriage to beautiful girls?" he asked as he sat down.

"I haven't done it yet! I simply asked her if she was *interested in marriage,* like you told me to, Sire!" Kazumae protested. Haise met his eyes and said nothing as the wind ruffled his long, wavy, dark hair. Genesis noticed the blood red streaks in it now that she had a better look at him. Kazumae released a frustrated sigh. "You see, Lady Genesis, 'tis custom for those in my country to marry at 16. I am now 17 and still have not found myself a bride. 'Tis a year of loneliness I should not have had to endure! My master told me if I waited 'til we started at the university, I would have a whole class full of lovely ladies from which to choose my bride. But now," Kazumae turned his gaze sharply toward Haise, "*you* keep telling me I cannot ask the ladies to marry me! You're going back on your word, Sire!"

"I was just telling you that, so you would stop whining about being a bachelor."

"I do not whine." Kazumae turned his head away to one side in a dejected manner.

"This world is different than ours, and since we are in this world we must follow their customs. You can't have just one conversation with a girl, decide you like her, and then ask her to marry you. You need to woo her first. Win her heart, start dating her, get to know her really well, then marry her...and you should probably wait till she's at least 18, 'cause they don't like to get married so young."

"But 'tis so far away since everyone in this class is younger than I!" Kazumae cried.

"Then start befriending upperclassmen."

"I feel as if you have my whole life plotted out for me, Sire."

"Not at all... I'm just making a friendly suggestion so that you don't keep getting rejected."

Kazumae remained silent for a moment as he drank his tea thoughtfully. The tap of ceramic cut the silence short as he replaced his tea cup again. "As I was saying before 'twas interrupted... Lady Genesis...are you perhaps interested..." Haise stood up and hooked his arms under Kazumae's, lifting him out of his chair so that his tea spilled all over the table. "Put me down this instant, Sire!"

"No more tea for you, Mister Kazumae." Kazumae reached toward the ground, which was pretty far away since Haise held him up and he was so incredibly short for a boy his age. "I know what you're trying to do, Mister Kazumae, and I purposely held you far away from the ground so that you could *not* start an earthquake in your rage."

"Why doth my power have such a handicap? Fine! I promise I shan't start an earthquake if you set me down!" Haise replaced him back into his seat, then took his own seat again.

"So what were you guys talking about with Lady Genesis? I assume it was quite a good conversation since it resulted in Kazumae asking her to marry him," Haise inquired.

Mae beamed. "Yeah, Genesis came to talk to us so that we could all be friends. Apparently the rest of the group doesn't hate us!"

"Oh, I see. Well, it makes sense they would send Lady Genesis then. She's the only one who will talk to us without trembling."

"'Tis quite annoying," Kazumae added as he cleaned the spilled tea off the table.

"So have you decided to be nice to them now?"

"Yes. I think the best course of action is to try and become friends when they are all still weak. Maybe, in that case, Sir Alric and Lady Misteria won't try to kill them when they become stronger. I think 'tis best that Lady Genesis and Lady Mae go speak with Lady Misteria on their own, while I speak with the rest of the class myself on the matter. Since Lady Misteria feels most wary of Lady Genesis, I think it would be good for them to have a little chat. Lady Mae shall attend such an occasion to vouch for her. I think 'tis the best course of action. Sir Alric is a fairly lost cause at this point, so put such ideas of drawing him in from your mind, Lady Genesis. He didn't really fit in at the House either, if it makes you feel any better."

He didn't get along with those at the House either? Genesis thought it made sense, but it also made her feel sad deep down within herself. He seemed to push people away, so it must be his own fault, but even so... Genesis wished she knew of something more she could do to help pull him into the group.

"That sounds like a good plan." Haise stood up. "Why don't the four of us get the ball rolling and go. Kazumae and I can go talk to the rest of the group... I noticed they were all gathered in the lounge right now. Misteria is most likely in her room studying, so why don't Mae and Genesis head on over there?"

"Good plan! First, let me clean up this tea," Kazumae said.

"Let me help you." Haise reached for a napkin.

"No, Sire! I would not wish for you to get your hands dirty!" Kazumae snatched the napkin away before Haise could reach it.

"It is quite all right. I like cleaning things," Haise interjected.

"But I said *no!* No way am I letting you lift a finger, Sire!"

"Please, Mister Kazumae..."

"So, what kind of relationship do those two have?" Genesis whispered to Mae as the two of them continued to argue on the issue.

"Even I get confused on that one," she answered.

"I have said it time and time again, Lady Mae dear, I am Master Haise's slave," he said in a matter-of-fact fashion.

"And I have told *you*, Mister Kazumae, time and time again that 'slave' is not the proper English word for it. Butler or hired servant would be a far better and more descriptive term to describe our relationship."

"But I have never once been paid for my services!"

"You don't see the money. It's all sent to your family."

"My brothers are getting it? My parents? All those sadistic blood artists???"

"Yes, the Amana family fortune is all kept together. You also have access to the rest of your family's hard-earned money as well."

"I knew that." He turned his head aside in irritation.

Haise sighed dramatically. "Sometimes I feel like you're more trouble for me than I am for you," he muttered as he shook his head.

"Say whatever you like. But I shall not let you lift a finger in the ways of cleaning." Kazumae returned to cleaning the spilled tea off the metal table top. Haise sighed again, which he seemed to do quite frequently.

"Let us go see Misteria. I am sure they have things under control here," Mae said with a wink. Genesis nodded and stood up to follow Mae away from the tea table back toward the dorms.

"What should I say to her?" Genesis asked as they climbed up the front steps onto the porch.

Mae twirled on her heel. "Anything you like! I'm sure you'll find the right words. After all, Mister Kazumae seems to have faith in you, otherwise he wouldn't have suggested we talk to her!" Mae answered then slipped through the front door.

Genesis still felt uncertain. How was she supposed to talk to someone as cold as Misteria and convince her that she was of no threat to her? Especially with how little faith Genesis had in her own social skills. Every step closer to Misteria made Genesis feel only more dread and uncertainty. They stood outside Misteria's door all too soon, and then, without any hesitation, Mae knocked upon it. Genesis knew she had to say something, but still, what should she say? Would the words come to her?

Mae threw open the door and dashed into the room even before Misteria had time to answer her knock. Misteria sat at her desk, as she so often did—every time that Genesis passed by her room, for that matter. As Genesis came very hesitantly over the threshold, Misteria's cold eyes lifted up past Mae to meet Genesis's. Mae fell into Misteria's lap with her arms flung around her neck, but Misteria didn't seem all that phased by her rambunctious behavior. She had grown up receiving Mae's hugs almost hourly.

Genesis swallowed and continued forward into the room. She wouldn't back down. Mae had said that Kazumae had faith in her abilities. She'd say something to convince her.

"Mist! I brought a friend here to have a little chat!" Mae chimed.

"I see." Misteria's words came out just as cold as ever as she set down her watercolor brush and turned her chair away from the desk so that she faced the room. No kindness emanated from her. The malice wasn't as great as Alric's, but it still felt malicious all the same to Genesis. She had faced Alric night after night, so she could face Misteria, too.

Genesis nodded slightly in greeting. "We haven't been directly acquainted with one another even though we are in the same group. I'm Genesis the shapeshifter. I wanted to speak with you." She somehow kept the tremor out of her voice, but that had to be some kind of miracle because her body shook all over.

"What is it that you have to say to me?" Misteria implored. Genesis had to keep her composure no matter how cold that voice came out at her. She was tempted to avert her gaze—to look to where Mae now stood staring into the fishtank that Misteria kept on top of her dresser. Instead, she lifted her gaze to look Misteria directly in the eyes again.

"I won't grovel at your feet. I won't deny that I'm doing my best at this school to improve myself. But I wanted to say this: I'm in no way trying to challenge you. I'm here...for another reason entirely. I'm sorry if I made you feel threatened because I got a scholarship into this school. It was not my intention at all to make you feel that way..." How was she doing? Were her words coming out right? Was she getting through? Misteria hadn't interrupted her yet, so she had to keep going. "I don't think any of the other girls feel that way either. Most of those in our group don't seem to have any intentions of fighting their way to the top of the class...except for maybe Alric and Hiero...but I won't speak for them... I will speak for some of the others, though. The others really want to get to know all of you from the House better. I would as well. I know we may not have started off on the right footing, but I would like for us to all get along...to be able to support each other instead of compete against one another. I don't know the details on what you're aiming for once you become an agent, but I'm sure you have good reasons...so I would like to support you as well, in any way that I can... I think that's what I wanted to say..."

Misteria's expression hadn't changed once the entire time Genesis spoke. Mae sat on the floor now with her eyes lifted up toward the girl she had grown up with. Thick tension hung over the room while they all stared at each other. Misteria took a deep breath at long last, and lowered her eyes.

"Words aren't enough... I don't trust people readily, because people betray one another and will say anything to get what they want... But...you were being honest the whole time and so...I'll take a leap and trust you, just this once. But..." Her eyes cut back up to Genesis again. "If you ever go back on those words and challenge me, I'm not going to trust you ever again... You mentioned the rest of the class as well, are you speaking for all of them?"

"Of course! They want to be our friends, too!" Mae chimed in.

"Friends..." Misteria muttered.

"Yeah! Isn't that wonderful? Some people want to be friends with us! Our upperclassmen were right. The people coming into the university *are* really nice! Not anything like we were told growing up!"

"I don't feel entirely certain of that. I guess I do consider Mae my friend. Not by choice, because she forces herself on me...but even so, my mother did tell me that making friends was important. I don't see much use for it though," Misteria stated, glancing over at Mae while she spoke. Genesis agreed with her, since she also didn't see any use for friendship.

The next instant Mae jumped to her feet, her hands planted firmly on her hips. "No use for friends? That's no way to see it! Having friends is super important! Friends share burdens with you! They help you through the hard times, and are there for you when you need them. If you don't have friends you'll have no choice but to bottle up all your emotions inside of you and that is in no way good! It would make me really sad..." Mae stared down at the carpet. "Plus having friends makes life a whole lot more interesting! You'll see!"

Misteria sighed again. "It will take more than *that* to convince me... But, I'll let actions speak in this scenario. Very well. I'll try this whole friendship thing. But I don't promise to keep it up for long if I don't like it. I'll at least try not to ignore everyone..." She turned her gaze back to Genesis again, but this time her eyes did not hold the malice that they had earlier. For the first time, Genesis didn't feel so intimidated. She wasn't sure how that was possible with the wacky plan they had come up with, but, in the end, it had all worked out, hadn't it? Misteria must have been on the cusp already. She would make an effort, but that only meant that they had to make just as much of an effort, if not more.

"So how did the plan go?" Reiss asked, leaning over on Ellie's desk—Dusk, Dawn, and Grisham were all gathered around her, talking with one another as they waited for class to start.

Dawn sighed. "I d-don't think it w-worked..." Dusk nodded quietly and they all turned their eyes to where Genesis sat at her desk alone. She didn't even notice Mae had come up behind her.

"She still ignored us all at dinner, and then went straight into her room and shut the door afterward. I tried knocking but I guess she had already gone to sleep," Dusk murmured.

"She's friendly with me in class," Reiss said.

"She isn't unfriendly..." Grisham clarified.

"Y-yeah. She j-just avoids everyone unless you c-corner her or t-talk with her d-directly, and we now know if you ask her f-for something, sh-she'll d-do it." Dawn stammered.

"We got River all hyped up to draw her into the plan," Grisham continued, "but he's kind of all over the place, too. I think he respects her, but I think because of that, he sees her like a mother and doesn't always want her around to cramp his style, if that makes sense."

"Yes," Dusk stated. "I think it's wonderful that we got the House students to be more comfortable with us...but that doesn't change the fact that we failed the true objective. How do we get Genesis to stop secluding herself."

"I guess the mission we presented to her was successful, but our true objective was not," Grisham said.

"'Tis something you must leave alone." The four Earth-side students jumped as Kazumae's voice suddenly addressed them from behind. Reiss, of course, had seen him approach and now stifled a laugh with his hand. "She must figure it out herself. You have planted the seeds, now wait for her to be ready. Do not declare failure quite yet, you have done what you can, and I do believe in time she shall change her mind about not making friends. Just be patient and wait. Focus on one another and show her kindness when you can... Just look... Now that you have Lady Mae in your ranks, she'll do quite enough bothering her for the lot of you." They all immediately turned their heads to see Mae had, without permission, started to weave flowers into Genesis's braid. Genesis looked back startled, and then, after a moment of eye contact with Mae, she started to laugh. "I believe pushing her too hard, too fast shall not be the answer. Did Sir River not mention she had the same behavior in middle school as well? 'Tis a deep-seated habit to avoid making friends, and such habits are not easily broken. So have patience with her, and wait for her to figure out how much she doesn't want to live her life here alone."

Chapter 26
The Duel

MONDAY ROLLED AROUND AND, before Genesis knew it, classes were over for the day, which meant the dreaded time quickly approached; soon she would have to face Alric in their duel. She headed back to the dorm with the new shapeshifting garb that Mister Cherith had given her. She had tried shifting with it on during her session that day and it had gone very well. Like Dr. Cherith had said, the shapeshifting garb became an extension of her body. That fixed the problem of her being naked when she shifted back into her own form, however, if she shifted into another person, she would still be naked in their form unless she had clothes on over the garb. At least she had no further intentions of shapeshifting into anyone again.

All that said, she still felt rather nervous about the duel, despite that major issue being resolved. Even though the garb would shift away with her true form, she was nowhere near being ready to use her valta to fight. A promise was a promise, though, and she would not go back on her word. At least she was more mentally prepared than she had been two weeks ago. She shifted pretty fluidly between forms after just two weeks and she still had the MMA training from her uncle, she just wasn't so sure she had enough strength back in her muscles to fight against a boy who had not recently been set back by an awakening. On top of that, she didn't know what kind of previous combat training he might have received at the House.

Back in her room, after dinner had settled, Genesis changed into her shapeshifting garb. Admittedly, she initially thought the skirt a bit short, but at least the shorts attached underneath made it far more modest. If she wasn't wearing a tracksuit, she generally wore only skirts and dresses, so the garb would be just fine under her normal clothes and her school uniform. She could also wear it alone as the school had designed it to be somewhat stylish.

Now dressed and ready, she headed down to the gym as she did every night. She wondered if he would let her have some time to prepare before they started the duel, or if the moment she entered the gym he would be ready to start. She could picture him running at her with his arms already ablaze the second she rounded the corner into the room.

She arrived down in the gym and, glancing about, realized Alric was nowhere to be seen. This was quite unusual because he usually got there before her. Had he chickened out? He had been reminding her daily about this duel!

She made her way over to the equipment and started her workout per usual. After several minutes had passed without Alric making an appearance, Genesis began to hum to herself, glad for the first time to feel no judgment while doing so. She even thought about playing her music out loud if he wasn't going to show up. After all, she didn't enjoy working out in silence or with her earbuds in and had begun to miss having her own space to do as she pleased, like back at Uncle Ferris's house. Could she have lucked out and he for some reason would not be able to come that night? The thought seemed too good to be true, but maybe it was and she wouldn't even have to spend an hour with his scowl either!

Then came heavy footsteps on the stairs and her heart sank. The rejoicing had been short-lived and now here he came. One couldn't mistake the sound of his stride; even it, like his eyes, was heavy with rage.

The footsteps ceased but the door did not open. She paused in her movements to listen. Had she been mistaken? No, she was sure that it was Alric. Like I said before, she already recognized the sound of his stride. He must be still in the stairwell. Was he delaying? Why, though? Hadn't he been so excited for their duel? She would have thought he would come running down into the gym the second dinner was over. So what was it now?

The truth of the matter was that Alric had indeed stopped on the stairs in an attempt to collect himself. He had a splitting headache and the ibuprofen hadn't taken effect yet. He seethed with anger as he stood in the stairwell, for, as Genesis had guessed, he had looked forward to defeating the shapeshifter in a duel for the entirety of the two weeks since she had agreed to fight him. The day couldn't come fast enough, and now that it was upon them, his body betrayed him.

"Pretend like it doesn't hurt. I'm fine. I am not weak," he muttered under his breath. Still, he couldn't bring himself to move any further for several long minutes. He couldn't let it hold him back. He had to do it. If he could defeat her even in his current state, then there would be no doubt that he was strong. He breathed in deeply and descended down the last few stairs.

As he entered the gym, he glanced about the room until his eyes encountered Genesis stretching on the floor. All remaining hope within her died. "I see you decided to show up tonight," he muttered as he stalked across the room.

"I've only ever missed one night here the whole two weeks we've been here, and that was because I fell asleep after class," she pointed out as she got to her feet.

"That one night is going to cost you. You better not have forgotten your promise."

"I didn't forget. I promised to fight you tonight."

"Yes, you did." He crossed his arms over his chest, his eyes almost wilder than usual, and a grin spread over his lips.

Genesis swallowed. The time had come, and despite all her wishing that it hadn't, she would fulfill her promise. She held her head up and strode away from the equipment as he was putting his belongings down. When she had reached a place on the sparring mats where they would have enough room, she stopped and stood pensively as her mind began to go over the logistics of a duel. Alric had fire, which was one of the most dangerous and destructive of all the valtas. That could become a problem. "Are you sure it's all right for us to duel down here?"

"Don't know, and don't really care. Probably not."

"Then maybe..." His eyes grew more severe, so Genesis stopped what she was about to say and glanced about the room nervously.

"The walls are made of cynthian stone. So is the main structure of the whole dorm. If there was to be a fire due to valta, the cynthian stone would grow active and put it out," Alric said, setting his hand ablaze before slamming it into the wall closest to him. The flames instantly snuffed out as if blown away by the wind.

"You just did that to convince me, didn't you?" she said.

"Did not! Try shifting while touching the wall!" he snapped. Genesis put his words to the test, and, much to her surprise, she couldn't shift while touching it.

"What about the floor? Also, I still don't understand the principle behind it? Why does it deactivate valta?"

"Why should I explain something so basic to *her*? We learned this in the first grade," he grumbled in Arshin under his breath. She tilted her head with a blank expression on her face. "We'll just learn it in class, so I don't see why *I* need to be the one to explain it to you."

"Because I don't know... I didn't grow up in this world and, therefore, I have less knowledge about it than you do. Wouldn't it just be easier for you to give a brief explanation? I think I have a right to know what protections are in place before we start fighting. Because the alternative is that I'll leave right now and go find Professor Glazunov to explain it to me. If I do that and dueling really is against the rules, I guess we won't be able to duel," she answered firmly.

He couldn't argue with her and so he sighed in an exasperated manner. "The floor isn't cynthian stone, so it won't deactivate our valta. Cynthian stone is rare and it probably already cost them a lot to build all of the dorm walls out of it, even though it is inactive. Active cynthian stone is more rare and expensive."

"If these walls are made of inactive stone then why does it still work?"

"Active cynthian stone emits energy, deactivating valta within a certain radius. To line everything with that would be nearly impossible because it's a lot more rare. Inactive cynthian stone works just fine to keep buildings from being damaged due to valta!"

"Why does cynthian stone deactivate valta?"

"It just does! Please, don't tell me you need the science behind it, too?"

"Do you know the science behind it?" she asked with a teasing smile.

"Yes, but it would take a long time to explain and I just want to duel."

"Very well. Thank you for telling me. I appreciate the information." She took her spot again to prepare for the duel. She supposed if there wasn't a risk of burning the building to the ground, they would be fine. She also noticed the large number of sprinklers on the ceiling as another safety measure. She still didn't like the idea that they didn't know for sure whether or not they were even allowed to duel in the dorm gym. Dr. Cherith said she was allowed to practice her valta outside of class, but that she still had to abide by the rules, such as not flying too high as a bird or going past the campus fence.

Alric took his place a few feet away from her. "Don't expect me to go easy on you! 'Cuz there's no way I'm going to!"

"We should avoid injuring each other so that we don't get in trouble with the school."

"No promises! After all, it's not easy to control what a fire burns," he said, fluttering a flame between his fingers.

She swallowed again, and wondered what she had gotten herself into. He had left her no other choice, and she wasn't about to step down now that she had promised. Plus, she wanted to see exactly how strong she had gotten after all the training she had done over the past two weeks. She still needed a lot of work, but it would be nice to see where she stood in terms of power.

All at once, her thoughts drew to an abrupt halt—she noticed his hands shaking at his sides. It was only for a split second before he crossed his arms over his chest again to conceal it, but she had noticed nonetheless. Something wasn't right and that worried her. She thought back to that moment when she had shifted into him. The heaviness of breathing, the exhausted cloud that hung over her the entire time she moved around in his form...she had had that small glimpse into what he felt, based on what transferred over with shapeshifting. But this looked like more than what she had experienced in his form. What more could be going on with him? Somehow she knew he was in no condition to fight at that moment, but this was Alric Ashford, a boy determined to be the best at the school. Even if he didn't feel well, there was no way he would admit that to her and step down. He would push himself, which just didn't feel right. Why should she help him abuse his body like that?

"Listen... Do you want to postpone this till tomorrow night?" she suggested without further thought.

His face twisted into a grin. "What? Are you getting all chicken on me? A promise is a promise!"

"Yes, and I fully intend on keeping my promise..." She paused again because she knew she couldn't ask what was going on with him. If he wasn't feeling well, there was no way he would ever postpone and look weak. She either had to pin a delay on herself, or she had to go through with it. It didn't feel right to help a person push themselves too hard, but he should also know his limits...and she had her own pride to think about as well. The whole thing was like a war, which meant that she had to try and push aside her emotions and treat it like one. He would never take notice if she wasn't feeling well and suggest it be postponed, therefore she had to try not to either.

"You know what, I was being silly. I'm not about to chicken out at all. I want to duel tonight. So bring it on." She grinned up at him, slumping forward to prepare herself. He looked pleased at her resolve, so he wasted not another second as he dove toward her, his hands lifted up by his face with flames bursting forth from them. The heat hit her at full force. She dodged away and hurried across to the far side of the gym. He dove at her again with a similar attack and she dodged in the same way, back toward the stairwell that time.

"Stop running away and face me head on, you coward!" he shouted as he let the flames die down into a simmer. To her surprise, even though the flames had definitely been licking up his arms to his shoulders, his shirt was not burned at all. Thinking about it, she had shapeshifting garb, so of course it made sense that other valta users had garb that was resistant to their valta, too. Alric usually only wore the pants of his flame-resistant garb, because he hated how the shirt felt on his skin, but he figured it was probably best not to risk burning his shirt off during their first duel.

He came at her yet again. She took a deep breath and dropped to the floor to shift into a cat. He stumbled, as she dodged swiftly right past him. She had somehow taken him off guard. He couldn't possibly have thought that she wouldn't use her valta after making him wait two weeks for her garb to come in, had he? She didn't stand a chance against him when it came to power. He could easily burn her to death with one touch of his hand. She, on the other hand, only had her physical strength. She knew some things from martial arts, so she was stronger than the average person, but she still had a long way to go, especially since her awakening had initially weakened her. Despite that, she really wasn't sure that she would ever have the strength to go against him.

He headed her way again, his flames blazing brightly. It dawned on her that shapeshifting into animals did come with some advantages. With that in mind, she went straight for him, swiping him with her claws as she passed. She managed to rip the hem of his pants, but she couldn't help thinking how painful a cat scratch could be. She did not want to risk drawing blood.

"Is that all you got?" he asked with a loud mocking laugh. "Stop making me use the same old boring attacks!" She wasn't making him use the same attacks, he had just never dueled someone like this before. No one at the House had ever accepted a challenge from him, and when they had combat training, he had been the kid stuck dueling with the teacher.

Genesis shifted again, this time into a bird, and flew at his face. He paused and brought up his arms to shield himself in his flames that sizzled up from his hands and forearms. She swiftly withdrew, knowing that he was more familiar with his valta after years of experience with it. Using it was second nature to him—like part of his body. She swung in for another attack with similar results, then dropped back down, changing into human form again.

"You know...I may be doing the same tricks because I'm new to this kind of rolling. But you also don't have to react the same way every time. I don't think I'm the only one to blame for the repetitiveness," she stated.

"Stop it! Don't say another word!" he snapped in response.

"You and the others from the House may have had your valta long before the rest of us, but I don't think you had much training in combat prior to transferring into the university."

His eyes grew all the more rageful and he ran at her again. She moved to shift into a bird, when a thought occurred to her. What was her one issue at that moment? Strength, of course! He had far more than she did. The way to possibly win was so clear. How had she not thought of it before? Had her mind dismissed it as a possibility? Well, of course. She probably would enrage him all the more, *especially* if it led her to win. But a victory over Alric would be pretty sweet...

She grinned as she locked eyes on him briefly, then hurried over to where his sweatpants hung out of his bag. He paused in his stride, his face filling with confusion as she proceeded to pull them on over her shapeshifting garb.

"What are you doing?! That's mine!" he snapped and hurried after her. She fled away from him while trying desperately to keep from tripping over the long pants. Then, with another backward glance, she shifted into his form and lifted her arm right as his flaming hand clamped down onto her. To her surprise, his flames did not burn her at all. Of course, it only made sense since he did not get burned by his own flames, but Genesis had little time to think of such things in the heat of the moment. Alric's eyes widened and his teeth gritted together.

"How dare you?!" he snapped.

"That's why I grabbed your sweatpants!" she snapped back, although in a much calmer version of his voice. Everything around her was so blurry now. She had to keep contact with him, although the hotter the blaze that welled up from his hand the hotter her skin felt.

She dove down, grabbing hold of his legs and yanking them out from under him without any difficulty at all. The light from his flames snuffed out in an instant and she tackled him, pinning him down to the ground. He tried hard to shove her off of him, but she had the far better position, with one knee pressed down hard into his chest and the other pinning one of his arms. He tried to push her with his free arm again, thrashing his legs about, but she swiftly took control over the free arm and continued to hold him down, pressing her knee harder and harder into his chest. He probably couldn't breathe well, especially with his already existent troubles with breathing. He'd have no choice but to give up soon. She glanced down at his face and could see he had already grown a bit blue. Guilt welled within her, but she held her composure. She shifted back into her own form, lifted her knee from his chest, and smiled down at him as he started to gasp for breath.

"I guess I win," she beamed.

He gritted his teeth together and shoved her off of him as hard as he could. Then he sat up, his whole body shaking in rage as she proceeded to take off his sweatpants. "Sorry to have messed with your belongings. I figured, in the moment, that you would be less angry if I at least put something on first before shifting into you. After all, I would have ended up naked in your form if I had shifted in just my shapeshifting garb. That would have been awkward as well!" She folded his pants neatly in her hands as she spoke.

"Why would you take my form?!"

"Well...I actually took it a few days ago... I guess I hadn't lost it yet..." She averted her gaze as she spoke.

"I'll kill you!" he snapped.

"Eep!" she cried, afraid he would actually hit her. She dodged, but there was no need, for his hand had stopped before it had come anywhere near her. He had no intention of actually hitting her. In fact, he even covered his mouth with his knuckles to conceal a short laugh over her reaction.

"I wasn't going all out tonight!" he swiftly covered. "That shorty told me if I ever hurt you while we were down here he would kill me. He could if he wanted to and I haven't become the best valta user yet."

She laughed. "I think you have more sense than I thought you did. Although, weren't you the one going on about not holding back?"

"Don't try to flatter me, Shapeshifty. I don't care what you think of me. I'll win next time!" He snatched his pants from her outstretched hand and scrambled to his feet.

That's right, like him, she shouldn't care what others thought of her. She wasn't there to make friends, so she shouldn't let their dislike get to her. She could stay right there in her own little bubble, focused on her studies and finding her parents.

He stalked back toward the door. "Wait....where are you going?" she asked. Quite contrary to what she had just been thinking about not caring, I'd say.

"Oh..." he stopped in his stride, trying to come up with an excuse. "Well, I was going to turn in for the night! But you be ready for the next fight! Because I'm going to win!"

"All right. I will be," she said with a kind smile. He then turned, grabbing his bag from the floor as he continued out of the room.

Once he was gone, Genesis did a twirl around on her heel and clenched her fists together in triumph. She had really done it! She had defeated Alric! Maybe he had been off his game that night, but that was still a victory for her!

As for Alric, halfway up the stairs he came to a halt and slumped forward, his hand clasped to his head.

Chapter 27
Siblings

GENESIS LEANED BACK IN her desk chair with a gentle groan of boredom. She had taken up writing since the start of classes, but she could only spend so many hours doing that, especially when she wasn't quite sure what she wanted to write. She had done all of her homework after class and had none left over for the weekend, so a hobby seemed necessary. She hadn't really had a hobby like writing before now because back at home she had always spent her free time with River. I guess that is just what comes with spending so much time alone...you pick up a new hobby. That's part of the reason why I decided to start writing up our story in the first place. Like Genesis, I also felt I needed a new hobby now that Dylas is always off with his girlfriend. Anyway, that weekend was actually Open Hall, although Genesis had forgotten the event. I tell you, although it had been mentioned on various occasions during the week, it seems the information had just flown right over her head. So when River appeared in her doorway, he certainly startled her.

"What the heck are you doing in my room? How did you get on the girls' floor?" she said with a start.

"Are you so upset to see me, dear sister?" he responded with a laugh.

"It's not that! Of course I'm always happy to see you, but I can't condone you sneaking onto the girls' floor!"

He laughed again, a wicked sort of laugh. Once he had quieted down again he proceeded to explain himself. "I didn't sneak onto the girls' floor. Today is Open Hall! Actually, everyone was wondering where you were when we were touring everyone's rooms. Gosh, your room is so boring! Why didn't you decorate it at all?" he muttered as he looked about at the bare walls of his sister's room.

"Oh... I hadn't realized... Was it mentioned in class?"

"Uh...yeah, several times. I mean, you had your door open so I guess that's good... Now...I know you had decorations here somewhere..." He opened up her closet to search some boxes she had shoved inside.

"Well, maybe I remember something being said about it... Oh well... I don't much care how everyone arranges their rooms... I would like to see your room at some point, though."

"You still have an hour left to do so. I'm decorating these bare walls first," he said, setting a box from her closet down on the carpeted floor. His sister leaned on her hand, watching him as he went about pulling out her fairy lights and pictures from the box. After a moment lost in thought, she tipped her head back to look at him now crouched on the ceiling as he strung the fairy lights up.

"That is pretty wild," she remarked.

"I know, right?!" He reverted his gravity back to float down to the floor again. "I'm not doing so well with the super strength side of my valta, but I'm absolutely loving the anti-gravity! It makes things so much easier! I've always been short, and now I can actually reach things!"

Genesis laughed. Some time passed before either one of them spoke again. River silently pulled out a large blue wall hanging with a white cross pictured on its center and proceeded to hang it up on the wall under the fairy lights. While Genesis, on the other hand, sat at her desk still lost in thought, mostly over the night of their parent's disappearance. That night had been on her mind more than ever since they had arrived at the school. She then remembered discussing it with Kazumae, and the memory of the agent who had concealed their presence came back again.

"Hey, River. Do you remember the name of that agent who protected us *that* night?" she asked at last. He glanced over his shoulder at her. Neither of them needed clarity as to what night *that* night was.

"You mean the one who almost looked under the bed?" he clarified. She nodded. He had such a sharp memory; she found it crazy the things he could remember from when he was only five years old. "I think it was something like Ash..." He paused. "Gosh, I can remember everything else about that night so well, but that one's hard."

"You were only five, so I don't expect you to remember such a thing," she laughed it off. His fingers had ceased moving, so that he just stood motionless with his hands holding up the one corner of the wall hanging. A name surfaced and he grasped it immediately with a gasp of surprise.

"Oh! Ashford! I think it was Ashford!" he declared. The wall hanging slipped from his hands to dangle from the corner already attached to the wall as he spun around to face her.

His sister laughed and shook her head. "You're silly. I'm pretty sure that's Alric's last name."

He stared at her with a blank look on his face and then he, too, started to laugh. The name had felt so right, but now that she said it, Ashford was definitely Alric's last name. He turned back to straighten up the wall hanging again. "Oh, you're right. I'm probably getting the two confused."

He continued to hang things up and set out her pictures on her dresser and bookshelves. He admired many of the pictures as he put them out, most especially the one he knew to be her favorite—one of the only pictures they had of their whole family together. River didn't remember when it was taken, but, whenever he had felt that finding their parents again was an impossible dream, he would go and gaze at that picture. He really couldn't remember them well at all, but the photo made him feel so warm. That's why no matter how uncertain Genesis's plans seemed, he followed her lead. He hoped more than anything that one day he would be able to fully understand her determination to find them. With that all in mind, he put the picture down on her desk beside her where she could easily see it. As he did so, however, he noticed that she didn't even look up at it or him.

Genesis was so engrossed in her thoughts that were taking her further and further back into that night...to the sound of that man's footfalls as he left the room. *"Agent Ashford, we must leave this instant. Did you find any children?"*

"No, sir, I think they told the truth. There are no children here."

The name fell into place so perfectly that her mind couldn't think it any different anymore. The man who had saved them that night was indeed Agent Ashford. Thinking harder about it, it only made more sense. Alric was from the House. The House was filled with orphans from Arisha as well as the children of agents who had died. She swallowed hard and turned her eyes to the photo her brother had placed on her desk.

"It was Ashford, though, wasn't it?" she said. Remaining where he stood beside her, they both stared at the picture as she continued, "I mean, it's not impossible, right? Alric's parents were agents before their death. I don't know how old he was when they died, but that could have been before they died. It would make a lot of sense why the guy would have protected children if he himself had a son our age."

"But that guy seemed nice. How could Alric come from that?"

"Easy, he died when Alric was young. Maybe Alric resents him for that. From what I heard the other day when I had tea with Kazumae, it sounds like his parents were more focused on their work than on him, and they died on a mission."

"That's really sad..."

"It is. I can't help but feel a little sad for all of them. It seems like those from the House have had it pretty hard. It kind of explains why they are the way that they are."

"Yeah."

Another silence hung over the room, as Genesis felt sadness well within her. "Dang, if it really is his dad, then I can't thank him one day like I wanted to."

"You could thank Alric," River jested.

She laughed nervously. "Hey, once we're finished in here, do you want to show me your room and then maybe take a walk around campus?" she suggested. River nodded quickly. "All right, it's a plan then!" She then got up from her desk to help her brother finish decorating her room.

Chapter 28

Alric

GENESIS SAT ON A bench down in the gym lost in thought. She had been sitting there awhile but had made no move to work out. She couldn't get her conversation with River out of her mind.

She was suddenly aware that a silence had fallen over the room, and she could feel Alric's eyes upon her. She looked up to meet his gaze. "What?" He didn't say anything as he continued to examine her with his bright eyes. "Do you have something you want to say to me? We're not dueling today, right? I thought we were going to duel every two weeks... So we still have a week."

"No. I don't want to duel right now," he answered. She was honestly slightly baffled to hear something like that come out of his mouth as he was always ready to fight. She wasn't sure how to respond, and so she said nothing. Surprisingly, the tension between them seemed less than usual. He appeared calm tonight compared to most other nights, and she noticed he looked a bit pale.

At last, he sighed. "You've been sitting there for a while not doing anything but occasionally sending weird looks in my direction. Are you tired? Or maybe sick? It's not like I'm worried about you or anything, so don't give me that look." She straightened up and fixed the bewildered expression that had come over her face. "I'm only asking because you keep looking over at me so much!"

Despite her attempt to look neutral, she still felt bewildered that he had initiated a conversation with her in the first place. Even if he had done that by just standing in front of her and staring until she noticed. Sure, he gave her reminders that they had another duel coming up in a little over a week, but otherwise, he wouldn't say more than two words to her most nights. Truth be told, she couldn't stop thinking about the possibility that it had been Alric's father who had protected her and River that night. She had glanced over at him working out and pondered if that gentle voice could really belong to the father of this hotheaded teenager. In the end, she had to remind herself that, when it came down to it, she really knew nothing about his father.

The longer Genesis sat thinking about how to respond to him, the more on edge Alric seemed to get. Finally, Genesis decided she must say something, make up some sort of excuse. She decided to brush it off first, as if it was nothing for him to be concerned about. "I just have a lot on my mind tonight," she answered. She watched as he shifted from one foot to the other, the tension growing between them. Her eyes then wandered away from him.

"That's not it, and you know it. A lot of people have been saying weird things about you. But I see you down here every night and I don't agree with them. You seem different to me than they make you out to be."

"They say weird things about me?" she questioned, turning her attention back to him.

"Uh... Yeah... Sometimes not far from you, so I assumed you had heard them," he answered.

"I see... Is it very bad then?"

"They say you're really kind, just quiet and aloof. That second part is true—you seem to think you are better than everyone else so can't be bothered to talk to anyone. Plus, you never seem to know what is going on around you."

"Hey!" she objected.

"But when you're down here in the evenings...I don't know... I mean, you act like you were the other day during our duel. You were totally mocking me. You shapeshifted into me, and then proudly declared you won after nearly suffocating me to death! I thought you were the one who said we shouldn't hurt each other, then you were the one doing most of the hurting! No way! I won't believe you're kind for a second!"

She stared at him for a moment, before she burst out laughing. "I *can* be pretty cruel, can't I? I wasn't meaning to mock you... I guess I got a bit carried away—your determination energized me. Should I have let you win?"

"Of course not!"

"Then, I guess using your form, when I had it, was my way of doing everything I could and not holding back. And you *told* me not to hold back. I really thought you would win." She lifted her eyes again to meet his.

"Well, are you kind or are you not?"

"I wouldn't know how to answer that," she laughed, shaking her head. "I don't really understand myself right now, to be honest. I feel so lonely, but I want to be alone all at the same time. I want to have fun, but I also want to focus on my studies. I want to know the truth behind everything, yet I'm so scared to find out..."

He took a seat beside her on the bench, something he had never done by choice with any girl before now. He couldn't help it though, because he knew the feeling of being pulled in two different directions himself. He knew what it felt like to push people away while wanting to know what it was like to be close to someone at the same time.

Before he had time to realize what was happening, she had placed her hand on his forehead. "Are you all right?" she asked.

He drew violently back away from her. "What are you doing?" he snapped.

"Sorry..." she continued hesitantly. "You're burning up, though... Is that just your valta...or do you have a fever right now?"

"I don't..." He stopped and looked away. "Don't touch me."

"I don't mean to be nosy... I was just concerned because you look so pale..." She paused. "Wait... Is that why you asked me if I was sick? Were you worried that I might have gotten you sick? Or maybe that you had gotten me sick?"

"You ask so many questions."

"Yes... I know I do. I'm sorry you're not feeling well. If you want me to get you anything..."

"No, I'm not weak!" he snapped.

"I wasn't suggesting..." She bit her lip and looked down at her hands in her lap.

"It does make me weak. If I didn't get sick, then maybe my parents would have changed their minds about not wanting me." His voice had gotten so low that she barely caught his words. His eyes looked tired, as he leaned forward to rest his head in his hands in a defeated manner.

"Your parents?"

"Don't."

"Sorry! I won't pry! That's your business. But don't listen to anyone who tells you that being sick makes you weak. Throw that thinking out. Sickness happens in life! It doesn't mean you are weaker than anyone else! I just hope you feel better soon!"

"Why should you care?"

"I wouldn't wish misery on you, even if you can be pretty cruel!" She smiled kindly at him. He was far too exhausted to really be upset about it. Maybe if he felt better he would have been offended by her expression. Could she be belittling him? He didn't care at the moment.

"There isn't really anything to say about them..." He stared down at the floor, which looked foggy as his vision blurred a bit from his fever.

"Them?" she echoed, and it really did sound like an echo to him, for everything was growing more hazy.

"My parents... They didn't want me, and no one has, for that matter. They died while they were on a mission when I was three years old. Before that, they never once came to visit me at the House. But why would that be a surprise? My mother tried to kill me before I was even born so that the school wouldn't find out that I existed... D-does that clear up your curiosity now?" He turned his gaze back to her, and was half startled from his feverish daze by the expression on her face. It wasn't pity he saw in her eyes, like so many others when they learned about his parents. No, she looked almost angry; in fact, she trembled. He tore his gaze away and tense silence began to envelop them again.

"How could she do that...to her own child...?" she whispered. He could hear a tremor in her voice. Was she crying? Why? Why would she cry for him?

He stood from the bench and slowly sauntered out of the room. Genesis remained, left with her own thoughts. She knew she shouldn't pry any further, but she did know that he couldn't possibly be the son of whoever it was who protected her and her brother. He had said he was three when they died, but she had been seven the night her parents disappeared. She and Alric were the same age, so that didn't add up. Once he felt better, Alric would probably hate her more than ever... But, thinking back to Agent Ashford, she was beginning to realize that it wasn't just to thank him that she wanted to find the man. If anyone had answers about what had happened to her parents, it had to be someone who had been there that night...which meant she had to find another lead in that direction. She knew that, based on what Alric knew, his parents had died before that time. That didn't mean there couldn't be other Ashfords at the Agency. That or she and River had gotten the name wrong. She just had to dig a little deeper.

Chapter 29

Freecia

RIVER AND ZURI REMAINED close from the first day of school. For River, their friendship meant the world to him. He had many friends back at home before coming to Arisha University, but things were totally different here. He liked to think that he fit right in with everyone else, despite his younger age, but that was not quite the case. In fact, he suffered greatly because many of the students in his class did treat him differently because he was only 13. Zuri held no such prejudice at all and neither did Freecia.

Ah, Freecia. I know now is the first time I have mentioned the name, so bear with me. Freecia approached River shortly after gym class one day following their first month of school. She was in Group B so River had not really interacted much with her. That said, he had taken notice of her as she seemed to be a total sunshine...and he also thought that she was rather cute. She had beautiful bright red hair, cut in a bob, and wore huge round glasses. He felt most drawn to her eyes because despite her being a fire user, she had the deepest blue eyes he had seen in his life. Yes, I tell you the truth. Despite her being a year older than he, he had developed a bit of a crush on her from a distance. So, after gym one day when he was seated on one of the bleachers, tying his shoes, he was quite surprised and nervous when she sat down beside him. That bright smile of hers he admired so much was directed at him!

"I heard your name is River Deadlock. Is that correct?" she asked.

River nodded, his head spiraling out of control at the notion that a cute girl was really talking to him. "I also heard you're the youngest student currently in the university... You must be pretty smart! On top of that, you're friends with Zuri Whitlock, correct?" River kept nodding. "Cat got your tongue? You can speak to me, you know." She giggled with a tilt of her head.

"Sorry... I-I'm not very good at talking to strangers...at times..." he stammered. *Especially really cute girls he was interested in.*

"Oh come now!" She placed her hands on her hips. "Have we really been in class together for a whole month and you still label me as a stranger? Also, you ask the most questions in class out of everyone, so that's got to be a lie!"

"Oh... Well, of course you're not a *stranger*! I was only meaning this is the first time we have spoken to each other... Sorry, maybe I'm just making excuses!" He laughed. "I really don't know why I'm nervous!" He bowed his head to her, partially out of respect and partially because he wished to conceal the color rushing into his face.

"No need to get nervous and formal! I hope you don't think of me like a stalker, but I keep noticing you and Zuri in class and around campus. You hang out at the Entertainment Center after class a lot, right?"

"Yes! All the time! We have a blast!"

"Well...I've been looking for people to go with... I'm actually kind of from the House, kind of not. My mother is an agent, so she ended up sending me to school at the House, but I always went back to Arisha for the night and on weekends to be with her and Dad. Glad they live close to the Gateway, but still that commute was something else! Anyway... I'm kind of friends with the House students, but I also don't think I can relate to them all that much since we grew up under slightly different circumstances... I'm looking to make some friends with some other students who enjoy things like playing games at the Entertainment Center...and aren't so rigid and focused on studying and training all the time..."

"Of course you can come with us!" River blurted out.

"Really?"

"Of course! You're welcome anytime! Some games are more fun with more than two people! Oh! Also, I heard they're opening up the ice skating rink soon! Zuri and I are planning to go ice skating in the future... Although, I'm guessing you're a fire user so you might not..."

"I'll bundle up real snugly-like!" she declared.

A smile fluttered over River's lips and he gave an enthusiastic nod. "I'm headed to the café for lunch right now with Zuri... If you wanted to join us..." River started, his face getting warm again. His mind kept repeating over and over again that he was not asking her out on a date so there was no use getting nervous about inviting her. Zuri would be there, too, after all. She was an absolute ray of sunshine!

"It would be my pleasure to eat with you two! Let me change out of my gym clothes first. Don't leave without me!" She jumped up and hurried away, her sneakers squeaking on the gym floor.

Zuri watched her as she darted past him. Curious about what had just transpired between them, he walked over to the now-glowing River. "What did you two talk about... If I may ask?"

"She wanted to join us... I invited her to lunch... I hope that's all right?" River asked, a sudden wave of anxiety rushing over him. He had made all of the decisions for himself, without thinking at all about how Zuri would feel.

"Oh, of course! She seems really sweet! Plus, the more the merrier!" Zuri answered. Relief swept over River and, pleased by his friend's equally glad reaction.

"Your sister is in our class, too, right? Genesis Deadlock?" Freecia asked River. The leaves of the trees rustled overhead as they walked over to the campus's café. The leaves were still mostly green, but the temperature had started to yoyo every few days.

"Yes! She's about two years older than I am, but we get along pretty well—as far back as I can remember! She always claims she treated me terribly when we were little and insists on apologizing now! I can't remember that, though, so I don't think it matters that much!"

"She sure is beautiful, too!" Zuri added, as he walked backward ahead of them so as not to lose touch with the current conversation, even if he had little to add to it. Freecia wished he would walk beside them instead, because the wind coming from behind him was blowing the coldness he exuded right into her face. Being a fire user, she got easily chilled. They were having a warm day so she was not well dressed for cold air. Despite that she was happy to be with Zuri, too.

"That's so nice! My mom and her younger brother both went to this school, but he was a few grades below her. They didn't get along at all, though! I've never even met my uncle. I heard he either died a long time ago or he was stationed overseas in Arisha under some kind of agent protection program for a while! Can't really remember, my mom seemed pretty adamant that he was dead! I just know for sure there was some major drama!" She said the last word in a sing-song manner.

"Really? Who's your uncle?" Zuri asked.

"Elwood Ashford. He's actually Alric's old man."

"You're Alric's cousin?" Zuri gaped.

"Yeah... You wouldn't realize it because we rarely talk to each other."
She chuckled. "I used to try and talk to him at the House, but my mom
caught wind of it and told me to be friends with anyone but him. She
hated her little brother and wanted nothing to do with his 'illegitimate
child,' as she would say. Apparently Elwood was far too childish and silly,
according to her..."

"What's an 'illegitimate child?' What is that supposed to mean?"
Zuri questioned with uncertainty.

"You know... Um... A child born outside of... Nevermind..." She
laughed nervously. Zuri stared at her blankly for a moment and then
turned around to continue walking.

"Here we are!" River declared to break the awkward silence.

"Yay! I'm so ready for a muffin with lots of whipped cream! The
barista does it especially for us! It is quite delicious, Miss Freecia," Zuri
explained.

"A muffin for lunch?" She laughed again. "I will get fat hanging out
with the two of you!"

"The potential is certainly there. All River does it eat. I've probably
gained some weight since getting here, too, all thanks to him. You'll see!
He would buy out the whole pastry stock if the barista would let him."

"I might as well indulge today! I'll try to be good the rest of the
week," Freecia answered, clapping her hands together.

"Yes, let's celebrate new friendships!" River declared.

The two of them continued on through the front doors of the café
ahead of him, seeming not to acknowledge his last words. Even so, a
bright smile spread over River's face as he skipped in behind them, happy
to be forming a new friendship with another of his classmates. I fear
River was too distracted by his crush to remember to tell his sister later
the new information he had learned about Alric's father.

Chapter 30
Advice

LIFE STARTED TO BECOME normal for everyone at the university. Genesis no longer felt anxious as she continued to duel with Alric every couple weeks and pushed herself to improve just as hard as he pushed himself. As he got better, so did she. The results never ceased to surprise her. Since their first duel, she had managed to win every time, even without using his form. In her free time, she would strategize ways she could catch him off guard, and each and every time her strategy would work! She was certain she was only making the tension between them greater. Yet each night he came down into the gym, his expression seemed a little less severe, and he didn't glare at her as much. He kept challenging her and she was certain he would keep that up until he finally won. He never brought up what he had told her about his parents, and so she wondered if the fever had affected his memory. With that in mind, she never dared to bring it up herself.

Before she knew it, she realized they had been at the school for over three months and, in that time, not much had really changed for her socially. She still kept to herself as she had decided to do at the beginning of the semester, much to the dismay of several of her classmates. She was naturally close to Reiss, since they were the only two in their valta training class. He was friendly with everyone, however, and they never hung out together outside of class. I tell you the truth, I have heard many stories about Genesis and Reiss's training sessions, and while he made her laugh a good deal, due to his silly antics, those are not important to our tale.

Mae often came around, and I suppose they were close, although Genesis would never see it that way. She was kind to her classmates, but never went out of her way to spend time with them.

She also sat with Roland Watts at lunch on a couple other occasions. All such occasions turned out exactly like the first time. She kept it up until Roland flat out told her to leave him alone. After that, Genesis ate with Ellie every day, who for some mysterious reason started going to the cafeteria later than everyone else, too.

Since Genesis had always kept her distance from kids her age, it proved to be only natural for her to continue doing so now. She had her brother, after all. With each passing day, however, it grew increasingly obvious that, as River got more independent, he spent less and less time with his older sister. As a result, she grew more lonely, especially because she had assumed they would always be close. That assumption had made it all the easier to never make new friends, but now he'd far rather spend time with Zuri and Freecia than with her. She kept telling herself it didn't matter that much, but, even still, every time he rushed off to be with his friends, leaving their unfinished conversation hanging in the air, she couldn't help but be filled with loneliness. She felt as if the last piece of her family was drifting away from her bit by bit, her dreams of reuniting all of them floating with it. She would do it all alone in that case. She would continue forward to find their parents with or without her brother's help.

The last few weeks of class before the end of the semester approached and Genesis could not believe how fast the months had gone by. Next semester would probably be completely different from this one, although Genesis couldn't know for sure, since she had not heard anything from the faculty about the schedule yet. In fact, Professor Glazunov had gone over this thoroughly during their morning class , but she had not paid attention.

Genesis sat on a bench in the gym staring up at the clock that hung in the center of the back wall. Curfew was fast approaching and Alric still hadn't shown up for their duel... She tapped her foot on the floor nervously. Would he want to do it tomorrow night? What if he chose not to duel at all? Maybe he hadn't shown up because he had decided to give up? She shook her head. She shouldn't be upset about such a thing. Wasn't having the gym all to herself for one night what she had wanted since the beginning? That intense feeling of loneliness welled up in her again. No, she had begun to look forward to the evenings, because she felt less lonely working out with Alric.

She slumped forward. Why couldn't her mind just think as she wanted it to? Getting distracted by her own loneliness wasn't helping anything. She hadn't made any progress on finding her parents... What was she supposed to do next? She felt imprisoned in her own body. There wasn't a single other person she could be herself with, now that River had grown distant from her... He looked so happy all the time... So why did she feel so miserable?

Finally giving up on Alric, she stood and gathered her things. She might as well go upstairs and do homework if he wasn't going to show up. She walked through the first floor lounge into the foyer/dining area. She had intended to continue into the elevator room, but she came to a stop, her eyes fixed on the telephone that was used to call up to the floors above. She could call up to the third floor and ask to speak with Alric and see where he was...

She grasped the telephone, paused, then drew her hand away again. No...if she did that, she would be giving in to that loneliness, even *admitting* it to someone like Alric. She just had to start hanging out with Zuri, River, and Freecia, even though the high energy and childish innocence of that group was a bit much for her. She started to regret refusing all of Kazumae's offers to have tea with him, Haise, and Mae. After her adventure with shapeshifting into Alric and talking about uniting the class, the three of them had invited her to do things with them many times, but she had always had an excuse not to. Was staying so focused on her studies and training all the time really helping her toward her goal of finding her parents? Was it too late to make friends now? Would forming friendships help her toward her goal? Mae still talked to her on occasion, as did Dawn, Dusk, and, of course, Ellie during lunch, but they had stopped inviting her to things now, so that ship had probably already sailed. They were more focused on Wayland and Hiero, who seemed more likely to join them.

Hiero spent most of his evenings with his girlfriend from Group B on the front porch, and when he did grace them with his presence, they all remembered why they had chosen not to invite him to things in the past. He dominated the conversation, and got flirty with the girls despite having a girlfriend. The others also found him terrible to play video games with, as he was a sore loser. On a few occasions they asked him to play guitar for them, as it would allow him to be the center of attention while not subjecting them all to hearing a long story that they had already heard five times. That plan failed, however, as he refused to play for them, and even left without another word. All were quite baffled by the response, since River had been sure to tell them again and again how great Hiero's passion for music was.

Wayland, on the other hand, was more of a quiet, observant type. He didn't say much of anything, but didn't seem entirely opposed to being friends with Group A. Several of them had carried on fairly good conversations with him, although Mae said that the conversations were either very deep or very shallow as he awkwardly answered questions about the weather or the quality of his meal. There was one subject that he seemed unwilling to discuss, however, and that was why he had come to school a week late. Whenever anyone asked him about it, he would either answer "just because" or "it's not important." There were a few rumors circulating, but none had been confirmed.

Genesis heard voices on the stairwell above. Maybe Dawn and Dusk? She thought she heard stuttering. She couldn't make out what they were saying, so she stepped closer and listened, even though she really ought not to have been eavesdropping.

"P-please! Y-you're intimidating so...so..."

"I will have no part in your games. Just leave her alone." That sounded like Wayland's cold voice.

He came through the doorway alone, and briefly made eye contact with Genesis. He sighed and shook his head. "It's not my business," he muttered under his breath.

Genesis smiled sheepishly and turned to walk back toward the phone. She felt awkward, and wasn't sure if she should just go upstairs, or... She stared at the phone again.

The running of the sink in the adjacent kitchen drew her attention. Wayland stood there fixing up some kind of drink that he made himself every night before bed—something that was high in iron and helped his valta recharge itself in his sleep. She watched him as he cut his eyes in her direction.

"It's almost curfew," he stated.

"How does your valta work?" she asked. Iron was one of the few she hadn't seen in action yet. He seemed to have good control over his valta upon arrival, so he didn't have the accidental valta slips that many of the others still struggled with—just another thing that made his first week absence more curious. One of the rumors about him was that the reason why Wayland already had that control was because he was a faculty member's son and so his valta had already been awakened before he got there. While it was only a rumor, it seemed more than likely.

Genesis was glad that her valta was shapeshifting. She'd only accidentally shifted a handful of times at the very beginning. One time she had accidentally shifted into a cat while she was with River, and he had been absolutely delighted about it. She didn't have her shapeshifting garb on, and he had run around campus showing her off to every one of their classmates. Reiss got a good laugh out of it, and said that that was the reason he always wore his shapeshifting garb under his clothes, so he didn't get stranded in a form. Finally, River let her go into one of the bathrooms with her school uniform to change.

"I can harden my skin," Wayland answered with a lift of his hand so that she could see a sheen of metal spreading over the surface of his skin. "I can make things as well, but I'm a little low on power right now, so it would be difficult."

"That's interesting..." she answered. A silence proceeded as Wayland continued to drink what he had concocted for himself.

"Listen," he muttered after a while. Genesis lifted her gaze. Was she about to be a part of one of his deep conversations for the first time? The idea kind of excited her, because she would love to have a deep conversation after all these months of being alone. That was something she missed most from back home: the deep conversations she used to have with Uncle Ferris.

"I don't know if it's my place to say anything...but I have noticed some things... I think you should stop fighting yourself, because I think whatever you're doing right now is more distracting to you. I don't mean to sound blunt, but I feel like you don't always pay attention during class or to anyone else around you for that matter...especially during our first class of the day with Professor Glazunov."

"What do you mean?" she asked.

"Like...hmm...maybe that's not exactly it." He gathered his thoughts. "Here's an example... Did you hear about the class trip?" Genesis shook her head. "Once the semester is done we'll be taking a class trip to Arisha for a week in December. See...a lot of our classmates have been talking about it for weeks now since Professor Glazunov briefly mentioned it during class, but, even so, you don't know about it... Almost like you've trapped yourself in your own little bubble and nothing can penetrate it. I think it's a guard you put up. I'm not really the person to be pointing out this kind of stuff. I personally don't tend to talk to people. I haven't really done so in the past, because I didn't have many opportunities to do so..."

He glanced down at the glow of the under-cabinet lighting and tightened his lips. "But I think...that human beings need each other... We can't live trapped in our own little bubbles no matter how much we don't like other people or how much we think that being close to people will distract us from what's truly important. I'm starting to really come to terms with that myself... In the end, what will be far more painful and far more distracting is being completely alone and blocking out all their voices. Don't block them out. Listen to them from time to time...and listen to that loneliness inside yourself. Don't neglect it, because if a time ever came where you were truly isolated and unable to make contact with another person, how many regrets do you think you would have looking back on how you pushed all the opportunities away? You have no grounds to argue. Everyone can see it, and everyone is worried. Mae has mentioned several times how you keep getting more and more distant, and while you apparently helped bring Misteria, Haise, and her together with the rest of the class, they've never been able to return the favor because you won't let them. Stop wallowing in your own loneliness and accept the hands they are reaching out to you. If you think it's too late, it's not. They've only stepped back because they know that they've done all they can, and that you have to come to them on your own now."

He took a deep breath and swallowed down the last of his drink, then turned to rinse out his cup in the sink. "Again...these are just my thoughts... I still don't talk to people much, but you don't have to be that way if that's not who you are. Just be yourself... I'm sure you'll feel a lot better if you do..."

Genesis stared at the dark wood floor as his footfalls faded away out of the room. After another moment, she heard the elevator doors ding. She was left alone again, but yet something felt different. His words continued to repeat themselves again and again in her head. She thought of Alric not showing up in the gym and River as he ran away from her to meet up with his friends. Then her shoulders began to shake and tears started from her eyes. She didn't move from that spot as she continued to cry gently, even as the grandfather clock that stood by the door to Professor Glazunov's office chimed to mark 10:00—the start of curfew.

Shortly after, Genesis turned and went back over to the dorm phone. She paused in front of it, half wondering if she was allowed to call someone after curfew. She wiped the last few tears from her eyes, drew in a deep breath, and selected the "3" for the third floor. She waited as it rang on the other end. Why was she doing it exactly? Had what Wayland said influenced her? That she could not answer, but it was something she suddenly wanted to do more than anything.

"Good evening, 'tis Kazumae Amana at your service," Kazumae answered on the other end of the phone.

"This is Genesis," she answered. Her voice shook a bit at first, but she managed to calm it as she continued. "I was wondering if I could speak with Alric for a moment."

"Sir Alric?"

"Yes."

"Okay, I shall get him." A silence proceeded as she waited. The lights automatically went out, save for one light above the stove that was always left on for anyone who might need access to the kitchen medicine cabinet in the middle of the night. Still she waited with the phone held to her ear. What would she say? Did she plan to ask him if he was all right? Or should she take a different approach? She would be talking to Alric after all.

"Who's calling me at this hour?" Alric answered at last.

"Hey, Alric!" she chimed.

Silence.

He stood in the hallway directly above her, thoroughly confused by her random call. She, on the other hand, thought his silence was because she had said his name, which always seemed to make him tense.

"You know...you always stress to me about not skipping out on our duels...yet tonight...you were the one who skipped out..."

"I did not!" he tried to defend himself.

She laughed, her hand clutching the phone tighter. "Well, it was a no-show, so I'd say..."

"I had the worst migraine ever, so it's not my fault I couldn't fight! I couldn't even keep my dinner down! We'll just do it tomorrow!"

"Okay then, well, you better be there." She twirled the phone cord around her fingers.

"Yeah! Because tomorrow I'm going to win!"

"I'm sure you will. I'm just a weak girl, after all."

"You're always shaking in your shoes before every single one of our matches...so..."

"There you are wrong. I think it is you that is always shaking."

"I can't help that, it's just my muscles having spasms because I work them so hard."

"Okay, okay, I get it." A silence proceeded. She continued twisting the phone cord around her fingers unsure of what she wanted to say next.

"Why did you call me in the first place?" he asked at last.

"I don't know. No reason. I guess I was just lonely and wanted to talk to you."

"Why?"

"*Why?*"

"There are 12 other people in our dorm so why don't you talk to one of them instead?"

"Oh...well...because they're not Alric Ashford," she answered. The phone clicked, leaving her standing in silence with the phone still held to her ear. She hung it back up slowly. For the first time ever, his abrupt behavior didn't matter to her in the slightest. She had always been quiet, but that was not who she really was. She wasn't all that serious a person either. Studying and training were a whole different story, but life had grown dull and lonely there, always staying quiet and distant from others. Even if Alric had hung up on her, she still had clung to his words as he spoke.

"Why be something I am not?" she muttered. Wayland had said some interesting things. He might have been right. She was far more distracted by trying to block out her surroundings than she would be if she let people in. She'd try to change that. She'd make sure she didn't have regrets later. She could do both. She'd find her parents, but she would do it while surrounded by others. Finally, she turned to go up to her floor for the night.

Above on the third floor, Alric stormed back to his room. "I suppose your chat with Lady Genesis did not fare well then?" Kazumae called out of his doorway as he passed.

"Absolutely the worst! She's the worst and I hate—" He stopped.

Kazumae leaned against his doorway with his cup of tea in hand. "Hate is quite the strong word. For that matter, if you were to ask me, I'd answer that, based on my observation, the red in your cheeks does not look like anger to me," he remarked. Alric came at him, his hand bursting into flames, to which Kazumae reacted with a startled squeak, and shut his door with great swiftness.

"Of course, I am not blushing over *her*." Alric growled in Arshin under his breath. He clenched his teeth as he turned to his room. Her voice had been normal on the phone, and she sounded fine. So why, when he had been headed down to the medicine cabinet in the kitchen a few minutes before her call, had he seen her crying?

Chapter 31

Trio

ONE'S FIRST CRUSH... SUCH a painful experience—it usually goes nowhere. Except, of course, for the few lucky enough to succeed the first time around, which is truly impressive. Oh!—but I don't refer to Alric in this talk of first crushes. No...supposing he did indeed have a crush upon our dear Genesis, he is still far from ever admitting that even to himself. Who I speak of is none other than River. Although, keep in mind he is a bit younger than the rest of the class, and personally I think 13 is a bit young to dip one's foot in the dating pool. Although I do know there are some who will, those are just my personal thoughts on the matter.

Freecia, unaware of the false signals she gave off—River was merely the cute little genius boy in their class—held onto River's hand as they hurried to meet Zuri at the university's entertainment center. River's heart pounded faster now whenever she came close to him, and especially when she held onto his hand. Snow had started to fall gently around them, freezing as it gathered on the sidewalk, so River had to run cautiously beside her to avoid slipping. Even through her gloves, her hands felt so warm, partly because she was a fire user and naturally exuded heat.

He intended to express how his feelings for her had grown over the past couple months, but didn't know how to broach the subject. He had never asked a girl out before and hadn't liked a girl in that way either, for that matter. He knew his sister had the stance that such relations should wait until at least the age of 16, and he had agreed with her for a long while...but that was until he met Freecia... He couldn't help but be dazzled by her brightness and also her kindness toward him. He thought there just might be a chance that she felt the same way—she *was* holding his hand right now—but he wouldn't know for sure unless he tried to talk to her. It would be better to discuss now before they met up with Zuri...but—

"Zuri!" Freecia called, her hand releasing River's so suddenly that he nearly tripped. Too late—he had delayed too long and now he probably wouldn't get another chance that day. Zuri came up to meet them, clapping his bare hands together to break up the sheen of ice gathered on them. He was not at all pained by such cold weather; in fact, he rather enjoyed it.

"Man, how do you dress like that in this weather? You even have your sleeves rolled up and everything! It's so cold!" River lamented.

"Of course you're cold! You're just skin and bones!" Freecia declared.

"But aren't you cold? You're a fire user..." River murmured, reaching for his scarf as she nodded. His words wouldn't come out, but maybe he could show her how he felt by offering his scarf to keep her warm. She wasn't wearing one... The next moment her back turned to him so that she faced Zuri and River lost his nerve. How embarrassing would it be to wrap his scarf around her neck without a word?

"I'm very cold, but that doesn't mean I'm not ready to do some ice skating now that the ice rink is officially open!"

"I know, right? I'm so excited!!!" Zuri said.

"Then let's go in!" River suggested. The other two nodded in agreement and the three of them hastened in through the front doors of the entertainment center.

The entertainment center was a favorite hang out on campus. It had a lounge, a large gymnasium, a theater, an arcade, an outdoor swimming pool, and a roller skating rink that was currently covered over in ice to form the skating rink. The man seated at the front desk gave the three students a bright smile. "Here for the ice rink?"

"You bet!" River declared.

"Let me see...skates for Freecia Leo and River Deadlock..." He went into a bin beneath the desk and pulled out two pairs of skates. "Enjoy your time."

"Thank you very much, sir!" River turned to see Freecia already hurrying to catch up with Zuri. He took a deep breath, then quickly followed after them, anxious to not miss a moment of their new adventure together. You see, he had, in truth, never been ice skating before, but he supposed it to be very similar to roller skating, which he had mastered over the course of the semester. He was determined to look like he knew what he was doing.

"Do you like ice skating a lot?" Freecia asked Zuri as he tied up the laces of the ice skates he had brought with him.

"Very much! It is my favorite activity! I loved to skate out on the lakes back in Southern Country," he answered.

"Oh! I had heard you moved when you were very little."

"Yes, but the government would send us home every summer when it got too hot in the Shield Alliance. A lot of SSA guards would come with us to make sure none of us wandered away too far. We all loved it there, but most of the guards had a miserable time in all that snow." A sad expression crossed his face, and he shook his head. He glanced down at Freecia's untied skate laces. "Let me..." He knelt down on the floor in his skates, his fingers already at work tying her laces for her.

"Oh...you don't have to do that..." Freecia blushed as he lifted his pale eyes to her and gave her one of his innocent smiles that she had grown to love so much.

"No, it is my pleasure to serve." He stood as he finished, cutting his eyes briefly in River's direction and then hurried onto the ice. Freecia jumped up to follow him, leaving River to struggle with his laces alone.

When at last he finally got them tied, the other two were already gliding over the ice in smooth circles. Freecia's delighted laughter filled the air. Her laugh always brought such warmth to River, even in that cold room. He stood swiftly and took a step forward, but the strangeness of walking on blades made him fall over after his first step. He felt heat rise up in his cheeks and he lifted his eyes to ensure the others had not seen his stumble. He knew then and there that ice skating would not be a skill he could easily fake. Ice skating was most definitely *not* the same as roller skating.

He took hold of the bench behind him and hoisted himself off the ground to sit for a few moments and observe the way Zuri glided fearlessly over the ice. Freecia was not quite as skilled, but she had experience from ice skating on the lake behind the House a few times.

Zuri waved to River to coax him to join them. River nodded in response and finally pushed himself off the bench, taking the pace very slow as he crossed the carpet to the entrance into the rink. Once there, he paused again, white-knuckling the side rail and then stepped out onto the ice.

"Come on...I can do this...fake it," River muttered under his breath as he balanced himself on his skates. It took him a few seconds to find his center of gravity so that he could let go of the rail and drift forward a few inches. He watched Zuri's swift movements and tried to mimic them precisely. His biggest difficulty was maintaining balance and he fell on his first try to glide forward. I am sure all who have gone ice skating for the first time understand his struggles.

Upon seeing River fall, Freecia slid over to him and helped him back to his feet, holding onto his hand as he regained his center gravity. She had come to help him up. He felt embarrassed for falling, but still, she was holding his hand again.

River laughed nervously. "I guess I'm a bit rusty."

"You're standing on your own pretty well, though! Now all you gotta do is glide!" She skated backward away from him then turned forward to glide across the rink to Zuri.

"It's just like being weightless... Staying upright is difficult, but once I find that center, it *can* be done." He took a deep breath and made another attempt. After another stumble he finally found a rhythm and was able to glide ... I couldn't say it was with ease—each and every muscle in his body was clenched into the position where he found he had the most balance. He also tried to activate his valta to keep him from falling quite so hard when he did. He could not rely on his valta, though, because he wasn't good yet at adjusting the amount of valta he released at a time: he either started averting his gravity too much and lost touch with the ice, or he didn't avert his gravity at all and ended up falling ever so gloriously.

After a while, he noticed Freecia and Zuri gliding ahead of him close together. They spoke in low voices that he could not quite make out. Curious as to what they were talking about, River tried to speed up to skate with them, but in the process lost his balance again and fell hard onto his bottom. His body stiffened from the shock of the sudden fall, then Freecia was before him with her hand held out to help him again. She helped him back to his feet once more, a bright smile curling her lips upward as if something good had just happened.

"I must be going. It was nice skating with both of you!" she informed him.

"Oh...it was nice skating with you as well, Freecia..." he responded. She spun happily and then glided off toward the entrance to the ice. River looked after her for a while, his heart weary as she went. He had failed to tell her how he felt and now he wasn't sure when he would get another chance. If he knew what had really happened at the rink that day, I don't think he would have continued to skate with Zuri. All he knew was that Zuri's skating had suddenly slowed and lost its spark.

Chapter 32
Ally

ZURI AND RIVER TRUDGED back through the fallen leaves that same evening as the sun was just about to fade beyond the horizon. The flurry of snow had passed, so now the air was just cold. Zuri seemed distant and lost in his own thoughts as River talked about how much fun ice skating had been. He had truly enjoyed it by the end, despite how bruised he knew his behind to be. He really didn't have much cushion between his bones and the ice.

"So, yeah! I agree with you now! I think it *is* better than roller skating..." River paused.

"I wanted to discuss something with you, River... Since we're a trio... I think it's important..." Zuri's words came out with much hesitation.

"Of course, pal! What is it you wanted to say?" River asked with a grin.

They had just reached the dorm, so Zuri stopped for them to talk alone before entering the building. He stared down at the light dusting of snow on the sidewalk as he considered how to begin. River stood patiently in front of him, waiting until he was ready to speak. Finally, Zuri began hesitantly, "Listen... Today...at the ice rink..."

"It's okay, Zuri! Whatever it is, you can just say it..." River urged as Zuri continued to hesitate.

"Well... You see... Freecia asked me if I would be her boyfriend..."
The second the words had been said, River felt his heart dive into the pit

of his stomach, but he kept his composure and refused to let the dread and shock show on his face.

"Oh, really? I could see you two seemed pretty friendly today... Actually you're always pretty friendly and she's always excited to see you..."

"Yeah... That's what she said..."

"Well?" River prodded.

"Well... Honestly, I hadn't thought about dating anyone at all... It's just not something I've really thought over... Sure, I can say girls are attractive...like your sister..." he half jested.

"My sister is off limits!" River declared, trying to make a joke of the situation. Zuri didn't sound all that interested in Freecia, so maybe he had turned her down. Even so, that didn't change the fact that now River knew that Freecia liked Zuri, not him.

"Yeah... Well, even though I'm not all that interested... I said *yes*."

"You did?" River's heart sank again. Why would he...

"Yes, she's our dear friend after all, and we do get along nicely, so I thought I had no reason to reject her. Am I right?"

River hesitated for a long time. Zuri's question lingered between them in the cold air. "Yeah... I guess you are..."

"Well, since the three of us always hang out together, I thought I'd let you know. I don't want you to feel uncomfortable because you're my best friend first and foremost. So..."

"Of course it's fine, Zuri... If it will make the two of you happy, I'll cheer you on! You're both the closest friends I've ever had! So why wouldn't I be happy for you?"

"I see. I'm glad it's all right. That should take those lingering doubts from my head... Shall we go in?" Zuri turned toward the front porch.

"Actually... I'm going to go buy something for my sister real quick,"

River blurted, turning away from Zuri to face the empty sidewalk ahead of him. His heart was pounding so quickly and he could feel a large lump forming in his throat.

"Oh... Would you like me to come with you?" Zuri asked.

River didn't even turn around at the sound of his friend's words. He merely shook his head hard before he spoke, swallowing back the lump so that his voice would come out steady. "Oh no, no, I'll be fine on my own! It might take a while, so you just head in without me..." He paused, remembering he had just said he would be quick. He had panicked and contradicted himself, but he knew he just had to be alone for a moment so that he wouldn't take any of his anger out on Zuri. His sister had taught him that after a time he had upset a friend by lashing out at him when he was angry about something entirely different. She said that if he felt himself getting angry, he needed to either go and be alone or say nothing at all.

"Dinner is probably soon..." he continued, "I wouldn't want ya to miss it on my account!"

With those final words, River's footfalls faded quickly away through the crisp air. Zuri remained in the path watching as he went, his lips tightly drawn together. He wondered if he had made the right decision with regards to Freecia. "You're so bad at faking it, River... I know you like Freecia... I just don't know what else to do... I'm so sorry..." Zuri muttered.

The instant River was alone at last, he could not fake the smile any longer, and before he had time to get too much further away, tears started to pour down his face.

"I'm such a fool," River muttered under his breath, brushing the tears from his eyes as he slowed his walk. "I'm still the youngest in the class... What girl a year older than me would be interested in dating me? Plus, I'm so skinny and short..." He sank down on a bench and clutched his arms against the cold. "I shouldn't even be sulking... So smart that I got accepted into this school? Why does everyone think that but me? Maybe I read books, but I'm not smart... I only got accepted because they wanted my sister so badly...and because I could endure the awakening process..."

His shoulders slumped over as he clutched his head. He shook his head again and again, trying to wipe away the images of Zuri and Freecia skating ahead of him. She always had that bright expression on her face, but when she looked at Zuri, it got even brighter. How had he not noticed that until now? The evidence had been right there in front of him the whole time. He just didn't want to admit it to himself. He wanted to continue to dream that he had a chance with her, so he had ignored all the signs. "I'm a fool..." he muttered again, still shaking his head.

The crunch of the fall leaves startled him out of his despair. He lifted up his head to see the principal of the school, Mr. Johnathan T. Watts, approaching him. River had only seen him in school pictures up until that point, but in meeting his kind gaze River knew immediately who he was.

"P-principal..." River stammered, then remembered with great embarrassment that he had just been crying, and swiftly began to wipe the tears from his eyes. The principal held out a handkerchief without a word. "Th-thank y-you, sir..."

"No need to grow tense. Take your time to recover." He spoke with kindness as he took a seat beside River on the cold metal bench. River dried his eyes and blew his nose with the handkerchief. He'd recompose himself and pretend like nothing had happened. He was fine.

A long time passed as River tried to take his mind to better places. He gazed up at the few leaves that still clung to their branches, and at the occasional snowflakes that fluttered down from the sky. Some students passed on the sidewalk across the street, their laughter and light voices making River only sadder. That was how he, Freecia, and Zuri always interacted. His little crush aside, what would a relationship between Freecia and Zuri mean for their trio? Would things stay the same? Or would River be a perpetual third wheel? There he went thinking about the thing he was trying not to think about again, which only made the tears sting his eyes once more.

"Are you all right, River?" the principal finally asked.

River snapped out of his thoughts and he turned his head quickly toward the principal. "You know who I am?"

"Of course I do! I make sure to know all of my students by name!" The principal chuckled.

"I'm all right now... I guess I just needed a good cry..." River laughed it off.

"Is the school not to your liking? May I ask for a suggestion to improve your experience?"

"Oh! No, no, it's not the school at all! Your school is absolutely wonderful! I love it here! Actually, this is more related to social stuff! You see... I'm the youngest university student right now, so it can get tough at times! But when the new freshman class enters next year, there will be lots of kids my age, so that won't be a problem anymore!"

"I see..." River glanced over at the Principal's face. His eyes were filled with a strange distance that he couldn't help but notice. "How is your sister faring? Is she doing well?"

River's lips drew tight and he lowered his eyes. Everything was always about his sister. Everyone always asked him about her...the girl who had gotten in with a full scholarship...one of the most beautiful girls in their class...one of two shapeshifters attending the school...a girl naturally gifted with valta. Why was she so perfect? Why didn't anyone seem to care about how hard he was trying to prove himself? No matter what he did, he would always be in her shadow. They would always ask him about her, because she was so perfect in every way.

The smile upon the principal's lips faded as he sensed the stirring of negative emotions within the boy. "Forget all that. It was quite rude of me to bring her up when you have suffered from heartbreak... Believe me... I know it well myself..."

"How did you..."

"I am the principal of this school. Did you not know that the role of principal came with a built-in broken heart sensor?" The principal let out a hardy laugh, which made River smile at the man's joke. "In all seriousness, I am here to listen if you need an ear on such matters. I know adolescence is no easy time in one's life, and I want to make sure every single one of my students is well both in mind and body. Do you understand?"

"Yes, sir..." River broke off as a car pulled up in front of them. Dr. Cherith got out of the driver's seat, and made his way around the vehicle to open the car door for the principal.

The principal's gaze lifted and he heaved a sigh. "That seems to be my car... I must make a brief trip back to Arisha, but I will return shortly for the end-of-the-semester party." He grasped River's shoulder. "You can do this, River. The heart will heal... I know it can be difficult, but you are a strong. You endured the awakening process, did you not? So you will be able to endure this matter of the heart as well. Remember *I am your ally.*"

Chapter 33

Announcements

TWO WEEKS LATER, THE day of the end-of-the-semester party arrived. With all their first semester classes behind them, the students now looked forward to this festive event. The school seldom had celebrations of any sort, and so this was an occasion that even the upperclassmen got excited about—they served pizza for dinner, along with brownies for dessert, which they hadn't had for months! Dessert was rarely served in the dorms, although Zuri would sometimes bring Group A snow cream that he'd made during valta training. Otherwise, the school tried to keep them in shape through a healthy diet. Furthermore, there was dancing at the party and the opportunity to go with a date.

At the beginning of the evening, several students from Freshman Group A found a corner of the crowded party hall, and all of them, even Alric, stuck together for the rest of the night. Overall, students from Earth-side enjoyed the party far more than the other students. Arishian students tried to enjoy experiencing a small piece of Earth's culture, despite feeling the lights were too dim and the music too loud, but the House students were an entirely different matter. They had never experienced something like that before and were not used to being around so many in a closed, dark space.

Mae, on the other hand, was one of the few in Group A who would take off from time to time to converse with other students. She enjoyed the party because she loved positivity, and the atmosphere was more positive amidst all the Earth-side students who were enjoying themselves at the dance, unlike the students huddled in the corners of the room.

Kazumae also attempted to enjoy the party and danced with every girl who agreed to it. He had attended nice parties on Arisha before he had come to the school with Haise, and was quite good at socializing and making girls blush. He thought this type of party rather inelegant, however, and, with how Arishian the school tried to be on many matters, he would have expected them to have hosted a more traditional Arishian ball instead. The party planner was American, so I guess it only made sense that this was not the case.

Genesis found Alric's skittish behavior quite amusing, to say the least, and several times even teased him, until she realized he was actually developing a migraine from all the noise. After that, she searched for a gap in the crowd and swiftly ushered him out onto the back deck of the party hall where it was quiet. He seemed not in the least bit appreciative, though, but should that surprise us? Eventually, after he told her to leave him alone for the fifth time, she returned to the party hall to rejoin the others.

Genesis spent most of the party with the rest of the class, Ellie in particular. After her talk with Wayland, she had found it easiest to approach Ellie as she had been eating lunch with her every day since the beginning of the semester. She had trouble with the others at first. She felt it was too late in the year to have a total personality flip and still felt awkward going out of her way to talk or spend time with them. They all had their routines, but part of Ellie's routine was with Genesis, and so Genesis only had to start conversing more with her as they ate. Ellie had obviously told everyone that Genesis was becoming friendlier because soon other classmates began approaching her more frequently. She wasn't sure when she could consider herself friends with them, but she supposed that what she had right now was a start.

In the middle of the party, the students were directed into the auditorium for some short announcements from Principal Watts. The principal got up on the stage and strode across to the microphone set up for him. His son, Roland Watts, shadowed him, as he always seemed to do when not in class. I think the system of passing down the role of leadership through the Watts family very strange, like passing a crown down the generations of a royal bloodline, don't you think? But then, a lot of things the school did were strange.

"Good evening, students," Mister Watts said into the microphone. Cheering rang through the hall. "Congratulations on making it halfway through another year at Driscoll University, especially to all our freshmen who are here for the first time! I'm going to keep the announcements short so that we can get you back to the celebrations in the ballroom. We will continue the music and dancing until 9:00. That gives you all another two hours to have fun and an hour afterward before your curfew!"

"Oh gosh, I'm only halfway through this nightmare?" Alric muttered beside Genesis.

"You could head back to the dorms alone," she suggested. He shook his head violently and glared at her, as if she were suggesting him weak for needing to dip out early. She wouldn't have minded leaving early either. This kind of party really wasn't her thing.

"I've decided upon four students from each of the freshmen classes to help out at the House in the spring semester." All the students from the House tensed up in fear of being selected. "For those of you who don't know, we select students from the university that have not previously been called on and have them help out with the House kids who have not yet entered the university. Responsibilities include helping with the younger children, doing chores around the House for the House Ladies, and facilitating valta control. Without further ado, from Freshman Class 1: Group A... Alric Ashford and Genesis Deadlock. From Group B Reiss Gatlin..."

"Gosh, it keeps getting worse..." Alric muttered, his head falling into his hands as the principal spoke.

"... and Toseul Franks..."

Mae leaned over to Genesis and explained quietly, "Alric hates Reiss! Reiss tried to become his friend one time and Alric didn't like that. Reiss will try again with a lot of people, if they put up a fight about being his friend, but Alric is the one exception. Reiss will never try to be his friend again."

"Besides Genesis, they're all students from the House this year," Misteria observed, as the Principal continued to call off names from the other freshman groups.

"Why me? I freaking hate that blasted place," Alric grumbled.

"Well, you got picked," Misteria stated.

"And I'll have to see stupid Reiss all the time again."

"You already see him every day during class, silly Owl!" Mae chimed.

"At least I don't have to interact with him in class, but now I'll have to see him on the weekends, too!"

"I think seeing more of Toseul is far worse... She already comes to our dorm too frequently to see Hiero," Misteria murmured.

Genesis, on the other hand, was all right with being chosen. She felt she twiddled her thumbs far too much on the weekends anyway. She wondered about her language class on Saturday mornings. She struggled as it was in that class because she wasn't good at picking up languages. She sighed deeply. Maybe she didn't initially mind, but she still didn't like drastic changes to her routine. However, every semester would be different at Driscoll, so what had she expected?

"Another announcement is about graduation, which we will be going over next semester with the seniors. You will be given your badges at the graduation ceremony and then from there you will receive your first assignments as full-fledged agents. We will go into more details in your homeroom classes.

"Next up, we will soon begin freshman introductions to Arisha. During your introduction to Arisha, each class will spend one week in Ferris City in the country of Lyre—a beautiful city that our school has rejuvenated and that serves as a main base of operations for the Agency. You'll have to stay at the Agency's housing, so space will be a little tight. However, it will only be for one week, and I am sure you will spend very little time in your sleeping quarters, as some of you will be in another world for the first time! So for this year, Freshman Class 1 will be a week from now at the beginning of December, and Freshman Class 2 will be the last week before Christmas... Then, moving over to summer break: Freshman Class 3 in mid-June, Class 4 the last week in June, and Classes 5 and 6 consecutively the first two weeks in July. I know it's frustrating that some of the classes will have to wait so long, but, like I said, we only have so many available sleeping quarters for students. Moving on, the bus will be outside of Group A's dorm Monday the 9th, so make sure all of you in Class 1 are ready."

Haise lifted his hand to his mouth. He had gone very pale and his chest felt tight at the thought of returning again through the Gateway after all that time. Of course, he knew the time would come eventually, he had just hoped it wouldn't come so soon.

Kazumae had been watching his master as the details of the trip had been announced and he could see the emotion on his face. He rested his hand gently upon Haise's shoulder in hopes of easing his master's anxiety even the slightest.

"I was hoping for a nice winter out in the snow. Not a trip back home, and in Lyre of all places! The seasons are reversed from here, so it's going to be super hot," Zuri complained, his eyes cast down to the snowball he had been forming in his hands as the principal spoke.

"Don't be a downer! It's going to be fun! Also, it's only for a week! You'll have plenty of snow this winter when we get back! I'm excited about the holiday coming up—Christmas! The House helpers used to tell us younger kids how Earth students love that holiday! I want to celebrate it like Earth people do!" Mae said with great enthusiasm. At that point, the sophomores in front of them began to turn around in their seats to shush them, since the whole freshman class was being quite talkative in their excitement about the announcement. Chastened, they fell silent until dismissed from the auditorium.

After the closing of the party, Group A returned to their dorm together. In the end, Alric had waited on the back porch for everyone, because Kazumae told him he wasn't to leave. Not even Alric felt keen to go against Kazumae. Kazumae could act like a bossy older brother at times. Genesis really couldn't see why he had to stay if he wasn't enjoying himself.

"So I guess we should pack tomorrow?" River asked as they walked under the darkened night sky.

"We still have a week..." Genesis started to say, but Mae spoke overtop of her.

"Yeah! We should totally start packing! We're really going to go to Arisha in a few days!" she declared, hopping backward on the sidewalk ahead of them.

"I honestly can't believe we're going so soon," Genesis said to River. "We've learned about the place for the past four months but now we're actually going to go there. I feel like part of me still doesn't believe it's a real place yet."

Mae giggled. "I've been hearing about it my whole life, but have never gotten to go! It's crazy to think I finally will! I can't even imagine what it is going to be like! I saw the Gateway once on a field trip from the House... Oh, but Misteria has gone through a bunch of times! Haven't you?" She turned to Misteria who was in deep conversation with Haise.

"Yes, yes..." Misteria answered, a little disconcerted by the interruption.

"I guess this trip is no big deal for you because you always travel through the Gateway."

Zuri chipped in, "I wish I didn't have to go back, honestly... I think I'll take the extra classes so I can live in Mirrorick after completing my term as an agent."

"Then I'll go to Earth-side, too!" Freecia spoke up. The others looked at her as she made her presence known.

"I thought you were in Group B?" Misteria questioned.

"Yeah...but I wanted to walk back with my boyfriend," she said, squeezing Zuri's hand tighter.

"Oh! Really? You're dating?!" Mae said. She clapped her hands together in excitement, flowers springing up from various places in her hair.

"Yes! We have been for two weeks now!" Freecia announced. Dawn and Dusk exchanged secretive glances as their own relationship had been going on for an entire month now, little to anyone else's knowledge, although Genesis had suspected that to be the case. She glanced back as she saw River take off across the lawn away from the group. The tone of everyone's voices filled the air around her, but the words did not register in her mind as she watched her brother disappear into the night.

They arrived back at their dorm and many of them filtered into the lounge. Miss Nenna and Professor Glazunov had not yet returned from the event center, and so no one was there to remind them that it was almost curfew.

Genesis stopped as Alric sank down at the dining room table and thumped his head upon the table's smooth surface. She glanced ahead into the lounge then back at the door in hopes that River would reappear and put her mind at ease. But he did not, so she heaved a sigh and made her way toward Alric.

"Are you all right?" she asked, as she sat down beside him.

"I'm just swell. My whole second semester just fell apart, and my stupid head..." he groaned. She drew in a deep breath and reached out to rest her hand on the back of his head. He gave a start. "What are you—"

"Putting pressure on a person's head sometimes helps to relieve the pain a bit," she answered.

"I don't need that," he grumbled.

"Why not? If it makes you feel better..."

"Fine, if you really must." She smiled to herself and rested her head down on the table not far from him, her hand still resting on his head.

The door to the dorm suddenly opened and in came Principal Watts. "It's Daddy!" Mae exclaimed, as she ran back out of the lounge into the foyer to throw her arms around him. Genesis sat up to look back over her shoulder at the scene. She dropped her hand into her lap, her eyes drawn to River, who came in behind the principal and went straight upstairs without a word.

"Good evening! How have you been doing, my child?" the Principal asked as he patted her leaf-green hair.

"I've been great! I've missed you, though!" she beamed up at him. He released her as Misteria came from the kitchen toward them. Alric sat up, his eyes fixed on the principal as the man moved to embrace Misteria. Alric didn't move, his expression looked neither happy nor angry. The look didn't show jealousy either, but maybe something else indefinable. Genesis wasn't quite sure what it meant, but when the principal withdrew from Misteria he merely glanced in Alric's direction and then looked away again.

"You are like my own children. I've had you since birth, so it makes me so proud to see you grow and flourish in such beautiful ways. Has the rest of your group gone upstairs or into the lounge?"

"Yes, Daddy!" Mae beamed.

"Well then, pass this information onto them: Your group is truly exceeding my expectations... I'll be off now." He turned to leave but then stopped again. "Oh, and have fun in Arisha," he added with a glance over at Genesis. With that, he left as he had come.

"I don't doubt that he went to every dorm and said those very words to all the students: 'Your class 'tis truly exceeding my expectations... You're all like my very own children...'" Kazumae said from the doorway of the lounge.

"How can you assume something like that, Mister Kazumae!" Mae cried. "He certainly looked more tired than usual tonight, though..."

"I am going to bed," Kazumae announced as he departed from the lounge doorway. His footfalls seemed heavy over the floor. A few of the others could sense slight tremors through the ground with each step. They all thought it quite funny when Kazumae got even the slightest bit agitated and let his valta slip. He was so incredibly small to be shaking the room as he did.

"We'll ride halfway up with you!" Mae declared as she and Misteria followed him into the elevator room.

Alric and Genesis both remained seated after everyone left the room. She felt so weary. Something about the Principal had made her feel strange, but she could not decipher if the feeling was negative or not. He seemed a rather odd man. He had a sad air about him when she had seen him up on the stage, almost as if his smile was trying to hide something. But the way he had looked at Alric just now... She shouldn't assume anything. He probably had made no move to go over to him because Alric would not have wanted to be touched by him, or anyone else, for that matter. But couldn't he have at least acknowledged Alric? Mae had mentioned time and time again that all three of them had been there since they were babies.

Alric stood from the table just as Miss Nenna came in through the front door to enforce curfew. Genesis smiled and waved at her, before following Alric up the stairs.

"Are you feeling better?" Genesis asked after a moment.

"Just fine."

"That's good."

Alric's lips tightened and he stopped, spinning around to look down at her. "Why should you care?"

"Why should I..." she started to repeat. Then she remembered how the principal had not even greeted Alric, and her heart felt heavy in her chest. "Because we're friends, aren't we?"

"Friends?" he muttered.

"Yes... That's what we are. I know that is true, even if I haven't really had a friend before. You are my friend, and so I care about you," Genesis answered.

Alric turned his back to her, riffling his hand through his bright red hair. "We aren't friends."

"Why not?"

"Just because we aren't. I don't have friends. Now I'm going to bed." Alric continued up the stairs.

Genesis smiled to herself. Thinking back to that first morning, Alric the hothead was the last person in her class that she could have imagined being her friend. Now she knew that there really weren't any rules to how and when two people became friends. You just were and couldn't help it. And, if she thought about it, she was probably friends with everyone else in the class as well.

Chapter 34

The Gateway

A TWINGE OF ANXIETY and excitement filled the air as the students of Freshman Class 1 waited outside their dorms for the bus to arrive. The first week of their winter break had come and gone, which meant that after four months of attending school there, they were finally going to go through the Gateway and see the so-called world of Arisha. That was, if it really existed, which, I tell you the truth, some of the Earth-side students still had their doubts about.

As the time continued to pass, Zuri would occasionally sigh and fiddle with a wood necklace that he wore. Despite Freecia's constant reassurance that the trip was going to be fun, he did not show the least bit of excitement to return home. After a while, River couldn't take it any longer. Zuri's sighing became more and more irritating, especially as it seemed like he was doing it merely for attention. In addition, River could not stand hearing Freecia's sweet words of reassurance, nor could he stand his own thoughts about the couple in general. He hated how negative he had grown toward his best friend because of the whole situation. He wanted to still be friends with Zuri, and so he worked hard to completely diminish all traces of his crush on Freecia. He knew that once he did that, things could probably return to semi-normal with Zuri. Although...being a third wheel and having to listen to Freecia say some of the sappiest things to Zuri would have been annoying to anyone. With a nearly imperceptible shake of his head, River set aside his negative emotions and began to run laps around the dorm to burn off some of his excess energy. He thought it was good preparation for possibly sitting still on transportation vehicles for the rest of the morning—they had been warned that they would spend time on a bus, train, and in a small boat. With the force of his valta, the speed at which he ran was much greater than the average person, so about every five seconds the other students would feel a gentle swish of air as River dashed past them again and again...and again.

Meanwhile, Hiero was in the midst of his fifth self-aggrandizing story, all while he sat stroking his girlfriend's earth-brown hair, by the time the bus came around the corner and pulled to a stop in front of the dorm. Saying everyone was relieved to see it would be an understatement, for even the people who had blocked out Zuri's sighing, River's dashing, and Hiero's story-telling had gotten tired of waiting.

Usually such a situation would have been the perfect opportunity for Mae to cheer everyone up by asking them questions about themselves to pass the time. No one had realized until that moment how much Mae's mood could affect the entire group. Mae was currently in the dumps because the little flower garden she had planted on the porch the night before had withered by morning. One of the vegetation users from Group B tried to explain to her that it was because she had planted summer flowers that could not survive in the cold of winter and suggested she should look into some winter Arishian flowers so that she might plant some upon her return. The boy's words of comfort were of little use, as she pointed out that they were not supposed to plant Arishian flowers outside of their classroom due to rules against mixing the worlds.

Now that the bus had arrived, Professor Glazunov began to organize the students for the journey. "Okay, I'll have you all board the bus in the following order in groups of six. Please go to the first available seat at the back of the bus... Alric Ashford, Mae Driscoll, Misteria Remington, Kazumae Amana, Haise Immogen, and Genesis Deadlock..." He paused to give the first six students time to board and find their seats before calling out the next group.

Genesis climbed through the bus doors and up the steps behind Haise, who turned around to lend her a hand. "Thank you," she responded.

"And like that, there was romance!" Mae said, clapping her hands together. With Haise's one small gesture, Mae's fog seemed to have lifted, raising everyone else's spirits as well. If there was one thing the flowery girl liked more than flowers, it was the prospect of romance blooming between her classmates.

"I was helping her onto the bus, not proposing marriage," Haise answered quickly as he walked back to sit down in the first available seat next to Kazumae. Genesis was nice, but suggesting he could have romantic interest in someone when he had already given his heart to another, felt wrong to him. Who had he given his heart to? Well, I shall not unveil that quite yet, my dear reader. You should simply know that it was no one in their class, or at the school, for that matter. It actually might not even interest you all that much, now that I think about it.

The three true House students in Genesis's group took up the back row that seated three across. Alric looked out the window in irritation at being stuck next to Mae and Misteria for the whole ride, which, while short, was too long a length of time in his mind. Genesis took her seat across the aisle from Kazumae and Haise, sliding over by the window so she could look out while the next group was called to enter the bus. The bus driver was loading their luggage for the week into the side of the bus. She swallowed nervously and peered out to see who she would ride next to, which soon became clear as the last person she wanted to see came down the aisle toward her and plopped into the vacant seat with a sigh. Alric's head shot in his direction and he started to get up from his seat, but Mae and Misteria simultaneously grabbed him to hold him down. "No! Don't start a fight on the bus...please!" Mae pleaded. He sank back down with a sigh and crossed his arms over his chest.

Genesis felt a small zap at her shoulder as Hiero bumped against her. When she finally met his eyes, he gave her one of his most flirtatious smiles—I've mentioned he had a girlfriend, right? Yes, yes, keep that in mind. Genesis responded with an extremely brief smile in return. The view outside her window was far more appealing, so she turned to look out again, hoping he would catch the hint that she did not want to talk, or, for that matter, to listen to a sixth story about when he was famous. She felt extremely guilty for feeling that way as storytelling was his way of trying to make friends with everyone, but today was already off to a rather exhausting start.

After the other students had taken their seats, Professor Glazunov got onto the bus with a handful of the valta trainers, including Dr. Cherith, who waved to Genesis and Reiss as he sat down at the very front. The driver did a quick check to make sure he had everyone, before he closed the doors and started up the bus.

"We don't know how long this ride is going to be...so why don't we get to know each other a little better?" Hiero said as he leaned toward her. She pressed herself against the window and tried to ignore him. "Genesis, right?" he whispered into her ear.

"Please back off," she muttered. He drew back. "You're very pushy, Hiero. Last time I checked, you had a girlfriend, so I don't know what you're trying to gain here."

"Oh, Toseul? She doesn't care. Just because we're dating doesn't mean we can't flirt with other people. We aren't the over-possessive types.

Personally, I think you're the prettiest girl in our class." He snapped his fingers so that a spark of electricity would flutter before her eyes for a brief moment...at least that was what he had been picturing in his mind. Genesis did not turn around to see it, however.

"I doubt that. Misteria is far prettier, and I think Mae would be more your type with her figure."

"Nah, I've thought about both of them. Mae's too childish and so she just gets confused when I flirt with her. Misteria, on the other hand, is no fun—she's too uptight, and has no shape to her whatsoever. You have all three traits that I want: a nice figure, a pretty face, and a serious personality." He moved in close to her face again and breathed down her neck.

She let out a short laugh. "I still don't see what you're trying to gain here. You really are making me think far lower of you. Even if you were single, I wouldn't be interested. You're not my type, and I'm not going to date anyone until after I turn 16 anyway, even if I were interested. Also, I may seem serious to you, but that is not how I really am. I want to work hard, but I'm sure you'd see that I can be pretty silly once you get to know me. Now, I would appreciate it if you'd leave me alone. Maybe you should think more about your girlfriend's feelings, because I doubt she's really okay with this." She gave him a nudge away from her, but grossly underestimated her own strength. He had to catch himself on the back of the seat to keep from falling into the aisle.

"But I'm handsome, what woman *wouldn't* fall for me? Besides, don't you girls like it when a guy gets all up in your face all dominant-like? Toseul does..."

Genesis shook her head. "Not me. I don't care if you have a nice face. I have to fall in love with a person before I would consider dating them, and while I don't dislike you, I also don't love you either. Getting all up in my face and flirting with me while you are currently in a relationship, is *not* the way to do it."

The others looked in their direction, stifled giggles coming from various places in the bus. Everyone had heard the whole exchange as clear as day due to the silence that had descended on the bus after everyone had settled into their seats. That included, Toseul—Hiero's girlfriend—who now sat glaring back at him with her arms crossed over her chest. Genesis kept her head turned away from Hiero and continued to gaze out the window as they drove through campus. Either Genesis's firm words or Toseul's obvious displeasure had worked, for he did not attempt to speak to Genesis again during the bus ride, not even to tell her a story. Hiero was not happy in the least. He sank down low in his seat in embarrassment at being treated like that in front of everyone. Toseul seriously didn't usually care, he had seen her flirting with guys on many occasions. He knew she was simply acting that way because everyone was watching. I feel I must say that I do not agree with such behavior. I would leave out such details entirely if I were not trying to convey the characters of these individuals.

They drove through the gates of campus and down a steep gravel road for about five minutes. The bus came to a stop by the docking area that Genesis and River had seen when they arrived at the school months earlier. I fear it has been so long now that you might not remember, but that is all right! The dock extended over the water, as the stream was wider and calmer here than downstream closer to the Gateway. Along the dock, many small boats were tethered, bobbing ever so slightly up and down with the movements of the water. The teachers and bus driver got right to work loading one of the boats with all of the luggage, while the students were instructed to stay in their seats until they were called. Only one of the teachers embarked on this first boat, starting away downstream alone.

"Okay. We'll have the first six students from earlier come down to the boat now. That's Alric Ashford, Mae Driscoll, Misteria Remington, Kazumae Amana, Haise Immogen, and Genesis Deadlock," Professor Glazunov instructed from the front of the bus. The six students moved to get up. Genesis practically had to climb over Hiero to get out of her seat because he refused to budge from his place.

Genesis finally jumped down off the bus onto the rocky path, which crunched beneath her feet. She had to move swiftly to follow the five House students who had gone on ahead of her. They were directed toward a boat, which held Dr. Cherith and a woman—the fire instructor, Venessa Alex, or Professor Alex, as she was called by most of her students. Professor Alex had bright red, curly hair and a dark complexion like that of hazelnuts. The lively air around her was like the bright blaze of a fire, but she rarely got truly angry. She was firm, though, so perhaps that is why most who knew her had the utmost respect for her.

Dr. Cherith reached out to help each one of them into the boat to take their seats. Genesis was seated beside Alric, facing Professor Alex, who smiled very kindly at the young girl. She had a soft, gentle smile, a thing Genesis had not expected from the fire instructor. She had assumed that the fire instructor would be short-tempered and mean. She had only heard about her from Alric, and he only really ever complained about people. Professor Alex was actually quite warm and friendly.

"Is this the shapeshifter girl you work out with, Alric?" she teased.

"Yeah, so what?" Alric grumbled.

"She's just so pretty and delicate. I always imagined you would be more into the tough, beefy ones."

"What are you saying?!" Alric questioned in a defensive manner.

"Now, now, what did I say about using that temper with me?" she cautioned good-naturedly.

"Well, you're getting the wrong idea, Venessa! She may not look beefy but her muscles are hiding somewhere!"

Professor Alex stifled a laugh and shook her head. "Now, now, at least a Professor or Miss before my name would be nice!"

"We'll start off now," Dr. Cherith said as he got back into the boat and took hold of the tiller. Professor Alex grinned at Alric and winked. In return, Alric gave her the stink eye, furrowing his brow at her.

The rest of the students and teachers loaded into the other boats. Dr. Cherith steered the boat away from the shore and out into more open waters so that their boat drifted along down the river with the current. The ride was rather peaceful along that stretch, with the overhanging trees that dipped their branches into the swift-flowing water, and the chill breeze as winter approached. Mae kept her hand down in the water, talking about how she hoped a fish would come up and nibble her fingers. Misteria responded that all she would get was frostbite.

Soon the mouth of a cave came into view ahead of them. Mae clapped her hands together in excitement, while Haise, Alric, and Genesis all began to feel a little uneasy. What awaited them in the dark reaches of that cave? Haise knew, and that was why he felt apprehensive.

A lantern fixed to the bow of the boat, automatically flickered on to light the dark waters ahead of them. The little light was only enough to light their way, the rest of the cave was still shrouded in darkness. Professor Alex looked at Alric. "Why don't you give us some light? We won't reach the Gateway immediately," she suggested. Alric lifted his hand and flames flickered from it. "Good, nice and gentle, that's what we have been working on." Alric scoffed and turned his head away from the lot of them.

The boat glided along in the gentle glow of the lantern and Alric's flames. The current wasn't as rapid in the cave and he knew the waters well, so Dr. Cherith was able to steer the vessel with ease through the water, even in the dim light. Despite that, Genesis felt strange sensations run through her entire body, sensations that she really didn't like in the least; a feeling of dread descended over her, which made her want to jump out of the boat and return to the school. She couldn't shake it no matter how hard she tried to focus her mind on anything else. As they drew further and further into the cave, the sensation only increased until she felt she could not stay still in her seat. She clutched the edge of the wood panel she sat upon so hard that her knuckles whitened.

"There haven't been any Sirus in the caves lately, right?" Professor Alex asked Dr. Cherith. Genesis focused on the professor's words to keep her mind off of her rapidly rising panic. Dr. Cherith just shrugged in response. "Easy for you to just brush it off! This boat is half full of women!"

"I don't think Principal Watts would let us make the journey today if there had been any recent sightings. Sirus tend not to attack if there are too many men present, and besides, part of the reason we have agents stationed around the Gateway is to make sure to keep Arishian creatures like Sirus out. They typically stay out of colder waters, so they don't usually venture through the Gateway when it's winter in Driscoll. I know people treat them like animals, but they are intelligent enough to know that," he answered her.

Misteria stared off into the darkness as they spoke. She didn't much like the current subject of conversation. While no one in the class knew at that time, Misteria was actually half Sirus, a race of vicious merfolk. Unlike merfolk or sirens, Sirus are mostly male, and only return home once a year to where their women dwell, in either a place called Merbrook or Sirus Cove. Merbrook was a huge gulf to the west in Arisha, while Sirus

Cove was a small outlet in Lyre. Sirus are forbidden from forming bonds with humans, as humans are seen only as a source of food. Misteria's mother did research for a long while on the Sirus, and during that time she formed a bond with a Sirus. A bond that led to him being devoured by his own kind.

Professor Alex nodded to Alric, "Best to put that out now. As we near the Gateway your valta power will spike and you might have trouble controlling it after that," she said. He let his flames flicker out, but the cave wasn't nearly as dark as it had been earlier. In fact, a dim light now filled the cave. The three who had not been to Arisha went on high alert as they presumed that they drew near to the Gateway. Genesis could feel an intensity of valta in the air—the strongest valta presence she had ever felt. Kazumae smiled to himself as he awaited their reactions to the Gateway itself.

The river grew narrower and bent around a mass of rock. Genesis's chest started to throb and her hands shook. She wondered if everyone experienced the same thing at the same time, and, more than that, she wondered if the Gateway was really safe if it made her feel that way just by being near it. She was, in fact, the only one in the boat that felt that way, however.

Alric noticed her shaking body and clenched hands. Was she scared? But she had never shown fear that strongly, not even when he threatened her during their duels. Truthfully, her lack of fear was an inspiration to him, so her fear now made him feel a bit afraid as well, even though he had not felt that way previously.

Dr. Cherith guided the boat around the bend, and, as they rounded the corner, they all held their breath in awe. A bright light filled the chamber. An aura so dark and so light at the same time. A tear in the fabric of our worlds. A wide open doorway of light and darkness stood right before them to block the path, pulsing, as it painted strange light on the walls, ceiling, and water of the chamber. The boat headed straight for it. Even Alric had awe in his eyes as they drew closer and closer to the vortex of the Gateway to Arisha.

Genesis's whole body trembled all the more as the boat drew closer and closer to the vortex. The nose of the boat disappeared into it, first Kazumae and Haise, then Misteria and Mae. Genesis's levels of fear welled up to their peak and she reached out to take hold of Alric's hand as the Gateway consumed her. She shut her eyes but in that instance she felt power surge through her entire body. Her eyes were forced open and she was surrounded by a blinding light. The power was so intense she thought her body would be torn apart. Voices filled her head—voices calling her name. She could hear River, Zuri, Mae, Kazumae, Reiss, her mother, her father, and so many others that she did not yet recognize. She hadn't seen her parents in so long, but she knew their voices anywhere. She distinguished a particular voice above the others. Was it Alric's? No, it didn't sound angry enough to be his. The words reached her ears in broken sentences, ringing through the air in a wispy, dreamlike way.

"What I wanted to say, Genesis...give me a third chance...please...come back... Let me pull you out of there again..."

Then she was thrust into an open void, but not like the void during her awakening, which had been so dark and black. This void was the stark opposite—light and white. A woman with long, rippling, navy hair that cascaded down to her feet, rose up from the ground, her body bent and her lips moving as she murmured. She turned, her head twisted to one side like some kind of undead creature, and blood seemed to spill from a wound in her stomach, but also it did not flow at all, as if she was stuck in a state unchanging, never aging, never dying from her wounds.

"Genesis, Genesis," the woman said through her murmurings, and like a flash of light she was upon her. "Save me," she hissed. Her eyes wild as she clutched at Genesis's throat. "I'm trapped here in the Gateway! You have to let me out!" The fear rose in Genesis's chest making her want to scream. But no scream would escape her lips. Then she realized she could still feel Alric's hand even though she knew she was alone in that void with the disturbed woman. She tightened her grip on it and was suddenly jerked away from the woman. The coldness pulled away from her in an instant and she fell out through the Gateway into the water. Still she held fast to Alric's hand, and, in a moment, he yanked her up out of the water and back into the boat.

Chapter 35

Arisha

"ARE YOU ALL RIGHT?" Dr. Cherith asked as he bent over Genesis. She lay in the bottom of the boat, her clothes now soaked through. Her whole body felt as if it had been wrung out and dragged through the mud. She couldn't move for a while afterwards.

"It's going to be okay, Genesis; try to take some deep breaths," Professor Alex soothed. She pulled a dry cloak over her. Genesis gasped for breath—it took several minutes before she could breathe with ease again. Fortunately, unlike the air they had just come from, the air on this side of the Gateway was warm, like that of summer.

"I have gone through the Gateway with many people, and never have I seen anyone get stuck in the vortex like that..." Dr. Cherith observed. "It was truly a sight. If Alric hadn't been holding onto your hand, I'm not sure how we would have gotten you out again."

"Oh, Alric, I didn't think you would need to hold a girl's hand your first time through the Gateway!" Professor Alex teased him. She partly did so to lighten the mood in the boat, for it had grown very tense. Alric did not respond, much to the professor's surprise.

"Gen-gen, are you okay?" Mae said as she bent over Genesis. Genesis gave her a confused look—she thought she might be hallucinating, for she was sure that Mae had just addressed her by the nickname only River called her.

Genesis finally caught her breath. "I think I'll be okay in a moment, once we get further from the Gateway," she responded weakly. Mae nodded with concern apparent on her face. Dr. Cherith's eyes had remained fixed upon Genesis since she had emerged from the Gateway. Perhaps out of apprehension or perhaps in wonder.

"Let us drop the issue for now," Professor Alex said. "Everything is all right. We will just need to keep a close eye on her next time she travels through the Gateway. I'll report the incident to the higher-ups once we get to Ferris City."

"Don't worry about it and enjoy your vacation from work. I'll get it all taken care of myself," Dr. Cherith told her.

Carefully, Genesis ventured to sit up and observe her surroundings for the first time. She found that they were in a ravine with cliffs on either side. The river passed between them out from the Gateway, which appeared just as it did on the other side, painting its dark lightness on the cliffs. At first glance, the greatest notable difference from Earth was the deep gray color of the nearly cloudless sky. The few clouds they could see were black like puffs of smoke. The scenery proved just as bleak as Zuri had made it out to be, but it did not really look that much different from Earth otherwise. Those who had never been there before were quite perplexed: were they really in another world? The idea was still quite hard for them to wrap their minds around, even now as they dwelt in the very world that they had learned about over the past few months, or, for Alric and Mae, their entire lives.

Another boat came through the Gateway with River, Zuri, Hiero, Dawn, Dusk, and Ellie. Upon seeing the first boat stopped in the middle of the river, a teacher called out to them as they glided past. "Is everything all right?"

"Yes, I think we are okay. Miss Deadlock had a scare, but I think everything is fine now," Dr. Cherith informed them.

Haise looked down, his stomach turning as Kazumae held onto his arm. His senses were reeling as the distinct scent of the Arishian air hit his nostrils. Many memories that he had wished to forget suddenly came rushing back into his mind. Kazumae knew that must be the case and so he held onto his master tightly.

"Is my sister okay?!" River called out.

"She's fine now; it was only a strange occurrence," Dr. Cherith called back.

The next boat now came through with Wayland, Grisham, and the first of those from Group B, along with a few more of the teachers. "Let's go. We need to keep moving. We only have a little further downstream until we reach the base, and then we have the train ride into the city," Professor Alex said.

Dr. Cherith nodded as she spoke. He looked over at the others in the boat and took notice of how pale Haise looked. "Are you feeling all right, Haise?" he asked. While Haise was always very pale, his lips weren't usually so white, and his expression wasn't usually so sickened. Even so, Haise nodded as he did not want to make a big issue out of his ill feelings. "Just a little motion sick?" Haise hesitated, then nodded again. Satisfied, Dr. Cherith moved the boat to follow the others downstream.

They traveled out of the ravine, and were soon surrounded by thick black-leaved trees on both shores. The world seemed starkly black and white except for the sharp contrast of some red flowers gathered amongst the gray blades of grass. The scent that they exuded was like none on Earth: a bit sweet, but not entirely pleasant.

They passed under a round stone archway—something built by Arishians who worshiped the Gateway—and then a structure built over the river came into view. The boats drifted into an opening, one after the other, entering into a chamber with many other boats docked within.

Some young agents helped the students out of the boats and onto the docks. Genesis's body still trembled from her passage through the Gateway, so she needed extra assistance in order to join her classmates.

Kazumae drew in closer to Haise not far from her. "'Tis all right, Sire. Your grandfather shall never go near a city run by Driscoll, such as Ferris City. You have no reason at all to have fright over the situation," Kazumae whispered. Haise nodded, then paused as he contemplated asking a question that lingered in his mind. Kazumae saw the expression and grabbed his master's arm with a look of inquiry in his eyes.

"While we're here...may I...may I see her?" Haise whispered.

"Her?"

"Seripha..."

Kazumae grew silent. He had asked, but knew all along of whom he spoke. "I already fear enough with the exchanging of letters between thee that our location shall be compromised. I am quite sorry, but 'tis not possible for you to meet her just yet." He lifted his head to smile up at his master. "Eventually I shall make it happen. I promise, Sire."

"Thank you, Mister Kazumae..." Haise's voice faded, as the others came up the dock toward them.

"Let us speak no more on this matter." Haise nodded in agreement.

The others stood in a cluster on the docks and waited for those in charge to tell them what to do next. None of them spoke as they took in their surroundings, although the room they were now in provided little to see, just many boats like the ones they had come in and a few doorways leading out. The walls and floor were all the same boring iron gray stone. Eventually, as they all lost interest, they grew aware of how much stronger their valta felt on this side of the Gateway. River might have started running laps around the room if he had not felt uncertain about their current situation. Mae couldn't help but grow some flowers on her arm as she felt ill at ease letting her valta lie still.

A woman in the Agency's uniform approached them. "Second year Agent Bertha here, would you all please follow me?" She smiled as she saw the wonder on their faces. "You've noticed! The surge in valta is not just because you are in Arisha where valta is widespread. You'll feel the same way when you first go back to Earth. Passing through a portal constructed of valta energizes your own valta," she explained. When she received no immediate reaction from any of them, she turned and strode swiftly up the steps that led off the docks. The students looked at one another in consternation and followed her lead.

They first stopped in a break room where their luggage was brought to them. The journey wasn't supposed to be too much longer, but they all took the opportunity to make use of the bathrooms. Genesis was also able to change into some dry clothes, much to her relief. After they had all finished up, Agent Bertha led them up a long, sloping hallway and through some glass doors that opened up onto a train platform. There, in the station, awaited a train to take them on to their final destination. The agent stepped aside.

"What order are we supposed to sit in?" Mae asked quickly.

"It doesn't matter, just get on," Agent Bertha urged.

"It wasn't like that before..."

"It's fine, Mae," Misteria muttered and pushed her onto the train ahead of her.

Genesis got on last and found everyone already in their seats in pairs. River sat beside Reiss because Zuri and Freecia had sat together leaving River out. His sister's heart clenched at first, but seeing Reiss smiling at him and talking to him in a gentle voice eased her concern a bit. She would have liked to sit next to him herself, even though his energy earlier that day had been a bit much for her. He seemed somehow off in recent days, and that worried her, especially when his best friend had just started going out with someone.

Alric sat by himself at the back of the train car. The two likely scenarios were that either everyone had avoided sitting beside him, which was the most likely scenario, or he had told everyone he didn't want them to sit next to him, which was also very probable. Genesis decided to sit down beside him, and, since he didn't say anything to her, she assumed her presence to be acceptable. He did not speak, however, as he continued to stare out the window at the gray landscape that stretched on for miles away from the train.

She leaned over him to look out the window herself. "It's so gray... Do you think a storm is coming...or is it always like this?" she questioned.

"How should I know?" he muttered.

She shrugged her shoulders. "You're from the House, so I always assume you are more knowledgeable about these kinds of things." He didn't answer, so she sank back in her seat again to wait for their journey to continue.

The train's engine started up after several minutes had passed; it was so loud that the voices of their classmates sounded muffled and indistinguishable, like on an airplane. The air felt heavy around her as if she had been closed in a bubble that contained only Alric and her.

Alric glanced surreptitiously at her as she stared at her brother several rows ahead of them. A strand of her hair had come loose from the braid she wore and lay ever so delicately upon her face. His eyes wandered down to where her hand rested on the seat between them and he clenched his jaw as he remembered passing through the Gateway. His natural reaction was to be angry, but at the same time he was confused. When Genesis had gotten stuck, the boat had continued to move forward with the river yet his hand remained inside the Gateway with her, nearly pulling him out of the boat. Before they passed through, he had felt so angry when she grabbed his hand. But, on the other side, he was filled with dread.

"About what happened earlier... Why did you grab my hand?" Alric suddenly asked. He lifted his gaze up from her hand to see her scarlet eyes fixed on him. Her emotions didn't betray her. He couldn't tell at all what she was thinking. "Just forget about it." He looked back out the window and tried to forget her stupid face.

"What?" she prodded, a mischievous grin creeping over her lips. "Are you blushing, Alric?"

"You think I would blush over a girl touching my hand? You obviously don't know me well even after all these months," he answered, his face growing hot with anger. Why did she have to tease him like that? It was so infuriating! She laughed, but he continued to ignore her antics. She soon stopped and only then did he glance over at her again.

Her face was pensive as she stared down into her lap. "I was just scared, for no apparent reason..." she started. "You were sitting next to me...and...I thought I would feel safer if I grabbed your hand. I'm glad I did, because for a moment there I just wanted out of that place in the Gateway and I wasn't sure how to get out... Then I felt your hand and the next thing I knew...you pulled me out..." She turned her gaze back toward him and met his eyes. "You did that... I know you did... Because all I did was tighten my grasp..."

"You're probably just reading into things. No way would I have pulled you out. I'd have let go if I could have, then I would have finally won a duel..." A smile broke over Genesis's lips and she burst into another fit of laughter. Alric turned his head away to conceal his own smile. "Cut it out, Shapeshifty!" He tried to keep his irritated tone, but Genesis could hear the hint of laughter behind his words.

Chapter 36
The Train

THE VIBRATIONS OF THE train kept Alric awake. His eyes felt heavy from his sleepless night, but even though Genesis dozed beside him, he could not do the same. Meanwhile, the train continued on through the gray Arishian countryside. Almost an hour had passed before Genesis opened her eyes and glanced over at Alric, who continued to gaze out the window with nothing else to do.

"I thought we were going to Driscoll's main base of operations. So why does it seem so far from the Gateway?" Genesis asked.

Her voice sounded muffled beneath the loud train engine, so at first he didn't move. When his brain finally registered that she was talking to him, he withdrew his gaze from the outside to glare at her. "Are you asking me?"

"You're the only one here to ask."

He sighed. "Two reasons. One, not many train tracks can be built through the forests in this region, because the forest floor is a twisted mess of tree roots that grow over the tunnels of a certain race of small elvish folk. I don't know much about them, so don't ask. The second reason is because most Arishians don't know the exact location of the Gateway. The school wants to keep it that way, because there are some people who oppose us for some reason. They don't want to advertise the Gateway's location by having our main base right by it. That's why they just have a small docking facility on the river, and even that isn't right next to the Gateway. I know one of the school's next big projects will be to build a facility around the Gateway, since some Arishian countries are getting more advanced and will probably have aircraft that can perform aerial searches. That could be a problem, but building a facility around the Gateway is not going to be easy."

"I guess that makes sense..." Genesis said.

"For most of my childhood all I could do was read books, so I learned a lot about Arisha. Now, I enjoy looking out of the window in silence..."

"But there isn't anything to do on this train. How interesting can the gray countryside be? Let's have a conversation." She smiled at him as she tucked her hair behind her ear.

"That's what we're having right now, and I am *not* enjoying it," he answered.

She laughed briefly and lifted her eyes to the ceiling, thinking of what to say next. She knew she would have to work pretty hard to carry the conversation if she was going to make it happen. "We hang out after dinner, don't we? Why don't we talk more?"

"We duel and work out. That is not hanging out after dinner. That is war." She sighed and let her head sink back against the headrest. "We are not friends," Alric clarified.

"Fine, if that's what you say... I just want someone to talk to until we get off this train."

"Well, I don't feel the same way."

"All right. Again, whatever you say, Mister Ashford."

"Gosh! It's always something new with you! *Mister* Ashford? You're making me sound like an old man! Can't you just call me Alric?" Part of him was angry, but the other part of him kind of liked the way she teased him. She had been particularly bold in approaching and talking to him as of late, ever since that night she had called him on the dorm phone.

He still wondered why she had been crying alone in the foyer.

"So I may drop the formalities then?" she asked.

"What are you getting on about? You've always called me Alric in the past. Also, just because I said it was all right does not make us friends. I don't need friends because I can do everything by myself."

"I used to agree with you about that...but I'm starting to wonder if I was wrong. Why not try our hand at friendship? The two of us haven't really had friends before, so maybe we should be each other's first... See what happens..."

"Sure, that totally sounds like a great idea," he uttered sarcastically

"Well, I guess I don't expect you to just say 'cool' and we are instantly friends, but I'm just going to secretly hope you make a friend with someone and that that friend flips your world upside down, even if that friend isn't me."

"Keep living on in that fantasy world of yours. I won't ever let any woman seduce me, so you better not be trying to—"

"I'm not trying to seduce you! I'm just trying to befriend you. There is definitely a difference! Although I'd love to see what happens when you fall head over heels in love with a girl... Mister. Ashford." He glared back at her, but the smile did not waver from her lips. Who was this girl? Was she really the same withdrawn one from the start of the year? There was no way someone could change that much, right?

All at once the train came to a very short, hard stop. The students gasped as they were flung forward in their seats. Naturally all conversations ceased and the students began to look about, wondering if they had arrived. Of course, if they really had arrived, wouldn't they have stopped more gradually at the station?

"We apologize for the sudden stop. Please remain seated while the issue is resolved. We will be in Ferris City shortly," the announcer said through the speaker. Everyone settled back in their seats, too confused to speak. The engine cut out and a deafening silence fell over the car. After so long with the continuous white noise of the engine, the quiet felt almost unbearable.

Then, almost as quickly as it had descended, the silence was broken by a loud crash that shook the entire train. There were loud gasps about the room, followed by the rustling of the leather seats as everyone leaned toward the window closest to them to look out.

"There! I see something outside!" Mae cried. In the next instant, those on the left side of the train all had leapt from their seats and crowded over by the right windows to see what was happening outside the train.

A huge animal-like creature raced past the windows, causing the students to draw back again in horror. Genesis, however, still leaned over Alric to look out as the animal rammed itself into the side of one of the cars again, shaking the entire train with its force. Atop the creature sat a rider covered from head to foot in black armor. Genesis watched the rider pull on the reins to bring the animal around close to the edges of the nearby forest, before going back in for another charge. Then, several others appeared, racing down a nearby hill and shattering windows with their beasts' large horns.

"We should get back..." Alric said, taking hold of Genesis's shoulder.

"Mister Kazumae! Get down!" Haise shouted at Kazumae as he attempted to open the window. "You'll get hurt!"

"I shan't just sit here and let our manner of transport be destroyed! Someone shall be seriously hurt!" Kazumae declared as he threw open the window.

"Those animals will crush you in a second!"

"Have you no faith in yours truly? I lived in this very world for seven years of my life. Do you think I know not how to handle myself? Do you think me an inexperienced guard with no means to protect who I must?" Kazumae inquired of his master. Haise reached out to try and grab him, but Kazumae had already jumped out the window.

The beast charged at him. Those within the train assumed that he would use his valta to counter the attack, but he didn't. He continued on toward the beast and rider, running as fast as his small legs could carry him. Truly, none of them thought that someone so small could cover such a distance in only a matter of seconds. The closer he got to the large beast the more tense his classmates became. They were all certain that they were about to watch the beast trample little Kazumae, yet they also felt too afraid to look away from the scene. I assure you even Hiero wanted to cover his eyes, although I am also sure he thought the scene would make a good story for later.

At the last second, Kazumae leapt from the ground, so that where he had stood cracked with the force of his valta. He scaled over top of the creature and its rider with ease at a height that seemed unnatural for anyone, but especially someone so small. The rider reached up as if to grab him, but Kazumae caught the corner of the rider's helmet and yanked it off. The rider's head was thrown back with great force and only for a brief moment could they see her elegant elvish face. The beast spun around and charged into the trees as three other riders came at Kazumae. He remained crouched motionless on the ground watching the riders advance.

"Kazumae..." Haise muttered.

Large rocks and earth ripped from the ground around Kazumae and seemingly hurled themselves into the faces of the charging beasts. In an instant, Kazumae had darted behind them while they were still blinded by the dust and jumped on the back of one of the riders, grabbing his throat and flinging him to the ground. He took hold of the reins and crashed the creature into the other two. One of the men grabbed Kazumae by the collar and yanked him off the animal. At that same moment, Haise jumped out the window and bit violently into his own arm with his sharp fangs. His blood solidified into a bar, almost like a spear, and he raced after the rider who still held Kazumae. Meanwhile, Kazumae drew a knife out of his cloak and thrust it between the plates of armor into his captor's chest. As the rider fell, rolling to the ground under the beast's feet, the small Arishian somersaulted through the air to land elegantly on his feet in the black grass.

The last remaining beast now raced toward Haise at full speed. Haise stopped, and it was at that moment that Kazumae caught sight of him outside the train. His eyes grew wide with horror, as the absolute worst that could happen sprang into his mind.

"Haise!!!" Kazumae shouted.

The other rider used Kazumae's distraction to draw a bow. His valta ignited the end of his arrow and he aimed for Kazumae, all while still plunging on toward Haise. Haise moved swiftly, tossing the spear so that it pierced the soldier between the plates of armor covering his elbow. The arrow went wild as his arm became stiff and immobile; Haise had activated his blood art to solidify the blood running through the rider's veins. Kazumae's beast collided with the rider's and he jumped from the animal, leaping onto Haise to protect him. Dust flung up around them, clouding the vision of those who still dared to watch through the windows of the train.

Another rider appeared at the top of one of the hills not far from the scene. This one wore white armor, rather than the black of the others. He held a flute to his lips and a melodic trill pierced the air. At the sound of those notes, the riderless beasts seemed to fall under a spell.

The ones on the ground stood up, and the ones galloping about slowed. They moved to where their riders lay on the ground, at least one or two probably dead. Another trill sounded and the beasts responded by opening their mouths wider than anyone thought possible, and lifted their riders' bodies gently in their jaws. The white rider played a third trill, and then yanked on the reins of his beast to return to the forest. The other beasts quickly hurried after, and then they were gone, leaving behind only their destruction as evidence that they had been there.

By that time, the dust had cleared away outside the train. Haise stood and held out his hand to help Kazumae up. Kazumae did not immediately accept his master's hand, however, as his mind seemed to be elsewhere. He looked calm as he gazed out at the vast Arishian landscape. He had protected his master, and now it had fully set in that he was back home in his own world, a world that he actually loved quite fondly.

Chapter 37

River

DURING THE COMMOTION OUTSIDE of the train, River flung himself away from the window and gagged, almost vomiting from the gruesome sight they had all just witnessed, but he managed to keep it down. Most of them felt similarly ill, so they couldn't blame him for this reaction. At that time, Reiss withdrew from the window as well and put his arms gently around River's shaking shoulders. Reiss was numbed to such sights; he was used to the sight of blood. Most of the rest of them hadn't imagined they would witness such brutality, at least those who were not from Arisha... They had only been in this world for a few hours, and already such sights awaited them?

After the battle was over, Mae crouched down beside River. "Are you all right?" she asked. River now lay curled up on his seat in the fetal position, his head on Reiss's lap.

"That was awful! I've never seen so much blood!" he cried.

"It's going to be all right, River. Haise and Kazumae are fine," Misteria reassured him.

"Those knights aren't okay, though! How can I see Kazumae the same way if he can do that to people?"

"It's okay, River! He wouldn't do that to *you*!" Mae tried to assure him. But River shivered, his hands clasped to his head.

"Is everyone okay?" Agent Bertha asked as she entered the train car. When her eyes encountered River whimpering in the fetal position on his seat, her expression changed and she decided this was not her area of expertise. "Let me get Mister Glazunov..." she mumbled and exited the car quickly.

A long time passed before the train was ready to move again. Several teachers had emerged to collect Kazumae and Haise but they had not been allowed to return to their classmates. All the remaining students sat whispering with each other. The air felt dense, like a cloud, and not even Mae felt right speaking loudly. Many actually gathered around Hiero seeking a story to distract their minds, and, of course, Hiero obliged. He kept tripping over his words, though, and, based on the excessive amount of electrical sparks he produced as he snapped his fingers, the others could tell that he, too, was disturbed under his carefully held composure.

At last, Professor Glazunov and Professor Alex came back into the train car to assure them all and help River, who had not moved from his place beside Reiss. Genesis had joined them and had spent half an hour quietly running her fingers through his navy hair or holding onto his hand when he reached to take hers.

"I must thank you all for not jumping outside of the train to put your valtas to the test," Professor Glazunov began. "Haise was not trained well enough in his valta yet to be allowed to do such a thing. He will be reprimanded for his actions." He kept glancing over at Alric as he spoke, for he was surprised that Alric had not even tried to jump out to join the battle. In fact, the others were pretty surprised, too.

"What about Kazumae?" Dusk uttered from the shadows. "He jumped out of the train."

"Kazumae presents a slightly different case, as he is well-trained for conflicts such as this," the professor explained. "Before he came to the House, he was trained to defeat creatures such as these. He grew up very differently from anyone else here, so we can't really reprimand him, since he's primarily at this school to protect Haise. That is all I will say on the matter now." A hum of understanding followed. "Now, River. Would you please come with me? I'd like to talk through some of what happened, and make sure you're doing all right."

"Yes..." River started, his fingers still clutching his sister's tightly. The Professor motioned for River to follow him from the train car. Genesis held out her hand as her brother's thin fingers slipped away. River paused in the doorway briefly, to turn and gaze back at everyone over his shoulder. He looked longest at Zuri, then Freecia, and last of all, his sister, whose heart weighed heavily in her chest. She was so worried about her brother, and him leaving only made her feel all the more concerned. She wanted to do more for him. She wanted him to come to her and talk to her. She wanted to continue to hold his hand and comfort him. But River smiled, waved, and then followed after the professor.

A stillness lay over the room for a few moments. Finally, Professor Alex began to move about the car to check in with a few of the other students. Her demeanor now was very different than it had been earlier that day. Still, she kept her composure and smiled at the students as she listened to how they were feeling about what they had seen.

Genesis tucked her knees up to her chin and rested her head on them as she tried to sort out her own emotions. She hadn't taken well to the sight of so much blood either, but, up until that moment, her concern had been solely for River and his reaction to what had occurred.

Alric's eyes moved from the torn-up earth outside the train to where Genesis was seated beside Reiss a few rows up. The two of them spoke in low voices that he could not make out from where he was seated. A few times Reiss reached out his hand to gently brush it through the back of her hair. Alric looked away from them and back out the window. He just wanted the train to start moving again.

Professor Glazunov led River to the next car over, where many of the agents and teachers had been riding. Now the car was empty, as all of them had gone out to see to the situation and help clean up the train so that they could get moving as soon as possible.

The professor directed River to be seated, and was just about to sit beside him when, from outside, Agent Bertha hurried up to the open train window.

"You're needed," she said to Professor Glazunov.

"Right now? I'm with one of my students..." Professor Glazunov said.

"It's the head of security who needs you."

"Very well... I guess I can't go against the orders of someone with a higher rank. Will you stay with River until I get back...?"

"Of course," she answered.

Professor Glazunov turned to look at River. "I'll be right back, will you be all right?"

"Yes, sir," River answered. The professor gave him a bittersweet smile and departed.

A sinking feeling washed over River as he watched the Professor heading through the dark grass away from him. He only pulled his eyes away when Agent Bertha stopped beside him, and gave him a strange sort of smile.

"The principal is on the train if you would like to see him," she said.

"The principal?" River gave a start. The sinking feeling instantly left his chest and he nodded enthusiastically. "I would like that very much!"

"Wonderful. Why don't you follow me then?" Agent Bertha said. River gave another energetic nod and jumped up to follow her.

Agent Bertha walked a few paces ahead of River as they passed through the next car. Broken glass crackled beneath their shoes and the stench of blood filled the air. The blood was mostly outside, of course, but a few of the agents that had been passengers in that car had been injured when the windows had shattered. Drops of blood sprinkled some of the seats and floor. Such sights and smells only made River feel sick all over again. At last they came into the next car—a private car just for the principal.

The principal looked up from his seat at the window with a plastered smile on his face. River's first reaction was to wonder if Mr. Watts was trying to fake composure, despite the destruction to his very own property. That thought was quickly replaced when River met the principal's eyes, and that sinking feeling returned to his chest.

"Far more comfortable in here, if I do say so myself," the principal quipped with a light-hearted chuckle. The private car smelled very nice, with a hint of pine needles, or perhaps it was from the Arishian wood that had been used recently to refurbish it. The color scheme was very similar to that of the school: red cushions on the chairs and dark cherry wood.

"Yes, sir," River agreed. His mind wandered back to his sister, and his stomach began to turn as he curled and uncurled the fingers of the hand she had been holding. How long had it been since she had done something like that? He suddenly wanted to go back to her very badly. He wanted to go back and hug her as tightly as he could. Like back home. Why hadn't he gone to her more often, even just for a hug? Why hadn't he shared his heartbreak with her and let her comfort him? Had he really been the one to draw the distance between them? It was fine. Now that he had realized it, as soon as he returned to the others he'd make sure he talked to his sister. He'd give her the tightest hug that he could manage with his skinny arms.

"Come, sit beside me," the principal requested. River nodded and went over to where the Principal sat at a table beside one of the windows, while Agent Bertha remained stationed at the door like a guard. River turned his gaze up to the sky and watched as some Arishian birds soared across it. Unlike the gray landscape, the birds were brilliantly colored. Purple-feathered parrot-like creatures.

Another agent entered the room and offered drinks to the both of them.

"Something light on the stomach, I think. It will make you feel better in no time at all." The principal set a glass down on the table in front of River to draw his attention away from the scene outside.

"Thank you, sir," River answered as the principal nudged it toward him. He held the glass to his lips, but withdrew it before he had taken a sip. The drink had a rather strange odor that only made him feel all the more queasy. "What is this?"

"A type of Arishian tea. I know the smell is a bit misleading, but I promise it tastes quite good and will do wonders for your stomach in an instant."

"I'm not sure...if I can drink anything right now... Sorry, sir..."

A suffocating silence filled the car, as River's last words hung upon it. Very slowly River turned his eyes toward the grinning face of the principal.

"I tell you the truth...the tea will do wonders for your stomach. Just take a sip, you'll see..."

"Al-l right..." River stammered. The principal was smiling at him, and River worried that if he refused the principal might be upset. It might be rude if he did not drink the tea. "Well...I'll try it then..." River held the glass to his lips and very slowly took a sip. The liquid inside was warm and smooth. The feeling that washed over him was like none other, complete tranquility...he felt it washing away all his anxieties and frustrations. None of it was important anymore. His vision blurred so that he fumbled the glass and it toppled over, spilling the rest of its contents all over the table in front of them. His head slumped sideways onto the principal's shoulder, to which the principal responded by gently resting his hand upon him.

"Have no fear, my sweet boy. You will be of much use to me..."

Chapter 38

Ferris City

THE SUN WAS STILL high in the sky when they arrived in Ferris City an hour later. They had only been about 15 minutes away when the attack delayed them. After they started moving again, it had not been long at all before the sea coast appeared in the distance, and then, after passing by an area surrounded by trees, they saw a town. That town, of course, was Ferris City.

Ferris City, which despite being called a city was more the size of a small town on Earth, was situated along the shores of the Scarlet Sea—called that due to the fact that the country known as the Kingdom of Scarlet was located just across that sea. Ferris City was built along the edges of the sea, sloping down from sea cliffs to a quaint harbor. Why have it built in such a precarious manner? Well, the sea cliffs ran for miles on either side with no other low points from which to easily access the ocean. From a distance, one could easily see the town's stark whiteness standing out against the surrounding black turf and trees. Tall, gold lightning rods stood up high above the white buildings, glimmering in the sunlight.

The train chugged along the last stretch of tracks that ran through the farmland surrounding the town. Their approach to the station was far more gradual and gentle than when they had stopped so abruptly earlier, which helped the students feel a little more at ease. They had arrived at last and should be safe within the city limits. They still felt a bit rattled after what had transpired on the train, but upon seeing the city, their initial excitement for their trip was rekindled.

The students gathered on the platform while waiting for someone to guide them to the next place. In that time, they looked around to take in their surroundings, but the station had been constructed by the Agency, and so proved a disappointment to Earth-side students who wanted to see something more interesting and otherworldly. A typical train station? How boring!

Once they had gotten more comfortable speaking again, Mae and a few of the more sheltered House students started to go on and on about the train and how fast it had been moving through the countryside. They had been on the bus back on campus a few times, but because it usually only traveled up and down a gravel road to commute between the House and school, they had never gone at such a speed before. Genesis marveled at how little those students had seen of either world.

Finally, they were instructed to follow Agent Bertha again. When the students questioned her about the whereabouts of their teachers, along with River, Kazumae, and Haise, she only answered briefly that the teachers had been instructed to go straight to the Agency to report on the incident. She would join them after showing the students where they would be staying. As for the missing students, Kazumae and Haise were being examined by a doctor to be sure they had not sustained any injuries. They would join the others later at Agent Housing. River, on the other hand, had been taken to see a mental health specialist in the city to talk over the incident. The others wondered why they all couldn't see a mental health specialist, but they supposed River had been the only student noticeably traumatized. Later, Professor Glazunov expressed great disdain for them taking River away while he was otherwise occupied, without even talking to him first.

Agent Bertha led them down a street, bustling with mid-day activity. The streets were quite narrow and far too crowded with pedestrians for automobiles to pass down, so the only vehicles allowed were carts pulled by animals that in every regard resembled horses. They were horses, in fact, but the students tried hard to pick out any differences as they felt this world could not possibly have some of the same animals as on Earth! They were not left disappointed for long, however, when they caught sight of a strange cat-like creature that was perched upon one of the agent's shoulders as he passed them by.

They quickly were able to discern who were agents amidst the crowds, for they all wore the same black uniform that Agent Bertha did. Actually, the uniforms were made of materials that were resistant to the wielder's valta. For water users, a material that dried quickly. For fire users, a material that did not burn. For the few shapeshifting agents, their uniforms were made in the same way as Genesis's. The shadow uniform was quite interesting as well! With further training, shadow users could actually warp into shadows and vanish. So when they became agents, their uniforms were constructed much like shapeshifting garb so that their uniform would not be left behind when they vanished.

Although Agent Bertha seemed in quite a hurry to reach Agent Housing, the students could not stop being sidetracked. There were simply too many unique trinkets, clothing, strange fruits, colorful birds like none other they had seen, and all sorts of pleasant smells and sounds in the air. The agent wished she had chosen a different route that didn't take them through one of the market places, but it was the most direct route to their destination. When she finally got them all together again, a few were drawn away by the pleasant aroma of Arishian pastries sold outside a bakery. Then more students began to wander off, leaving only the overwhelmed House students, Zuri, Genesis, and a few other serious individuals. Genesis knew that if River had been there, he would certainly be all over the place.

Bertha finally gave in and purchased all 28 of them some small cookies, with the promise that they would stay on track to Agent Housing. They graciously accepted her gift, as it was the first food they had managed to get since breakfast that morning. They would have a late lunch as soon as they reached Agent Housing. Mae looked forward to the food they would get once they arrived, but complained that there were too many hours left in the day for them to be stuck in some building for the rest of it! They all got the impression that with what had happened on the train, all activities would be delayed until the next morning. They were correct about that: Agent Bertha was merely dumping them somewhere safe for the rest of the evening until the teachers returned around dinner time.

They at last reached Agent Housing, where Bertha immediately handed Group A off to another lady who led them to two rooms on the fifth floor. She briefly informed them that one room was for the boys and the other for the girls, then she left without further word. After how organized the first half of the day had been, now they felt thrown to the wolves. Although, I suppose being literally thrown to the wolves is a lot different, and far more dangerous, than being left to settle into cramped dorm rooms where you must bunk with many others like inmates.

Genesis felt quite uneasy that her brother was away, more so than she usually was. More than that, she still couldn't believe they were not on Earth anymore, although the day had been so strange and surreal.

Genesis and the other girls entered the girl's room, which had three bunk beds. As you are well aware, five girls made up Group A: Genesis, Dusk, Mae, Ellie, and Misteria. Due to very conflicting personalities, they very quickly began feeling even more disconcerted by the lack of space they had been given for all of them to share for the next week. At least each got her own place to sleep in the L-shaped room, even if sharing the three wardrobes would be a necessity. Given that the room was shaped like an L, two of the girls could sleep in the bunk that resided around the corner, out of view of the door. It came as no surprise that the girl who would claim such a place quickly was Misteria, and only Mae dared to ask if she could share the bunk with her. That left the two bunks that ran along the left wall from the door for the rest of them.

"It's going to be a long week..." Misteria muttered.

"It will be like one big, long slumber party!" Mae chimed, in an attempt to think positively.

Dusk set down her stuff and crawled in under one of the comforters, to escape the brightness of the sunlight that filtered in through the window.

Ellie glanced about the room. "If you have trouble sleeping, I will hypnotize you," she announced and left the room without another word.

Mae and Genesis stared at each other in awkward silence for a moment before Genesis placed her suitcase on the last bunk and also left the room to go explore, mostly because she felt uncomfortable. She had been a bit spoiled and hadn't had to share a room with another person since she and River had moved in with Uncle Ferris. The thought of being in that room much longer made her feel a bit overwhelmed.

She wandered down the hall and glanced into open doorways along the way. Her interesting findings on the fifth floor included a lounge and a very small workout room. The workout room didn't have all the equipment that they had at their dorm back home, but she was sure it would serve its purpose so that she could keep up with her training while there. Unlike the school back on Earth, everything seemed so stark and white. The carpets were a light golden color, while the walls were just plain white. Decorations were quite scarce, so it was a bit harsh on the eyes.

Genesis went downstairs to the lobby to see if she could figure out where the dining hall was located. At that particular hour, the lobby was still and empty, save for one lady seated at the desk speaking to an individual who Genesis knew quite well: Alric Ashford.

"You want the agent records?" the woman clarified.

"That's what I said," Alric answered, obviously trying hard to keep his tone polite.

"They would be at the Agency. You would need your student ID card to be allowed to look at them."

Alric held out his card to her. "This will do, right?" he asked.

"Yes..."

"How do I get to the Agency?"

"Why don't you wait until tomorrow? You're visiting, so your teacher has to go over some instruc—"

"No, I want to go now."

"You're a brat," she muttered. "Fine, if you go out the doors and head down the street to your right, eventually you'll come to a building that looks sort of like a bank. That will be the Agency."

"Thanks," he said and strode away from her. He came to an abrupt halt in front of the doors. "What in Arisha does a bank look like?" he murmured. Genesis stepped out of the doorway toward him, grabbing his attention. She might know what a bank looked like. "You coming, Shapeshifty?"

"Sure... I've got nothing better to do," she answered, surprised at the impromptu invitation.

"Then come on. There's too many people in that room," he grumbled as he moved to the doors. Genesis swiftly caught the door behind him and followed him into the street.

"That was my problem, too. I found the gym, though," she told him.

"It's too small for our duels. I don't like it."

"That's all right! We'll only be here for a week," she laughed.

"Don't think you can chicken out now just because we're on vacation," he gave her a sharp look. She only smiled back in return, so he looked away. She always smiled whenever he glared at her, and he couldn't understand that. Usually people would just leave him alone after that, but not her. He clenched his jaw. He couldn't say that he hated it, though, and that only made him angrier.

"I wasn't going to chicken out. I guess we can find somewhere—maybe outside?—to do our next duel. But, I also don't see any reason why we can't skip a week and do it when we get back..." Genesis suggested tentatively. Alric didn't answer.

Sure enough, after a short walk they found a huge building that did remind Genesis of an old-fashioned bank. A large sign over the doorway read "Driscoll Agency."

"She coulda mentioned the sign..." Alric grumbled.

"With people attacking the school, why advertise the base of operations so boldly?" Genesis asked.

"Arishians are still pretty afraid of Driscoll...because of our technology. When the Watts family came into Arisha, most Arishian countries didn't have trains or aircraft, and they had barely figured out making use of electricity valta for power. I guess they're still pretty cautious about attacking the main base of operations. Also, Arishians used to like the school a lot more before Johnathan T. Watts became principal. The attacks, like the one we experienced today, are relatively new. Now come on already."

Once in the foyer, the students took a moment to observe their surroundings. They were in a large open room with ceilings that stretched
high above them. The room was fairly empty except for a reception desk
straight back from the doors, and some sitting areas on either side of the
entrance. There was a large stone staircase going up on the right side
of the desk, and on the other side were several desks with computers
on them. Everything seemed to be made of a white marble material.
Genesis wondered if they were confident enough in their agents' control
over their valta to not have to construct the whole place out of inactive
cynthian stone.

When the two students appeared, several agents, who were sitting at
the tables in the sitting area, shot strange looks in their direction. Seeing
the student uniform was a rare sight in Arisha outside of Tryss—the
country where the seniors studied for a year. This indicated it was
Driscoll University's "December Introductions to Arisha," which meant
the next two weeks would be filled with naive children wandering around
the streets of Ferris City.

Alric strode straight for the reception desk. "I would like to see the
agent records," Alric requested as he held out his student ID to the
receptionist.

"For what reason?" the woman asked.

Alric's grip on his ID tightened as his stomach knotted itself. He
needed to come up with some kind of excuse. After all, he didn't want
to say what he was actually looking for, because he felt foolish. Both the
lady from the housing desk and this woman's voices were so reluctant
that he knew he would have to convince her to give him what he wanted
without revealing what he was really looking for. "I just want to look up
someone I used to know at the House. I want to see if they're still alive,"
he explained.

The woman sighed. "Very well. Over there..." She pointed with her pen toward the area with computers. "You'll need to scan your ID card and type in your code to get in."

Alric mumbled something under his breath, and turned to go to the computer desks without a word. "Thank you," Genesis said on his behalf, before following him.

The chair legs squeaked on the marble as Alric took a seat in front of one of the computers. The hum of agents' voices filled the air. Occasionally bits of conversation passed them, as agents came down the stairs or in through the front doors. The computer was taking quite long to boot up and so Genesis shifted from one foot to the other as she stood behind him waiting. She supposed she could pull over one of the other chairs, but she had been sitting for the majority of the day. She still wasn't a hundred percent sure why they were there, but she was happy to be along for the adventure.

The sign-in screen popped up, and Alric held his student ID under a scanner next to the computer screen. He held his breath for a moment as the computer continued to load. It then asked for his passcode which he swiftly typed in. After that he was in and so heaved a heavy sigh. Several options were listed on the screen's table of contents, Alric, of course, selected the agent records, and it led him to a search screen. Now he paused with his hands held over the computer keyboard.

"Looking for a friend of yours?" Genesis asked to break the uncertain silence.

Alric blinked a few times as he had started to zone out. "No... I don't have friends... I'm actually looking up my parents..." he muttered in a low tone so that only she could hear him. For a while he contemplated whether or not he really wanted to know, but he couldn't shake a feeling that had eaten away at him since the night that Genesis had questioned him about his parents. He had to know for sure.

While Alric was stuck in indecision, Genesis realized this might also be an opportunity for her to see if there were any other Agent Ashfords who could have been the man who protected them that night.

At last, Alric started to type, and so she leaned over his shoulder to look as he hit the enter key with "Silverstone" now typed into the search bar. Nothing came up, so he tried typing in Sarah, which obviously produced a lot of results. He tried her full name, her middle name, various different spellings, but still nothing.

"Where the heck is she?" he grumbled.

"Your mother?" Genesis asked.

"Yeah, I was told her name was Sarah Silverstone," he mumbled.

"Might her name be under Ashford instead?"

He shook his head. "My parents never got married."

"And you're sure your mother was an agent?" she asked.

"That is what I was told... Why would they lie to me and tell me that she was an agent if she wasn't? And why wouldn't she be an agent? I was told that she and my dad both became agents and were very focused on their work. That's why they never came to visit me before they died." His voice had taken on a calm tone, so that Genesis barely recognized it. For once, he didn't seem angry whatsoever, just deeply sad.

"We can ask the lady at the front desk if there is any reason an agent's name would not make it into the records," she suggested.

"Maybe..." He started to search for *Ashford* now, and so Genesis leaned in closer to the screen as one result popped up. Alric moved the computer cursor over the name and clicked on it. The computer chimed as a notification popped up. Both students leaned in closer to read it.

"*File is restricted for the agent's safety...*" Genesis read off of the screen.

"Huh?" Alric responded. "What does it mean 'for the agent's safety'? He doesn't need protection if he's dead," he muttered under his breath. The expression on his face became more angry and his shoulders began to tremble. "Unless...he's not dead."

Genesis drew back, her mind racing. If Alric's father was still alive, she knew what that meant for her as well: the agent that night may very well have been Alric's father, after all. No other Ashfords came up on the page. But... She glanced over at Alric.

"The shriveled old man must not have wanted the responsibility of coming to see his own son anymore...just told them to tell me he had died with my mother."

"I mean, his information is restricted...so there might be a legitimate reason..." She trailed off as Alric turned his face away. She could feel his body shaking with anger, and so didn't feel like she should try to defend his father. She didn't have the details either, so who was she to say he was innocent. She could not help but feel a little confused by the idea that he could be everything Alric made him out to be. If the man really was awful enough to abandon his own son, then why on earth had he protected her and her brother that night? It didn't make sense to her...especially because she had held the man in such high regard for all these years. She didn't want to think the same man was capable of abandoning his own child. As an aside, you should know that, while Alric referred to him as a shriveled old man, his father was in fact not all that old.

"Do you have anyone you want to look up?" he asked, in an attempt to turn his thoughts away from this new discovery.

"Nah, I wouldn't know anyone who had become an agent here. My brother and I aren't from the House after all. We just entered this world now," she said with a short laugh.

"Can't hurt to check, Shapeshifty. Might as well while we got this stupidly slow computer on," he said as he started to type again. "Let's see Deadlock... Deadlock..." She smiled to herself, as he repeated her name. So he actually knew it? She had assumed the reason why he called her "Shapeshifty" all the time was because he had forgotten what her real name was. He seemed like the kind of person who wouldn't care enough to remember a person's name. But if he knew her last name, then he probably knew her first name as well.

"There is a Deadlock here. Maybe he's not related to you, just has the same last name, but looky here!" She leaned over to look at the computer screen again, giggling at the thought that he had actually found someone with her last name. Then she gasped and time stopped in the now painfully silent room. Her mouth opened and her lips began to quiver.

"But... Turmentic Lee Deadlock... that's... that's my father's name..." she stammered at last.

Chapter 39

In the Garden

RIVER'S EYES FLUTTERED OPEN and he found himself lying on a soft velvet sofa. Only then did he realize he had been unconscious, and with that realization the memory of his vision blurring as he sat with the principal on the train jolted him up with a start. His chest heaved as his breath came out in short, hard gasps.

He scanned the room he now found himself in—a sitting area filled with great finery. The room was very similar to one of the sitting rooms Uncle Ferris had back in Mirrorick. But his eyes did not linger on the white marble floor, or the fine chairs and sofas, nor the porcelain vases situated in the alcoves in the walls. Instead, he stumbled over the oriental rug on the floor, his head still swimming, and clutched the gold door handles, giving them a jiggle to no avail.

He spun around to face the room again, his eyes catching a large window on the opposite wall. He attempted to rush toward it in desperation, but, partway across the room, he had to grasp the back of one of the chairs for support. Dark splotches darkened his vision for a time before he could regain his proper footing. At last he reached the window and undid the latch to throw it open. That done, he prepared to revert his own gravity with the intention of floating down from the window into the garden between the house and the thick forests that surrounded it. His heartbeat quickened again as he tried and tried again. No matter how hard he concentrated on his valta, nothing happened. It was as if he had become a normal boy again with no special abilities.

He clutched the windowsill, his body trembling as he realized he could not escape. Why? Why had the principal betrayed him like that? Mr. Watts had seemed so kind the first time he met him. Had he missed something sinister in his behavior because he wanted so badly for someone to pay attention to him? The principal seemed to care about him and how he felt when no one else at the school did. Had he ignored everything deep down inside of himself all for fake comfort? How stupid! His jaw trembled as he clenched it so hard his head began to ache.

As he stood at the window, his tear-filled eyes caught sight of a woman walking along the iron fence that surrounded the house. It was the beginning of summer in Arisha, so the garden beds below were lush, still blooming with life. The woman paused and slowly knelt down in the soil with her back to the fence. She was very lovely. Not too old, maybe in her late thirties or early forties. She had long, dark hair, and wore a nightgown and robe. He could sense a great sorrow exuding from her entire body, despite her eyes not once lifting to look up at him.

River lifted his hand to his mouth about to call out to her for help. Perhaps she could come up and unlock the door for him, or maybe she could help him down from the window somehow. The ground wasn't that far away, but having someone to spot him might keep him from injury. But before the words could come out, he stopped, for he heard her humming, and the moment he heard it, a lump formed in his throat and he lowered his hand to clutch the windowsill once more. She couldn't help him, because she was trapped there as well...because it was no coincidence that she suddenly reminded him so much of Genesis and why she was humming the same song that Genesis had hummed to him so many times before. She was his mother. The mother he had wanted to meet so badly.

Then, the next moment, a voice called out from a doorway below, and she got up quickly to depart through the rows of flowers. As she fled away, a cry welled up into River's throat, choked by his tears so that he couldn't utter a word until she was nearing the far corner of the house from his window. "Wait! Don't go! I'm right here! I'm your son, River! Come back!" he shouted, but she was gone. River continued to tremble as the garden stood in silence below him. "Please help me..." he murmured as he sank down under the window to the marble floor.

His sorrow was interrupted when the door opened and Roland Watts stepped inside. River dashed across the room toward him and caught his classmate's jacket in his hands. Roland tensed, his gaze fixated on River's fear-stricken face.

"Please, Roland! You have to help me! You have to get me out of this place! I want to see my sister!" he pleaded with him. Roland didn't speak, nor did he move under River's tight grip. He just stood there, blank-faced, unsympathetic yet not cruel either. He stood like a stone statue that had been chiseled into form by his father. "Roland..." Tears began to pour down River's face and sobs shook his small body as he continued to clutch his classmate. "I'm so scared... Please save me... You have to save me... Your father..." As soon as the words left his mouth, he drew back, his fingers releasing Roland's clothes, but still stiffened into place as he stared at him wide-eyed. "Of course... I can plead with you, but you're on his side... How foolish of me... Why would you help me?" River backed away, bumping up against one of the chairs. "What are you going to do to me? What is it you want from me? Why do you have my mother?"

"You shall be used as a tool. Come." Roland turned away as he spoke, his voice stiff. River didn't see any other choice and so followed him from the room into the similarly marbled hallways beyond. River stayed close to Roland despite his fears over where he was taking him. Even with his stony face, there was something in Roland that did not give the same feeling as his father...something beneath that cold exterior that provided a little comfort.

Roland paused briefly in front of a set of large, white doors. When he opened them, River could see that some sort of guest room awaited them on the other side, and by the windows with their long transparent curtains draped over them, stood Principal Watts himself. In his hands was a strange container from which a faint light emitted through cracks in its surface. As soon as River saw the principal, he quickly began to backtrack out of the room, but the doors slammed shut behind him and he was grabbed by two agents who had waited on either side of the doorway. Roland turned back around, his eyes growing very sad as he watched them drag River toward a chair not far from where the principal stood. With an outburst of cries, River continued to resist as the agents tied him down to the arms and legs of the chair. The closer that strange container got to him, the more panicked he became.

"Please don't do this! I'll do anything you say! Please don't hurt me! Please let me see my sister!" River cried, thrashing in the chair. With every bit of strength left in his thin body, he pulled against his restraints.

"Sedate him," Principal Watts ordered coldly. One of the two agents picked up a syringe from a sterilized tray. As he drew near, River's cries only grew worse as he tried all he could to resist them. His voice crackled and he grew hoarse with his screams. Still, no matter how hard he tried, he could not activate his valta to escape. It was as if it had been shut off and there was nothing he could do about it. His eyes met Roland's as he stood motionless in the center of the room observing what was happening. Then the sedative took hold and River's muscles all relaxed at once so that he could not even move his fingertips. Only then did the principal begin to unscrew the lid of the container he still held. Tears poured down River's face as the bright light began to escape its container and came to rest in the principal's outstretched hand.

"Come, my dear child, Cassian. From this day forth this boy's body now belongs to you. In exchange, you must do as I tell you. Understand?" he asked. River stared at the light and was instantly reminded of the stories his mother had told him and his sister about how once, long ago, a spirit had taken his mother's body and cast out her soul to wander the Earth alone for hundreds of years. A story he had always thought was a mere fairytale she had made up for their entertainment. But now...

The spirit drifted from Principal Watts's hand and descended upon River...

Chapter 40

Family

GENESIS COULD NOT BRING herself to speak as they both glanced over her father's record in disappointment. The record was not restricted, but it might as well have been. There was nothing listed there other than that he had received his agent badge four years ago. His position, location, age, education were all blank. So truthfully they had nothing more than that he was alive and an agent for Driscoll.

"What are you two doing here?" Both students jumped and turned swiftly to see Professor Alex standing a few yards away from them. She approached swiftly, the heels of her boots tapping the marble floor.

"You're not to leave Agent Housing at this time," she said in a lower voice. "You both need to get back right away before Professor Glazunov finds out that you're gone! I'm inclined to let it slide, since we haven't gotten the chance to go over the rules yet, but still... You will get free hours to explore the city on your own each day, so having a little patience would be—"

"Do you know where Agent Turmentic Deadlock is stationed?" Alric interrupted. Genesis's eyes widened, and she reached out to grab his arm. Why? Why had he asked about her father instead of his mother? The reason he had gone there in the first place was to learn about his parents, not hers.

"Agent Deadlock? I've only heard that last name a handful of times, so I don't know, and even if I did I wouldn't be authorized to share that information with you," she answered. Alric stood as if to leave, but Genesis thought it far more likely that Professor Alex might have information on Alric's parents than her own parents. They couldn't just leave without learning anything more about his mother!

"What about Sarah Silverstone? Do you know anything about her?" Genesis asked quickly.

Professor Alex really didn't strike Genesis as a stern person, but the expression that came over her face looked quite stern. "I see you've been poking around to find information about your parents... I can't blame you." She looked over at Alric. "Sarah and Elwood are your parents, and I don't think that situation was handled very well. I can't tell you much of anything, either, not just because it's restricted information, but also because I don't know much more than you. Most of us who went to class with Elwood—me and Zenry Glazunov—and his sister, only found out he was alive recently. Your mother isn't in the records because she was merely a receptionist here and not an agent. For that matter, she was a complete lunatic. Now, you two need to go straight back to Agent Housing."

Without another word, Alric strode heavily across the room toward the doors. "Thank you...and sorry for breaking any rules," Genesis said to the professor, then hurried after Alric.

She reunited with Alric where he stood waiting at the top of the stairs outside. He said nothing to her as he continued down the steps. Her chest felt so twisted, and she began to wonder if it would have been better if she had not asked and just let the absence of his mother's name remain a mystery.

Alric started off down the street moving quickly enough that Genesis was not sure how to match his stride. When she glanced back at the building behind them, she could see Professor Alex following to make sure they made it all the way to Agent Housing, even though she still had things to do at the Agency.

Genesis stared at the back of Alric's bright red hair. She pursed her lips, but the words didn't come out immediately. "Th-thank you for asking about my dad for me..." she said at last.

His gaze remained fixed forward. "Don't thank me. I wasn't trying to be nice or anything, so don't get the wrong idea." His voice softened a little as he continued, "But I guess... Thank you for asking about my mom, too. I was honestly too afraid to ask myself."

"Yeah... I understand... I'm sorry she turned out to be..." She stopped as she finally fell into step beside him.

"No, it makes me feel better. At least now whenever I feel like I'm going crazy, I can just blame it on genetics," he answered in a serious tone of voice. Genesis looked up at him and their eyes met. A smile broke over his lips and then they both burst out laughing. After the spell had subsided, Genesis smiled to herself.

Alric's thoughts turned to his father as he kept up the walking pace. The story he had been told about his parents must have just applied to Elwood; *his* work had been too important for him to continue to raise the child of some nut he had dated at his first station. That made sense to Alric at least. The school must have grouped his mother into it because they didn't want him to know the truth about her being a nut. What kid would want that information? Telling him that his father was dead fell into line with that. A kid would probably be better off just thinking his parents had died rather than that they didn't want to raise him. Now knowing that his dad was under some kind of restriction, there was the possibility that he was not *allowed* to raise a child. Or, perhaps the restriction was because of some crime his father had committed, in which case the school might have been protecting him. He wondered if learning more of the truth had really made anything better, or if everything was just worse now. At least Genesis had been along with him. Honestly, that made him feel better, because there was someone else to bear the truth with him.

With that last thought, Alric turned to Genesis in the lobby of Agent Housing. He immediately stopped for he had not expected the sight that awaited him. The normally composed Genesis had tears pouring down her face. He wasn't sure what to say or do for a second. Why was she crying again? Like that time down in the lobby of the dorm... That time had been completely different, though, because she had believed she was alone. Now she unashamedly and openly cried in front of him.

"W-what's wrong with you?" he stammered. She didn't answer as she wiped the tears from her face with her shirt sleeves. "Don't cry, for goodness' sake! I don't know what to do!" He looked about the room quickly, as if to try and find someone to help console the girl. How was he supposed to make her stop crying? Should he make another joke about him being a lunatic? She had laughed earlier when he had.

"I don't know why I'm crying... I'm sorry... I guess I'm just shocked... I don't know what to do now... This is more than I had hoped for... I have a lead! My father is alive and he's an agent..."

Her voice warbled but he could still make out every word she said. He didn't feel like he followed her train of thought, however. "If you don't have a reason to cry, then don't."

She tried to wipe her tears away again, but they kept coming from her eyes. Part of it was because she had bottled up her emotions for too long. She had tried so hard not to cry since her awakening, so now it all just rushed out of her at once...everything she had pent up. I tell you the truth, I think it's best just to let things out in the moment instead of bottling them up for so long. Shedding a few tears now and then doesn't make you weak, and, in some cases, it can bring relief.

Alric sighed. "I'm not showing you any pity, if that's what you are looking for."

She turned her back to him, embarrassed because of the harsh biting tone of his words. Of all people to cry in front of, he must be the absolute worst. "You're such a weird girl. Fine!" He grabbed her wrist and yanked her back, embracing her tightly to him. She was so stunned that she stopped crying in an instant. His arms were so warm, which was no surprise since the temperature of his whole body was a lot higher than a normal person's. She grew aware of how nice he smelled, like a warm campfire. The rapid beating of his heart sounded against her ears, and she felt at peace again. She could stop crying now. Everything was going to be all right. No matter what happened.

"Why are you acting like that? Keep crying, otherwise it's awkward!" he snapped. She started to laugh. "Now I don't know what to think. You're crying, then laughing? Which is it?" He grabbed her shoulders and pulled her back to look down at her tear-stained face.

"You're just so mean, Alric," she half-teased.

"Are you done crying yet?"

"Maybe..." She looked down.

"Now don't you start up again!" He sighed and hugged her again so that the sound of his racing heart returned to her ear. She wondered if his heart was always racing—was it so fast with rage? Hesitantly, she moved her hands to hug him back, but the second her hand rested on his back, he pushed her gently away from him and turned to leave. Something she had wanted to say popped into mind and she reached out her hand.

"Wait," she blurted out. His movements ceased, and she could feel his gaze back on her again as she stared down at the white stone floor of the housing lobby. "I don't know if you want to hear this...but I think your father saved my life."

"What are you talking about, Shapeshifty? Why would that guy save you?"

"It was when I was seven years old... I've only told a few people from our class about this. But—River!" She stopped as River appeared in the doorway to the stairs, and her heart leapt in her chest. He was back! Thank goodness! All else left her mind, and so her words remained suspended in the air.

Alric glanced from one Deadlock sibling to the other. He knew she wouldn't continue now. After all those months, the one thing he knew for certain about her was that her brother was far more important than anything else. He sighed and took a step away from her.

A wave of heat washed over River as Alric sauntered past him into the stairwell. River sent a cold look back at him and then redirected his gaze to his older sister. She remained where she had been when she saw him, her eyes fixed on him as she smiled.

"River!" she repeated as she finally moved to close the gap between them.

"Genesis," he muttered and in a moment he took hold of her hands. "Are you okay? Did Alric make you cry?" His tone was strange, but even stranger was the dark look in his usually sparkling, energetic eyes. "I'll go fight him if you like." His hands withdrew from hers as if he would go after Alric. Her heart twisted as something didn't feel quite right. Was it because of everything that had happened that whole long day? She grabbed River's arm to keep him from going.

"No, he actually cheered me up..." she told him. River narrowed his eyes at her. "What? What are you thinking?"

"Do you like Alric?"

"Well, he's not actually that bad! I mean, he's definitely short-tempered, but most of the time it seems like he's just pretending to be mean..."

"So you *do* like him?"

"What do you mean by *like*?" she questioned.

"I mean, do you have feelings for him?"

"What?! Of course not! Sure, I think he's not *really* mean, but I think I'm far from feeling *that* way about him... I mean, I like him as a person. Not like *that*..."

"I don't see what there is to like about him as a person either, but I'm glad that's cleared up. I would be concerned if you had a crush on that sort of person." River's foot struck the stone and he turned to leave as he now found the conversation with her to have grown tiresome.

"Hey!" She started after him through the door.

"*Hey* what?" he answered without even bothering to glance back in her direction.

"I just think that was a bit harsh..."

"Stop sticking up for him. He obviously doesn't like any of us. So why should you defend him?"

"Because he's... He's my friend, River..."

He let out a short laugh. "Like you know anything about what a friend is. I think you should stop hanging out with him. Hang out with Zuri, Freecia, and me instead. We are a far better crowd, don't you think? Why would you hang out with someone like him over your own little brother?" He tilted his head to the side, his red eyes boring through her.

"What is wrong with you, River? Why are you suddenly being so controlling over who I am allowed to be friends with? You're acting really strange right now, too... What's going on...? Who are you?"

"Your little brother River, of course! Why would you ask that? I just think you have the wrong idea. You've never had any friends before, while I have had plenty. So I feel like I have way more knowledge in this department. I'm going to say it right now: Alric is the last person you should be friends with. That's going to be one toxic friendship, and I don't think you know what you're talking about."

"Stop it."

"But what about Zuri? He would make a way better first friend. I've been friends with him since the first week of school and I really think you should hang out with us more."

"I said, stop it!" Genesis strode angrily past him toward the staircase. He followed a few paces behind her. She had asked for it—she was the one who had continued the conversation when he had deemed it trivial. She would get what she wanted.

"Really, Genesis, you're being unreasonable! You must think about it like this. All of those from the House have made it clear that he's not a good guy. Why not take their word for it? They have known him a lot longer than you, after all." Genesis didn't answer as they reached the fifth floor and continued down the hallway toward their designated dorm rooms. "Come now, you think being silent can wash away your problems? Answer me right now. You know the right answer and that's why you won't say it!" he snapped. She grasped the handle of the girls' room, her rage building, so that the glare she shot back at him was far more harsh than she intended it to be.

"You're not thinking clearly, so I think you need to rest. Have a good night." She then entered the room, shutting the door firmly behind her. River stood in the hallway, glaring angrily at the closed door.

Chapter 41

Rift

GENESIS OPENED HER EYES the next morning to find Mae and Dusk curled up on either side of her on her bed. Mae muttered something in her sleep and snuggled up closer; it was then that she remembered Dusk and Mae being a bit wild last night. Misteria and Ellie had gone to bed early despite their wildness, but Genesis, on the other hand, could not easily fall asleep with such noise. As a result, she had stayed up until at least 3:00 in the morning before the two of them had passed out on her bed. Apparently Dusk's dark aura slipped out even more when she fell asleep, because Genesis had nearly rolled Mae off the bed in response to her nightmare-riddled sleep. She was curious to see what else shadow valta did other than send chills up the spines of others around them.

Genesis shifted position causing Mae to bolt upright and, as she was on the very edge of the narrow bed, she tumbled backwards onto the floor. The loud thump that followed made Genesis gasp and sit up quickly herself to ensure Mae was all right. Mae was fine, but she lay on the floor with both hands clasped to her head.

"I fell asleep!" she exclaimed.

"That you did," Genesis answered as she rubbed her eyes.

"Dusk! Dusk! Dusk!" Mae shouted as she practically pounced back onto the bed and shook Dusk awake. Dusk groaned and vanished beneath the covers. "We fell asleep on Genesis's bed! I'm ruined! My purity is gone!!!" she cried.

Dusk sat up and chucked a pillow as hard as she could at Mae's head so that Mae tumbled back off the bed onto the floor again. "What on earth are you saying? Pull yourself together..." Dusk rasped, her trembling hand extended out like that of a zombie. Genesis slipped out of bed, still feeling half asleep and too tired for their antics so early in the morning.

Ellie and Misteria had already gotten up and had left the room, so the three of them hurried into a bathroom across the hall to get ready for the day. Once downstairs, they found most of their class gathered in the lobby with Professor Alex. They were just in time for roll call. They didn't usually have roll calls before class, because Professor Glazunov always seemed acutely aware of who was absent. A few of the girls from Group B were missing, so they had to wait a few minutes for Professor Alex to fetch them.

At last all the students and Professor Glazunov were there, and so the two professors went over the rules and scheduled activities. The meeting was brief and to the point. No school activities were scheduled for the first day, so the students were free to explore the city. The next day, they would have a tour of one of the city's research laboratories, as well as a lecture from a research agent, who would be going into further details on what they saw in the laboratories. For the remainder of the week, they would have lectures presented by research agents every morning to learn about some of the Agency's current projects in Arisha. In addition to the lectures, the students would spend their evenings aboard an Arishian vessel docked in the harbor, where they would eat local cuisine served by Arishians and practice speaking Arshin with native speakers. They would have several free hours in the middle of each day.

The students were anxious to get to breakfast by that point, so Professor Glazunov dismissed them, reminding them that the rules were in place for their safety. It was at that point that Genesis felt rather ashamed of herself, because she had zoned out in the middle of the meeting, thinking about yesterday's events.

"What are the plans for today?" Dusk queried as they all gathered around one of the cafeteria tables.

"Freecia and I will be heading to Ferris Tower to admire the view," Zuri said with a smile in Freecia's direction. She sat a few seats down with a bunch of other students from Group B.

"Some of the others mentioned going to the library to do some more valta research!" Mae chimed.

"Where are you going, Dawn?" Dusk asked.

"I-I d-don't know, d-do you w-want to do something t-together...? L-like... like a date?" He blushed, which only made the light aura around him shine all the brighter. In fact, his valta started to slip out and so he was quite literally glowing. His stutter hadn't gone away despite getting to know everyone better... He was still too nervous.

"I would love that..." Dusk answered in a hoarse whisper.

Mae grabbed Genesis's arm. "It's the beginning of romance!" she whispered excitedly.

"Haven't they already been dating for months now?" Genesis whispered back.

"What? How did Dusk not tell me of this?!" Mae drooped.

"Would you like to go to the library with me?" Genesis suggested in an attempt to cheer her.

"I'd love to... But...Levine and I were asked to do some work today after breakfast... We're both Driscoll girls so there isn't really a choice on the matter... Maybe some other time while we're here?"

"Sure!" Genesis agreed and began to walk toward the buffet counter. She paused when it occurred to her that she hadn't seen River. She looked at the empty seat beside Zuri, but he wasn't there. Concerned, she strode back and rested her hand down on the table next to Zuri to get his attention. He stopped chewing and lifted his eyes to her.

"Where is River?" she asked.

Zuri glanced first to his side then back up to her. "I... I don't know... He was here a little while ago... He had to be for the meeting, of course..."

"I-I th-think h-he left-t on his own," Dawn stammered.

Genesis straightened and took another glance about the room before she departed without grabbing anything to eat. Once she had gone, the others exchanged awkward glances.

"Was not Sir River acting rather strange last night?" Kazumae spoke up.

Zuri nodded, his eyes wide. He felt relieved that he was not the only one who had thought such a thing. "Not just strange—he was acting really weird... Not like himself at all..."

"Like how weird?" Mae questioned.

"Like...like he was a different person entirely... He had no energy and his eyes... I don't know how to explain it, but his eyes felt so heavy on me..."

Alric glanced up from where he sat by himself a little way down the long cafeteria table. After a while, in which the others began to chatter on about another matter, Alric got up with his plate and set it in the sink area at the back of the room.

Genesis wasn't sure where to begin to look for River in such an un-familiar place so she decided to start by wandering down toward the sea, because she knew River liked the sound of moving water when he wanted to be alone. As she neared the water, she found herself in the midst of a marketplace where farmers and artists sold their creations, such as jewelry, fine cloths, byproducts from the nearby farmlands, and many other little trinkets. The Arishian craftwork was truly unique and beautiful compared to that of Earth, but Genesis was on a mission to find her brother, so she did not bother to look very hard as she hurried past.

She came to an abrupt halt at the edge of the marketplace when she caught sight of River's thin figure seated at the very end of one of the docks that extended out over the harbor waters. She made straight for him, her footfalls rapid on the worn, white boards of the dock. To her surprise, he didn't turn around or even acknowledge her when she sat down beside him. His eyes were shut and his body rigid as he swayed ever so slightly from side to side in rhythm with each low hum that emanated from his throat. Her stomach ached with anxiety at the sight of him and his strange behavior, but for several minutes she was not sure what to say.

"River..." she started at last.

No answer.

"River." She rested her hand on his shoulder and his eyes swiftly opened to glare at her.

"What is it that you want?" he snapped. She drew back, her heart in a tumult as her nerve almost left her. All she could think about was the boy she had grown up with...the spastic boy who could not stop smiling. The expression he now wore was like none she had ever seen upon his joyful face, not even when they had argued as children.

"I-I..." she stammered, unsure of what she really intended to say. She was his older sister, she had always stayed strong for his sake. She had to stay strong even now...even while she was terrified of him. She took a deep breath to regain her composure. "What's going on, River? What has happened?"

"Nothing happened. I'm fine. Actually I'm better than fine. I'm absolutely great." He stood, a sinister grin spreading over his lips as he looked down upon his sister's fear-stricken face. "What's with that look? You don't like this? But this is who I really am, dear sister. So get used to it. Anyway...I'm not in the mood to hang out with a person who doesn't know the difference between someone who is true friend material and someone who is not. I'm going to go hang out with Zuri and Freecia, or find somewhere peaceful where you won't come and bother me!" He stalked off swiftly. Genesis wasted no time jumping to her feet to chase after him. She could feel him slipping away from her and wanted to stop him from going.

"River!" She lunged forward to grab him before he could disappear among the market stalls. "River, wait!" she cried out as he just barely slipped out of reach. He spun around and gave her a hard shove backward with the force of his valta. He flung her so hard and fast that she had little time to think of the way that she fell, her wrist twisting under her. Despite all her duels with Alric, she hadn't been prepared for such strength from her little brother. She gasped and turned to look up at him in shock, but River had already vanished into the crowd.

Chapter 42

Encounter

NO MATTER WHAT DIRECTION Genesis looked, she couldn't find him amidst the marketplace crowds. What had gotten into him? Why was he behaving so strangely? Had it only been yesterday that he had been acting like her fragile little brother, overwhelmed by the sight of blood and conflict? Now he was causing conflict and acting like he wanted to draw blood! Had hearing her call Alric her friend really upset him that much? Or had something more happened that she didn't know about?

She had landed in front of a fabric stall, so, when she stood up, the merchant approached and started to speak in fast Arshin. Even if she hadn't been terrible in language class, now was just not the time for her to focus her mind on his words. All that he said passed right over her as her chest began to feel overwhelmingly heavy. Everything was her fault. She hadn't checked in on River regularly. She shouldn't have assumed he was fine with only Zuri and Freecia for companions, especially after it became clear that they were dating, and she shouldn't have expected that he would come to her if he needed to talk about anything. She should have gone to him and asked how he was doing. Maybe he resented her because she hadn't. Her mind was reeling as she rubbed her aching wrist.

The fabric merchant dragged her closer to his stall to show off his products. He suddenly used a questioning voice and stopped to stare at her expectantly. Genesis stood in front of him lost for words. She knew how to say *yes* and *no* but wasn't sure which to use in this situation. Plus, in their language class, they had learned that saying just *yes* or *no* wasn't considered polite in Arishian society. Her mind drew a blank on the phrases the instructors had told them to say instead, and she still didn't know which to use anyway since she didn't understand the question.

Genesis glanced about the market for some aid, but the crowds were indifferent to her plight. The merchant grew impatient and kept shoving a bright red fabric in her face. She didn't even have any money with her, neither Arishian coins nor Mirrorickian dollars. She wasn't prepared to buy something.

"What a unique shade of olive green," a voice said in English behind her. She turned just as a man in a hood strode to her side and began to speak to the man in fluent Arshin. She sighed and was about to walk away, but the man grabbed her wrist to prevent her. She wanted to get away and she knew she could easily do so by shifting into a cat or a bird...but he was helping her out, as far as she could tell, so she thought she might as well wait for him to be done.

"Sorry, I speak only English. Can I please go?" she asked. He held onto her sprained wrist so tightly it hurt under his grasp. "I don't know what he is saying, but I don't want to buy anything."

He ignored her and spoke to the man for another moment. The conversation seemed a bit tense, for the merchant got angrier and angrier as the talking continued. She wished that she hadn't come down to the market in the first place. She had been chewed out by River, attacked by a merchant, and now she was being held firmly in place by a hooded stranger.

At last the man turned from the stall, dragging her along with him. Only when they were well away from the merchant did he loosen his grip and face her. His hood was pulled down over his face, but she could see the tips of his blonde hair peeking out from under it.

"Think nothing of it," he said in English. "He was claiming to sell fabric made of authentic dragon scales and thought the bright red color would look excellent with your eyes. However, there are far too few dragons left in Arisha for his claim to be true. The fabric was clearly made of scales from a common reptile. He was a fraud and did not like being called out on it."

"Ah..." Genesis answered.

"Your wrist seems to be sprained..." he whispered. She examined him as he continued to hold her wrist, light radiating from his hands. "Does that feel any better?"

"Who are you?" she murmured, as she withdrew her hand. To her amazement, her wrist didn't hurt at all anymore. The power he had used was strange, and she did not know of a valta that could heal.

He let out a lighthearted laugh. "I suppose it's rude of me not to introduce myself to such a lovely lady." He reached out, twisted a lock of her olive green hair around his finger, then leaned down to gently kiss it. Genesis thought it a rather strange greeting, but he really did seem quite enamored with the color of her hair. After a moment, he let her long hair fall slowly from his fingers as he drew back his hood just enough so that she could see his kind, golden eyes peering out from beneath it. "My name is Shireu. What would the fine lady's name be?" he asked, clasping her hand between his. His accent was very similar to Zuri's, so she knew at once he must be a true Arishian.

"My name is Genesis," she answered.

He had such a soft expression on his face, and he seemed to radiate light and kindness but in a different way than Dawn did. "You are one of the students from Earth who came here for the week, correct?" he asked.

"That I am..." She glanced down at his white cloak trimmed with gold. He also appeared to be a bit older than she was. "I don't suppose you're an agent since you aren't wearing the uniform..."

He chuckled. "No, I am not an agent. I am just another Arishian. I am from Shield Alliance, but I'm in town for the weekend visiting a friend. If you're a student, you must be pretty young then." Shield Alliance...that was the same country where Zuri had grown up.

"Yes, I'm 15."

"Fifteen isn't all that young! Arishians usually get married at 16, so you're technically almost of age on this side of the Gateway. Although I can't say I was able to do much at 15 either. I can do lots of things now..." Her stomach dropped as she noticed the neck piece of the white armor he wore under his cloak. Something that she had seen before. "Although I am 18 and still haven't thought about marriage yet. I suppose if I don't hurry up, I might miss my chance..."

"Were you one of the people that attacked our train yesterday?" she blurted out without thinking.

His grasp on her hand tightened. "Smart girl," he said so nonchalantly that it seemed to Genesis that he wanted her to figure it out. "Did that little Amana boy tell you of the SSA by any chance? It's really a shame we had to fight him as we did. The Amanas are a force to be reckoned with."

"No, he did not say anything... I don't know anything about whatever the SSA is, but, based on yesterday's events, I'm gathering that you are not good people. I am sorry—I'm jumping to conclusions..."

He laughed and took hold of her shoulders. "You're very sharp, my dear." His voice was harder now. "Yes, I am a general-in-training in hopes of leading a special unit of the SSA army. The same group that attacked your train yesterday. Do you want to know why we did it?" She made no answer. "The roundabout answer is that your world has no right taking over ours. Our world can take care of itself and I wish your agents would stop sticking their noses in other people's business. I wish they would stop ruining the lives of innocent people. We are going to stop Driscoll and drive your people out of our land one way or another. Before you join their side, maybe you should think hard about what you will be doing. You are not in the wrong *yet*, but you will be if you let them turn you into their pawn. I've chosen the side I think will most benefit my people: to free them from constant fear, to take revenge for what was done to my comrades... I will do everything to defeat Driscoll..." His face had grown very serious as he spoke, but so had Genesis's.

He paused for a moment, and then his cheerful smile returned. "Sorry... I spoke out of turn... I hope you can forgive me for speaking of the school you attend in such a manner... I can never forgive them for what they've done... I'll speak no more." He released her shoulders and took a few agile steps away from her. "I have to go now. It's taking a lot of effort to put my soldier who got trampled back together again. Until next time, Genesis..." He then hurried away.

She stood in silence as she watched him disappear between the market stalls. What should she do? He was already gone so it wasn't like she could report him... I mean, she *could*, but he didn't seem like the kind of person that would be found again easily. Should the school know that an enemy had been spotted in one of their main cities of operation? He was on the opposing side, so she knew he could say anything to make her believe she was in the wrong and he was in the right, but it was too early in her time at Arisha for her to jump to conclusions. She needed to know more, but what about River? If Shireu was right about the school being the enemy, then had the school done something to River yesterday to make him act that way? River was always so gentle, even when they had rolled in MMA class. Yet he had pushed her down so hard that she had sprained her wrist. If he wasn't the River she knew...then who was she to trust?

Chapter 43

Alone

GENESIS WAS QUITE GLAD now to have the first day off. She needed some time to collect her thoughts, and so she skipped lunch to walk around the city alone, admiring the beautiful view of the sea from various lookout points. She also used the opportunity to people-watch. The few Arishians who seemed to live there all wore long, white robes, and many of them had very long hair, even the men. That was not how all Arishians looked, however. Like Earth, each country had its own culture, races, and religion. Those who dwelt in Ferris City were referred to as "Earth worshipers." They believed that Earth was a holy place, and that those who came from there were holy beings. They worshiped the Gateway and the school itself due to its many peace-keeping accomplishments in their world. The Earth worshippers flocked to Ferris City in particular, as well as other Agency offices in various cities around Arisha.

Genesis took in the sights as she wandered, lost in her own thoughts. She didn't want to go back to Agent Housing to find her friends, yet she felt so alone now that her brother had pushed her away. Something lay beneath the surface of the school—it had only been a suspicion before, but now it seemed more of a reality. She just couldn't yet put a finger on what it was. Whatever the truth about the school was, however, something definitely wasn't right with River. He had changed too much too quickly.

She stood at a guardrail looking out at the sea. From Ferris City, one could see land far off in the distance just barely visible on the horizon. That land was the country called the Kingdom of Scarlet, the country of blood artists, and the place from which Kazumae, Haise, and Reiss had come.

She leaned on the railing, strands of her olive green hair blowing ever so gently around her in the light breeze wafting up from the sea below. The things that had happened the night before, her brother, and then her Uncle Ferris back at home, passed through her mind again and again. She wondered if Uncle Ferris ever worried about them, or if they had been forgotten.

Alric came up the path but stopped when he caught sight of Genesis. He didn't say anything at first, but, upon remembering he had been looking for her since she had rushed out so quickly at breakfast, he shook his thoughts back into order again and approached her.

"What are you doing, Shapeshifty?" he asked casually. She straightened up, startled, and redirected her gaze over her shoulder at him. He seemed so calm as if the sea breeze had a soothing effect on him. "Stop giving me that look..." he muttered. The moment he said it, Genesis realized she had been smiling at him.

"In that case, I will give you that look *harder*," she teased. He sighed in response. "I was just looking at the sea. What about you?"

"I was looking for you," he grumbled as he leaned down on the railing next to her. She noticed he held a paper box in his hand, but because the material and packaging were quite Arishian, she hadn't the faintest clue what could be inside.

"Well, I feel honored," she answered.

"Not because of any of that friendship stuff. It doesn't matter if you cry and get your snot all over me. We're still not friends."

"I got snot on you?" Her eyes widened.

"Just a little bit, but it was still nasty. You should control your emotions."

She looked down, slightly embarrassed. "Yeah, that was one of the few times that I've cried in months, and I'm a girl, so that says something about how I handle my emotions..."

"Fine, whatever," he growled. "Anyway, I was wondering if you'd fight me. I want to go out of the city. Kazumae was telling Freecia and Zuri not to earlier because there are monsters in the woods, but I want to go try out my valta while in Arisha! Plus, I thought you could come with me so we could duel."

"Are we even allowed to do that?"

"Probably not, but they never said we couldn't." Actually they had, but Genesis had missed it during the meeting, and Alric wasn't about to admit the truth and have her refuse to go. He knew Genesis well enough to know she wasn't going to break that kind of rule, but to him it made it all the more exciting. How much more dangerous could the forests be here than back at home?

"I mean, sure, I'd like something to distract me... So why not? I just need to get my shifting clothes before we go..." she mumbled.

Listening to her response, Alric grew acutely aware of the sadness that radiated from her and lifted his hand from the railing bringing it inches from hers. The instant he realized what he was about to do, he drew his hand back swiftly.

Genesis, unaware that Alric had almost taken her hand in his, swayed a bit and caught herself on the railing. Only then did she realize how faint with hunger she now felt due to having missed both breakfast and lunch. Without thinking, she placed one hand over her empty stomach.

"I figured as much." he grumbled, the box now held out to her.

She stared down at it for a second before she took it from his hands.

"What is..." she started. Without a word, he strode over to a bench that resided alongside the guardrail. She undid the box's clasp and flipped it open. Inside she found some of what had been served at breakfast, which she had not gotten around to eating. Her lips tightened and a lump formed in her throat. "Th-thank you so much..." she stammered.

"It's...whatever. I wasn't doing it to be nice. You just better have your full strength if we are going to duel. When I win, I don't want it to be while you're half-starved to death!"

She smiled and plopped down beside him on the bench. "Very well! Let me eat up then, so that we can go on our little adventure!" She clasped her hands together, said a quick prayer over her food, picked up the fork, and took a bite of the eggs. They had such an unfamiliar flavor—they looked like eggs but tasted almost like some kind of fruit, although she wasn't sure which fruit they tasted like. She took another bite to see if she could pinpoint it, but found she couldn't. She could only guess that it was the difference between Earth and Arishian eggs.

"I also wanted to know what you were going to say to me last night about my old man... There shouldn't be anyone outside the city so we won't be interrupted this time..." Alric mumbled.

Alric and Genesis left through the city gates a short time later, after their brief stop at Housing for her shapeshifting garb. They crossed a meadow toward the nearby woods and stopped just out of view of the city behind some trees where they prepared for a quick duel.

The duel went down as usual—after their initial surprise when they were reminded that grass was flammable. I heard the scene was quite funny with both of them shouting at once as they tried to stamp out the flames before they spread. They did get them out shortly thereafter, and Alric tried to be careful not to catch the grass on fire again. He claimed that to be the reason why he lost that day, but, of course, since he had never won a duel with her, his claim was questionable. How typical of their duels: every time, he made up some sort of excuse as to why he had lost.

When they had finished, the sun was still in the sky—although a bit low—so they then set off to explore the forest. The duel had kept her mind on other things for a while, but as they walked mostly in silence, all of the events of the past 24 hours resurfaced again, and her stomach began to turn over and over on itself once more.

Alric captured an Arishian bird and managed to retrieve one of its feathers before it got away again. He thought bringing her the new stronger bird form might make her smile, even though it would un-doubtedly give her more of an advantage in their battles. She did laugh at the sight of him wrestling with the bird, but the second he returned to her with scratches all up his arms, the brief moment of laughter subsided and was replaced by the sullen look again. She wasn't herself at all. That look had been in her eyes since that morning. Was it still about her father? Or had something else happened after he had left her in the lobby the night before?

When they emerged from the forest again, the sun began to set be-hind the trees, painting blue and purple light across the gray sky. Neither Genesis nor Alric made any move to return to the town yet. Dinners in the harbor didn't start until the next night, so with that in mind, neither felt in a hurry to go back to those crowded dorm rooms. Instead, they sat down on a grassy slope from which they could see Ferris City, now beginning to light up for the night.

Genesis had never gone on an adventure with anyone before like she had with Alric that day. Not even River, because "nature was gross and he would much rather be home reading a book." She smiled at the memory of his words, but thinking of River made her mind go back to him shoving her in the marketplace...and then to her father's name in the agent records. Her parents were somewhere on this side of the Gateway now...

A small insect fluttered about her like a butterfly, its wings glowing in the dim light. Alric held out his hand and it came to land on it, the light swelling up and then fading again. Genesis's eyes grew wide in wonder at the strange creature—it was so beautiful, like nothing she could ever have imagined seeing in her lifetime.

"You said last night my father saved your life. While I absolutely despise the man, I want to know what you meant."

"Alric..." she started then stopped. What was she planning on talking to him about? Was she going to spill out everything that had been swimming in her mind about the school? She was reminded that he was a House student, so how could he not be offended by any criticism of the people who had raised him? Genesis sighed and a brief silence followed as she contemplated this line of thought.

"I have many questions..." she started. Then, changing her mind, she began to answer his question. "As for what I was going to say last night..." She paused again, debating if she really should continue to tell him. He waited intently for her to speak, though, and so she decided to proceed with the truth. "The truth is my parents were taken away when I was seven years old. I have reason to believe that the people who took them were agents from this school. That would also be the reason why I came to the university with my little brother...because I want more than anything to find my parents again. That night, my brother and I should have been caught as well, but we weren't, because an agent they called

Agent Ashford concealed our presence. He saw quite clearly that we were hiding under the bed, but when his superior asked him if he had found any children he said *no* without hesitation, and I think that's the only reason that River and I didn't get captured as well that night. I really wanted to thank your father for what he did, but when I came here to Arisha, it seemed quite unlikely that I could, since you had told me he was dead. Still, I can't understand how the man who spoke so kindly to us that night could just abandon his own son like he did."

"Because I was weak." She turned her head toward him. He clutched his hands together, his eyes lowered down to stare into the dark grass. "If he had only waited around to see how strong I could become, even though I was cursed with this body, then maybe he wouldn't have... But who would want a weak son?"

"Alric..."

"Don't say my name like that. It's weird."

"I'm sorry..." She looked away, resting her chin on her knees as she continued to stare across the grassy fields between them and the city. The sounds of insects and small creatures filled the night air around them. Gradually Genesis's mind began to wander again. She thought of that night in particular, and then of her father's name in the agent records. That didn't make sense to her. She wondered why he couldn't have at least sent a letter to their uncle telling them he was all right...and she still didn't know what had happened to their mother. She thought of that feeling she got around some of the faculty members, as if a cold hand clutched her heart. Was the school evil? That seemed to be the only explanation for it all—and maybe they really had done something to River... Her precious little brother...

"Do you trust the school, Alric?" she asked at long last. He was someone who aspired to become the best agent, so he must trust the school a great deal.

"They raised me. They took me in when my parents didn't want me."

She looked over at him again. "But do you trust them?"

"Of course I do, Shapeshifty!"

Another silence.

"What about that attack on the train yesterday? What if those people are actually good and see the school for who they really are?"

"The SSA?" he snapped in horror. "No way that organization is good! They've gotta be the worst of the worst!"

"What is the SSA?" she asked.

"Right, you students from other places wouldn't know anything about them." He spoke more calmly. "Okay, well, I'll try to tell you, but my memory is pretty awful so don't take my full word for it!" This was a lie as he had spent the majority of his childhood with a book in his hands and was well-versed in the history of Arisha, remembering even the minutest of details.

"I know. You can't even remember my name..." Although he had known her last name when they were looking at the agent records, so she knew that was probably not actually the case.

"Whatever. I don't see the point in remembering such things. Anyway, Shield Alliance is a country across the sea to the southwest of Lyre and it is split up into the various countries of the Shield. When it was founded, it was much like the United States. There was Southern Shield, Northern Shield, Westward Shield, Eastward Shield, and Central Shield. They fought for their own freedom and each country had their own government under the main Shield Alliance government. That government was supposed to have minimal power over the countries of the Shield, but things eventually changed and the king, who was the equivalent of the United States president, slowly gained more and more power until a civil war broke out and the alliance crumbled. I hear the government became more and more corrupt as time went on, and craved more power until they began to take over other countries such as the Southern Country where Snowboy was born. Their goal is to take over the entirety of Arisha. That's where the SSA—which stands for Secret Shield Alliance—comes in. They have tried to keep their plans for taking over all of Arisha on the down low, so the Secret Shield Alliance was put together to slowly start carrying out their goals. They took over the Southern Country, the islands of the Southern Seas, along with the country of the Sunken Islands and Merbrook where the sirus live. But their main objective is taking down the Agency. I think eventually the Agency will have to stop ignoring their aggressions and there will be an all-out war. Their attack on the train earlier was just one of those terrorist assaults, and the war will probably happen around the time we become agents, so we have *that* to look forward to."

"Why does the SSA want to take us down though? I thought they wanted to take over Arisha, but we're from Earth," she asked, half-hoping he would start to see the strangeness in that.

"Because the Agency's goal is to resurrect their fallen world. The Agency will try to prevent the SSA from taking over Arisha, so they have to take us out before our numbers grow too large, especially since our agents are so well-trained and well-armed. The thing is...if there is an all-out war, I don't know how high our chances are, despite our better technology... The SSA army is a lot bigger than ours, and few Arishians will stand by the Agency. A lot of Arishians don't like the school at all."

She stared down into the grass where a small rodent with huge round eyes stared up at her through the darkness. She knew she had to create her own opinion on the Agency, but she had also just found out her father was an agent. All that information in only two days was too much for her to handle, so she buried her face into her hands. Alric watched her as she tried to keep a hold on her emotions. She still felt sick to her stomach. She knew that for now she had to keep studying at Driscoll. She had to continue with how things were and keep her doubts and suspicions to herself. They were training to be agents for Driscoll. That meant she would continue to train her valta and shoot for that goal. For now at least.

"Are you sick or something? You've been acting strange," he pointed out.

"I don't know what to do... I don't trust the school..."

He gave a start and looked at her sharply. "What?! Why wouldn't you?"

"Because they took my brother last night and now he's a totally different person! Because most Arishians don't like the school that claims to be helping them! Because they tore apart my family for what seems to me like no good reason! I just want to live a happy, normal life with my parents! Does some of that not seem strange to you? Why would most Arishians not like the people who are trying to help them, unless they aren't really helping them?" She stood now, her fists clenched.

Alric's face twisted with anger as the impact of her words struck him. "What are you talking about? Took away your parents? You were seven at the time! What did you know about your parents? For all you know, they could have been leaking secret information or attacking the school somehow. Just because they gave birth to you does not make them good people! I am sure the school wouldn't have taken them away without good reason!"

She drew in a deep breath in an attempt to remain calm. How could he be so insulting? *Her* parents in the wrong? Of course, he couldn't possibly understand what it was like to have parents. Finally she spoke again, trying to keep her voice as steady as possible. "And yet you brought me out here for this discussion on a sensitive topic because you realized there was a risk faculty could overhear us talking in the city. Do you not see the contradiction there?"

"Contradiction? I brought you out here so we wouldn't be interrupted! It wasn't for any stupid reason like worrying someone from the school would overhear, although I'm glad I did, because if they did overhear you, they would probably have to lock you up so you can't brainwash any of the other students with your corrupt ideas! In fact, I should tell them your doubts in order to get you removed! You could be a risk to the whole mission of the Agency!"

"Yeah...of course you would do that, because you just roll over and do everything they tell you to."

He sprang to his feet. "Whatever! You're just getting stupid ideas in your head! It's all stupid! You're blaming your brother's change on the school, when maybe it's just because he's changed!"

She let out a cry of frustration and turned away from him. They both trembled with anger. The beauty of the setting sun had completely faded now and all that was left was the darkness and the faint glow from the city.

Genesis spun back around. "Tell me this, Alric. If the school really is good, then how come you turned out the way that you have?"

"What did you say?!" he thundered, turning fully around to face her.

"You're angry and resentful all the time. But was it really your father who did that to you? Also, you never met your father, so therefore, all you have to go off of about his nature is what the school has told you about him! Your mother died after giving birth to you. Did it ever occur to you that maybe your father never even knew you existed in the first place? The school has been lying to you from the start... At least that's what I'm beginning to think! Also, tell me this. Parents are evil in your eyes, right? Because you were told your parents left you for their mission. But if the school is really your savior who raised you, did they coddle you? Did they embrace you when you fell down? Or sit by your bedside when you were sick? Or were you just raised as another pawn in their army?"

He struck her hard across the face. Her cheek stung from the blow and tears burned in her eyes as she glared viciously back at him.

"Shut up! How dare you?!" he snapped.

"You're angry because I'm right, aren't I?" she cried, her hand covering up her throbbing cheek.

"Shut up!" he repeated.

"I thought we were friends, but it seems as if we can't even have a civil conversation!"

"And who's fault is that? And like I've said, I don't have friends, and I never will! So just leave me alone already! I don't even like you, you stupid shapeshifter!" He turned completely from her and stalked away through the dark grass leaving her standing on the hillside alone.

Tears spilled from her eyes—tears of rage as he continued on away from her through the darkness back toward the city. She then wondered why it had to be *her* family? Why had the school torn apart *her* family? It wasn't fair. Images of a childhood spent with her parents and her brother flashed through her mind. If only they hadn't been pulled into this world!

She bit her lip and sank back into the grass, her body still overwhelmed by the rage she felt. "Friends? Yeah right, like I could ever have friends. I didn't want any in the first place... But now..." she covered her eyes with her hands. "Why do I have to go through this all alone...? Why River...? Mom...? Dad...?" Her mind thought over all of her classmates, but all seemed so loyal to the school. "Why do I have to do this alone…?" she repeated.

Chapter 44

Rage

GENESIS SLID AN ENVELOPE across the post office counter. The man seated behind it lifted his eyes. "I would like to send this to Agent Turmentic Lee Deadlock, please," she requested.

The man lifted the envelope, a half suspicious look in his eyes. A smile flickered over his lips and he released a lighthearted laugh. "This sure doesn't feel like a letter..." he chuckled.

"No...it's a Christmas gift." She averted her gaze to the black and white stone floor. Unlike most of the buildings in Ferris City, the post office was dark on the interior.

"For Agent Deadlock?"

"Yes."

He took a minute to look something up on the computer, while Genesis grew more and more anxious about the small package. Inside was the cross necklace that her father had given her for her sixth birthday. The necklace was her message to her father to alert him to her presence in Arisha. If she could be reunited with her parents, then they could all figure out what to do together. Yes, in fact, they could ditch the school completely and live out a happy life as a family, just like she had always wanted. Our poor sweet Genesis... If only it were that easy...

"Are you Dale Deadlock then?" he questioned.

She hesitated a moment, then nodded. "Yes..."

"I don't know... The name seems more like a boy's name to me... But

I guess Arisha is full of things that force me to flip my way of thinking!"

"I know... I get that a lot..." she said sheepishly, her mind boggled by the name "Dale Deadlock." But she couldn't think of that right now. She just needed to send the envelope somehow, and if that meant borrowing someone's name, she would.

"Well, I guess that's approved then... You often send letters to him from the Earth-side campus's post office. Is that correct?"

She felt terrible about lying but knew her only option was to move forward. "Yes, that I do."

"All right then... I'll get it to Agent Deadlock for you as swiftly as possible! I don't think it will be long at all. He might even have it in his hands before the week is up!" She bowed quickly and then turned to exit the post office.

Once outside, she took a deep breath and worked her way along the crowded streets. The volume of people had not let up since the beginning of the week. The students had now been there for almost six days. In the free hours before dinner, Genesis decided to be alone with her thoughts, as she had the previous days. She approached the outer gates through which she could leave the city.

Nearby, Reiss paused as he followed a group back from the library to Agent Housing. He had caught sight of Genesis walking away alone and his brow furrowed with concern for her. Kazumae drew up beside him with a deep sigh escaping his lips. "'Twould be quite the shame if our Lady Genesis was to put her life in danger. I think she knows not the dangers of Arisha, but perhaps 'tis her own lesson to be learned," Kazumae said to him.

At his words, Misteria, Mae, and Grisham, the wind user, stopped to stare after her. Misteria shook her head. "Seems like a storm is brewing... She could get sick, especially being in another world for the first time.

They're making us take those supplements every night to try to keep us healthy, but even those won't help in this scenario. She could get into other kinds of trouble as well," she mused.

"Quite so..." Kazumae agreed.

"What should we do?!" Mae cried. "I don't want Genesis to catch her death! I'm just now starting to feel like she's becoming part of the group and not isolating herself so much... But the last few days she's been acting so sad! And wandering off on her own! I don't want her to get hurt or sick!"

Kazumae seemed thoughtful for a moment, before he gave them all a nod of affirmation. "Quite so indeed. I have a rather frightful feeling about the matter, today especially. Let us..." He stopped as Dr. Cherith approached them from a sidestreet.

Meanwhile, Genesis departed through the city gates. Since that first day in Arisha, she had spent a great deal of her free hours wandering the forests by herself, because that was the only place where she could feel alone, like she had no watchful eyes or ears upon her. That day the sky was particularly dark with great black storm clouds gathering. She realized she would not be out long before the rain came, but still she went, and in no time at all she wandered into the forest alone, listening to the strange sounds of Arisha. The bird calls were different than many she had heard on Earth, and so were the scents of the forest. Arisha seemed to have an overall sweeter scent than Earth—some were pleasant, but others were sickeningly sweet.

She neared a small lake that she had discovered on a previous adventure and sat down on the trunk of a fallen tree. There she could watch the strange fish-like creatures swimming round and round at the surface of the lake, poking their heads up from time to time to look at her.

Her thoughts, of course, wandered back as they always did to everything that had happened since arriving at the school. For the sake of not getting redundant over her internal thoughts, I shall merely say she came to no new conclusions and just spent the time pondering over what she already knew.

Her attention was abruptly brought back to reality by the breaking of a branch nearby. She looked behind her to see Alric not far away, grumbling as he made his way through the trees alone. He had actually been doing the same thing each afternoon, but this was the first day they had crossed paths in the forest.

Genesis's heart plummeted in her chest and she swiftly took off from the clearing. Avoiding him had become a part of life for the past few days. As she fled away, fearful that he had seen her, she came to a short stop just out of his view behind a great, black tree trunk. She waited, hoping he would move on and ignore her. No luck, however, for he immediately stalked forward in her direction until he stood beside her, his eyes filled with rage.

"Why are you here?" he asked with scorn.

"I was taking a walk by myself," she answered just as scornfully.

"Why?"

"Because I wanted to!"

"Why couldn't you do that in the town?"

"Because I wanted to come to the forest. So let me be!" she snapped back, glaring equally as hard as he did.

"Fine! Whatever! Just stay out of my way!"

"I had already intended to do that, Alric!" She spun away but he caught her arm before she could go.

"Don't call me that!" he growled, his grip growing so tight on her arm that it began to hurt.

"What? Your name? Let go of me!" she snapped. He did not move to do so. "I said, let go!" She spun around, striking him as hard as she could across the face. His grip twisted and he shoved her violently against the trunk of the tree. His face burned with anger and his teeth gritted so tightly, she was sure it must hurt. She hastily shifted into a cat and bound away from him through the black undergrowth that carpeted the forest floor.

"Get back here, you stupid shapeshifter!" he shouted as he began to run after her. Once she had gotten a distance away, she shifted back into herself, but she had underestimated his speed and he was upon her again in an instant. She tried to avoid his attack but he came at her with his hands in flames. She had become very swift with switching between forms, so she was better at dodging him. He went in for another attack, but she took the form of a bird and tried to quickly fly past him. He grabbed her by the tail and flung her to the ground. She changed back and darted forward to throw both her arms around his waist in order to knock him off his feet, but he held his footing and did not yield under her. He lifted up a flaming hand and then froze just as he was about to bring it down upon her back. He realized he had fully intended to burn her, and knew that no matter how angry he got, he could not stoop to such a level. In the next moment, his legs gave out beneath him, and she shoved him down onto the forest floor on his back.

"Seems like you have a bit of sense after all! For a moment there, I thought you really wanted to kill me!" she cried vehemently. He turned his head away with a scowl.

A low, rumbling growl sounded behind Genesis and she turned her head right as a large jaw closed down on her shoulder. Alric's eyes widened in shock as she was yanked off of him and dragged a few feet away through the rough mixture of grass, fallen leaves, and tree branches that littered the ground. She gasped as her back struck either a stone or root that bumped up out of the ground. The creature held her so tightly within its jaws that she could not break free, and she was afraid if she struggled too hard her arm would be torn off. I fear her mind was too much in a whirl to think of the obvious solution of shapeshifting to escape.

Alric snapped out of his initial shock and sprang up toward the creature, thrusting his flaming hands into its fur. The beast cried out in pain and Genesis's arm slipped from its mouth. She scrambled away through the detritus to get some distance between her and the beast. Her chest heaved in pain as blood ran down her arm and dripped into the grass. She felt dizzy, but whether from blood loss or simply the sight of her own blood, she wasn't sure.

Alric was thrown from the beast's back, landing near her. Then it turned and charged at both of them. The creature's long tail thrashed wildly, knocking down a tree. Genesis's brain completely blanked on what she should do, so she just stood motionless as Alric stepped in front of her, his arms lifted in front of his face as he cloaked himself in flames. The beast veered away from him in an instant. It was enormous and wolf-like, with long horns like a ram and sharp claws like a cat. It circled through the trees for another charge.

Genesis held her hand over her shoulder to try to stop the bleeding, but she felt so dizzy and weak now from seeing that much of her own blood that she couldn't think what to do. Even thinking about losing that much blood made her whole body feel strange and tingly.

"Alric..." she muttered weakly.

Alric turned and took hold of her wrist. His face filled with terror as he truly saw the amount of blood dripping from her shoulder, staining her hair and clothes. She had lost so much now, he knew he had to get her back to the clinic in Ferris City as quickly as possible. Even so, he knew she probably didn't have enough time left.

"We have to get away!" he urged. Her face went ghostly pale, and she began to nod lethargically. How could she possibly run in her current state? He grabbed her around the waist and swung her over his shoulder as he darted through the trees.

"It's coming back too fast," she gasped, clutching the back of his shirt and staining it with her blood. The creature still charged toward them. Of course, it wasn't going to just let them flee—it had chosen them for its prey! Alric's head snapped back to look, and then he shoved her roughly onto the ground. He thrust a flaming arm out to the side to detour the beast again.

"Stop bleeding so much!" he shouted at her in frustration, as the large beast circled through the trees.

"How am I supposed to stop?!" she gasped, holding her bleeding shoulder.

He pulled his burnt hoodie off and began to wrap whatever he could salvage from it around her wound. His hands shook uncontrollably, but he had to try something to make the bleeding stop. He felt absolutely powerless. The situation was his fault—it was all his fault for arguing with her over something so stupid and attacking her in such a violent manner. They had been distracted and hadn't heard the creature coming. In fact, all their shouting was probably what had drawn it to them.

He turned as the beast came in for another charge. "I'll get rid of it!" he growled.

"We should call for help! We aren't authorized to do this!" She sat up, trying to grab his arm to prevent him from leaving, but he stood just outside of her reach.

"Help?! How are we supposed to call for help?"

"I... I don't know..."

"Good, we're on the same page for once!" He darted at the beast, his arms blazing again. The beast ran away obviously afraid of fire.

Genesis slowly got to her feet. The ground felt as if it rocked beneath her. She was in so much pain that she wasn't sure if she could move any further, but she thought that the monster might kill Alric if she didn't do something. The situation was too much for her to take.

She didn't think things could get much worse...but then she felt a raindrop hit her face. She lifted her eyes to the sky in horror. The clouds opened up, sending down torrents of rain, and in moments the flames on Alric's arms sizzled out and he became powerless to produce them again. Still, Alric continued to fight the beast without his valta. His attacks had become desperate and not well thought out as he swung his fists and shouted at it in his panic. The creature did not find him intimidating anymore, however, and with a swift motion of its paw flung him to the ground where he lay motionless.

Genesis started toward him, stumbling in her panic, but he suddenly jumped up and ran at the monster again. He looked completely exhausted from fighting, first her and now the creature. He had scrapes and cuts all over himself and his head bled from being struck when he was thrown. He didn't have his glasses anymore either and so she knew that he was blind to the creature's precise movements. The beast shifted his trajectory to charge at Genesis again. She knew she had to use her valta, but she knew her valta abilities: what good would a bird or a cat be against that massive creature? Her mind clouded and she wasn't sure what to do. She could almost feel herself slipping. She would pass out from blood loss soon.

Alric stepped between her and the beast once more. But the creature effortlessly threw him into the trunk of a tree, and, to Genesis's horror, he didn't rise again, for he had been knocked unconscious that time. In desperation, she looked down at her shoulder and noticed the beast's glistening saliva, which had remained there after its first attack. That was it. The power of shapeshifting. She could feel the DNA of the creature coursing through her veins. She could shift.

Chapter 45

Friends

GENESIS'S BODY WARPED, AND in moments she had assumed the form of the beast. The two beasts growled and circled each other as the rain poured down in sheets between the tree branches. Finally, she pounced upon the creature and swiped her claws at it. She was timid at first, striking gently, afraid to hurt another living creature...but then she saw Alric lying against the tree, and that image brought a wave of determination over her. She stopped holding back and attacked the beast with all the strength left in her.

She tore its face and it cried out in pain. Blood began to pour from the deep wounds she had inflicted. Genesis growled menacingly and it shrank back from her fury. She kept coming at it. She had trained all those months, and now she could finally use her full potential.

She charged at the creature again, but it shrank further back, its eyes darting around the clearing. She let out another deep growl and continued forward as it snapped its jaws open and closed repeatedly in defense. Suddenly, in the next moment, a scarlet red wolf leapt into the clearing, his jaws sinking into the creature's neck. The beast tossed its head to send the wolf flying so that it fell at Genesis's feet. Then the raindrops began to tremble midair and were swept up to one side forming a wave of water that crashed on top of the monster. In the next instant, the ground opened just beneath the creature and swallowed it up so that only its head could move. Only then did Genesis see Misteria and Kazumae around the edges of the clearing.

Behind them Dr. Cherith approached through the trees, giving orders to Grisham and Mae as the rain poured down all the harder. Grisham hurried to where Alric lay and created a pocket of dry air around them with his wind valta. Having regained consciousness, Alric looked up at Grisham's blurry form beside him.

Meanwhile, Genesis watched her friends finish securing the beast in a prison of vines and earth. She shifted back to her own form now that the situation was under control. Her hand immediately went to her shoulder but the wound on her arm had vanished.

She must have been relieved, but her legs trembled so much beneath her that they gave out and she would have sunk into the mud that now coated the forest floor if Reiss had not swiftly shifted from his wolf form and rushed to her side to steady her.

"I'm so glad you're not dead!" Mae cried over the rain as she rushed over.

Misteria joined Grisham to see to Alric's injuries, but he slapped their hands away. Misteria didn't much like his attitude, and, due to being almost like a sister since they had grown up together, shouted back at him and told Grisham to just let him get soaked to the skin.

"Thank goodness you are both all right..." Dr. Cherith told Genesis. "I worried something like this would happen... The forests are even more dangerous right before it rains and your classmates saw you leaving the city as the storm was looming... Are you all right, Miss Deadlock? Are you injured anywhere? Sorry...silly question. Did I fail to mention in training that you could shift out of your injuries?" He smiled at her so kindly that she couldn't help but burst into tears.

She caught hold of Reiss's clothes and buried her face into his shoulder. "Pretty cool, right?! We're virtually indestructible!" Reiss declared.

"It's all right... It's over now..." Dr. Cherith soothed. "Now...we have to get you all out of the rain..."

No sooner had they reached the shelter of the city gates, then the rain ended just as abruptly as it had started. The black storm clouds swiftly rolled away leaving only the puddles and damp scent in the air as a reminder that it had been raining. The Earth-side students had never seen storm clouds as dark as those in Arisha. Reiss came bounding down the pathway behind them in his scarlet wolf form surprising them, for they had assumed he had been with them on the walk back from the woods.

Dr. Cherith sighed. "And where in all of Arisha have *you* been?" In response, Reiss released his jaws to drop Genesis's boots and socks down on the stone street at her feet.

"Th-thank you... You didn't have to do that..." she said in surprise. She had actually forgotten all about them due to the chaos of the afternoon. Her shoes did not shift with her so they had fallen off at the very start of her fight with Alric when she had first shapeshifted. Luckily, the only other thing she had been wearing was her shapeshifting garb due to the heat of the Arishian air, so she had not misplaced any of her other belongings.

Blue light enveloped Reiss's form and he straightened up as himself again only seconds later. "We'll have to talk Dr. Cherith into getting you some of these!" he said, tapping the toe of his boot on the stone path. He side-eyed the doctor who was still staring at him in disapproval. He probably should have alerted the doctor before taking off on his own. Dr. Cherith didn't need to say it out loud for all of them to figure out that much. "They're expensive but I'm sure he can be convinced!"

"I'm sure you will convince me quite easily after all the trouble you've caused, Miss Deadlock," the doctor teased.

Genesis shook her head. "I will not ask you for anything of the sort. I don't intend on doing much shapeshifting away from the school after all that has happened here... I'm very sorry," Genesis bowed low to the doctor apologetically.

"Don't apologize to me, I'm just glad you're safe, really. Rules are in place for a reason. They aren't to hinder your fun but to protect you. You were told during the meeting that you were not to leave the city without permission, but I'll see what I can do to make the consequences less severe." He glanced at Alric. "Principal Watts and Professor Glazunov will not be happy with either one of you, and I'm certain Professor Alex will have a thing or two to say to you, Alric." Alric muttered something in Arshin under his breath. "That said, and jokes aside, you won't receive any harsh punishment from me. So don't feel the need to punish yourselves or feel you owe me anything. I am happy to look after my students in any way that I can." The doctor's kind eyes put her mind mostly at ease.

Genesis's shoes were dripping wet when she picked them up. She'd just have to carry them back—the streets were not at all rough on her bare feet. "Oh! This won't help your shoes, but you should shapeshift into something else and then back again!" Reiss interrupted her thoughts. "You'll be dry again if you do! Also you might need to get your dress mended," he gestured to where it had been torn around the shoulder by the beast's teeth. "It's like our hair in this regard. If you cut or dye your hair, like I have, it won't be longer again or change back to its original color when you shift back into yourself. Likewise, your garb won't repair itself like your skin will!"

Genesis laughed sheepishly as she fingered the hole in the shoulder of her garb. "I guess that makes sense... But it also hurts my brain a bit with everything that happened...."

Alric suddenly uttered some words of protest in Arshin as Misteria grabbed his head while both Kazumae and Mae restrained him. "Come on, Owl, quit being such a baby," Misteria said, proceeding to absorb the moisture from his hair and skin. Alric stopped resisting and waited for her to be done—he supposed having Misteria touch him was a small price to pay for being less wet and cold. Once she was done with Alric, she also dried off Kazumae, Mae, and Genesis's shoes. Of course, that was far more water than even a water user's body could hold, and so between each one she had to release the stored water onto the ground again. Genesis took the opportunity to shapeshift as Reiss had suggested, so that she was also dry.

"All right, now that everyone is dry again, would you all please follow me back to Agent Housing? I have some reports to make to the Agency. Even though you are dry, I suggest you change out of those clothes. The moisture may be gone, but any foreign bacteria that might have been in the rain still remain," Dr. Cherith instructed.

As they started walking, Genesis fell into step beside Alric at the back of the group. Mae was singing up ahead as she ran over to some garden beds to lift the heads of some flowers that had started drooping from the rain. All was quiet between them until they came close to the marketplace. Then the streets were busier, as merchants were milling about trying to put their wares out on the sidewalk again, now that the rain had ended.

"If the school truly were evil, then why would Dr. Cherith come to save us like that?" Alric asked, breaking the silent spell between them. Genesis glanced over at him but he did not return her gaze, instead he moved quickly to catch up with the others. She didn't know what to say on the spot. She needed time to collect her thoughts. It was too soon after the incident in the forest to think straight—she was too scared about what had happened and too grateful over being saved. One thing she knew for sure was that she trusted Dr. Cherith, Professor Glazunov, and Miss Nenna completely. Therefore, it wasn't the entire school that was evil; she needed more concrete information in order to draw any further conclusions.

The small group came to a stop outside Agent Housing. Alric muttered something under his breath in Arshin and continued past the doors, kicking his foot through a rain puddle as he went.

"And where do you believe yourself to be going, Sir Alric? I shall see to it myself that you make it to the clinic. Do you not agree, Sir Willliam Cherith?" Kazumae spoke up.

"Yes, with Alric's health history, he definitely needs to be looked at," Dr. Cherith agreed.

Genesis stood by herself, gazing at the others. At Grisham, who she still didn't know well because he didn't speak much; at Kazumae, who smiled his slim charming smile all while still trying to pull the resistant Alric away to the clinic; then over to Reiss, who at the moment was being unintentionally flirty with some Arishian girls; to Mae, who was trying to convince Alric to go with Kazumae; and last to Misteria, who Dr. Cherith was personally thanking for everything she had done that afternoon. Genesis thought about how alone she had felt the past few days, but she wasn't really alone, was she? She had started to get close to other members of her class as well. She had no idea what was going on with River, but she most certainly wasn't alone.

Mae hurried to Genesis's side and linked arms with her. "That's it! I've determined you have to hang out with Misteria and me for our last day here! I don't want you to ever almost die again! We're all friends, aren't we?" Mae demanded.

"Yes... That sounds quite nice," Genesis answered.

"Yay!" Mae chimed.

The others who remained began to excitedly make plans with one another, but Genesis caught sight of Dr. Cherith taking his leave—probably to head over to the clinic to explain the state Alric was in. "Wait...Dr. Cherith?" Genesis started after him. He paused. She drew in a deep breath of the sweet, damp air. She knew what she needed to do.

"Yes, Miss Deadlock?" he asked.

"Um... Well..." She shifted from one foot to the other, her eyes fixed on the white stone path. "It's about my brother... A few days ago...he started acting really strangely. I don't want to believe any ill toward the school...but because it was right after he went away for a few hours after the train incident...I was worried something might have happened. He's not himself at all... It's like he's a totally different person, actually...and I don't know what to do... I want my brother back."

The chirping of a bird sounded in the distance and the soft laughter of her classmates erupted behind her as Misteria teased Reiss over how flirty he had been with those girls. Dr. Cherith—the man who had taught her everything she knew about shapeshifting—said nothing at first. Genesis continued to stare at the ground, finally lifting her gaze to see a thoughtful look on his face. "Like a different person you say?" he clarified when he felt her eyes upon him.

"Yes... He's always been so positive and enthusiastic and doesn't really let anyone—or anything—get to him at all. He's always been so kind and respectful to me, and we've not really fought much at all since we were little... But that's been different this week... He's been anything but kind and respectful... He's said truly terrible things to me..."

"Hmm... well... I don't know if I can really say much on the matter, since I don't know your brother well... But, it could be possible he's having an off-week... I heard he had a recent heartbreak and also the Arishian air will often make students depressed their first time here..."

"A heartbreak you say?" Genesis interrupted.

"Yes... I've heard from other members of the faculty...the principal actually...that he may have had some feelings for Freecia Leo, who recently started dating your classmate Zuri..."

"Oh... I did not know..." She averted her gaze. How had she and her brother drifted so far apart that he didn't even come to her when he was hurting? She wanted to be there for him through times like that, even if she did think he was a bit too young to be dating. One could not control the human heart, and love for another wasn't something so easily contained.

"That all said, the situation does seem rather suspicious, and—just between you and me—I have been unsettled by some rumors about the principal recently. Will it ease your mind if I investigate the situation for you? As I am a long-term member of the faculty, I might just be able to pull some strings and find out the truth."

"You would do that for me?"

"Of course! If you're really concerned about your brother, I think your mind should be put at ease. Stress isn't good for the human body after all."

"Thank you. I don't know what to say, sir..."

"Nothing at all. It gives me an excuse to do some digging for myself as well... I have had a few questions in more recent years for Principal Watts. Now you should probably get back to your classmates and Professor Glazunov. I'm sure he wants to reprimand you for your actions, plus, you should probably get yourself into some clean clothes."

"Yes, sir." She hurried back to where the others still waited for her outside the doors to Agent Housing. Her heart felt lighter in her chest. For now, she'd trust that everything would be all right. It was in the doctor's hands.

Chapter 46
The Message

FRESHMAN CLASS 1 REACHED the end of their week-long introduction to Arisha. Only one full day in Ferris City had remained after the battle with the beast. I fear that day was rather uneventful, especially for Genesis and Alric, who were not permitted to leave Agent Housing. Genesis was a bit disappointed that she could not spend the day with Mae and Misteria as they had planned, but she didn't mind spending the day inside, after such a long, busy week. She took the opportunity to spend some time catching up on her journal, reading some Arishian books, and working out in the gym. Then, the next morning, exactly one week from their arrival, they all boarded the train to head home.

The trip back to the Agency's base on the river was rather uneventful. As they pulled into the station, they saw the members of Class 2 waiting on the platform with their luggage ready for their own adventure in Ferris City. Class 1 was then divided up into the same groups they came in, and embarked on the boats. Professor Glazunov took Alric's place next to Genesis, however, and Alric rode back with the luggage due to having a fever of 102. He was truly quite miserable.

Genesis knew she ought to be anxious to pass through the Gateway again, but those feelings of dread had not returned. Professor Glazunov held onto her arm the whole time they drifted through the Gateway to Earth-side, but nothing happened that time, much to everyone's relief. Instead, she experienced it like everyone else, as if she had just passed through water without getting wet. The experience was not pleasant, but it was not as unpleasant as the first time. She guessed it had just been a random phenomenon with no real significance.

The ride back was not as smooth against the current, but eventually all the boats had made it safe and dry up to the docks. After disembarking, all 28 of the students in Freshman Class 1 waited together by the road with a few of the teachers. River sat down as the time became lengthy and pulled at the green grass that now looked so vibrant compared to the black blades in Arisha. His fingers dug into the dirt until the underside of his nails were blackened with it. Genesis couldn't help but notice that her brother hadn't been biting his nails like he usually did.

Professor Glazunov, who had been speaking with someone on the phone for several minutes, ended the call with a long sigh. "Sounds like some kid ran away from the House this morning, which is why they're taking so long to send the bus," he told one of the other teachers. Genesis's stomach dropped. Was it not strange that a child had tried to escape the House?

"That's a silly reason... Why would that delay the bus?" Professor Alex asked.

Professor Glazunov shrugged his shoulders. "Those kids are very important to the school," he answered.

At last the bus arrived and the tired students boarded quickly, anxious to get back to the dorms. Genesis took Alric's seat in the back row with Mae and Misteria this time, to avoid sitting next to Hiero, which made for a far pleasanter ride. Getting off the bus, Genesis caught sight of a small boy who sat on the steps of their dorm. Professor Glazunov rushed over to him. With his navy hair and bright red eyes, much like River's, the boy appeared to be an energy user. For that matter, he looked strangely familiar to Genesis.

"Dale, are you aware of how much trouble you're in?" Professor Glazunov demanded. Her heart jumped in her chest upon the mention of his name, and she took a quick step forward.

"I'm sorry, Mister... I just wanted a day out," he said as he shoved his hands into his pockets. He must have been around eight or nine years old, but his eyes were filled with such seriousness that he seemed years older.

"The faculty are looking all over for you."

"I know!" the boy responded, impatience in his voice. "I'll go back now." He trotted toward the class and wove uncertainly through them. His eyes seemed to search their bewildered faces as he examined each and every one of them. When his gaze met Genesis's he stopped, then he lost his balance on the curb and fell over onto her. Genesis looked startled as she caught him to keep him from falling onto the asphalt. The boy looked up at her face as he slipped a small note into her hand. He then let out a short laugh. "Whoops! I'm always such a klutz. Sorry! Farewell!" He then climbed onto the now empty bus behind them.

Genesis looked after him in bewilderment, as she gripped the slip of paper in her hand. She wondered what the note he had passed to her could possibly say, but restrained herself from even acknowledging it had been passed to her. Instead, she closed her hand tighter about it, hoping it was the response to the envelope she had sent their father. A response this soon didn't make sense, though. She had only sent the envelope two days ago... Unless her father had been in Ferris City...

"All right, everyone into the dorm. Don't worry, we'll get the boy safely back to the House," Professor Glazunov instructed.

"I always thought Dale was the cutest of the younger kids at the House!" Mae said happily as they all filed into the dorm—I tell you the truth, she would have said that about any of the other children.

When she reached the stairwell, Genesis glanced down at the piece of paper in her hand and saw her name scribbled across it. She closed her hand again and glanced over the railing into the elevator room below her. Her eye caught River staring intensely at her fist, so she smiled at him, then continued up the stairs feeling uncomfortable under his strange gaze.

She entered the girls' dorm area and slipped into her room at the end of the hall. Relief filled her as she was back in her own private space. She did not like sharing a room with four other girls in the least.

After she shut the door, her bag slipped from her shoulder with a thump and she could finally turn her attention to the small slip of paper in her hand. Unfolding it quickly, she found a brief note written inside. She took a deep breath, her eyes scanning the words written there. When she was finished, she sank down to the floor with a sigh. "If only this were possible, Father... I don't know what to do now..." She crumpled up the note, determined to burn it later. But the words kept repeating themselves in her head:

Don't use your valta anymore. You are in more danger than you realize. Run away and disappear from Driscoll.

Your Father.

To be continued...

Acknowledgements

I spend so much time with words, yet I am not sure any words can express the depth of my gratitude toward all of those who helped make this journey possible. I could not have done any of it if I had not had two very supportive parents, sisters who encouraged me along the way, and a God who is merciful. First, I must thank my sister Juliette for all the hours she helped me process every possible wacky idea in my brain. Her patience and interest in my stories has always meant the world to me. I am thankful to my sister Charlotte for always being the first to read all of my stories no matter how rough the draft. I want to thank my father for helping me strengthen the plot. While I do believe he has some wackier ideas than I do, I know that the plot would not be where it is now if he had not given his initial thoughts on Gateway to Arisha as a whole. I am so grateful to my mother for the countless hours she devoted to this story despite having her own life and responsibilities. Without her editing, the story would still be quite a disaster. She is my harshest critic but also my greatest supporter, and for both I am very grateful. For the final proofreading, I must thank both my sisters Juliette and Anna, most especially Anna. She was able to view my story with a fresh set of eyes, and with her comments and questions I was able to finalize this book. Lastly, I must thank my Father in Heaven who is the real Creator behind my stories.

Cast of Characters

Alexander Viotto / Dawn (al-eks-AND-er vee-OH-toh / Dahn) *The light user with a stutter in Group A. He came from Mirrorick with Dusk.*

Alric Ashford (AL-rik ASH-ford) *The short-tempered fire user in Group A. He grew up at the House, but he is half Arishian, half Driscollian.*

Drydan Das (DRY-dehn DAZ) *A fire user who works as a doctor-in-training under Dr. Cherith. He was born in Arisha but raised at the House.*

Ellie Blanchet (EHL-lee blahn-SHAY) *The French psychic user in Group A, who specializes in hypnosis.*

Freecia Leo (FREE-shee-ah LEE-oh) *A fire user from Group B who befriends River and Zuri.*

Genesis Deadlock (JEH-nuh-sis DED-lahk) *A shapeshifter from Mirrorick. She enters the school from Earth-side in hopes of finding her missing parents.*

Grisham Ferrari (GRIH-shuhm fur-RAH-ree) *The quiet wind user in Group A. He came from an art school in Italy.*

Haise Imogen (HI-say ee-MAH-gen) *A blood artist from Scarlet who grew up at the House with his hired guard Kazumae.*

Hiero Caddel (HI-roh KAD-duhl) *The electricity user in Group A. He was a child prodigy, famous for acting and singing before entering* *the school.*

Johnathan Watts (JON-uh-thuhn WAHTS) *The principal of the school. He has no valta and was born and raised at the school.*

Kazumae Amana (KAH-zoo-may uh-MAH-nuh) *The very short, yet very elegant earth user in Group A. His duty is first and foremost to his master, Haise.*

Levine Arisha Driscoll (luh-VEEN ah-RISH-uh DRIS-kuhl) *An electricity user in Group B.*

Mae Arisha Driscoll (MAY ah-RISH-uh DRIS-kuhl) *The vegetation user in Group A. She's Arishian, but was born and raised at the House. She and Levine are both Driscoll girls—girls of currently unknown origins who will eventually perform special duties for the school.*

Misteria Remington (mis-TEE-ree-uh REM-ing-tuhn) *The water user in Group A, who was raised at the House while her mother did research in Arisha. She is half Arishian and half Driscollian.*

Nennisa Glazunov / Miss Nenna (nen-NEE-suh GLA-zuh-nahv / NEN-nuh) *Professor Glazunov's wife and the housekeeper for Group A's dorm. She possesses no valta, despite being Arishian, and speaks only a little English.*

Olivia Elrod / Dusk (uh-LIV-ee-uh EHL-rahd / DUHSK) *The shadow user in Group A. She came from Mirrorick with Dawn.*

Reiss Gatlin (RICE GAT-lin) *The only other shapeshifting student at the school. He attends special valta training with Genesis but was placed in Group B. He was born in Scarlet but transferred to the House when he was seven.*

River Deadlock (RIV-er DED-lahk) *An energy user also from Mirrorick. Despite being a bit young for the school, he enters with his sister Genesis.*

Roland Watts (ROH-lund WAHTS) *The only son of Principal Watts* *and heir to the school. He has been placed in Group B. His valta is unknown at this time.*

Shireu (SHEE-ree-oo) *The mysterious young man Genesis meets in the marketplace.*

Venessa Alex (veh-NEH-sah AL-eks) *Dorm director of Group B and the instructor for the fire user's special valta training.*

William Cherith (WIL-yuhm CHAIR-ith) *Genesis's shapeshifting instructor and the doctor she met during her awakening. He was born in Lyre in Arisha but raised at the House.*

Zenry Glazunov (ZEN-ree GLA-zuh-nahv) *Freshman Class 1's main teacher and the dorm director for Group A. He was born on the Island of Ice in Arisha but was raised at the House.*

Zuri Whitlock (ZER-ee WIT-lahk) *The ice user in Group B. He is from Southern Country in Arisha.*

Milton Keynes UK
Ingram Content Group UK Ltd.
UKHW040840140624
443986UK00003B/13/J